Australia's Son

The Man with the Golden Voice

GARRICK JONES

This is an IndieMosh book

brought to you by MoshPit Publishing
an imprint of Mosher's Business Support Pty Ltd

PO Box 147
Hazelbrook NSW 2779

indiemosh.com.au

Cataloguing–in–Publication entry is available from the National Library of Australia: http://catalogue.nla.gov.au/

Title:	Australia's Son
Subtitle:	The Man with the Golden Voice
Author:	Jones, Garrick (1948–)
ISBNs:	978-1-922440-49-5 (hard cover)
	978-1-925959-77-2 (ebook – epub)
	978-1-925959-78-9 (ebook – mobi)
Subjects:	Fiction Mystery & Detective, Private Investigators, Historical; Fiction LGBT; Fiction Action & Adventure.

Cover design by Garrick Jones

Cover images copyright free from Pixabay and Clean PNG

Editing by Victoria Milne Professional Editing

Author's Note and Acknowledgements

The opening scene of this story takes place in the principal male dressing room of The Theatre Royal in Castlereagh Street, Sydney, on Thursday the 17th April, 1902.

*****

The first few years of the twentieth century were difficult times for theatre-goers in the city, as many theatres had either fallen into disrepair or had closed their doors. For example, Her Majesty's Theatre, which is mentioned frequently in the text, burned down on the 23rd of March, 1902, a few weeks before this story takes place. It wasn't rebuilt until 1903.

I hope the reader will understand that I've used artistic license to change performances and venues in Sydney, using theatres that weren't in operation at the time of the narrative, or had already been demolished, or more commonly, destroyed by fire. This is a work of fiction, so although the performances of operas, dates and theatres in Melbourne are historically accurate, I've moulded the history of the theatres in a way that suits the narrative of Edward and Theodore Murray and their busy lives in early Edwardian Sydney.

Buildings and places mentioned in the story are all from the historical record, some of which still exist today and others that are no longer in existence were so during the lifetime of the author. Sydney underwent a major overhaul during the 1960s and many historical buildings of great beauty, like the Hôtel Metropole, were demolished and replaced by glass and steel.

I'm eternally grateful to John Wregg, international opera director and theatre historian, for the time and effort he put into the background checks on theatre history and the operation of theatres at the time in which Australia's Son is set, and also to my dear friend and fellow-baritone, now also retired from a life upon the stage, Dr. David Brennan, who was fastidious in his observations regarding the performances and the repertoire of Edward Murray.

The behind the scenes life of an opera singer at the turn of the century was not unlike the earliest years of my own professional performance in the days when theatres depended on manpower, when we used greasepaint, and when we worked in theatres whose wings bustled with stagehands, flymen and other mechanicals, all going silently about their business.

I hope you enjoy a glimpse into the life of a performer as it was, well before computer technology took over the operation of nearly everything behind the proscenium arch. In those days the magic of the theatre happened not only in front of the house curtain, but also by the hands of men and women backstage, in the wings and in dressing rooms all over the world.

Garrick Jones

CHAPTER 1

"It's your half-hour call to stage, Mr. Murray."

"Thank you," I shouted to the call boy through my dressing room door.

A second knock followed almost immediately, and one of the assistant stage managers poked his head around the door. "May I bother you for an instant, Mr. Murray?"

"Of course. Come in ... Simon," I replied to the young man. He was a new arrival in the theatre, barely a week now, and I had trouble remembering his name.

"Close the door," Howard Talbot, my dresser, snapped.

"Sorry, Mr. Talbot," Simon said and then winced as the door slammed shut behind him. We were used to its over-oiled hinges and how much force was needed to close it—he was not. "I beg your pardon, Mr. Murray, but your manager, Mr. Solomon, called by earlier and gave me a list of things to remind you to do."

"Give me a moment before you reveal the contents of this list, please," I said and then spoke to Howard. "Would you fetch me more spirit gum from wardrobe please? And, while you're there, get someone to iron out this hank of crêpe hair. I've made a right mess of the beard tonight, and I'm going to have to redo the left-hand side."

"Yes, Mr. Murray," he replied and was about to leave the dressing room when Simon stopped him.

"The list of reminders concerns Mr. Talbot, sir. Your costume fitting for the new *Don Giovanni* tomorrow morning, Mr. Murray—will it be you, or will Mr. Talbot go in your stead?"

"I'll be attending," Howard replied. Ah, what a joy it was to have a dresser whose measurements were exactly the same as my own. Poor man had a huge appetite and I ate sparingly, so it was a constant struggle for him to maintain the same weight. "Ten o'clock, isn't it?"

"Yes, Mr. Talbot; at Tanning's, at Railway Square."

"Does your list say I shall still have to stand in for Mr. Murray at the rehearsals for *Die Fledermaus* tomorrow afternoon?" Howard asked.

"Yes, sir," the young man replied. "It's at the Criterion and starts at two in the afternoon. The rehearsal is to fit Miss Blanchard into Act Two. She's not done the production before, and Mr. Solomon says Mr. Murray doesn't need to be there."

"Very good," Howard said to me. "I've remembered all of your moves, Mr. Murray, and for good measure I'll go over my notes of the stage business in my score in the morning while I'm being fitted at Tanning's."

There was to be a revival of *Die Fledermaus* at the Prince of Wales early next week and the young woman was a replacement for the role of Adele. I noticed my dresser looked a little uneasy.

"You know the songs well enough don't you, Howard?" I asked.

"Yes, Mr. Murray, well enough. Signor Cantieri doesn't like it much when I sing your lines, but I assure you they're accurate and in tune. He makes a huge play of yawning and looking bored. It makes me feel uncomfortable, that's all. He'd much rather it was you there than me."

"Signor Cantieri can 'rather' in one hand and piss in the other and see which gets filled first," I snapped.

"He seems to have all the attention in the world when I'm rehearsing the new *Romeo and Juliette* in your place ..." Howard said with a wink. "It's been done so often even the prompter knows the choreography of the sword fight."

"That's because when either of us are in tights and have an épée in our hands, his attention is focussed on what's below our belts rather than on what's coming out of our mouths."

Howard laughed.

I swear Cantieri drove me to distraction. Were he not a generous employer, if a rather dreadful theatre impresario, I'd refuse to work for him. He insisted my costumes were as revealing as possible and then pretended it was the designer who'd drawn them up so. *Romeo and Juliette* required a complex fencing scene, and he insisted I rehearse it bare-chested and in tights—and far too frequently for my taste. "To get used to the costume and the unaccustomed freedom of working without a tunic," he'd said to me before the first rehearsal to mark out our planned positions in the scene.

In recent years, it had become quite the rage for me to appear partly clad on the stage. Last year, in the first mounting of *Hérodiade* by Massenet, I'd even appeared wearing only a loincloth and sandals. It had created such a stir, the season had sold out in one day—and most likely not because of my "manly looks", but due entirely to the sensationalism of the newspaper reporting. I suppose I should have been flattered. A man of thirty-nine has to work very hard to maintain his physique. Makeup helps, of course, and Howard was a master of the art of shading. My chest looked like it belonged on a Greek statue when he'd finished blending and finessing greasepaint strokes to accentuate my pectoral muscles and those of my abdomen. However, I hated both body paint and body wash, the choice between the two depending on whether the theatre still had gas or the new electric lighting. The washes, easily removed with a white spirit, didn't read that well from the front in the old gaslit theatres, so in those venues I had to apply heavy oil-based body paint that took forever to remove and which came off on the sheets for days afterwards, no matter how hard I scrubbed at my body under the shower bath. We used pig fat to remove the oil-based products—it was the reason cheap comedians were called "hams". However, if not rendered carefully, the thick grease could leave a lingering, unpleasant odour, which was as difficult to remove as the blasted paint itself.

"More tights tomorrow morning, Howard," I said, and then, when he looked puzzled, added, "at the costume fitting."

"More tights? For *Don Giovanni*?"

"Even though he won't be directing the stage business, Cantieri has supplied the costume designs. So, don't forget to take your ballbag and a dance belt."

"I'll pop a set in my pocket before I go home. I sincerely hope he won't be there."

"He wouldn't dare appear at a costume fitting. I've forbidden him. He'd love to catch either of us in the altogether, and I for one can't stand his constant ogling. Your wife would come at him with her kitchen knife if she knew how his hands like to wander—"

"Thankfully, she knows little of what goes on when I'm at work these days."

"She's best kept in the dark, Howard. What goes on in the theatre, stays in the theatre. Anyway, it's to be Mr. McDaniel from the Palace who'll be doing the mise-en-scène, and he won't be at the fitting. There'll just be you and Gideon, the costume maker's assistant."

"I like Mr. McDaniel. A quick pat on the bum and that's all there is to it."

"Unlike our overly familiar Italian, you mean?"

"Quite so, Mr. Murray," Howard replied, and then added, with a large smile, "And Mr. McDaniel gets so guilty about his 'accidental' caresses of my backside, there's always an envelope with ten shillings in it for me at the end of the run."

"Good heavens! Ten bob for a grab at your arse? How much does he pay for a sniff of your knickers?"

Howard laughed. Our banter had been for the benefit of Simon, who'd been waiting patiently for us to send him away. Wide-eyed and red-faced, he'd been standing with his back to my dressing room door, squirming at our theatre talk. It was backstage nonsense; within a few more weeks it would be water off a duck's back.

"Don't worry, Simon," I said, smiling at him, as I leaned into the mirror to apply a dot of red greasepaint to the inner corner of each eye. "We'll keep you safe, and if we can't, we'll give you a cut of the takings."

The young man's mouth dropped open, and then, when he'd recovered, nervously cleared his throat and then pointedly looked at his fob watch. It would be the beginners' call shortly, and he seemed mindful of what else he had to do before the performance began.

"You'll get used to me, Simon; pay no heed. The fact that I can tease you as I have done is merely my way of welcoming you to our lives—our true lives—our lives here in the land of make-believe which is the theatre. I hope you'll forgive my levity at your expense."

The young man blushed and then gave me a bright smile. "All is forgiven, Mr. Murray. There's no need to apologise."

I smiled at his shyness and confusion. I'd felt much the same during my first few weeks as a "grown-up" performer in this very theatre, almost sixteen years ago. Dealings between those of us who worked backstage often held more than a hint of teasing; it was our way of showing friendship.

"Is that everything on Mr. Solomon's list, Simon?" Howard asked.

"Yes, Mr. Talbot. I'd better get a hurry on, if you'll excuse me; unless you have something else for me, Mr. Murray?"

"Well, if you'd like to earn an extra half-crown, you might stay behind tonight after the performance and help Mr. Talbot into my new *Faust* costume. As I've a guest appearance at my brother's benefit performance at the Adelphi to raise funds for the boys' home at Petersham and will have to leave the theatre before the end of the opera, it's been arranged that he'll do the curtain calls for me next Wednesday. My manager made the arrangements with the theatre, confirming I could leave, before he'd allow me to sign the contract."

It was traditional for the full cast to appear onstage and to take final bows only on the first and the final performance of an opera. However, if a character died or was killed before the end of the evening, the performer usually only did a curtain call at the end of the act in which he or she "passed away", and then went home early.

In *Faust*, Valentin perishes at the end of the fourth act. Normally, I'd take off my makeup and be at home with my feet up while the rest of the cast were taking a final curtain at the end of Act Five. But, due to my prior engagement to appear at my brother's benefit, which coincided with the last performance of our run, I'd arranged for Howard to take my place in the bows with the rest of the cast. He was the same build and height, and had learned to mimic my bow to perfection. No one in the audience had ever been any the wiser on the times he'd stood in my shoes.

"Two and six pence is two and six pence, Mr. Murray," Simon said. "I'd be up for that like a shot."

"Come here to Mr. Murray's dressing room half an hour after the theatre is cleared, Simon," Howard said. "That will give me time to replicate Mr. Murray's makeup for *Faust*, and then you can lace up the back of the doublet so I can check to see I've got the colours right. I had to mix new ochres this morning."

"I'll see to it, Mr. Talbot," the young man said, glancing once more at his timepiece as he left my dressing room.

It was unusual for a new costume for the last performance of a run, but my normal *Faust* costume had seen the last of its days. As I'd taken it off last week, the fabric had given way at the sides, and the lacing panel had torn clean out of the back. Wardrobe had informed me it could not be saved, so I'd gone to Tanning's the following morning with a few sketches and a bolt of fabric from our private store, and they'd knocked up a magnificent pair of costumes in golden silk within three days; they'd fitted both Howard and me like a glove.

No sooner had Howard left to sort out my crêpe hair and fetch more spirit gum, than Arnold Willings, the theatre manager, knocked on my door.

"Come!" I called out. I'd been rotating my head to loosen my neck muscles, and at the same time humming softly to remind my voice it was still there. I'd warmed up for a few minutes an hour ago, not long after I'd arrived at the theatre.

"Sorry to disturb you, Edward," Willings said. "I thought you'd like to know the final performance of *La Bohème* on Saturday is already fully subscribed."

"Really? That's wonderful."

"I was wondering if you might be interested in an extra 'by request' performance next Thursday? I know it's a day after your final *Faust*, but *La Bohème* is hardly taxing for an artist of your quality—and, as my theatre is dark that evening?"

"I'm sorry, Arnold, but on Thursday I'm already engaged. However, I seem to remember I have two unbooked weeks in August after my brother and I return from our New Zealand tour, if you'd like to remount the production then, for a more extended run?"

"How many performances were you thinking to show?" he asked, rather too eagerly.

After having travelled to Melbourne to see the Australian premiere of *La Bohème* last year, my brother Theo and I had obtained the performing rights for Sydney and Brisbane from Ricordi and Company. I knew the opera would become a popular performance piece, and so we'd decided to act as impresarios, despite the rather exorbitant royalties, which ran at about forty pounds per performance. My brother and I had funded this evening's performance of maestro Puccini's new opera, the third of our four presentations at the Theatre Royal. We'd hired the theatre and its staff, and had paid for the sets, costumes, orchestra, and the other performers ourselves. It had been a gamble, but with the house full for every performance, we'd already covered our costs. So, the receipts from the final showing on Saturday would be profit in our pockets. I couldn't have been happier ... unless Signor Puccini had written a nice aria for the baritone, as he had done for the bass. Still, I didn't mind. Marcello was a decent, strong character, and I enjoyed performing him. The work was charming; and despite the lack of a showpiece, I had a marvellous quartet to sing in Act Three, and a truly ravishing duet with the tenor right at the top of Act Four.

"How many performances in August, Arnold?" I asked. "Well, it depends—"

"What if I fund the mounting costs, and you, your brother, and I split the profits?"

"No outlay from Theo and me?"

"At my cost."

"I'll speak to my brother about it tonight when I get back to the hotel. We'll want full artistic oversight—including casting, of course."

His face fell slightly. I knew he'd wanted his mistress for the role of Musetta, but I couldn't bear her. She overacted and had no spatial awareness on the stage. Besides, who wanted to perform with a footlight fanny of her propensity? Not me, that's for sure.

"Very good, we'll talk of it later. *In bocca al lupo*," he added, wishing me good luck for the performance.

"*Crepi il lupo*," I replied.

It was considered bad luck to wish performers good luck before they went onto the stage. In opera, we used arcane expressions in lieu of saying those actual words. *In the mouth of the wolf,* he'd said to me, to which I'd replied, *may the wolf die*. It made no sense to an outsider, but it was a tradition for performers. Theatre was the most superstitious place in the world, no matter the country—and I'd been backstage as both a performer and a visitor in many.

Howard returned with my spirit gum and ironed crêpe hair as Arnold Willings was leaving, and I'd barely had time to stick on my beard when the call boy knocked on my door to announce the beginners' call. In an age of beards and fine moustaches, I was conspicuously clean-shaven. One could not perform certain roles—Mozart for example—with a befurred face; belief could only be suspended so far.

I gave myself one last quick check in the mirror, tugging at the sidepieces of the wig to make sure it was on tight, and then picked up my chair and knocked it twice on the dressing room floor. Another ritual for luck.

"Have fun, Eddie," Howard said.

"I will do, my friend," I replied, and then kissed his cheek, as I'd always done before countless performances over the years, the formality of our exchange when Simon had been in the room forgotten. When we were alone, he never called me Mr. Murray. To him, I was Eddie, and to me, he'd always be Howie. It's how we'd called each other since the first day we'd met, in 1871, thirty-one years ago.

He opened my dressing room door and called out into the corridor for it to be cleared, to allow me to proceed to the stage. As I pushed open the green baize door at the end of the passageway, the smell of the theatre hit me. I adored that first smell of the hemp fly ropes and the canvas of the cyclorama; no matter what had occurred before I walked onto a stage, it instantly transported me into the world we called theatre. I knew precisely at that moment, when that fresh, hay-like odour hit my nose, I was about to perform, and it filled me with excitement.

A dampened handkerchief still pressed to my freshly glued whiskers, I made my way along the prompt side of the wings, passing by the dozens of line sets that made up the rigging system, muttering thanks and acknowledging the greetings of stage hands, assistant stage managers, and machinists as I headed to shake hands with Braxton Miller, the stage manager, who waited for me in prompt corner.

"New tails suit, Braxton?" I asked.

"Yes, Mr. Murray."

"Very dashing," I replied. "Dinner after the performance, I suppose?" Only the stage manager and the theatre manager wore evening dress backstage; it was their right and privilege. Braxton had a perfectly presentable set of tails, which he wore every night, but this new garment was beautiful. Even in the sparse backstage worker lights I could see the sheen on the moiré silk of its lapels.

"Sir H. has reserved a private table at the Café de Paris," Braxton said.

"I shall be eating in the hotel with Theo. I've ordered a late supper to be sent up to our rooms."

"Why don't I send a telegram to your brother and you could both join Sir H. and me for dinner? He'd love to see you … he's out front tonight in fact."

"Another time," I replied. "Your evening sounds a little too romantic to intrude upon."

It was a badly kept secret, known to everyone who worked in the theatre, that Braxton Miller was the special friend of Sir Horace Blake, the Surveyor-General, who attended the opera frequently with his wife on his arm. Sir Horace usually dropped her at home after the performance and then went on to spend the evening with our stage manager in an apartment he kept at the Metropole Hôtel. It was on the same floor as the suite of rooms I shared with my brother. At times it could be quite comical when we four met unexpectedly in the elevator or in the corridor. Polite exchanges of greeting, all the while pretending none of us was aware that Sir Horace had been, or was about to spend the night with Braxton.

"Please tell Mr. Harcourt he's not to hum my lines along with me during the big ensemble in the first scene, otherwise I shall kick his arse and then shove him head first into the orchestra pit," I said.

"Yes, Mr. Murray," Braxton replied.

"Inform him if he wishes to study my role, he can pay the rehearsal pianist her fee instead of driving me to distraction by trying to learn it by ear while I'm singing it myself. He's paid to sing Schaunard, not Marcello. You may be as blunt as you wish. You may also inform him the direction came from my mouth with the warning I shall spread the word he's an undisciplined performer."

Braxton smiled. The ultimate threat. Undisciplined performers in a world of hundreds of aspiring young singers got no work.

"That's harsh, Mr. Murray," he whispered.

"He's already tried to entice me into an inappropriate and unwanted liaison. Came into my dressing room unannounced during the run of *Don Pasquale* last year sporting a johnny in his tights and asking me some nonsensical thing about one of the moves while attempting to rub his erection against my shoulder. No doubt he'd already dipped his prick in poison in readiness," I said with a small laugh. "He's desperate to take over my roles."

"I think you'd be safe there, Mr. Murray. I hear he likes his visitors via the scenery dock."

"I don't get your drift."

"Where is the scenery dock situated in the theatre, Mr. Murray?"

"Well, it's—"

"Yes! It's in the rear."

"Braxton! Really?" I said, trying not to laugh. "And how do you know this?"

"I heard tell he offered his rump to Signor Cantieri in exchange for your Mercutio when you sicken of it."

I laughed and then put my hand over my mouth—I was always the first to call for quiet in the wings. "Signor Cantieri is interested in no man's rump unless he's clutching it with both hands," I said. "And he never speaks with his mouth full and when he's on his knees, so he'd be in no position to offer anything."

"How very vulgar, Mr. Murray," Braxton replied, almost helpless with laughter.

"Well, between you and me, Cantieri would have a great deal more success if he wasn't so lascivious and over-ardent in his attentions. He's hardly plain to look at."

"Please, may we discuss something else? Even talk of the man makes me feel quite unwell."

We were interrupted by the arrival of our Rodolfo, Signor Greco, a taciturn man, possessed of a beautiful, unforced voice, but prone to eating an excess of foreign smallgoods, which not only gave his breath a noxious odour, but caused endless bouts of loud flatulence from the other end. It was rumoured he wore a pad in his underwear to help muffle the sound. I was not unused to having to turn my head upstage whenever I performed with him to hide my laughter from the audience, as his voluminous farts nearly always erupted at the most serious moments during the opera. His nickname among theatre folk was The Euphonium.

I hugged him and we pretend-spat over each other's shoulders, three times in all. Another good luck wish, but without the need for words.

Howard arrived at that instant with a mug of warm water for me.

He handed it to me and then took the cloak I wore to protect my costume. "Thank you," I said and then excused myself to him and to Braxton, as I needed to prepare myself for the performance.

I stood quietly next to one of the tormentor legs and did twelve toe-raises, breathing long and deeply between each one, at the same time stilling my mind. After that, I took a few sips of warm water while standing first on one leg, and then on the other, grasping the opposite ankle in turn up behind my back to stretch out my calf muscles.

Then, I felt ready. I was in my role. Edward Murray had walked from the dressing room into the wings, and now Marcello the painter strode onto the acting area of the stage and took up his opening position in front of a tall easel placed at centre stage, opposite prompt.

"*Questo mar rosso mi ammollisce assidera...*" I whispered to myself, while running my eyes over the large oil painting my character Marcello was to be dabbing at when the curtain rose. I'd no need to repeat the words—it was another ritual. We all had them, we creatures of the theatre—and some of us more than others. I placed my cup of warm water on a stool behind the easel, and then cursed. "Tiddly-fuck-bum," I said, swearing quietly and to myself. The last of my rituals.

A loud round of applause from the other side of the house curtain was the signal the conductor had entered the pit and was bowing to the audience. There was no overture to *La Bohème*. I picked up a paintbrush and stepped close to the easel, the brush in place on the canvas, and held my position.

"Stand by, Mr. Murray," I heard in a soft whisper from one of the assistant stage managers in the wings.

All at once the lights went out on the stage, plunging us into near darkness, and then I heard the whoosh of the curtain as it was raised swiftly into the flies. After a few seconds, the stage was flooded with light, and then, as soon as the tableau was revealed, the auditorium exploded with the sound of thousands of pairs of hands clapping with delight. One could also hear distinct gasps of astonishment given up by hundreds of enchanted patrons; it rippled through the theatre over the sounds of their tumultuous applause.

The scene was a marvel, costing us most of the budget we'd put aside for the construction of the set pieces. We had perfectly recreated a students' garret in Paris in the depths of winter.

The rear wall of the impoverished artists' studio consisted of one large paned glass window that stretched across the entire width of the stage, through which could be seen snowflakes falling softly in front of a precisely reproduced panorama of the famous city itself—anyone who'd ever been there would have recognised it instantly. Clouds rolled gently across a full moon, and silver light bathed the entirety of the back of the stage, flooding over the cut-out rooftops of the capital city of France.

"*Ba-dum-dum-dum,*" the orchestra played. Signor Greco and I at once broke from the frozen positions of our opening tableau vivant.

I forced my body to relax, preparing for my first breath, and readying myself to fill the auditorium with rich, round, and sonorous tones. I wasn't known as Australia's favourite baritone for nothing, and I was in my element.

*****

I eventually fell through the door of our apartment at the hotel a little after eleven thirty. I was exhausted.

"Hello?" I called out. Theo was home already; my brother's clothes were spread out over the sofa in our living room. There was no answer, so I went to his bedroom door and knocked. He didn't often invite partners back to our rooms, but I wanted to make sure. The bed was still made. I knew where he'd be, and I wanted to join him as soon as I got out of my own clothes.

The Metropole upper-floor suites all had the most splendid new bathrooms. White marble tiles, gleaming polished brass accoutrements, and equipped with the latest gymnasium-style shower baths— semicircular in shape, like a half-cage, with copper and brass tubes that sprayed water on all sides from one's feet to the top of one's head through adjustable nozzles. There was also a central, large showerhead a few feet above head height. When the water was turned on full, it was like a body massage—wonderful for tired post-performance muscles.

"Hello there," he said as I elbowed him out of the way to get under the stream from above. "I didn't hear you come in?"

"It's because you were soaping your hair when I came into the bathroom. I picked up your clobber and put it on your bed, you messy layabout."

He didn't reply, but smiled, and then goosed my behind. I pretend-yelped.

Theo was two years older than me, born in 1861. My best friend, my childhood protector, my mentor, and my surrogate father. Although he'd branched out into a different form of theatre than I, he was as equally well known. Actor, singer, raconteur, he possessed a lovely melodious Irish tenor, not only famous for his rendition of heart-warming ballads, but also for his portrayal of both heroes and villains in all of the standard theatre pieces. His Hamlet was as good as any I'd ever seen, and that had included performances in London and in Paris we'd attended on our European tour two years ago.

Not only that, he could knock out a rendition of "I'll Take You Home Again, Kathleen", delivered with such artistry and beauty of tone, it could reduce strong men to tears—I'd seen it happen myself, and more than once.

"How was the house tonight?"

"Standing room was filled and then some," I replied. "I was only grateful the theatre inspector didn't turn up."

"Well then, we've broken even?"

"Two hundred and fifteen pounds, eleven shillings and sixpence in the black as of tonight's takings."

"That means—"

"That means after Saturday night we'll have enough to pay the builder to finish our house ... what have you done to yourself?" I'd been soaping his back with a flannel. There were still stubborn streaks of makeup underneath his shoulder blades he hadn't been able to reach.

"That idiot, Mercier, didn't place the mat correctly in Act Two, and I came a cropper on my fall from the tower. Is it bruised?"

"Right down to your backside, Theo. Your right buttock is already turning black. I suppose you had stiff words with him?"

"Too right!" he replied and then sighed. "I'll be glad for the end of the run tomorrow night; I'm getting too old for all that tumbling. You're coming?"

"Yes, of course I'll be there for your last performance. If you don't mind, I won't come to the foyer for the celebrations after the performance. I've a busy day tomorrow and the last *Bohème* is on Saturday."

Theo had been performing the leading role of the magician, Ali Naqi, in a new dramatic version of *The Arabian Nights*, written by Mr. Horace Turkley from New York. It had received excellent reviews, mainly because of Theo's outstanding performance of a man brought to ruin by no fault of his own, who, after imbibing an arcane mixture, discovers he has hidden powers. Accompanied by his apprentice, Hussein, he uses those powers to recover his family fortune, making them both rich and happy. The story sounded trite, but it was an excellent piece, full of great drama, which required athletic feats from all of the main actors, and featured huge chorus numbers and astounding magic effects. The production had cost a fortune to mount and had included, for the first time on a Sydney stage in my memory, extraordinary changes of the scenery done in full view of the audience.

The final scene, in which Ali Naqi and Hussein fly off into the sunset on a very realistic winged horse, had been one of the most theatrical and bedazzling accomplishments I'd seen since returning from Europe. On the opening night, my brother had been recalled to the stage over fifteen times. I'd been so happy and proud of him I could have cried tears of pure joy.

"Tired?" he asked me as I squatted behind him, scrubbing at his ankles and the backs of his calves.

"Quite. But, we've twenty minutes more before supper arrives, and then it's off to bed for me, full stomach or not."

"I wonder if it will be Lucas or Ethan who brings up the trolley?" he mused, giving me a wink and gesturing to me to get to my feet. He twirled his finger in the air, indicating I should turn around so he could scrub my back. We had spent the entirety of our lives in each other's company, and had bathed together since we'd barely been old enough to talk.

"Really, Theo. You've more oats in you than is good for your well-being."

He laughed. "And you've not?"

"I'm more discerning than you."

That wasn't quite true, but my comment evoked a bit of playful roughhousing in the shower. He loved to tease me about my private life. His liaisons were opportunistic; mine were planned and conducted with a few, select partners—although I'd been known to ... well, let's say more often when I'd been in my twenties than in recent years, now I had a reputation to uphold.

Dinner, when it arrived, and much to my brother's disappointment, was brought up by neither Lucas nor Ethan, but by George, the elderly pantry butler who often worked night service.

Theo had opened the door wearing only a towel around his waist. George was oblivious to it. The towel was Theo's prepared signal to Lucas or Ethan he'd like some "after supper service". If either of them was amenable for a bit of joey or some bed-pressing, they'd ask Theo if he'd like them to remove the service trolley later that evening, rather than first thing in the morning. Theo would casually remark that he'd like that very much. The man would return for our dirty dishes an hour later, accompany Theo to his bedroom, and then leave with a smile on his face and five shillings in his pocket.

Such were the ways we middle-classes signalled our desires to the working-class men of our times. Theo enjoyed the game. When I had been slumming it, a wink and a half a crown peeping out between my fingers would get me what I wanted, no questions asked. One only had to be aware of who was up for it and to make sure it was in the right locale. As for the gentry? Well, there were always "negotiations".

Except among men of the same class, there was always a price to be paid. The middle class paid the working class, who could then make excuses to themselves they were only doing it for the money. The upper classes usually paid us middle-class men with gifts rather than vulgar coinage or pound notes. To them it was a ritualised form of prostitution, much like keeping a mistress—liaisons came with jewellery, or, as in my stage manager friend Braxton's case, by way of a splendid apartment, an account for clothing, expensive dinners, and a carriage. He was one of the very lucky ones.

As for the toffs skipping a social level, well, I couldn't imagine a situation in which that could possibly happen, unless it was by means of a third party and in the back of a carriage doing the rounds of the quieter parts of the city at night. Perhaps they had arrangements with their servants or stable hands? I really had no idea, neither had I ever wasted much time thinking about it.

All I knew was for someone like me, a labourer in the street might give me a nod and a wink and expect two shillings and sixpence in return, but I could never solicit someone a level above myself. In those cases, it was always a matter of waiting to see whether the nob would make the first move or not.

"You could always throw some strides on and go down to the boiler room," I said to Theo after George had left us. "There's that Mr. Carter, who's as well-equipped as the baker's Clydesdale."

"I can't be bothered, to be honest, Eddie. If it were to be room service, I wouldn't mind … but that Mr. Carter? Well, times aren't quite that desperate."

I laughed. Billy Carter was a rough and tough man who also liked it rough and tough, but only thought of himself while he was at it. He was for those occasions when one merely wanted a pint from a bottle instead of a convivial schooner of ale at the bar.

We'd barely finished eating when the telephone rang. It startled me, as we still didn't have it connected to the house we rented in Hunters Hill. We were building at Birchgrove, closer to town, but our new house was at least a few months from completion. The Hôtel Metropole was our home away from home during the busiest part of the theatre season, only because Hunters Hill could only be accessed by either a long carriage ride or by ferry—the first option arduous after eleven in the evening, and the second impossible, as the last paddle steamer was at half past ten.

I checked the clock on the chiffonier behind the sofa. "It's after midnight." I cursed under my breath and then looked to Theo, who was spread out stark naked in one of the sofa chairs, reading, sipping champagne, and trying to ignore the telephone. I didn't move, so he glared at me and went to answer it himself.

"Who was that?" I asked him after he'd returned to his armchair.

"That was Monsieur Hilaire and he's on his way up."

"Monsieur Hilaire, the hotel manager?"

"How many Monsieur Hilaires do you know?"

"At this time of night? What did he want?"

"He didn't say, except it was an exceptional circumstance."

"Aren't you going to put some clothes on?"

He shook his head and then looked at me from under his brows, dangling his champagne glass in one hand. "If Monsieur Hilaire objects to me as God made me, he can avert his eyes," he said. However, he did pick up his bath towel from where he'd flung it before dinner and arranged it over his lap.

I went to my bedroom and put on a robe in time to hear the sound of the apartment buzzer. When I opened the door, I found Monsieur Hilaire standing in the hallway, flanked by two other gentlemen, one of whom I knew, the other I did not. Chief Superintendent Abel Morris, head of the main branch of the Sydney police force, located in Philip Street, not far from the Metropole, was accompanied by a well-dressed young man, whose splendid blond moustache was so carefully groomed my eye went to it involuntarily—I immediately assumed it was an artifice, such was the precision of its symmetry. You could take the actor out of the dressing room, but you could never take the dressing room out of the actor.

"Edward?" the chief superintendent said, puzzled at my inspection of his companion's whiskers. The young man blushed at my examination and then cleared his throat, which caused me to return to the moment.

"Abel? I do beg your pardon." I turned back to the chief superintendent, painfully aware of my distraction and subsequent rudeness. "What on earth are you doing here?" I could not hide the surprise in my voice. As Theo and I had no living relatives, he could not have arrived at such an inopportune time in the evening to advise of a death in the family. My stomach went cold. Had the theatre burned down? Had there been a robbery and the evening's takings stolen?

"This is Chief Constable Andrew Bolton from the investigative unit, Edward," he said, introducing the other, younger gentleman. "May we come in?"

"Yes, of course," I stammered.

"Hello, Theo," Abel Morris said as he entered the room. "No don't get up, please. Stay as you are." My brother had made an attempt to rise, but had then remembered he was naked and had clutched at his towel to cover himself. "I'm afraid I have some rather bad news, Edward."

"Bad news? What sort of bad news?"

"I fear there's no easy way to say this, but Howard Talbot is dead."

"Dead?"

"Yes. Simon Collier, the assistant stage manager at The Royal, found him a little after midnight in a state of undress, dead in your dressing room."

"What? I'm sorry, I don't understand? He was in perfect health when I left the theatre …"

"He would have remained in perfect health until this very moment, had not someone stabbed him in the back."

"Good Lord!" Theo said, jumping from his sofa chair, his towel forgotten. Howard was as much Theo's friend as mine. "He was murdered?"

"Theo, cover yourself," I said, suddenly aware of the younger policeman's unexpected blush.

"Don't bother, we're all men here," the young man said, trying to smile. It was not hard to see he'd been taken aback by our reaction. Not many people knew how close Theo and I were to Howard and his family.

My brother began to pace, running his fingers through his hair. I felt like doing the same, but had decided one of us had to keep his wits about himself. I picked up his towel and threw it to him; he mumbled thanks and then wound it around his waist.

"Stabbed?" he asked, "and in the back? That's a coward's way of killing—"

"There's worse, Theo. Would you both mind taking a seat?" The inspector's request sounded more like an entreaty than an invitation.

"Why on earth would anyone have cause to kill Howard?" Theo blurted out. "It's beyond belief—"

"We believe the killer mistook Mr. Talbot for your brother, Mr. Murray," Andrew Bolton said, interrupting him, and then indicated we should do as the inspector had asked and take a seat.

I was too stunned at this revelation to say anything much. My open-mouthed stare probably made me look like the village idiot.

"Andrew is to be an important member of the investigative team, Edward," the superintendent said. He patted my back and shook my shoulder. I'd known him for years and supposed he was trying to make me feel at ease. "He's the newest and brightest at the station and has come to us directly after finishing his studies in law at Sydney University. He's also very fond of the theatre. I thought he'd be the best and most understanding person to keep you informed of whatever progress we're making."

"I'm a huge admirer," the young man said, "of both of you, of course. My parents and my sister and I have attended every one of your performances as far back as I can remember, sir. However, I promise not to get in the way, but I'm to be the barrier between you and anyone who may wish to harm you, Mr. Murray. As Superintendent Morris said, I'll look out for you. I promise."

"Look out for me?"

"Yes, Edward," the superintendent said. "I'm afraid both Andrew and I agree once the report appears in the newspapers tomorrow, whoever it was who made an attempt on your life will realise they've failed in their endeavour and could quite likely try again. Andrew will accompany you wherever you go during your normal daytime and evening activities. If he's caught up on other police business, we'll make sure to have a constable in street clothing at your side at all times, and another on guard outside your door of an evening while you sleep."

"I'm rather puzzled, Abel," I said. "Is this normal procedure? Surely you wouldn't go to so much trouble for any other person?"

"You're not 'any other person', Mr. Murray," Bolton said. "You're 'Australia's Son'."

"Australia's Son" was a song written by Leon Caron for his pantomime *Djin-Djin*, or *The Japanese Bogeyman*. I'd sung it so often during the lead-up to Federation, the public had christened me with its name, and it had stayed with me ever since. In concert halls, variety theatres, and at public gatherings, I'd been asked to raise the fervour of the nation by singing the stirring anthem. To most people, I was not known as Edward Murray, the opera singer, but simply as "Our lad, Australia's Son".

"Why do you think this person believed it was Édouard they'd killed?" Theo exclaimed suddenly. He only used my real name when he was emotionally charged. Our father, Jacques Marais, was a Frenchman. However, both Theo and I used anglicised versions of our real names— my brother's Christian name was Théodore, mine was Édouard. To distance ourselves from a man who'd abandoned our mother and who we didn't really know, we'd changed our surname from Marais to Murray. Few people knew.

"Well, for a start, Mr. Talbot was wearing Mr. Murray's wig and makeup, and was sitting in his dressing room chair," Bolton explained. "The room was quite dimly lit when we entered—Simon Collier explained Mr. Talbot had adjusted the mirror-frame lights to the level required for his attempt to reproduce your makeup. I've seen Mr. Murray countless times on the stage, and I had to pinch myself to believe it was not him when I inspected the body close to," the young policeman added.

"Simon … how is he?" I asked.

"Shaken, sir, but he's resilient. He'll be right enough in a day or two."

"There's more, though, Edward," the superintendent said gently. "If you would both be so kind as to take a seat?" It was the second time they'd invited us to sit. I couldn't help but think the news to follow was going to be shocking.

I sat on the sofa, and Theo lowered himself next to me, placing his hand on my knee. I could feel him shaking.

"The body had been defiled," the chief superintendent said after a moment.

"Defiled?" Theo said, trying to leap up onto his feet again, but I grabbed his arm and then put mine around his shoulder.

"I'm sorry, Abel," I said. "Perhaps you don't know this, but Howard, Theo, and I have been the closest of friends for over thirty years. We've known each other since we were children. It's a dreadful shock. Please, explain what you mean by defiled. We're both theatre people, we're used to dissembling. We can see you're trying to find a way of revealing something that's difficult or distasteful."

The chief superintendent sighed and then turned to his younger colleague and indicated he should speak.

"Someone had written your name across the top of Mr. Talbot's back in greasepaint, Mr. Murray, and under it a heart drawn around the hilt of the knife. They finished off their work with the letters RIP inscribed across the small of his back."

"Dear God—" Theo put his fist to his mouth to stifle a sob.

"But there's more?" I said. It was more a statement than a question; I knew the constable had not yet finished. I got to my feet, my hand remaining on Theo's shoulder.

Andrew Bolton nodded and then swallowed before speaking. "Your dressing room mirror had also been vandalised."

"What do you mean—vandalised?"

"We've yet to scientifically determine the substance, but we believe it's a man's ejaculate."

I was aghast. Someone had murdered Howard and then rejoiced in my presumed death with childish scrawl on his body, finishing his evil work by fetching off on my dressing room mirror?

"Eddie? Eddie?" I heard dimly. My brother's voice faded as my vision grew dark and my head began to swim. I knew I was about to faint with the shock of what I'd heard.

I couldn't stop what happened next. My feet seemed to be attached to a different body than my own, and I felt myself pitching forward into the arms of both Abel Morris and Andrew Bolton. My skull collided with the young policeman's chin with a resounding crack as we hit the floor. Superintendent Morris lost his balance and fell on top of us with a loud grunt; had it not been so unseemly, I might have laughed.

CHAPTER 2

"Good morning, Mr. Murray," a voice said quietly as light flooded into the room.

"What time is it?" I asked.

"It's half past six, sir. An early morning wake-up call, as you requested. Here's a cup of tea beside the bed."

I'd forgotten I'd rung down to the concierge last night before I went to sleep, asking to be knocked up at this time.

"Thank you, George," I said.

"There's a policeman outside your door, Mr. Murray. He's asked me to lock us in for five minutes while he goes to the butler's pantry on this floor for a moment. I wanted to check with you it would be alright for me to do so."

"Why on earth does he need to go to the butler's pantry?"

"It's to attend to a call of nature, Mr. Murray."

"Oh, for heaven's sake, tell him to use our bathroom. I suppose you've brought up a tea service? Please, offer him a cup. I'll have a full breakfast this morning—seven thirty should do me well enough. The policeman's name, do you know it?"

"Constable Cooper Haddley, sir."

"Ask what he'd prefer and bring enough breakfast for Mr. Haddley. It seems heartless to leave him outside while I eat. I'll check before I leave for the day to see what time my brother would like to have his. He has a performance this evening and will more than likely stay in bed until at least nine."

"Very good, Mr. Murray," George said and then closed the bedroom door.

I staggered out of bed and picked up my cup of tea, immediately placing it on the window ledge of my bedroom as I'd felt a powerful urge to stretch. After I'd stood on tiptoes and yawned my head off, I lumbered to the mirror on the front of the wardrobe to peer, bleary eyed, at my reflection.

Good grief! I'd a lump on my forehead. It wasn't spectacular, but it was obvious—round and reddened, although unlikely to bruise. I felt a slight twinge of discomfort; not for my own bump, but for the contusion I knew would be already showing on Constable Bolton's chin. He'd been most gallant about my collision with his jaw last night, assuring me it had been no fault of my own. "Accidents do happen," he'd said. Still, tumbling into the arms of two policemen was more fitting for a threepenny theatrical than for a man who'd been skilled at sports, acrobatics, and fisticuffs for the greater part of this life. Not that it mattered, neither of the men would pass judgement on me, but it felt distinctly un-manly. Mullins, our "stepfather", would have thrashed me for it.

I picked up my cup of tea and wandered naked into our lounge area, almost immediately colliding with a young man, who I took to be Constable Haddley.

"Oops!" I'd completely forgotten I'd told George he could use our water closet. Too late; he'd already copped an eyeful.

"All right then, sir?" he asked with a very broad grin.

"I do beg your pardon, Constable—"

"No need, Mr. Murray. Youngest of six boys. Nothing's new to me."

I laughed, and then, after I'd retrieved my robe from my bedroom, returned to shake his hand and introduce myself. He was a nice enough young fellow; very keen to meet Theo, who he'd seen regularly at The Variety theatre last year in the melodrama *Keeney's Last Hope*, which had played there for six weeks. He'd never been to an opera, and when I offered him a ticket to *Faust* next week, he politely declined, explaining "high-class" music was not to his taste, but adding he'd heard me perform countless times in other forms of theatre and at concerts.

I didn't ask if he'd enjoyed it, nor did he offer comment. I assumed that my type of singing was also off his list, due to the "high-class" type of voice I possessed. One couldn't please everyone, and I had no need to fish for compliments.

Even though I'd had one last night after returning from the theatre, I showered again to soften my beard and then shaved slowly and pensively, dressing in a new, dark suit, appropriate wear for my sombre mood and for half-mourning. Howard was not a relative, and full mourning would certainly have been unseemly and inappropriate. I grumbled a little at the height of the collar of the shirt I'd put on—so high it almost touched my chin. However, it was the latest fashion, newly delivered from our shirt maker, and looked very smart once I was fully dressed. It was with a great deal of sadness I slipped a black crêpe armband over my jacket sleeve. I sorely wanted to weep for Howard but now was not the time. That's the way I was. I saved up my sad and my happy moments for private times when no one else was around. It had to do with Theo's and my upbringing and formative years. We never showed extreme emotion except when alone with each other and when no one could chance to see or hear us rejoicing or grieving. At first, until new acquaintances became friends, we could both come across as unfeeling—removed. It could not have been further from the truth.

I checked the time, deciding I could wait no longer, and phoned Braxton's apartment, which was on the same floor as ours but at the other end of the building. I apologised for calling so early, but then told him there'd been an accident at the theatre and asked if he could come to see me after he was up and about.

Immediately after, I put through a call to our manager, Elias Solomon, to inform him of the tragic news. He was devastated. Howard had come along with us as part of our team when my brother and I had accepted Elias's offer of theatrical management. As there was much to sort out, I arranged we'd meet downstairs in the hotel palm room at half past eight to discuss the problems associated with my schedule now Howard could no longer substitute for me.

As I sat down to breakfast with Constable Haddley, Braxton arrived. When the policeman showed him into the room, he almost collapsed into my arms.

He'd already phoned the theatre and had heard the news.

*****

Elias Solomon and I both walked into the palm court at the same instant, but from different directions.

He ordered coffee, but I demurred. I'd already had so much tea I knew I'd be peeing all morning. As I revealed what I knew, his face became more and more drawn, until finally, when I divulged what Inspector Abel Morris had told me—that I'd been the intended victim—he gasped, white-faced, and reached across the table to clutch at my arm.

"I have a constant police guard, Elias, there's no need to worry," I said. "You see the young man in the corner reading the newspaper? Well, that's Constable Cooper Haddley and he's been standing guard outside our hotel door since one in the morning. He'll accompany me on my rounds for another hour or two and then hand over his vigilance to the detective who's to be my liaison with Abel. His name is Andrew Bolton; he's fresh out of law school and is a whizz of an investigator, so the inspector told me."

"Being a 'whizz', as you call him, is not going to help if someone attempts violence towards you, Edward."

"Have no fear, Constable Bolton was not only the junior wrestling champion of Sydney University but is also a sculler, and an expert with a pistol. I think between the two of us, I should be safe."

"The 'two of us'? Which two?"

"He and I, of course," I said with a smile.

"Honestly, Edward," he replied, smoothing his moustache into place, "I don't know how you can be so flippant about your own safety."

"Because I won't let a coward, a man who stabbed my closest friend in the back, intimidate me. That's why I shall go about my business as I ever did, with one eye on my work and the other on the lookout. No one will hurt one of mine in an attempt to get at me."

"In your shoes, I fear I would not be as brave as you. But then again, I didn't lead the life either you or Theo did."

"We've faced far worse, Elias. Now, let's talk about what's to be done."

"Well then, you'll have to go to the costume fitting, I'm afraid. Otherwise none of your clothes will be ready. There are five costumes for *Don Giovanni*, each one extravagant, and they'll need a lot of work."

"Five?"

"One for the opening scene, en déshabillé, after violating Donna Anna, which you'll wear for the murder of her father. Then will be a second for when you run into Donna Elvira and for the next scene for the seduction of Zerlina. After that, the third will be something outstanding for the ball at the end of the first act. An act two costume for the serenade will make four, and then the fifth for the meeting in the graveyard with the Commendatore, and a pièce de résistance for the final scene … oh."

"That makes six—"

"Oh, dear. Yes, I'm sorry. Six costumes in all. And they must be ready in two weeks from tomorrow. So, you see—"

"Yes, I understand. I've already made arrangements to meet Constable Bolton at Tanning's for the fittings. I shan't be able to do the *Fledermaus* rehearsal at the Criterion this afternoon; I simply must visit Eileen. I was best man at Howard's wedding and Theo is the eldest boy's godfather. She and the children will be devastated."

"Cantieri won't be happy," my manager said.

"Oh, yes he will."

"So, you've something up your sleeve?"

I nodded.

"Aren't you going to tell me?"

"I know you'll disapprove, so I'll wait until it's a fait accompli before I let you know. In any case, it brings me to the next bit of business I wanted to discuss with you. I spoke with Braxton Miller earlier this morning and he tells me the Theatre Royal is dark on Sunday afternoon. I'd like you to approach Arnold Willings and ask if I could hire the theatre for an afternoon subscription concert to raise money for Eileen and Howard's children."

"He'll ask for an arm and a leg ..."

"Not with the tantalising promise dangling in the air of a possible repeat mounting of *La Bohème* in August when Theo and I return from New Zealand, he won't."

"Well, I think a subscription concert is an excellent idea. Will you set up a fund?"

"I think everyone in the theatre will not only donate their performances for the benefit, but will also throw a few shillings in as well. Everyone loved Howard."

"As did I. I'll subscribe ten pounds and personally stand the costs of the theatre."

"My word!" I said. "That's incredibly generous, Elias."

"Well, were it not for him, I should not have made quite so much money from you, young man. I'm sorry to be blunt, but his death is going to leave us in a predicament on Wednesday night."

I cleared my throat. I couldn't let my brother down, and yet I had to make a final curtain appearance at the end of *Faust*. "I tell you what, Elias. Tell Willings if he'll release me early, at the end of Act Four, I'll give him a free *Lucia di Lammermoor* at the end of next month. You'll still get your management fee; I'll perform pro bono."

"Now who's being generous? You'll do no such thing. I have the man at my mercy. Don't forget who manages nearly every singer in Sydney. I'll come to some arrangement. Now, we need to think about finding you a dresser. I'll put an advertisement in the Saturday papers for open auditions on Monday morning."

"If you make it late on Tuesday morning, I can be there, and then we can compare physiques. Make sure you put in the advertisement they need to be able to fence—"

"And do gymnastics, be able to read music, sing a little, and have had dance training … yes, yes, I know."

"Thank you, Elias. Thank you very much. What would I do without you?"

"I think you'd manage quite well, Edward."

"Will you be my spokesman to the press? In the theatre world, there's no secret kept longer than it takes to walk five yards. Someone will have rung the rags for a half-crown on the sly."

"Of course. I'll fend off the jackals—"

"Perhaps you might let slip that despite the terrible incident, Mr. Talbot would have insisted the show must go on. Therefore, I'll still be attending Theo's performance of *The Arabian Nights* this evening."

"Do you think that's wise?"

"The coward stabbed Howard in the back. Do you hear me? In the back! He's hardly likely to repeat John Wilkes Booth's extravagant gesture and shoot me point blank in the manager's box at the theatre. Besides, I'll have my detective with me."

"I suppose that's something …"

"I've sent a telegram to his home inviting him, his parents, and his sister to join me tonight as my guests at the performance. If the detective is to be at my side for however long, it would be unfair of me to impose a situation on him for which he might not already be prepared."

"Prepared?"

"It's the last performance. He's a policeman; who knows if the man owns evening clothes? I offered the expense of hire of tails for both him and his father. I'm sure his mother and sister will have something suitable; however, in my experience, it's the men who are always lacking."

"Listen to yourself, Edward," my manager said. "I think you're underestimating Mr. Bolton without really knowing him. If, as you say, he has completed a degree in law at Sydney University, he's bound to have formal evening clothes. What do you think they wear when they attend house dinners? Cow cocky hats, bushies' swags, and stockmen's strides?"

I felt instantly ashamed of myself. I'd fallen into the trap most men in our new Edwardian period were, at times, guilty of. The trap of assuming something about a man by the clothes he wore. Admittedly, although Andrew Bolton's suit was patently not bespoke, it was certainly well-cut. However, the collars and cuffs of his shirt were celluloid. Of all the things I should have had my mind on, I'd wondered about it last night when I'd finally got to bed. Instead of dwelling on poor Howard, or on the attempt on my life, I'd spent what seemed like an age trying to marry up the policeman's beautifully groomed moustache and immaculate haircut with the quality of his garments.

"Well?" Elias asked.

"I owe the man an apology. You are right, of course. It's the slum boy come good inside me making judgements that aren't mine to make. There's nothing worse than someone who's moved up in the world when it comes to judging social niceties."

"Just because you have starched linen collars on your handmade shirts and all your clothes are lovingly crafted by a tailor, it says nothing about who you are inside, Edward Murray. When you and Theo turned up at my auditions, when was it? Eighty-one, I think. You both wore hired, ill-fitting clothing. You were living at the time in a doss-house in Redfern and looked like you hadn't eaten in three days. Had I judged you by appearances—"

"Very well. I surrender. You are quite right. I'll get to know our Mr. Bolton first and then make my assumptions afterwards."

"There's one thing I guarantee already, my boy."

"And what's that?"

"If he has a *Legum Baccalaureus* from my old alma mater, then he'll have a better handle on Latin and Greek than you do."

"Well, that's hardly difficult, Elias. As you know, I have none!"

"Quite so, my dear boy," he replied with a knowing smile. "Quite so."

*****

"Who was that?" Constable Cooper Haddley asked me, holding open the carriage door.

"Who?"

"The gentleman who so politely tipped his hat to you a moment ago."

"Ah! That was Lester Palmer; he's the chief writer on the arts for the *Freeman's Journal*. He's extraordinarily well mannered, unlike some of the other members of his profession. No doubt Mr. Solomon will make an appointment for a special interview."

"Regarding Howard Talbot's murder?"

"No, Cooper; regarding the premiere of *Don Giovanni* two weeks hence."

"Where to, sir?" the carriage driver asked.

"Number forty-three Rawson Place, if you please. It's on the corner of Pitt Street."

"Right you are, sir. The Gulgong Private Hotel it is, then."

"I thought your costume fitting was at Railway Square, Mr. Murray?"

"It is, Constable Haddley, but I need to make arrangements for the rehearsal I'll have to miss this afternoon."

He nodded but with no real understanding. I think he was overawed at the carriage. It was Braxton's, who'd loaned it to me until lunchtime. Sir Horace had gifted him a splendid open phaeton, and as Braxton was working in the theatre most evenings, he used it infrequently, so Theo and I were often its most frequent passengers.

The streets were very crowded, and when we passed by the town hall, we had to stop and alight as a hearse was leaving St. Andrew's cathedral next door, and the cortège after it was very long. Both Haddley and I stood beside the phaeton and removed our hats until the last carriage had disappeared down Bathurst Street.

"This is where I first heard you sing 'Australia's Son'," Haddley said out of the blue. "In Sydney Town Hall, on Thursday the third of January, last year. We couldn't get to Centennial Park for the Federation declaration on the first. My mother was very ill at the time."

"You wouldn't have heard me there had you arrived in any case," I said. "There were countless thousands of people, and I doubt if any, other than the official party, would have heard anything. Open air concerts are a futile exercise for vocalists."

"Well, you were very stirring at the Town Hall. We all shed tears."

"Thank you, Constable. It's very kind of you to say so."

"Father has some of your Edison cylinders. You sounded quite different in real life."

"Why don't you take up my offer of a ticket for *Faust*? Even if the music's not to your taste, the story is very moving and the costuming is wonderful."

"If you'll beg my pardon, Mr. Murray, but perhaps I might oblige myself of your generosity at another time, in view of having to stand guard outside your hotel door from eleven in the evening until the following morning."

"Of course. Once this nonsense is over ... but you'll get to hear me in the flesh quite a lot over the next few days, as I need to rehearse nearly every day."

"Well, Mr. Murray, that will be quite a treat."

"You may change your mind after you hear me singing scales for half an hour."

He smiled and then turned his attention to the sights of George Street as Braxton's coachman manoeuvred the phaeton along the street through heavy traffic, weaving in and out between trams, omnibuses, handsome cabs, and delivery drays.

My friend was dead; and yet the world continued as it had done yesterday.

*****

"I'm sorry, Mr. Murray," the concierge at the Gulgong Private Hotel said, "but the internal speaking tube mechanism is being replaced by electric telephone. I can take you up to Mr. Harcourt's room if you wish? There's a smoking parlour on his floor you may use if you need to hold a meeting," she added, looking at Constable Haddley over my shoulder.

"There's no need, Mrs. Jamison. I'll only need a moment and it's nothing private, I can speak to him either in his room or in the corridor."

It took three attempts at knocking, followed by the rattle of his door handle before Julius Harcourt responded. "Who's there?" he called out sleepily.

"You have a visitor, Mr. Harcourt," the concierge said, her ear to the door.

"Tell them to go away," he replied.

"Is the door locked?" I asked.

"No," she replied.

I excused myself to her, removed my hat, opened the door, and entered his room, closing the door behind me and leaving her and Haddley outside in the hallway.

"Mr. Murray!" he squeaked, jumping up in bed and holding the sheet up to his chin.

"Good morning, Julius," I said, sitting on the edge of the bed. I shook the leg of the bed's other occupant, who pretended to play possum. "Good morning, Chase," I added.

"Morning, Mr. Murray," the head mechanist from the Theatre Royal mumbled and then groaned and placed his pillow over his head. He'd made such an effort to be known as a ladies' man, with no real evidence of it, that Theo and I had thought as much about him for years before we discovered he and Harcourt were casually involved.

"No need to look so startled, Julius," I said, forcing myself to put on a faux-smile. "It's common knowledge you know. You and Chase ..."

"I—"

"I'm the last person in the world to pass judgement, and I'm here for another matter. I'm sorry to have to tell you this, but Howard Talbot was murdered last night in the theatre—"

"Murdered?" Chase Osborne poked his head from under his pillow, his eyes wide with shock.

"Yes, I'm afraid I haven't the stomach to go into details. If you'll forgive me, I'm still rather upset myself."

"We were here—"

"No one's suggesting you had anything to do with it; either of you.

I spoke with Braxton Miller this morning and he said he saw you both leave fifteen minutes after the final curtain. As I said, I'm here for another matter. I remember you stood in for me for two performances of Signor Cantieri's *Die Fledermaus* at the Prince of Wales last year, Julius?"

"Yes, I did, Mr. Murray. You were indisposed with the influenza at the time."

"I heard tell you did a good showing."

"Why thank you, Mr. Murray."

"I need to visit Howard's family this afternoon and I'm scheduled to rehearse Miss Blanchard into Act Two—she's to sing Adele. I'd be grateful if you could revisit the score and refresh your mind on the moves. I'd like you to attend as my replacement if you'd be so kind. I'll offer you the usual fee from my own pocket—a crown, isn't it? And, as an enticement, I can offer you something else. There's to be a subscription concert at The Royal on Sunday afternoon for Mr. Talbot. In return for the favour I've asked of you, I'll make sure you get a nice song for yourself—a solo, not a duet or an ensemble piece."

"Why, Mr. Murray, I had no idea you held me in such regard—"

"I'd hold you in even higher esteem if you'd mind your place and come to understand your position in the theatre community needs to be earned, not merely bestowed upon you because you happen to be able to sing and have a comely face. You have talent enough, but you try too hard. Your time will come, and the more self-effacing you appear to be among your peers, the quicker it will arrive."

Julius Harcourt reddened and then swallowed. I doubt if he'd heard such plain speech, but his was an incipient talent that needed careful fostering. His voice would be irrevocably damaged if he pursued repertoire currently beyond his reach.

"What shall I sing … at the concert, I mean?"

The fact he'd asked my advice was a good sign. Normally, I'd have expected him to choose one of the larger dramatic works I might have sung myself. "Perhaps you might choose one of the Donizetti arias, Julius? I've heard you practising the Belcore aria from *L'Elisir D'Amore*?

Or maybe you'd like to sing the aria that won you the *Fuller's Journal* competition two years ago, from *Don Sebastiano*?"

"You mean, '*O Lisbona*'? You think I'm ready to sing it for an audience?"

"Yes, a few years will have allowed it to mellow in your voice. The theatre has the orchestral parts."

"He said 'thank you', Mr. Murray," Chase piped up, speaking on his behalf while climbing out of bed. "I'm sorry, sir, but I have to get into the theatre; there's bound to be chaos in there."

"Yes, thank you, Mr. Murray," Julius added. "I promise I'll repay your generosity."

"You can do that two ways, young man," I said. "Firstly, make sure you know your lines this afternoon and don't put on airs and graces. You are representing me, after all. Please don't forget it."

"Of course," he replied. "And the second?"

"Just keep in mind Signor Cantieri only desires things he cannot have. Once he's tasted forbidden fruit, it's invariably cast to one side."

"I have no idea what you mean, sir," he said, casting a furtive glance at Chase, who was pulling on his trousers. He could not see it, but I was sitting at an angle and noticed the mechanist's knowing smile.

"I think you know exactly what I mean, Julius. Now, I'll bid you good day. I have costume fittings at Tanning's in fifteen minutes. Good morning, gentlemen," I said and then left them.

"Everything all right, Mr. Murray?" Constable Haddley asked me when I joined him in the corridor. The concierge was nowhere to be seen. I supposed she'd returned to her position at the reception desk.

"Everything's as it should be, Constable," I replied.

"Very good, sir," he said and then followed me down the hallway to the elevator.

*****

"It's such a dreadful thing, Mr. Murray."

Gideon, the costume maker's assistant, was on his knees, adjusting my gaiters and pinning the rosettes in place.

"Thank you for agreeing to step in for Howard as my dresser,

Gideon," I replied. "It's only until we can find a replacement, and you know how the costumes fit better than anyone. If you come in at six tomorrow night, I can talk you through the changes."

"Well, it's not as if I'd be doing anything else, Mr. Murray. My eyes are tired enough by the time the sun goes down. I gave up hand stitching at night when I was sixteen."

"And you're all of what … nineteen, now?"

"I'll be twenty in three weeks, Mr. Murray."

"Barely legal," I said, winking at him.

He returned my wink with a smile. "Not even, Mr. Murray."

We both laughed, interrupted by a knock at the door.

"Who is it?" Gideon called out.

"It's me, Cooper Haddley, Mr. Murray. Letting you know Detective Bolton has arrived and so I'll be off. Shall I send him in?"

"Thank you for looking after me, Constable Haddley. Have a good rest; I know you deserve it … and you can tell Detective Bolton he's welcome to come in, or to stay outside the door as he wishes, but that if he's coming in, there's due warning I'm naked."

"Very good, sir. Have a good day."

"You're not entirely naked, Mr. Murray," Gideon said, still on his knees. "You're wearing red stockings and gaiters."

I'd barely stripped them off when Andrew Bolton poked his head around the screen that shielded the room from the doorway.

"Good morning, Chief Constable," I said, noticing the detective's shy glance at my furry backside. "This is Gideon Hawking, who's the main costume fitter for Tanning's."

The two men greeted each other, and then Bolton drew up a chair and asked if he might smoke. I did so myself and asked him if I might have one of his. Many people thought it odd professional singers smoked; but it was as much a social event as anything and most of the medical profession thought it beneficial to the throat. I, however, only partook in moderation. Theo smoked like a chimney, ordering beautiful hand-rolled cigarettes from the tobacconist on the ground floor of the Metropole, the packages stamped with his name. The smart packets raised not a few eyebrows, but also generated a lot of sales for the merchant, who supplied them to my brother for free.

"Nice shiner you have there, Mr. Bolton," Gideon said cheekily.

"Well, technically it's not a shiner, Mr. Hawking; it's a bruise to the chin."

"I didn't know you coppers liked the turps that much. Walk into a door then, did we?"

"I signed the pledge so that's not the reason. Some clumsy boofhead tripped and whacked me with his noggin."

"Likely story."

Gideon's wry smile and raised eyebrow made me chuckle. I'd arrived feeling melancholic, but the round of light banter and the detective's charming glance had cheered me up a little.

"I hope you slept well, Mr. Bolton," I said while making a mental note that he didn't drink alcohol. It was odd. He didn't have the usual demeanour of a temperance man. They were normally plain faced dour creatures who spouted bible verses at the drop of a hat. No, Mr. Bolton had other reasons for his choice of sobriety. It was intriguing, but none of my business.

"Fairly well enough," he said. "Until I was rudely awoken by the boy from the post office."

"Oh, dear. I'm sorry," I replied. I doubt if I'd be as good-humoured as he seemed to be after what could have only been a few hours' sleep.

"Mother thought something terrible had happened when your telegram arrived this morning." He opened his cigarette case and offered one to me and Gideon, who took it, stood up, and then stretched his back. "My telephone number is Camperdown twenty-nine," he added, handing me his card. "I should have given it to you last night, but what with the confusion, it completely skipped my mind."

"I had wondered whether to ask whether you were connected, but as there are so few private telephone lines in use as yet …"

"It was connected to the house because of my job. It's a party line with four other callers on the wire. But as so few of us receive calls, it's relatively private. Anyway, Father and I both thank you for your offer, but we do have our own evening wear. He's a regular speaker at our local Oddfellows club, and I have mine because of—"

"Hall dinners at university?"

He laughed. "Yes, for those, *and* for opening nights at the theatre, Mr. Murray."

"You must think me terribly patronising," I said, leaning forward so he could light my cigarette. As he was still seated, I suddenly became aware my private parts were at eye level when I stood back up again. He glanced quickly and then looked up at me as he flicked his match safe closed.

"I thought no such thing, Mr. Murray, only that you were being very kind and considerate. As you don't know me from Adam, both Father and I thought your gesture solicitous in the extreme."

"It's his middle name," Gideon said with a dry smile.

I scuffed the back of his head with my palm and laughed. "Neither Theo nor I have middle names, you ragamuffin; you know that very well. Now, I'm beginning to feel uncomfortable standing here stripped to the skin while you two are fully clothed. Let's get this fitting underway, Gideon. What's next?"

"It's the opening costume, Mr. Murray, and I know you're going to complain, but let me tell you the house will swoon when you make your first appearance. You're to be bare-chested, in duck-egg blue tights, with a silver-embroidered jacket worn à la Russe."

"À la Russe?" Andrew Bolton asked.

"Like a hussar," I explained. "Over the shoulder, only one arm through the jacket sleeve."

"How will you fight Donna Anna's father like that? Won't it be awkward?"

I suddenly realised I'd made another dreadful mistake in my summation of Mr. Bolton and would once again have to re-evaluate my opinion of him. "You know the story, then?"

"I've seen you perform it probably six times in all, Mr. Murray. Twice in ninety-seven and then again at least four times in last year's new production at Her Majesty's."

"Really?"

"I'm sorry; you must think me an awful show off. But I'm not really. I simply love music. Father is blind, you see, and he loves to go to concerts and the opera."

"Good heavens! I'm terribly sorry to hear that. Has he always been so?"

"No, it's been relatively recent—he first noticed it about ten years ago. The doctor said it was an age-related degeneration of the retina, and although it was unusual for someone as young as he was at the time, there's nothing could be done. But it hasn't stopped him. He still works in the family tonsorial parlour."

"He what?" I wasn't sure I hadn't misheard. I had my head down, pulling on the tights. They were indeed a splendid shade of pale blue.

"He still cuts hair and grooms moustaches and beards. He's a wonder."

"Well, if it is he who attends to your head and whiskers, then I shall more than likely call upon him myself. The man's an artist."

"He'd fall over himself with nerves, Mr. Murray. After my sister, he's your greatest admirer."

"Nonsense, Andrew," I said. "May I call you by your first name when we're not in public? I hate all this mister this and mister that nonsense."

"But of course, although I'm timid to use such a level of familiarity so soon after making an acquaintance."

I laughed. "You must call me Edward, if I'm to use your first name. And, as for level of familiarity, I'm standing here before you, completely naked, my bollocks blowing in the breeze, and you're the one who's clothed; so, it should be me who is shy."

"You're not quite naked," he replied with a grin. "But you may as well be."

"Is there a codpiece?" I asked Gideon, aware of the detective's meaning about being almost naked. The tights left nothing to the imagination.

"No, Mr. Murray," he replied.

"Then fetch me my ballbag and dance belt, if you wouldn't mind. They're in the satchel I brought with me."

I turned side-on to the mirror. The tights had been beautifully made and fitted perfectly. I had rolled the top around a length of cotton cord so they were pulled up tight and were wrinkle free. I undid the cord and then pulled the waist down around my knees. Gideon handed me the soft kid-skin pouch.

"That's a ballbag?" Andrew asked.

"Yes. With a codpiece I don't normally need one. But for decency's sake, especially when sword fighting, I need the bag. You see," I said, as I dropped my private parts into the sac and then tightened the drawstring, "all neat and tidy. The dance supporter goes over the top, like this."

Gideon draped the triangular piece of multi-layered fabric over the bag and then tied the ribbon that ran along its top edge around my waist. I threaded the ribbon from the lower point of the triangle between my legs, and he tied it at the back with the other ends.

"Et voilà," I said, pulling the tights back up and securing them around my waist with the cord. "There's certainly a mound, but nothing that would give offence to the eye."

"Isn't it uncomfortable?"

"A little, but you get used to it. Nothing near as uncomfortable as the thought of what the audience might think were I prancing around the stage wearing nothing under the tights at all."

He laughed gently. "I understand the dance what-you-may-call-it, but I'm still puzzled about the need for the bag?"

"It's because Mr. Murray has big bollocks and they pop out the side of his belt if he moves around too energetically," Gideon said.

"Gideon!" I laugh-protested, but Andrew Bolton already had his head back and was laughing heartily.

"Well, it's the truth," the costume fitter said as I pinched his ear, trying my hardest not to laugh at his sauciness.

"It may be the truth, but now I've no secrets," I said.

"I'm a gentleman," Andrew Bolton said, "and a gentleman doesn't kiss and tell."

I thought it an odd comment, but there was something so affable about him I simply smiled and then asked him for another cigarette.

*****

"I must say you took everything in your stride, Andrew," I said.

We'd elected to eat a catch-as-you-can lunch in the restaurant of the first-class waiting room of the Central railway station, across the road from Tanning's.

"Everything?"

"My state of undress; it didn't seem to bother you?"

"I'm not sure why you think it would. You're not embarrassed, are you?"

"I'm mostly used to theatre people around me when I'm having costume fittings. I did invite you to stay outside. Some people are more prudish than others when it comes to the human body, that's all."

"Phht! I swim naked at the Corporation Baths three times a week and was in the army for four years. I've seen more than you in your birthday suit, Edward."

"One never thinks of it, you know. It was only as we were leaving, I wondered if you were being blasé or incredibly stoic."

"It takes a lot more than your splendid physique to startle me. For a man of thirty-two …"

I smiled into my soup. "Thirty-nine, if you please, unless you're purposely trying to flatter me."

"My information is incorrect. I'm sorry."

"I'll take thirty-two any day."

"I've left my evening clothes with your concierge. I thought I might change at your hotel if that's not inconvenient? Perhaps, after that, you might agree to be my guest for dinner before the performance this evening? I said I'd meet my sister and parents in the foyer of the theatre at quarter to the hour. If we sat down close to half past six, we could have a decent meal, unless you'd rather eat in your room at the Metropole."

"We could go to the Café de Paris if you like. The food there is excellent."

"I was rather thinking of my club, Edward. The Australian? But, I'm sure you're already a member. Maybe you're tired of the place?"

"You're a member of The Australian Club?"

"Yes. Since leaving the army. The regimental commander put me up for it."

"I've eaten there, and I admit it's splendid. However, I'm not a member."

"Oh, is that because of your religion?"

I had no idea what he meant. Theo and I were Roman Catholics. There were admittedly some doors closed to us because of our faith, but not The Australian Club.

"Religion?"

He blushed softly. "I have seen both you and your brother naked, Edward …"

I had to press my napkin to my mouth to stop my laughter. "We were both circumcised before being sent to India," I explained. "We're tykes, not Jews!"

"Oh, good God!" he exclaimed. "What a dreadful faux-pas."

I smiled and then reached across the table and patted the back of his hand. "It's not a faux-pas in the least. It was done for hygienic purposes—that was what we were told anyway. White boys in India and all that. I don't know what they thought we were going to do with our doodles that Hindu boys don't? Theo was ten at the time, and I was eight. I had a terrible time. My brother thought I might bleed to death or end up disfigured."

"I assure you from what I saw, you're far from disfigured."

I stirred my soup with the back of my spoon.

"You don't have to explain," he said.

"About?"

"India," he said and then shook his head, as if to say, "it's not important".

"No, it's all right. I have no shame in it. But Mother sold Theo, Maddie, and me to a theatrical agent—to go to India as child performers."

"Sold?"

"Yes, it was the custom back then. They called it adoption, but to tell the truth, he gave my mother ten pounds for each of us and asked her to make her mark on a contract."

He looked at me thoughtfully before speaking. "You came from a poor family?"

"Yes, we were the youngest three of eight children. Born and brought up in Ultimo—the most squalid slum in the city at the time."

"You said Maddie. I take it that's your sister?"

"*Was* our sister; she died in seventy-two of the scours. We were in Calicut at the time, and she was only nine. I cried for days. There's only Theo and I left now."

"Of eight children, there's only the two of you left alive? Good heavens."

"Yes, we came back in 1879—I was sixteen and Theo eighteen—to find the rest of them had died; some of the bubonic plague and some during the scarlet fever epidemic in the early seventies."

"And your parents?"

"Father left when I was three. I barely knew him. As for Mother, well the drink and loose living took her away."

"Loose living?"

"After we left, she did what any poor woman would do with five children to bring up on her own."

"Laundry?"

I chuckled. "I'm afraid in the stakes for who is the finer gentleman, I've no chance against a man of your tact and sensibility."

"It must have been terrible."

I shrugged. I wasn't insensible to what had happened, but had it not been for Lloyd Mullins, the man who became our "stepfather", Theo and I might well have gone the same way as our siblings. Their faces were blurred to me now. I couldn't remember them as living people any more, only as shadowy presences in my early life.

Theo, Madeleine, and I had begged. Street-entertainment they called it. But we'd sung outside the ferry terminals, accompanied by

Theo's clever accordion playing, dressed in our rags and with a hat at our feet. Mullins had seen us one day and had been impressed with our ability to sing in harmony and to dance at the same time, and that's what had led him to adopting us. Three lives for thirty quid.

"That's the reason I've never become a member of The Australian Club."

"What, you mean the circumstances of your birth? Surely not."

"No, Andrew. Despite being the so-called 'toast of the town', my past is my past. Someone with an axe to grind sent a letter to the board when my nomination for membership was before them. No place in their hallowed halls for a slum child whose mother was a prostitute."

"That's outrageous," he said, sinking back against his chair. "You're famous, Edward. Your excellent manners, your speech, your comportment show you're a true gentleman to anyone who cares to look."

"The gentleman you see before you is a confection, Andrew. One cobbled together by spit and determination. To those men born to it, I am an imposter."

"I can scarce believe it. It makes me shamed beyond words." He placed his hand over mine. It was a solicitous gesture, but I appreciated it. His hand was warm and his fingers supple and strong. I longed to look into his eyes but was afraid he might see something there I'd spent my life trying to hide from men I found attractive, but whom I thought unlikely to respond to my interest.

"Please, take no offence on my behalf. I've learned to make my life my own and to love those who care about me. The theatre might not be filled with the same class of people as one would find in society, but I can promise you their hearts are as true and their friendships quite as steadfast."

"And yet I saw a reproduction of you and your colleague Miss Blanchard at Government House in the newspaper two weeks ago? It's the most awful hypocrisy if what you say is true," he said, removing his hand and then smoothing his moustache with the backs of his fingers.

I smiled and then leaned back as the waiter arrived to remove our soup plates. "There's beef or mutton, gentlemen," the man announced. "Which would you prefer?"

We both elected to take the beef. Mutton at this time of the year, at the end of the season, would come from ewes and weathers not fit for anything but the glue works.

"Let me tell you something about that evening at Government House, Andrew," I said, shaking my head to his offer of another cigarette. "Miss Blanchard arrived at the front door and was met by the Governor. We'd been engaged to sing after dinner, but before we performed, she sat at table and dined with the other guests. I, however, was directed to the tradesman's entrance, was met by no one, and had a cold collation in the staff dining room by myself. That's how they see us—theatre people, that is. It's well and good to laud our praises after performances, and to mix with us on special occasions, to name drop that we're their friends, but we're tradesmen to them—like someone who arranges the flowers, or who cooks their food, or cleans their houses, polishes their shoes. We supply a service and that's it."

"But you said Miss Blanchard sat down to dinner."

"She's a woman, Andrew. One with an ample bosom and a ready smile. The rules are different between the sexes. She's an ornament to those men who run and rule our world; a pretty thing that exists to reflect their power and to reinforce their masculinity."

He sat silently for a while, puffing vigorously on his cigarette, staring at me. I met his eye. He offered no challenge but radiated an unspoken "how can you bear to put up with it?"

"May I explain how I continue to smile and be polite to those men?"

"I must say I'm staggered by what you've told me already; but, please, proceed …"

"For our two songs each and a duet, Miss Blanchard's fee was dinner, sitting at the Governor's right-hand side, a carriage ride to and from Government House, and perhaps the chance of an assignation and the hope of meeting a suitable, wealthy gentleman in search of a mistress. My fee, however, was ten guineas, a cold collation, and the pleasure of passing a stool in the Governor's water closet and not flushing the bowl."

Andrew burst into laughter, hastily pressing his napkin to his mouth, in case heads began to turn.

"The more patronising the crowd, the higher my fee," I added.

"Ten guineas? I can hardly believe my ears! That's a huge amount of money."

"Don't you think I'm worth it?"

"Every penny and more," he replied with a bright smile.

"I think you're wasted in your profession, Constable Bolton. You should take up as a professional charmer. Now, while we're waiting for our roast to arrive, tell me a bit about you."

Andrew Bolton gave me a quick résumé of his life so far. He came from a middle-class family whose patriarch, as I already knew, was a hairdresser of no small ability. His parents had purchased a small house in the new suburb of Camperdown, close to the centre of the city, and Andrew and his sister had gone to private schools. Immediately after finishing, he'd joined up in the N.S.W. Regiment, but after a minor accident to his foot, was shifted into an administrative position. The job had been to evaluate reports of theft of personal property and pilfering from the stores; something he'd soon learned he had a natural aptitude for.

Finding he'd tired of the army after four years, and after hearing of the news of his father's failing eyesight, he'd resigned and then applied to the police force, where his skills at investigation, rather than day-to-day policing, had brought him to the notice of the sergeant of his local station. Not long after that, the sergeant had moved on to the main branch in Philip Street where my friend Chief Superintendent Abel Morris was based. The sergeant had recommended Andrew, who had been transferred there; then, in search of greater knowledge of his chosen profession, had taken leave from his employment to complete a degree in law.

"That's about it, Edward," he said, finishing his story as our meals arrived at the table. "Graduated last December, and here I am."

"You didn't want to practise law—to become a solicitor or a barrister?"

"Not for me. I wanted to understand what was behind the job I was employed to perform."

We ate in silence for a while. I was digesting not only my delicious, tender beef but also what he'd told me about his life. It was so different from mine. I suppose that's what made lives so interesting—the contrasts. I caught his eye and he smiled at me. It was such a genuine smile that I couldn't help smiling back. *Careful.* I could hear Howard's voice in my mind. I had the habit of becoming too interested in very nice men, who were generally not of the same persuasion as I.

"What are you thinking, Andrew? Go on, speak your mind."

"Why did you come back?"

"From India?"

"Yes."

"My voice broke."

"I'm sorry, I don't understand."

"I sang all the soprano roles in Mr. Mullins's touring company. You think it odd? But boys often have more flexible voices than girls of the same age. In any case, it was considered charming by the British Raj to see performances in which the roles were performed by children of the opposite sex. We did not only variety performances but operas as well. It was quite the thing back then. Lilliputian Companies they called them. They toured everywhere: here, New Zealand, South Africa, Singapore, Hong Kong. Well, Mullins had a company that performed all over India. I sang most of those high, coloratura leading ladies, like Rosina in *The Barber of Seville*. So, when my voice broke, I was no longer any use to Mr. Mullins, so he released us from our contract and put Theo, me, and Howard on a ship with third-class passage back home."

"Howard? Howard Talbot?"

"Yes. I told you we'd known him for thirty years. He was an acrobat; fell badly from a trapeze in Panaji and broke his back. Theo was an alto as a child, so his transition to tenor was far smoother than mine.

My voice went from high, light, and agile one day to sounding like a squeaky gate in need of a good oiling the next."

"You must have been devastated," he said.

"You know the worst thing, Andrew? It was to arrive at home at Darling Harbour after five weeks at sea and find the area in which we had lived had gone. Totally! The whole street had been demolished and rebuilt. It took us weeks to find out the rest of our family was dead. We'd had six quid's worth of Indian currency in our pockets, which no bank would change."

"What did you do?"

"I'm afraid that's a story for another day," I said. "It must be Howard's death that's made me open up to you like this. I never talk about the past as freely."

"Perhaps it's that, or perhaps it's simply because I'm a trustworthy sort of chap."

"Perhaps you are, Andrew, perhaps you are."

*****

I simply couldn't talk about those first six months after we'd got back home. I'd never asked Theo or Howard what they did to earn money. I could guess at Theo's activities, but Howard had probably resorted to petty thievery.

It had been tough going, only alleviated when one day, a year later, I'd woken up and was able to sing a major scale in tune and without any cracks or breaks. The one saving grace of the whole hideous adventure in India had been Lloyd Mullins's wife, Florence. Florence Mullins had been a student of Maria Malibran, the famous soprano who'd ruled the opera houses of Europe in the early part of the last century. Mrs. Mullins had been a tough but thorough teacher who understood vocal technique perfectly. It was she who'd taught me everything I knew. So, with a robust understanding of how to sing already knocked into me, it didn't take me long to master my youthful and fresh-sounding baritone.

It was another year later, on the day after my eighteenth birthday, in 1881, that Theo and I had presented ourselves at open auditions for Mr. Elias Solomon's Theatrical Agency. We'd performed "Excelsior" as

Balfe had composed it, a duet for tenor and baritone, accompanied by Howard on the pianoforte.

I distinctly remembered the look on Elias's face when I sang my first solo line in the duet. His head had snapped up from notes he'd been writing. My voice had rung out in the audition hall:

> *In happy homes he saw the light,*
> *Of household fires gleam warm and bright*
> *Above, the spectral glaciers shone*
> *And from the lips escaped a groan*

Gradually, the impresario had settled back into his chair, his hands clasped across his stomach, staring at me intently while he'd listened through to the end of the duet.

"The baritone can stay. I've no use for the other two," he'd said after we'd finished.

"We come as three," I'd replied, bravely standing forward, but with my knees shaking.

He'd gone so red in the face I'd thought he'd have an infarction. But then, he'd swallowed and asked me if I had any classical repertoire. I asked him if he'd care for lieder or opera. He chose the former.

Halfway through Schubert's setting of "*Der Leiermann*", from his song cycle "Winter's Journey", I knew I'd touched the impresario, as when I'd sung these following words, tears had begun to pour down his face:

> *Keiner mag ihn hören*
> *Keiner sieht ihn an;*
> *Und die Hunde knurren*
> *Um den alten Mann …*

The room had been a perfection to sing in. It had supported the sound and made it easy for me to shape the phrases and the dynamics exactly as I'd wanted them to be. Mr. Solomon had continued to dab at his eyes with his handkerchief as I'd performed. It was often the case with vocal music deeply felt; the listener made some personal connection with the words, and as a result, emotions flowed freely and often uncontrollably.

I'd had to stop myself looking at Theo, who'd moved to the back of the hall. I knew he loved the way I sang it, and he too had been drying his eyes. When I'd finished, Elias had risen slowly from his chair and walked to me, holding out his hand.

"My dear boy—" he'd said and then his voice had broken, so I took his hand and shook it. A deal had been struck without the need for words.

We became business partners from that day forward. All four of us.

CHAPTER 3

Theo had already been at Howard's house for half an hour by the time Andrew and I arrived.

The front door was wide open, and when I walked into the living room, Eileen was sitting on the floor weeping, her head in my brother's lap while he stroked her hair.

As I stood in the doorway, my heart was in my throat. I didn't know what to expect. Even though we'd been friends for years before she'd married Howard, I was half-afraid she might rail against me. It was me the murderer had intended to kill; her poor husband had died merely because we'd looked alike and in the dim light of my dressing room Howard had been mistaken for me.

But when I spoke her name quietly, Eileen called out my name and jumped up into my embrace, clinging to me, sobbing loudly. To my brother's astonishment, and my own, I burst into tears too. It was the first time I could remember crying in front of anyone other than Theo since I was eight years old.

In the turmoil of our arrival, I'd completely forgotten about Andrew, and it was only fifteen minutes later, when the detective had come into the room carrying a tea tray and with Gertrude, Howard's youngest, perched on his shoulders, that I remembered my manners and introduced him to Eileen. I nearly cried again at his thoughtfulness. He'd gone out to the kitchen, had filled up the coalscuttle and stoked the range, found the tea makings and the biscuit tin, and had taken the children under his wing while I'd been consoling her.

He coloured slightly when she embraced him. Theatre people were far more prone to hugging strangers than most other folk—she'd been a seamstress at the Palace when she and Howard had married, ten years ago. Andrew vowed to her that he'd "set things right" and that he'd find the person responsible for what had happened to her husband.

Not only had he looked after her children but had also gone to the trouble of preparing tea to give us time together without a stranger present. Who did those sorts of things? I asked myself. Only the nicest and most considerate of men did, the answer came back.

We stayed for perhaps two hours, until the doctor arrived to give Eileen something to calm her nerves. He was followed shortly after by her parents, who'd driven in from Camden, in the country, where they owned and ran a peach orchard. They announced they were taking her home until she felt strong enough to continue by herself. They were incredibly moved when I informed them of the benefit concert, but had insisted that Eileen and the children should be kept away. Theo and I both agreed. Sensationalism was, in this circumstance, tasteless. I couldn't bear to see my friend's widow appearing in public to evoke pity. It could have been perceived to be a ploy to encourage more generous donations. The idea felt quite inappropriate and vulgar; Howard would have hated it.

Earlier that morning, not long after I'd woken him, my brother and I had already decided what to do regarding Eileen's and the children's futures. Theo handed her parents an envelope. He'd visited Howard's landlord on his way to visit her. In the envelope was a receipt for the rental on Howard's house for twelve months, paid in advance. He presented it to them with our promise that for as long as he and I remained alive, Eileen and the children would never go without anything they ever needed.

*****

The carriage ride home was sombre.

My brother and I sat in the back of the phaeton, quietly holding hands under the carriage rug, while Andrew sat opposite us, upright, his hands clasped on top of his cane, staring at a point behind us, in the direction we'd come from.

Occasionally, he worked his jaw and his eyes glazed slightly. Except that he seemed in either a reverie or following some sort of internal investigative process, I would have spoken.

It had been the first time I'd occasioned to have a leisurely inspection of him. Of course, I'd taken in the man as a whole, but with his attention upon other things, I allowed my gaze to travel over his face, from the clear hazel of his eyes to the line of his jaw. I could see nothing that was not, to my eye, less than perfect—other than the bruise on his chin that I'd been responsible for, and which would soon be but a memory. I searched for some small scar, a hair out of place in his eyebrow, a missed patch of beard when close shaving earlier in the morning … simply something to reinforce the notion that, as striking as I thought his looks, he was merely another man, like Theo, or myself.

I had a terrible habit of idolising those I admired—of ignoring their faults and praising their virtues. Perhaps it was the result of a desperately poor child thinking that anyone who wore shoes was somehow better than he was himself. I didn't understand it. What I did understand was, unlike other men I'd taken an instant shine to—and they were very few and exceedingly far between—Chief Constable Andrew Bolton was not only comely, but possessed the most disconcertingly charming personality.

As we turned into Park Street, to avoid the worst of the traffic in George Street, he caught my eye. At that moment I was grateful for my years of theatrical training. I returned his smile, dissembling, as if I'd caught his eye at precisely the same moment and had not been inspecting the line of his lower lip.

"Everything all right?" he asked.

And then I saw it, the slight imperfection that would constantly remind me he was a man, just like any other. One of his canines was longer than the other.

I knew from that moment forward that whenever he smiled, I'd look for that small imbalance to reinforce my notion that he was not perfect.

Perfection, and, quite likely, Mr. Andrew Bolton too, was unobtainable. It didn't stop me daydreaming about my rather far-fetched "what ifs".

"Everything's as well as it can be, under the circumstances, Mr. Bolton," I replied, touching the brim of my new black homburg—one gentleman's salute to another. "Thank you for asking and for being such a trooper this afternoon."

"It was my pleasure, Mr. Murray," he replied, returning my salute by raising his fedora slightly. "Any time you need me, please ask. I'm totally at your service for whatever you require."

Despite the serious nature of our recent occupation, I had to force myself not to smile. There were far too many possibilities in a candid reply to that offer.

As he looked away, my gaze returned to the shape of his lips.

*****

We arrived back at the Metropole a little after four, and I excused myself, saying not only I was very tired after the performance last night, but I'd only had a few hours' sleep after the police had left us. I asked Andrew if he could shake me awake at about five. We'd dropped Theo at the theatre; he had a cot in his dressing room.

I was having a beautiful dream when I heard my name spoken. I'd been floating on my back in the ocean, about a hundred yards off the shore. My hands were clasped behind my neck, and I could see an island off to one side, dotted with palm trees. Small fish were nibbling at my toes …

"Edward, wake up!"

The feeling of nibbling fish was the detective, shaking my big toe. I yawned and stretched.

"Sorry, I was having a dream."

"You were moaning and thrashing."

"It wasn't that sort of dream," I said. He smiled.

"It's half past five. I thought I'd let you sleep awhile longer than you asked. You seemed to slumber so deeply, it felt like a pity to wake you. There's coffee been sent up if you'd like some. Did you order it?"

"I asked for it to be delivered at quarter past five when I picked up the room key."

"I have news," he said a few minutes later, after I'd been to the bathroom and splashed water on my face. I didn't usually sleep that long in the afternoon and still felt drowsy.

"Go on." I poured a cup of coffee. I could see that he'd already had one. There were papers strewn across our dining table.

"These documents were delivered to me while you were asleep. My colleagues have been very busy."

"What are all these squiggles?" I asked, picking up one of the pages. There was a large glyph in its centre, labelled like a drawing in a book of anatomy, with figures numbered from one to fifteen.

"Do you know what forensic science is?" I shook my head. "I'd be surprised if you did," he continued. "It's a relatively new method of investigation, using scientific and medical procedures to augment the art of deduction. One of the most recent developments has been dactylography—the study of fingerprints. What you are holding is an enlarged drawing of the impression of someone's index finger."

"I do remember Abel holding forth about over dinner one evening at the beginning of the year. Something to do with everyone's fingerprints being unique?"

"Yes, that's it. Here, press your thumb up against the side of this glass."

He passed me a water glass, holding it by the base. I did as he asked and then he did the same with his own thumb, placing it right next to mine. He held the glass up to the light.

"See, if you look closely, you'll observe the patterns of our thumbprints are quite different."

He stood behind me, the front of his left shoulder against the back of my right, holding the glass in the air in front of us. I felt the closeness of his presence more than a little disconcerting. I could feel the warmth of his breath against the back of my neck and became exquisitely aware of every small sound in the room. I wanted to hold my breath, to luxuriate in the moment, but couldn't. I was too fascinated with the curious way in which our breathing happened to be synchronous, and I didn't want it to stop. He smelled of honey and tar. I recognised it as a popular moustache wax called The Old Brigade.

"Do you notice it? Your thumbprint has a distinct whorl, like a vortex in the sea, while mine has an arch. No one could mistake one for the other."

The ridges and valleys of our thumbprints were quite dissimilar; the more I looked, the more varied were their elements. "So, in fact, if everyone has differing fingerprints, then any person who leaves a mark like this anywhere can be identified as having touched it?"

"Yes, Edward, and there's the problem. One has to have an authenticated print on file against which to match one that's been discovered at the scene of a crime. There's a system being developed now that classifies the directions and shapes of the whorls and loops. We're hoping that we'll be able to use it ourselves to make up a card index."

"Really?" I said. "I can't imagine how it would work."

"The system was adopted in Britain only last year. Sir Edward Henry developed it."

"What, not Eddie Henry who was inspector general of police in Bengal?"

"You knew him?"

"Well, in those days I knew him as assistant magistrate collector at the Bengali taxation office. We performed *La Belle Hélène* in the Empire in Calcutta, and he attended every single performance."

"*La Belle Hélène?*"

"It's a work by Jacques Offenbach. They showed it in Melbourne years ago, but it's never been here."

"I'm not sure I've heard of the composer," he said.

"Ah, but you will, young man."

"Young man? Why thank you, Edward."

I winked at him. "If I get my way, I'll mount a production of his opera *The Tales of Hoffman* if it kills me. I'll be singing Dappertutto's song from the work on Sunday afternoon at Howard's benefit."

"I don't know it," he said.

I sang a few lines for him:

> *Scintille, diamant*
> *Miroir où se prend l'alouette,*
> *Scintille, diamant*
> *Fascine, attire-la!*

"Oh, good heavens," he said. "Your voice! I've never heard any such thing close up. It's such a cavernous sound, and it resonated right throughout my own body. How do you do that?"

"Years and years of hard work," I replied, not a little pleased with the joy on his face as I'd sung. "Now, about this fingerprint business. If you're telling me about it, Andrew, I suppose that you've discovered such a mark."

"The medical examiner found a clear print on the upper part of the blade that killed Mr. Talbot. It was underneath the hilt, initially hidden by the guard. Tell me, how many people do you think were in the theatre last night? People who worked there, I mean."

"What? You seriously think someone from the theatre may have killed Howard?"

He nodded. "Your Mr. Hobbson, the stage door man, said no one entered after the performance, and that everyone who had signed their way in had also made their mark when they left. So, unless there are two people involved, one covering for the other by signing himself or herself out, we're perplexed."

"Unless they signed themselves out, and then 'forgot something' and went back to a dressing room?"

"Of course. That's a possibility. I'll make a note and get one of the policemen to ask if anyone noticed anything like that happening. So, Edward, how many people in the theatre during a performance?"

"Something big like our *La Bohème*, there'd be upward of a hundred and fifty, perhaps two hundred."

"As many as that?"

"Well, there's upwards of sixty musicians in the pit to start off with. On top of that, apart from the ten soloists, we have a chorus of another sixty, plus stagehands, mechanists, wardrobe, electricians … and then there's another twenty or so carpet layers, not to mention ushers, staff in the three bars, ticket sellers, cleaners—"

"Carpet layers?"

"I'm sorry; it's what we call supernumeraries, or extras. People who fill out the scene who don't sing, but who wander around pretending to be vendors in Act Two, or fillers in the other scenes … snow sweepers for example, in Act Three."

"That's a damned enormous number to fingerprint."

"Damned?"

"I beg your pardon, Edward. That's the army in me speaking."

I laughed loudly. "You haven't heard anything yet. Wait 'til you hear theatre folk let forth. Everyone who has signed a contract for our run of *La Bohème* will have a name and an address on file. The only people paid by the performance are the supernumeraries, who are given a chit when they arrive at the theatre, which is signed when they leave at the end of the evening and then discharged for one-and-sixpence on the following morning in the manager's office. You could ask Mr. Willings if anyone didn't turn up to collect their money. But then again, they may not have given their real names."

"How do you employ the supernumeraries?"

"Oh, you'd have to ask Braxton Miller, the stage manager. But in the normal course of events, they go from theatre to theatre whenever there's a show with a need for 'extras', and we audition them. There are labourers, housewives, all sorts … even off-duty policemen. Theo and I did it for a bit after we returned from India. In those days it was nine pence a performance; but it sometimes meant the difference between eating and going hungry."

"I had no idea—"

"I've just thought of something," I said. "There's also a pass door behind the first level of boxes."

"A pass door? What's that?"

"It's a door theatre staff use when they need to come backstage. If you've been to The Royal before, you'll know the corridor that runs along the back of the dress circle?"

"I've never been able to afford such luxurious seating, Edward," he said with a smile. "It's usually the gallery for me and my family."

"Well, tonight you'll be on show, smack bang in the middle of everything, in the manager's box of the Palace Theatre."

He swallowed and looked a little taken aback. "I thought we'd be somewhere nice; the circle, or the stalls for example. But the manager's box?"

I answered his question with a smile. "As it's the last performance, I've been invited to sing 'God Save the King' from the box after the final curtain. I can hardly stand up in the stalls to perform."

"Good grief," he said.

"Now, about the pass door. At the end of that corridor, on the right-hand side of the theatre as you're looking at the stage, is a door leading backstage. Whoever killed Howard could have used that. I'm not suggesting anything; it's another possibility that's all."

"Dear me," he said rather forlornly. "I'll have to speak to the governor and see if we can't get some more police to interview people and take fingerprints."

The phone rang. It was Braxton, telling me he was leaving for the theatre and asking me what I'd arranged for dinner. I mentioned Andrew's suggestion of The Australian Club, but then he told me Sir H.'s wife had begged off to attend a reception at the art gallery, and his patron had wondered if I'd like to join him for dinner before the performance at Chiffonier's, the very exclusive and expensive restaurant not far from the Palace Theatre. When I explained that Andrew would be with me, he covered the mouthpiece briefly, and then said that if my companion would be dressed as a gentleman should be for dinner, then he'd see us there at six thirty.

*****

"Chiffonier's!" Andrew said, looking rather flustered. "I've only ever read about it."

"It's posh and grand and the food is wonderful," I replied. "There! Have a look at yourself in the mirror."

He'd forgotten both his bow tie and his set of cufflinks and studs in his hurry to pack his tails, so I'd provided him with a tie of mine and a set from my collection. I'd been presented with so many cufflinks there were several sets to choose from.

"Crikey, these are lovely," he said, standing back, running his fingers over the studs and turning his cuffs in the light to show off the links.

"Black opal," I said. "So dark blue they look almost like jet. Come here and let me do your tie."

"I feel a dreadful fool now I've seen how deftly you do yours."

"You'd be equally as agile if you had to wear one nearly every night. I suppose your mother does yours for you?" He coloured slightly and nodded. "What about when you were at university?"

"House porters."

I stood behind him, trying very hard to keep my nether regions away from his backside while I tied the tie. I had a very sudden urge to move forward and nestle against him, but despite the strength of my attraction, I'd met him less than twenty-four hours before, and as polite and flattering as he'd been, I hadn't noticed the slightest soupçon of anything but respect and affability. I idly wondered what it would be like to have a "pal", the word the moderns were using for a close friend, one who was not someone from the theatre. It might be very refreshing, I thought. The idea of anything more than friendship was a mere wisp of a daydream, one that would no doubt, like others I'd carried a flame for in the past, remain unfulfilled. However, I lacked friends who lived in the "real world". I wondered if he played tennis …?

"Voilà!" I said, snapping out of my fantasy and turning him around so I could tweak the ends of his tie and straighten the shape of the bow.

"It's really beautiful!" he said while craning to see over my shoulder into the mirror. I ducked; we were of a height. "Mine is starched linen," he added.

"Then you may keep it. I've silk bow ties aplenty."

"That's very generous, Edward. However, I'll accept the gift for what it is. Thank you very much. Every time I wear it, it will remind me of you. I love the straight cut. Butterfly ties are everywhere."

"I'd be grateful if you didn't mention what happened to me to Sir Horace …"

"Of course not. I wouldn't think about it. How do you know him again?"

I didn't answer. I was not ready to talk about my friends' personal connections as yet.

"We'd best be going," I said instead. "The carriage will be waiting."

"I'm really looking forward to this. Thank you so much."

"Don't mention it," I replied and gestured towards the door. "Shall we?"

★★★★★

"Did you have enough to eat?" I asked, as I saw him press his handkerchief to his mouth in an effort to disguise a gentle burp.

"More than enough, thank you, Edward. The food was delicious, and perhaps I've eaten just a little too much."

"Next time we shall have to have a more leisurely dinner … perhaps just the two of us?"

"Sir Horace is charming company."

I couldn't tell if his lack of response was an evasion or an acknowledgement that he'd liked the idea. His smile perhaps suggested the latter.

"You'll see more of him here tonight," I said, peering from the carriage window as it came to a halt. "He'll seek us out in the interval."

"With Braxton?"

"Ah, Braxton will tactfully arrive a few moments after Sir Horace comes to say hello. They don't sit together in the theatre. There's always a seat conspicuously empty at Sir Horace's side, as if his wife was unavoidably indisposed."

"It must make their friendship … awkward."

"I'm sure they've learned over the years how to manage appearances, Andrew."

We were saved further conversation, as the major-domo of the theatre opened our carriage door, greeting me by name, and doffing his hat to us both.

The footpath of Pitt Street, outside the Palace Theatre, was packed with theatregoers, many of whom had already heard the news of the incident at the theatre last night and who pressed around me, expressing concern for my safety, and murmuring their commiserations on the loss of my friend. I smiled and thanked them, finally rescued by the theatre manager, who'd appeared in the main doorway of the theatre and who had raised his hand in greeting, beckoning me to join him.

Several minutes later, I checked my watch. We'd arrived early and had almost fifteen minutes to spare before the five-minute warning bell.

Andrew had left me to fetch his parents and his sister, while I'd gone ahead to the private reception room opposite the manager's box to wait for them. I had the biggest surprise when I reached the top of the staircase; Constable Cooper Haddley was waiting outside the door to the box, nervously clutching a programme.

"I managed to get a ticket at the last moment," he said, and then whistled softly. The usher standing at the doorway, although maintaining his gaze directed ahead, smiled at Cooper's next remark. "What a swell outfit, Mr. Murray. You look a proper toff."

I laughed. He was dressed in a modern, finely checked charcoal grey suit, with a deep purple waistcoat. It was obvious he'd made an effort. "I'm anything but a toff, Cooper. But, thank you for the compliment."

"I couldn't miss tonight. Not for anything! Especially as your brother is my favourite performer … after you, of course, sir," he added, while blushing mightily. "Anyway, I'll be waiting down here after the performance to accompany you home, sir."

He gave me a brief nod and then turned to go. "Wait a moment, Cooper," I said. "Where are you going?"

"Up there." He pointed towards the ceiling. "Front row of the Gods. It's a treat to be so close."

"You'll do no such thing. Come sit with us in the box. We're only five and it seats eight."

He stopped, open-mouthed for a moment. "That's incredibly generous of you, Mr. Murray. But I simply couldn't … why, I'm not dressed for it."

"Nonsense!" I said. "You'll be out of sight. No one will know you're not in evening dress, only us."

"I—"

"No protests, please, Cooper. I insist." He smiled and shook my hand. "Here's Andrew and his family now," I added, peering over his shoulder.

The Bolton family made the most elegant and impressive quartet as they appeared at the top of the staircase.

Andrew's mother and sister wore beautiful, off the shoulder, fashionable gowns. Both had extraordinary complexions and were impeccably coiffed. I suspected that Mr. Bolton senior was not merely a barber, but a hairdresser of some extraordinary talent. I couldn't help but see Andrew had inherited his looks from his father, who was also very handsome and elegantly dressed in a very well-fitted, obviously bespoke set of tails. Unlike other gentlemen of his age—I took him to be in his mid-fifties—he had a short, well-groomed moustache and close-cropped hair, cut in a very modern style. Only that he extended his hand and waited for me to take it, I would not have suspected for one moment he was blind.

"I shan't embarrass you by gushing, Mr. Murray," he said, as I led him by the elbow towards the private salon. "But, I can't tell you what a pleasure and an honour it is to meet you in the flesh."

"Please, the honour and pleasure is all mine, sir," I replied and then noticed Cooper gawping at Andrew's sister, Louise. I smiled at him, and he coughed softly, swiftly turning his head and pretending to admire one of the paintings that lined the corridor in which we'd been speaking.

She was a very handsome young woman, who'd blushed prettily

as I'd kissed her hand. There was something about her eyes, the shine in them, which I recognised as a quick wit hiding behind an intelligent mind—Mrs. Mullins had had the same look about her.

I was proved correct within a few minutes, when she revealed that she'd already started to study *Don Giovanni* for my premiere in two weeks. She'd been at school at the time and had been unable to attend my last performances, but since she'd turned eighteen, she'd been allowed to go to the theatre with her brother, without her parents in tow. Since a few years after her father had gone blind, she'd played through the piano reductions of opera scores for him, speaking out the translations and describing the scenes from the libretti.

I thought it exceptionally clever, as she could have been no more than eight years old when he first lost his sight, so by the time they'd started their voyages through the repertoire, she must have been a very accomplished ten-year-old. However, she became acutely embarrassed when I told her as much. Her brother, on the other hand, could not have been prouder, and he regarded me kindly, with a smile and an unvoiced "thank you".

The usher opened a bottle of champagne and poured glasses. "May I, Papa?" she asked, hesitantly. He smiled and nodded, and her face lit up with such a glowing smile that I wondered if it was perhaps the first time she'd been allowed bubbly while out in company.

We toasted the king and then new friendships, Andrew raising his glass but then putting it down without taking a sip, and immediately picking up a glass of water, which he used for the toast.

Jacob Bolton, Andrew's father, was an excellent raconteur, managing to make me squirm with the most glowing description of my very first operatic performance, at the age of twenty-four, six years after our audition for Elias Solomon.

"At the time, I said to my wife, 'You mark my word, Wilma. That boy's one to keep an eye on'. I'd never heard such a beautiful, ringing tone in one so young."

The memory wasn't without a twinge of nostalgia. I'd never forgotten that first performance, singing the role of Malatesta in *Don*

Pasquale. Who could ever forget their professional operatic debut, and in such an important role? However, the memory was tinged with sadness this evening, mainly because on that occasion the silent role of Don Pasquale's servant had been played by my friend Howard Talbot.

The bell rang, announcing the audience should make their way into the theatre. The usher opened the door of the private room and then crossed to the other side of the corridor, standing with his hand on the doorknob of our box, waiting for us. I knew there were fifteen ushers ranged down the corridor, one for each doorway, seven on each side of the manager's box, which was placed centrally on the first level above the stalls. On some unseen signal, they opened the doors of their respective boxes simultaneously. I was a creature of the theatre and I'd never been able to fathom how they always managed to choreograph the movement so precisely. However, it was incredibly impressive to witness.

"You go ahead," I whispered to Andrew. "I'll join you right before the lights dim in the auditorium. The theatre manager has warned me that I must make an entrance."

"An entrance?"

I sighed. "I can only imagine that my manager, Mr. Solomon, has arranged it. It seems there's been much speculation about my welfare today, and the theatre manager will make a short announcement in front of the curtain, before the overture, to congratulate me on making an appearance in public when my life could be in great danger."

"But no one will dare!" Andrew said, grasping my forearm. "Not with me and Haddley at your side."

"I've never felt safer, Andrew, and that's God's truth. However, my Mr. Solomon, when he can see an opportunity to whip up some publicity ..."

And so it was that as I heard the theatre manager ask the audience to give me a round of applause for my bravery, I stood up in the box. Bathed in a flattering rose wash thrown down by the spotlight operator, I bowed to the public.

*****

"Hello!" I called out.

Theo poked his head around my bedroom door. "You're still awake?"

"I've been asleep," I replied, "but I suppose my nerves are on edge. I woke up when I heard you talking after you came in. Was it with Constable Haddley?"

"Yes, the man's an admirer. What could I do? He was so effusive in his admiration of the performance this evening I couldn't cut him short."

"It's a wonder he saw any of it," I replied with a chuckle. "He had eyes for no one but Andrew Bolton's sister all evening."

"I'm not surprised. She's a stunner, that's for sure."

"I'm so proud of you, Theo."

"Ah! A moment of weakness is it to be, then?"

We normally didn't flatter each other. The expectation was that we'd both excel in whatever we did. "I keep thinking of Howie," I said quietly.

"Give me a moment to get changed, and then I'll hop into bed with you. Is that all right?"

"All right? Of course it is, you dag. You've no need to ask my permission."

We'd spent nearly all of our lives sharing a bed. I couldn't remember a time when, as a child, I hadn't gone to sleep with my brother's arms around me. Before India, it was us five boys in one bed and the three girls in with Mother. And then, once we'd arrived in Calcutta, I had been so afraid of everything and my world was so upside down, I'd sneaked into Theo's bed every night. Despite Mullins's constant thrashings when he'd found me in my brother's arms in the morning, I wouldn't stop, so eventually, after a tongue-wagging from his wife and a reminder that I was the company's future drawcard, he'd given up and let us be.

I'd never forgotten the first time we'd spent any time apart, shortly after our successful showing to Mr. Solomon, when I'd been sent off on a country tour for six weeks, singing in town halls, country theatres, and school auditoriums, while Theo had been cast as Jimmy Quick, a name by which many people still knew him, in the vaudeville review *Jimmy Steals the Show*. Not once, in those entire six weeks, did I have an undisturbed night of sleep.

No more than five minutes after he'd gone to get undressed, he slipped into my bed and raised his arm. I nestled under it and lay my head on his shoulder, closing my eyes and taking a deep sniff of my brother. Instantly, I felt the world was at peace and all was right in our lives. He'd been a father to me, had looked out for me, and had loved me unconditionally. His love, I hope, I'd repaid in spadefuls.

"So, buttering up the Bolton ladies to soften up the young man of the house, eh?"

"What on earth do you mean?"

"After you'd left, I spent some time in their company—they are truly delightful—I can see why you're smitten with him."

"Me? Smitten?" He pinched my waist, which made me laugh. "He is nice though," I admitted.

"The bouquets for the ladies? Bit extravagant wasn't it?"

"I got Andrew to phone ahead to find out the colour of their gowns, and then, while we were waiting to be seated at Chiffonier's, I arranged with the desk concierge to have flowers sent, to be waiting for them in the manager's box."

"Andrew?"

"I can't keep constantly calling him Bolton, or Chief Constable Bolton now, can I?"

"If he wasn't such a buck, I think you'd find it quite easy."

We both laughed softly. "Ah, one day …" I said.

"I keep thinking that too."

"We're both already married though, Theo; married to the theatre."

"Pity it's such a possessive and jealous beau," he replied, kissing my forehead. "He wanted to know all about you, you know."

"Who?"

"Who do you think? It was subtle, but he certainly finds you interesting."

"He's a detective; of course he's going to be interested in the intended victim of a crime. If he gets to know me, he may be able to postulate a reason for someone wanting to kill me."

"Perhaps you're right. But it seemed more than that to me. Of course, I could be mistaken; it wouldn't be the first time. Perhaps I'm reading more into it than was there. I know you like him. I could have been looking for signs that he liked you too. Maybe his interest is simply because he doesn't know people like you or me?"

"What? Thespians? Or Uranists?"

"Uranists?"

"It's the new word for it. Men who find love in the arms of other men."

"I honestly don't think he's given one thought to our private lives, Eddie. Besides, as for finding love? I've yet to find love—all sorts of other things in the arms of other men, but love's been more than elusive ..."

"I've often wondered if that's because of me?"

"What?"

"You've always been there for me, Theo, and at times I feel that you've sacrificed your own life because of me."

"What nonsense. You must banish any thought of that from your mind this instant, do you hear? I've perhaps never met the right person."

"Or maybe too many of the not-right type."

"Heartbreakers."

"No, Theo, none of them were good enough for you."

He sighed and then rolled onto his side, encouraging me to do the same. He spooned up behind me, infiltrating one arm under my neck and the other around my waist.

"At least you have Sandford Clarkson," he said sleepily.

"You know that's one-sided."

He snorted. "A filthy-rich grazier who's been madder than a hatter over you for how many years now? Twenty? And yet you won't give in?"

"Oh, I give in plenty. He's more than adept in the boudoir. But, can you see me living my life out as a grazier's 'whatever' out in the bush?"

"If you loved him it wouldn't matter."

"Quite. But it's the 'if' in that equation that's most lacking. I like him a great deal. He's kind and generous, but I couldn't give up the theatre for anyone. Could you? If he cared that much about me, he'd be prepared to share me with the great love of my life. But, even having said that, there's no fire—not from my side anyway. I've often thought of breaking it off for the amount of grief I cause him, but I get lonely, Theo. A man has needs. Surely you understand that?"

"He's coming down next Thursday, isn't he?"

I sighed. "I'll write to him in the morning. If I still have a police guard, there'll be no getting away. It will be dinner, but no overnight stays at the Australia Hotel."

"He'll be disappointed."

"As will I, Theo. For everything that's missing, I still enjoy his company. Anyway, he'll be back again for a week for the opening of *Don Giovanni*. Hopefully, the police will have caught whoever killed Howard and life will get back to normal."

"Amen to that, brother dear. Now, get to sleep, you've a performance tonight."

"Thanks, Theo," I said, snuggling back against him. "Sleep well."

"Sweet dreams," he replied, and then added after a few seconds, "dreams of golden hair, fine moustaches, and a bruise on his chin. The man with the—"

I clobbered him. Playfully enough, but then threatened to smother him with the pillow if he didn't close his eyes and let me do the same.

He was well asleep long before I felt my own eyes closing. I'd needed something substantial to make me feel safe. There was nowhere more substantial or safer than in my brother's arms. I kissed the back of his hand, which lay next to my cheek, and then allowed myself to drift off to sleep too, desperately hoping I wouldn't dream of Andrew Bolton.

CHAPTER 4

"No one has ever explained what once stood here. Do you know, Mr. Murray?"

"How old are you, Constable Haddley?"

"I'm a little shy of twenty years old, sir," he replied.

"Then you won't have any memory of it, as it burned down in 1883, four years after my brother and I returned to Australia."

The next morning, I'd woken early, as usual, and had asked the young policeman to accompany me on a walk through the Royal Botanical Gardens. I wanted to look at the rose beds next to Government House stables before the sun got on the blooms, while they were still close-packed and before the warmth spread the buds wide open.

When I'd risen during the night to use the lavatory, I'd noticed Cooper fast asleep on our living room sofa, which had been placed hard and fast up against the doors to the apartment. I assumed that's what the conversation had been about between him and Theo I'd heard last night, when half-asleep. It was so like my brother to be so solicitous. It was in his nature to be a caregiver. With the sofa jammed up tight against the doorway, no one could have affected entry—unless there'd been a pack of assailants.

I'd also learned this morning that Cooper had called in a favour. As he'd been at the theatre before coming to stand guard, and knew his shift would be exceptionally long, he'd asked a fellow policeman to take his place in the corridor outside our door. I'd already mentioned to Theo yesterday that spells of twelve hours split between two policemen was not in anyone's best interest. We intended to hire a private guard for eight hours, so that every one of the three could be rested and vigilant—even though my brother and I thought it was a lot of nonsense. Neither of us felt in any particular danger.

"It was an exhibition building," I said in reply to his question. "Our version of London's Crystal Palace. It was a beautiful, tall, gleaming structure, parts of which were laid out exposition style, others as large conservatories. There was even a splendid concert hall and a restaurant. It went up in an enormous blaze. We had lodgings in Bridge Street at the time, and Theo woke me at four in the morning, the sky bright yellow and red. We ran up to Macquarie Street to see what was going on, and you'll never believe this, but the fire was so intense we had to retreat. Even the windows of buildings on the other side of the road, opposite the gardens, had begun to explode with the radiant heat."

"There's little left of it," he remarked.

"It was the size of the Queen Victoria Building, in George Street, the ceiling all iron and glass. It had a huge dome as well, which fell down with the most enormous crash. For years, only the foundations and one tower stood, like some romantic ruin, but then most of it was cleared. Only these footings remain."

"And that's why the planting is so new around this area, I suppose."

"Yes, all the tall trees were incinerated. Mind you, in a decade or two, no one will ever have known it had been here."

The morning was beautiful and not as cool as I'd expect it to be for this time of year. Although in Sydney we did not have a traditional European autumn, April mornings could often be quite brisk. The sun shone on the waters of the harbour and already ferries were plying their routes across the waters, belching black smoke.

"Look!" he said, pointing off to the west. "There's the *Brighton*."

The paddle wheel steamer was heading away from Circular Quay on its way to Manly, and had come into sight around Dawes Point.

"She's to be replaced soon," I said. "They're already building new, screw-propelled ferries in Scotland, so I've read."

"Wouldn't you have liked to travel all the way to Australia on something like that?" he asked dreamily, leaning on the sandstone wall that ran around the edge of Farm Cove. "The chugging of the engine, the sound of the paddle wheels smacking against the water."

"You make it sound very romantic," I said with a chuckle.

"Don't you think it is?"

I shook my head. "The ferry trip from Circular Quay to Manly on the *Brighton* might be sufferable, Cooper, but Theo and I travelled by steam paddle wheeler to and from India in third class. It was far from romantic. First class might be a different story, but for all of us crammed together like beans in a can, I can assure you it was awful."

"India?"

"It's a long story," I said. "I'll tell you another day. Now, let's get moving, I'd like to circumnavigate the gardens before we get back for breakfast. Your friend, the policeman on guard. What's his name again?"

"That's Russell, Mr. Murray. Russell Ward."

"We'll feed Russell Ward too. Remind me to order an extra setting for breakfast when we return to the hotel and when I pick up my mail."

We headed off at a brisk walk, following the pathway around Farm Cove up to Lady Macquarie's Chair, where we sat for a few minutes under an enormous Moreton Bay fig tree, admiring the view.

"May I ask you something, Mr. Murray?"

"Of course, Cooper."

"I need some advice from an older, more experienced gentleman."

"Mr. Solomon will be at the theatre after the performance tonight. You can speak with him. I'm sure he won't mind."

He laughed. "You'll think me very forward and perhaps impertinent, but I was thinking of you."

I supposed thirty-nine was old to a twenty-year-old. I smiled. "Ask your question, whippersnapper."

"I know I'm hardly worthy … in fact, it's probably an enormous presumption, but—"

"You'd like to call on Miss Bolton? Am I correct?" He reddened so furiously I thought he'd combust, and then nodded, twirling his cap between his fingers.

"My family's at the lowest end of what you'd call middle class. I'm not sure—"

"Has the young lady given you any encouragement?"

"She said she'd like to hear me play the pianoforte."

"You play?" I couldn't keep the astonishment from my voice.

"Yes, I do. Mother teaches the piano. I started learning when I was only four. I heard the discussion last night about Miss Bolton's ability to play piano reductions of the operas, and during the intermission I asked her which was her favourite to play."

"And her answer?"

"*La Pique Dame.*"

"The Tchaikovsky opera?" I was doubly astounded. Not only had he pronounced it precisely, but the score was exceptionally tricky. Young Miss Bolton must be quite accomplished, I thought.

"Yes. And when I told her I played sometimes for the local dance school—only cakewalks, marches, and popular music hall type music—she expressed a desire to hear some."

I smiled at him. "What's your favourite … the one you'd like to play for her?"

"Most of the pieces I play are not of the same order she plays—"

"You mean what you called 'high-class' music?" I laughed so loudly, I was sure heads would have turned at twenty paces. He'd reddened so greatly, more than before, that I was not only delighted, but it melted something within me. He was more than a mere copper. He appeared to be quite a sensitive young man.

"I should never have said that, Mr. Murray. Upon reflection, I must have sounded like a frightful clod."

"Not at all, Cooper. Both you and Mr. Bolton have managed to put my feet back on the ground, where they used to belong. Too much time nobbing with the toffs, as you said last night while examining my evening wear."

He groaned and put his head in his hands.

"So, Mr. Bolton's a would-be lawyer with a university degree, and you're a pianist, who, having learned from the age of four, must possess a modicum of talent on the instrument. I'd previously imagined our police force made up of ex-thugs, stevedores, and ne'er-do-wells."

"We're detectives, sir. That's an entirely different kettle of fish than the regular policing branch. I'm not a detective as such as yet, but I'm within the investigative branch. Andrew's a lot older than me. He's earned his place. I'm only a beginner."

"Well, I'm sure you'll do very well, Mr. Haddley. Now, back to your initial question, about Miss Bolton."

"Oh, it's a lost cause …"

"Do you know *H.M.S. Pinafore*? You told me you liked vaudeville and musical theatre."

"I play the paraphrases for Mother's student concerts, so yes, I know it well."

"May I quote from it? 'Fair heart never won fair lady'?"

He chuckled. "I think I may prove too shy."

"Here's an idea. I'll float the idea by Andrew in a casual manner, and then if he thinks his father might be agreeable to the suggestion, you can send your card around, and then call on the Boltons one Sunday afternoon. Perhaps you could take your music and perform something, and when Mr. Bolton senior realises there's more to you than a pair of hob-nailed boots, you might ask to speak with him privately, and then ask his permission to call upon his daughter."

The hope in his eyes gave me an ache in my heart. I'd never felt like that about anyone.

"Would you, sir? I'd be ever so grateful—"

"It's an initial step, and it would be my honour. Now, what will you play for them if Andrew is agreeable for you to send your card?"

"I'm not sure, Mr. Murray. What would you suggest?"

"As the family is oriented towards what you called 'high-class' music, perhaps something that's less ragtime and more refined?"

He thought for a moment, and then his reply left me speechless.

"How about one of the Gottschalk pieces?"

"He writes difficult music. You can play his scores?"

"Yes, Mr. Murray. I only choose not to play other types of music; it's not that I can't."

"Then, my boy, after my rehearsal this morning, and before you leave me in the capable hands of Mr. Bolton, I might ask my accompanist, Miss Fischer, if she'd relinquish her instrument to your capable fingers. I'd absolutely love to hear some Gottschalk ... unless you'd be too nervous to play for me, that is?"

He smiled. "I don't get nervous—much like yourself, so your brother told me. However, if Miss Bolton was to be there, it might be another thing altogether."

I slapped him on the back, pleased, and yet astonished. It was as if someone had casually tossed off the fact they could juggle elephants with their toes. I knew Gottschalk's piano music was famous for its technical difficulty, and yet this young man at my side had announced that although he preferred cakewalks, he could play music beyond the reach of the average accomplished amateur. Well, of course there was always the question of how well he played it. I couldn't help thinking of Mr. Harcourt, who I'd asked to take my place yesterday afternoon at the rehearsal for *Die Fledermaus*. He was of an acceptable standard, but also had his limitations. There were some arias that, despite the over-estimation of his own abilities, he'd never be able to successfully perform at his current stage of technical development.

In the world of classical music, there were degrees of ability. I wasn't making any assumptions on Constable Haddley's skill, but I had to admit I was very curious. I admired those who could play; how I wished I'd learned myself.

Miss Fischer had almost fallen from her piano stool when I'd once expressed the same desire, and had reprimanded me, telling me that God had bestowed me with the rarest of instruments, and that I should consider myself fortunate and be content with the gift that He had given me. "Able pianists are plentiful, Mr. Murray," she'd said. "Those with voices like yours, who are able to make the angels weep with the beauty of your artistry, are singular among tens of millions. Leave the piano playing to the masses. You are most fortunate among men."

I'd been humbled by her passionate speech. Still, it hadn't stopped me being envious of those who could play.

"Well, Cooper, let's get moving. I need to eat breakfast, and then, after that, you and I are going to make music."

"Very good, Mr. Murray. I'm starving," he said with a cheeky smile.

*****

At about half past ten, Andrew arrived at my rehearsal to relieve Cooper as bodyguard for the rest of the day.

The Metropole Hôtel had been very accommodating, reserving the upstairs reading room for my use to rehearse every morning from half past nine until eleven. It held a beautiful, if mostly unused, Bechstein full concert grand pianoforte. If, like yesterday, I was too busy to use the room, I'd let them know, and they'd remove the reserved sign from the door. As few guests occupied the top floor suites of the hotel, the room was usually deserted. In fact, in the years we'd stayed there, I don't remember seeing another guest in the room at any time of day, and I'd never heard anyone use the piano—not once.

In previous years, we'd hired a smaller grand piano for our apartment, but this year the hotel had offered me this arrangement. It was to their benefit as they used Theo's and my photographs for advertisements in the country newspapers, stating, "The Murray Brothers prefer the luxury of the Hôtel Metropole". We didn't mind, especially as they gave us a discounted rate on the apartment and room service at no extra charge whenever we needed it.

I'd done half an hour of scales and vocalises before Hilda Fischer had arrived at ten, and then, after introducing her to Cooper, we'd started work on some of my repertoire for the New Zealand tour in July. Not only was I to perform staged productions as featured guest artist with the Williamson's touring company from Melbourne who'd be there at the time, but on top of those, we had a fairly busy schedule of recitals and concerts.

Cooper was drying his eyes when Andrew arrived. I'd just finished working on "It Is Enough" from *Elijah*, by Mendelssohn, which was to be my first major engagement with the symphony orchestra and choral society in Auckland, and despite his protestations at not being fond of high-class music, it was obvious that he'd been much moved. I took it as the perfect compliment: if one could affect an impartial listener, one's job as a musician had been fulfilled.

For the next half hour, I worked through the role of the Conte de Nevers in Meyerbeer's *Les Huguenots*, which I was to perform four times in all, along with several presentations each of *La Traviata*, *Don Carlos*, and *Faust* during the course of the six weeks we'd be away.

"What will you sing at the benefit tomorrow afternoon, Mr. Murray?" Hilda asked me. Although she'd been my accompanist since 1881, we still referred to each other by Mister and Miss. It was a form of professional courtesy.

"In the first half, I'll sing Captain Corcoran's song from *H.M.S. Pinafore*."

"I hope you'll sing the top A at the end?" she asked, leaning forward and patting my hand, which lay on the top of the grand piano, next to her music.

"You know me," I said. "Any chance to show off those money notes. After that, it will be the Rosina and Figaro duet from *The Barber of Seville* with Miss Blanchard, who's to be the new Adele on Monday. In the second half, I'll perform the quartet from *Rigoletto*, and then two solos right at the end, immediately before our finale ultimo. The first will be '*Vision Fugitive*' from *Hérodiade*, and for the second, I promised Chief Constable Bolton I'd sing the Dappertutto aria from *The Tales of Hoffman*."

She clasped her hands in delight. "I can't wait. That sounds wonderful. There's no one sings either with such beauty of tone and elegance of phrasing. And what have you planned for the finale ultimo?"

"I know it's a pot-boiler, but we'll most likely sing the prayer of the Hebrew slaves from *Nabucco* as an ensemble, with everyone who's performed during the concert onstage."

"And then?" she asked, a twinkle in her eye.

"You know very well, Miss Fischer, what the encore will be."

"'Australia's Son'?" Andrew suggested from the other side of the room.

I laughed and bowed to him.

"And now, we're in for a treat," I announced.

"A treat?" Hilda asked.

"Yes, Miss Fischer. Our young friend here, Mr. Haddley, is going to play for us."

I had to hand it to him, he didn't seem one whit nervous, merely standing and removing his jacket before crossing nonchalantly to the pianoforte and asking Hilda's permission to take her seat. She and I sat next to Andrew. I honestly had no idea what might come next. I rather hoped it would be passable, and not embarrassing, but I was used to being on audition panels so nothing except a truly terrible rendition would throw me off balance.

He sat for a moment, blowing on his hands to warm them up, and then adjusted his sleeve garters, humming and hawing. Finally, he seemed to notice we were waiting.

"I wasn't sure which piece to perform for you. However, Mother has a salon next Saturday at the Academy of Music in Castlereagh Street. It's to give her more advanced students a chance to perform. She's asked me to be her guest artist, so I think I might test out what I'm going to play then … if you don't mind being my victims? Mr. Murray himself said to me only this morning 'faint heart never won fair lady'. It will do me good to give the piece an airing before I have to play it at the concert."

He said it with such self-effacement and with such a cheeky smile, the three of us chuckled. "What shall you play?" Hilda asked.

"I was thinking of the Gottschalk Grand Fantasy," he said.

"Which one?" There was a note of almost-hesitation in her voice, as if she couldn't believe what she'd heard.

"Oh, I'm dreadfully sorry, the 'Grand Triumphal Fantasy on the Brazilian National Hymn'," he announced.

"Dear God!" my accompanist murmured at my side; and then, after the four opening bars of the work, let out an audible gasp. For such a slight man, the power and dexterity in his hands was truly astounding.

Even I, who'd heard the work performed several times, was more than surprised he was intending to perform the more difficult version of the Grand Fantasy at his mother's concert. I think I'd only heard it once or twice played with all of the variations, the last time by the wonderful Russian pianist, Vladimir de Pachmann, who'd married an Australian pianist, Maggie Okey. The young policeman's playing was so accomplished it took my breath away, and I wondered if he'd attempt the famous, almost-unplayable, alternative ending.

At the end of the arpeggiated first section, I glanced at my companion. She had her handkerchief clutched to her mouth, slowly shaking her head in disbelief. Andrew, on my other side, who also obviously had no idea of Cooper's talent, sat spellbound and gaping. I'm not sure that I hadn't been in the same attitude until I'd turned my head. But then, when the young policeman began to play the gallop version of the main theme, with all the "unplayable" double octaves, Miss Fischer let out a soft, "Holy cow!". I'd never heard anything vaguely resembling an oath escape her mouth. It made me grin, which almost turned into a laugh of excitement at Cooper Haddley's extraordinary proficiency.

On the last two chords, he ended with such a flourish, his arms flying high in the air, the momentum caused him to rise from the piano stool to his feet. Not one of the three of us moved. I couldn't. I was too stunned even to speak.

He tsk tsk'd and then said, "I'm sorry. There were a few imperfections. Mother would have been furious. It's a lack of adequate practice time—"

At once, we three leaped to our feet and clapped loudly, Andrew cheering, "Bravo! Bravo!"

Cooper Haddley's reaction to our eagerness was at once charming and surprising. "Oh?" he said, as if our noisy acclamation had been a complete astonishment to him.

It was Miss Fischer who ran to him, grasping his hands, gushing in her enthusiasm to tell him how wonderfully he'd played. She announced she'd never heard anyone actually manage to pull off the more difficult version of the ending.

"Well, I never," Andrew eventually said to me.

"To my experience, Mr. Bolton, talent is to be found in the most unlikely places, and to come from the most unlikely people. I think I should like to attend Cooper's concert next Saturday. It's rare for me to have a weekend free, but I think it might be a strong sign of support for someone so gifted. Perhaps you would like to come with me, Andrew? And your sister too, if your parents will allow it?"

"I think she'd be thrilled to hear such playing, Edward. The boy's a phenomenon," he said.

Content that I'd perhaps killed two birds with one stone, I joined Constable Haddley and Miss Fischer, who was still gushing. It was unlike her to be so magnanimous about another pianist's abilities, so I knew it had taken her completely by surprise.

"How do you do it?" I asked Cooper, shaking his hand, more carefully than perhaps I may have done previously.

"Same as you, Mr. Murray. It's simply practice after all," he replied with a shrug.

I was about to say something when the door to the reading room burst open. It was my brother.

"Come at once, all of you! No, wait, Miss Fischer, you must stay here."

"What on earth, Theo?" I said. He was visibly upset, his face pale, one hand holding the door open, as if he was about to spring into action.

We followed him down the corridor to our apartment.

"There!" he said, pointing at the desk we used for our office work. "It was dropped off at reception earlier this morning. It's addressed to Edward, Constable Bolton, but we open each other's post."

On the desk was an envelope, next to it an opened letter. Draped partially over the two was a handkerchief, in the middle of which was a large, irregular, dark brown stain. I knew dried blood when I saw it.

I picked up the letter gingerly by the corner, mindful of Andrew's talk of fingerprints. On it, in a scrawl, was written:

I'll be more careful next time. Watch your back Édouard Marais!

CHAPTER 5

There were policemen everywhere, both inside and outside the theatre.

Not that everyone would know, because apart from two of them in uniform outside the stage door, the rest were placed strategically backstage in normal clothing. I'd been surprised to see how well decked out most of them were. I think my friend Chief Superintendent Morris had passed the word around they should wear their best.

On the way to the theatre, Andrew had told me four would be posted in the wings, a pair downstage, and the other two upstage. Cooper was to be on guard outside my dressing room, except for the times I was actually singing, when he and Andrew would accompany me and take places in the wings nearby, out of the way, while Russell Ward, the young policeman who'd taken Cooper's place last evening, would replace him outside my dressing room.

I thought it was too much and had protested. However, after half the afternoon spent being gently persuaded, and desperate to have a rest before this evening's performance, I'd given in and had reluctantly agreed to the police presence.

It was the superintendent himself who'd suggested Andrew should be my constant companion for the next week, to accompany me wherever I went, and both Cooper and Russell would share guard duty with other rostered police officers until the offender was either caught or was believed to have given up his or her futile attempt at my life—the reason for which, despite hours of conjecture, neither Theo nor I had been able to put forward any suggestions.

The adjoining small apartment to our own suite had been made available to the police department courtesy of the Metropole. It was merely a living room, bathroom, and one bedroom, but opened via a locked door directly into the sitting room of our apartment, allowing Andrew full access to our quarters both day and night. I couldn't have been more delighted, or more uncertain, when the suggestion had been made. It was somehow alluring, yet disconcerting. I knew I'd have privacy, as he'd discussed it with me before I'd agreed to the suggestion, and had promised not to intrude. I'd had to bite my tongue while I decided whether it was to be too much of a good thing, or if I might simply decide it would be too awkward. In the end, like the pressure to accept so many policemen as guardians, I'd simply given up, and then had given in.

Fortunately, upon arriving at the theatre, I'd found Arnold Willings had gone out of his way to find me a suitable replacement dressing room. The one in which Howard had been killed would be put to another purpose, perhaps a storage room—no other artist would ever be comfortable using it. Arnold had moved the conductor into a large room with a piano, closer to the stairs that led to the understage entrance to the orchestra pit, and had refurbished what had been the conductor's commodious suite into my new dressing room. Neatly in place on the shiny new paintwork of the door was a brass plaque upon which was engraved:

Room 1.
Principal Artist Dressing Room.

My name on a handwritten card, as occupant of the room, was pinned below it. Normally, that honour would go to the leading lady, but in this instance, as my brother and I had funded the performances, I had the privilege of being the first to inhabit the room, which, when

I opened the door, I found to be already full of flowers from good wishers.

New lighting fixtures around the mirrors, a comfortable armchair, a sink in the corner of the room, and, glorious to my eyes, a door that opened onto a water closet. Such luxury! I could only think of one or two dressing rooms in the entire country with private lavatories. Such amenities were usually thought unnecessary in our theatres. Unlike Europe, back lanes behind theatres were often christened "piss palaces". Male chorus members, theatre technicians, and supernumeraries emptied their bladders in the street, usually against the back wall of the theatre. Dear God, it stank in the summer when one arrived for a matinee performance.

Another of my agreements with Andrew was that as I was tired of talking about who might have it in for me, once we'd arrived at the theatre, he was not to discuss the subject until the following day. Both my brother and I had exhausted all possibilities. We knew of no one we'd ever fallen out with, either in our business lives or in our private lives. That left one major current theory among the cadre of detectives investigating the attempt at my life. They'd suggested it was perhaps a deranged fanatic, and there was no real reason other than insanity, or some kind of twisted, demented envy. The heart around the dagger hilt had been proposed as vengeance killing by a thwarted lover. Both Theo and I had burst into laughter, explaining that I'd never been in a liaison of that intimacy. Andrew had raised his eyebrow at me in friendly disbelief, but I'd returned my own "it's the truth" facial expression, one that so many of us actors could pull out at the drop of a hat.

"Stop looking at me like that," I said, grinning at Andrew in my dressing room mirror. He'd been watching me intently while I brushed back my hair and then wound a linen bandage around my crown, a little above my hairline, securing it with a safety pin.

"Why do you do that?"

"To keep my hair firmly in place, and to have a secure foundation onto which I can pin my wig."

"Do you always wear wigs?"

"Most often I do. Especially if the opera is set in periods when hair was long. My hair is fair and often doesn't show from the front. It's another reason I wear a wig."

"Show?"

"Sorry, it's a theatre term for something being clearly visible from the audience under the lights. We sometimes use the phrase 'read from the front', meaning the same thing. Even in the last *Don Giovanni*, which you told me you'd seen, my blond hair wasn't my own, but a wig."

"It's fascinating," he replied. "And, since you've forbidden me to talk about your welfare, I'm probably going to pester you about your makeup and the theatre."

"Have you always been this interested?"

"Not until Father went blind and we began to attend plays and operas more frequently. I became caught up in his enthusiasm. Who wouldn't want to know what goes on behind the façade of the stage?"

"It's called a proscenium," I said. "The frame to the stage, in front of the curtain."

"Ah, I understood that word immediately. It's from ancient Greek. Did you know that?"

"I always thought it was Latin," I replied and then handed him a small porcelain dish. "Put water in that for me, if you please, Andrew. If you're going to pester me about the theatre, you may as well help." Gideon caught my eye and raised an eyebrow, accompanying it with a knowing smirk. "And you can go to wardrobe and check to see whether Theo's here, Gideon," I added.

"Here's your water," Andrew said, handing the small dish to me, which he'd filled in the corner sink. "Why would Theo be here so early?"

"We both acted as impresarios on this production, my friend, and as a thank you gift for everyone's participation, we've arranged flowers for the principal artists, and a small card with a silver coin in it for everyone else in the theatre. We've spent most of the week writing short notes of appreciation and congratulations on the cards in our spare time. Five shillings for those with singing parts, a florin each for the chorus and orchestra, and a shilling for the rest of the crew and the carpet layers. All up it's not more than twenty quid—incalculable in terms of the goodwill it will create for future theatrical endeavours. We always do it when we're the impresarios. Theo's here early to start to hand out our gifts in person."

"That's incredibly generous," he said.

"It's merely like tipping a valet or a servant on a country weekend," I said and then bit my tongue. "I'll invite you to one later in the month, before we go to New Zealand, if you wish."

"There's no need."

"There's always need if you haven't been on one before. There are many wealthy people who invite me to the country for a few days and the invitation always includes a friend."

He blushed gently and then cleared his throat before taking out his notebook and scribbling in it. He showed me what he'd written:

Προσκήνιον.

"*Proskenion*," he explained. "That's the Greek word ... sorry, am I being a show-off?"

"Not at all. I like men who are well educated. I didn't have the opportunity to learn Greek and Latin, but I like to hear people talk on topics they know a lot about."

"I suppose your country weekends come at a personal cost?" It was a sudden jump back to our previous conversation, but I knew he hadn't let it go. I looked at him from under my eyebrows—I always had to sing for my supper. "What would I do ... as your friend?" he asked. "Hang about and try to look charming?"

"There's no effort involved in achieving that end, Andrew," I said. "You're a natural."

He laughed. "If I didn't know any better, I'd say you were—"

"Everyone in the theatre flirts. It goes with the territory and it doesn't mean anything."

He held my eye for a moment, smiling, and I felt something clutch in my stomach. His gaze gave nothing away. I couldn't tell if it was amused or bemused. But after a few moments, both the gaze and the silence unsettled me. "You could swim, or ride, or play croquet. You could read or simply relax. Perhaps go for hikes—ramble in the countryside? There's always plenty to do. I'm often invited not only to sing, but to make up the fourth for doubles."

"Tennis? Really? You play?"

"Of course."

"I'd love to play with you," he said at the precise moment that Gideon opened the door.

The young man stopped with his hand on the doorknob. "Am I interrupting anything?" he asked. "Should I come back later? Give you two a few minutes alone?"

Andrew laughed very loudly. It had broken the moment, and I decided the best course of action was to divert him onto more stable topics of conversation. Those in which I hoped I could not embarrass myself, or deal a hand in a game I wasn't entirely sure we both were playing.

"Andrew, in my bag, you'll find a lemon in a square of muslin; would you fetch it for me, please?" While I waited for him to find it, I opened my makeup box and laid out its contents on the same handtowel I'd used for the past ten years: a pot of cold cream, my greasepaint sticks, my brushes, paints, and powders, all lined up the way I liked them.

"What's this for?" he asked.

"Pull up your chair and sit next to me, and I'll explain everything as I go along. Or, would you prefer to watch?"

"The hell with watching. I want to understand the science behind it."

The science of makeup was all about the lighting in the theatre and the size of the auditorium, I explained, and then went through a short description of why makeup was needed. Features blurred at a distance and lighting either flattened features or bleached them out. We applied lighter colours to parts of the face that would normally catch the light from above during the day—cheekbones, nostril flares, foreheads, for example. Darker colours went underneath the highlights to accentuate where shadows would naturally fall. He nodded as I explained, once or twice uttering soft "ahs" and nodding. Eventually he began to scribble in his notebook.

"Thinking of becoming an actor?" I asked playfully.

"No, Edward. This is truly fascinating for an investigator. Disguise, either as a detective or as a criminal, has always been part of our repertoire. I've never known much about it before. Thank you. May I ask you about the greasepaints? Why there are so many? Why don't you only use one to colour your face?"

I held up one of my Leichner sticks. "These are relatively new. They didn't appear here until about ten years ago. They're manufactured in Germany and come in twenty-two different shades, numbered from one to twenty-two. One being the lightest colour, almost white, gradually getting darker through numbers two, and three, and so forth. Included in those shades there is china white, crimson, blue, chrome yellow, black—they all have a number."

"But why?"

"Let me show you and I'll explain as I go." I cut my lemon in two and wrapped one half in my square of muslin. I rubbed the cut edge over my face. "This is to clean off any natural oils before I start to apply makeup. Wet one end of that bar of soap in the washbasin, please."

"What's this for?" he asked, returning to sit at my side. I was agonisingly aware that our thighs were touching.

"This is to block out my eyebrows; at the outside edges. Several layers of soap will flatten the hairs down, and when it dries, I'll be able to put makeup on over it and then draw on new, slightly elevated eyebrows that will seem, to the public, to open up my eyes—otherwise, they can look like dark smudges with no expression if they're not well made up."

He shuffled his chair closer and rested his elbow on the dressing room table, at times making notes, at others leaning in to have a closer look at what I was doing. Once I explained why I was putting strokes of greasepaint over my face, varying the amount of number five, the light colour, and number nine, the darker colour, he understood that by varying the amounts of each, I could make any shade I wished. "Just like an artist who mixes his oil paints!" he said in a quiet, eureka moment.

Finally, when I was done, he looked at me and remarked, "You look unrecognisable, and yet, if this is always the way you do your makeup, out in the audience you simply look like you!"

I stood and bowed. "Now, Gideon, where's that crêpe hair?"

"Here you go, Mr. Murray," the young man said, handing me several sheets of folded paper. It was the way; to iron out the crêpe hair and then enclose it in several sheets of doubled-over quarto paper to keep it flat. "I learned more about makeup in those twenty minutes than I have done in my life in the theatre," Gideon added. "Thank you, sir."

"I completely agree, Gideon," Andrew said. "An artist both on the stage and in the dressing room."

"So, is it to be dancer's belt tonight?" Gideon asked.

"No, a posing pouch under my normal undershorts will do. I've not much running about to do, but no one likes to see things jiggling on the stage."

"Some people might," Gideon said with a chuckle, and then undid my trousers, which I stepped out of. I picked up the spirit gum from my dressing table and began to apply it to my face, while Gideon cut the crêpe hair into four-inch long sections.

"It goes under the chin first," I explained to Andrew, applying the cut edge of a three-inch wide flattened strip of the artificial hair along the underside of my jawline, and then pressed it into place before dealing with the rest of my chin. "Once that's all done, it's the upper jaw, up to the wig line at the sides next to the ears, making sure the strands of hair run the same way a normal beard would grow. Voilà. Now the moustache."

I stood back to admire myself in the mirror while I waited for the glue to dry, skimming off my shirt and then my undershorts. Gideon handed me the posing pouch, which I put on, and then he tied the strings behind me, at the small of my back.

"You look like a wild man from the jungles of Borneo," Andrew said, laughing at my bushy, as yet untrimmed, voluminous beard. He'd averted his eyes as I'd put on the posing pouch, but I'd noticed a quick glance in the mirror as he did so. I told myself that it didn't mean anything. Most men examined each other when naked. Some blatantly, others furtively. It was simple curiosity.

"I won't once it's dry and I've trimmed it," I said.

"Will you allow me?"

"I thought your father was the barber?"

"I know how to look after hair and facial adornments. What do you think I did while growing up?"

"Spent it at your father's side, watching?"

I handed him my scissors, which he opened and then ran his thumb along the edge of each blade.

"How do you want me? Standing or sitting—shut up, Gideon," I said, trying my hardest not to laugh in response to the young dresser's undisguised chortle.

Andrew shook his head but smiled.

"Theatre humour." I glanced in the mirror. My face was burning, and my ears, to which I hadn't yet applied makeup, were crimson.

"It's not that different from the army. Whole lot of men together. The air is often thick with obscenities and rank suggestions."

"Then you'll find the theatre no different." I sat on the edge of the dressing room table.

He nudged my knees apart and stood between them, leaning around me and clucking his tongue as he made do with my scissors and comb, telling funny stories as he went about his business. I soon relaxed, initially worried that his proximity might rouse something I'd rather keep neatly enclosed in linen, but after a few minutes, I couldn't help but warm to his good nature and excellent, sometimes ribald, conversation.

"It's never looked better." I ran my fingers over the beard, smoothing the moustache while I examined his efforts in the mirror. "Thank you, Andrew."

"As I said, my friend, anytime, anything, anywhere …"

I wasn't sure if he was being serious or teasing, and was about to say something less than circumspect when there was a knock at the door.

"Come!" I called.

It was Simon. He managed to tell me it was my half-hour call before bursting into tears. I pulled him into my arms and rocked him, trying to comfort him. What a shock for a young man to find Howard dead, and in such a state.

I caught Andrew's eye over Simon's shoulder. His look melted something inside me. It was a look of care, concern, and of understanding. The naked singer, with a face made up like a tuppenny trollop, holding a scared, miserable lad in his arms, shushing him and telling him all would be well.

"You're a keeper, Mr. Murray," Andrew said after I'd sent Simon on his way, and Gideon had left to get my clean shirt from wardrobe.

"I don't play cricket, Mr. Bolton," I said cheekily, my body flushed red with embarrassment.

"You know exactly what I mean, Edward. I don't think I've ever met anyone with such a big heart."

Don't you go breaking it now, Chief Constable Andrew Bolton, I wanted to say. But I merely smiled and thanked him, and then began to powder down my makeup.

*****

"Are you sure you know what to do?" I asked Andrew, half an hour later, as he followed me into the wings from backstage.

"Yes, Edward. Your Mr. Braxton Miller was quite stern, as he should be. I understand the dangers of moving machinery."

"I'll join you in the wings and hold your hand—figuratively, of course—once I've come off stage towards the end of Act One. We'll stand downstage, near the prompt corner, while the scenery change into Act Two takes place. As there's no interval, and the change is done in full view of the audience, there'll be a lot of the set already in place on wagons, which will roll in from the back of the stage when the lights on the stage dim. There'll be pieces of the scenery flown up into the gridiron, and not only will the wings be packed with chorus and supernumeraries, ready for the café scene, there's a brass band that will process across the stage—"

"Yes, yes, I came on the opening night, remember?" He smiled and clutched my hand in the dim light, squeezing it momentarily. "I've never been backstage before, and I'm really excited to see—"

"Watch your step, sir." One of the mechanists interrupted him, as baskets of properties were carried past us to be placed in situ on the stage.

"Very well. I won't say any more. You'll know when I'm about to come off stage—"

"When you sing '*Occhio alla scala, tienti alla ringhiera*'. Yes, I know. Louise and Father have been singing *La Bohème* at our pianoforte for months in preparation for this season."

I was astounded he knew the text, and his pronunciation of the Italian words was not far from correct either.

"Is there nothing will surprise me from you, Constable Bolton?"

"I think I'm full of many surprises as yet, Mr. Murray," he replied with a soft chuckle. "Some of them may reveal that I'm a shyer, less-experienced man than you believe me to be."

In the semi-dark, standing right up next to the prompt desk, we exchanged another of those glances; this time his was hesitant, questioning.

"I can hardly wait," I said, leaning in to his ear. "I have so many 'knowing' people in my life, I can't tell you how refreshing it is to meet someone who is so genuine and uncomplicated."

"Ah!" he said, turning his head to whisper in my ear. "I didn't say I was uncomplicated—merely shy."

"Here you are, Mr. Murray," Gideon said, appearing from behind us. "Warm water, in your mug."

"Thank you, Gideon. And now, gentlemen, the curtain is not far off, and I must perform my rituals and get myself into character."

"More rituals?" Andrew asked teasingly.

"They are never ending, my friend … and don't!"

"Don't what?"

"Say what you were about to say. It's considered very unlucky."

"Unlucky to wish you good fortune? What should I say instead?"

"Something vulgar and contrary."

"Very well," he said and then whispered in my ear. "Here's one we said in the army: *may your creamstick curl backwards in your sleep and stick up your fundament!*"

I laughed. "Thank you, Andrew, but it's supposed to be something that I might not enjoy."

I left him and went to my tormentor leg to start my toe raises. As I looked over my shoulder, he had the widest grin plastered across his face and was shaking his head slowly—the perfect attitude of silent laughter.

*****

"I've never seen such a thing! It's more magical than it appears from the audience," Andrew said the moment we closed my dressing room door after returning from the stage at the end of Act Two. His eyes were afire and he sounded almost breathless. "There was so much movement, not only in the wings, but during the scene change. I swear my chin hit my chest ... why are you looking at me like that?"

"I don't often get to see people marvel at the goings on behind the scenes in my world," I replied. I'd been captivated by his child-like wonder. It was as if he was a five-year-old, opening Christmas gifts and finding something unexpected, yet breathtaking. "I'm fairly used to appreciation after performances by those who've been in the audience. But not a reaction from someone who's seen what actually goes on backstage for the first time. It's truly delightful."

"There were so many people rushing around, carrying things, adjusting their clothing and their hair quite automatically, not a word spoken, merely the rustling of costumes and the soft swish of their feet milling around to get into place on the carpet runners in the wings, all ready to run onto the stage. It was almost military in its precision. And then, quite without warning, I was dazzled by the lights as they were turned on above me. At that exact moment, all those who'd been standing around me swarmed onto the stage, erupting into such a riot of colour and movement, faces turned into the light, singing or laughing as they moved hither and thither, and then, and then … and then there you were! Magnificent and commanding, surrounded by your fellow bohemians. I say, Edward, the stage lit up when you strode in from the wings. You have such a strong presence. Why, I couldn't take my eyes off you—"

"Stop," I said, bursting into laughter. "You'll embarrass me."

"No, truly, you were!" He grasped my biceps with both of his hands. "I was captivated. Even standing in the wings, far away from you, your voice projecting out into the auditorium, I heard every sound vibrate through my body. I may have imagined it, but I tell you I felt it as if you were standing right next to me. Your solo in the big ensemble—*gioventù mia, tu non sei morta*—"

His voice was light and high, but perfectly in tune.

"Keep that up and I'll be forced to drag you into a room for some lessons," I said and then coughed and turned to Gideon, who'd been watching our interaction with no small amount of amusement.

"Come here and put your arms around my chest, Andrew," I said, and then, when he had done so, "Now sing that again."

"Sing what?"

"What you just sang. Those few bars of my solo."

He did so, blushing, but smiling at the same time.

"I felt my chest vibrate while you sang. Do you know what that means?"

He shook his head. "Could it be that our vibrations resonate similarly?"

"Quite so. Like singing into a fine wine glass, or two tuning forks vibrating in sympathy. It means our chest measurements, and our body sizes, are probably almost the same."

"I'd watch it if he asks you to take your shirt off next to check, Mr. Bolton," Gideon said. "You can't trust these theatre folk, no matter how innocent they behave."

"Cheeky monkey," I said, releasing Andrew somewhat reluctantly and stretching over to clip Gideon's ear. He moved aside adroitly, passing a wink at me as he did so.

"Here's your hot water, Mr. Murray," Gideon said and then turned to Andrew. "Can I fetch you something, Constable? Tea, perhaps, or something stronger? There's champagne in the green room for some of the important guests who've come backstage during the interval."

"Tea would be perfect, thank you. A little milk, no sugar, and in an old tin mug if need be. I'm a simple man at heart."

Gideon's raised eyebrow said it all. Simple … yet not uncomplicated.

"I've been meaning to ask you why you don't drink?" I asked, once we were alone.

His smile became brittle and there was a slight change in his eyes. "I took a pledge, Edward. That's all. I'll tell you all about it another time."

"I'm sorry, I didn't mean to intrude …"

"If, as Gideon said a moment ago, there are guests backstage, don't you need to—?"

"I don't entertain during a performance. It's very well-known that unlike other performers, I don't welcome visitors to my dressing room until after a performance, and then only on opening and closing nights— that's why there's that 'no visitors' sign hung on my door. Nor do I usually leave this room once the curtain has gone up at the start of the evening, unless it's to go onto stage. I like to keep focused on my singing, and the sorts of guests who usually come backstage in the interval do so for reasons other than passing congratulations to performers."

"Ah! To be seen to be chummy with the performers."

"Precisely. I've already told you how the wealthy see us—as adornments."

"Surely there must be many who have a genuine appreciation for fine music?"

"Of course there are; but those are the ones who show respect and pay their compliments in other, more thoughtful ways, rather than intruding into our privacy in the middle of a performance."

"I'm sorry. You've said you like to concentrate, and I've been bending your ear. Does that mean you'd like me to go? I can wait outside."

"Heavens no! Your passion was uplifting, and I find not only your presence reassuring, but your affable nature calming and moresome."

"Moresome?"

I laughed. "It's an invented word. Theo and I own propriety rights to it. It means wanting more, not satisfied with a small portion. It's a literal translation of Bengali *yathesta na*, which means not enough. We use it when we're feeling mellow and we don't want whatever it is that makes us feel good to stop."

"Moresome," he said quietly, unable to meet my eyes. "I don't think I've ever been paid such a compliment."

I felt that I'd gone too far, not for myself, but for his level of comfort. "Here, help me off with these boots. I need to put shoes on for Act Three and change out of these strides."

"You speak Bengali?" he asked, kneeling on the floor and tugging at the heel of my boot.

"Not a lot of Bengali, but enough to get by and to hold a conversation with an educated native speaker of that tongue. We mostly spoke Hindi. It was as widely understood as English all over most parts of India."

"Why?"

"Why what?"

"Why did you learn native languages if everyone spoke English?"

"Because the people who 'owned' us spoke no other languages than English."

His face dropped. "Was it that bad?"

I nodded. "Like the story behind your pledge not to take alcohol, I'm afraid that's a story for another time and in another place."

He smiled and then grasped my foot and massaged it briefly. "It's a pact," he said and stood up, grasping my shoulder. "At another time and in another place. Deal?"

"Deal!" I said and placed my hand on top of his. "Andrew …?"

"Yes, Edward?"

"Anytime you'd like a ten-shilling note in your pocket, I've a job for you."

"Doing?"

"Half an hour at massaging my feet will do it."

"Cheeky," he said, laughing.

"It's my middle name."

"What rubbish. Gideon already told me your middle name … it's 'solicitous'."

"That's what he thinks it is. He misheard and used the adjective in place of the verb."

"Oh, so you pay for it?"

"Didn't I just offer you ten bob?"

Our raucous laughter was interrupted by Gideon, who we hadn't heard arrive, but who'd knocked and was standing in the doorway carrying the manager's fine tea service on a silver tray. He placed it on the small whatnot next to the armchair in the dressing room, shaking his head and clucking his tongue.

"I'm sure I didn't hear correctly," he said. "But in case I did, I'll be outside for another ten minutes."

He left us both speechless with mirth. I think I may have even slapped my knee while clutching my stomach and trying not to cry with laughter.

*****

The performance was a resounding success. We gave at least a dozen bows as a company.

When I judged the audience had had enough, I beckoned Theo to come onto the stage from the wings where he'd been waiting to join with the full cast in a final bow. Along with the other principal singers and the conductor, we held hands and then moved forward right to the edge of the orchestra pit. Our hands still connected, we men bowed and the ladies curtseyed—the obeisance while still holding hands was called the performers' bow, and audiences loved it.

And then, as the applause rose to a crescendo, my fellow performers moved backwards, leaving my brother and me standing at the front of the stage. I raised my hands for silence and then gestured to the first row of the circle, where the Governor of N.S.W. and the Lord

Mayor of Sydney sat with their wives, and on either side of them, the patrons of the theatre.

"Your Excellency, my Lord Mayor, ladies and gentlemen," I said, sweeping one hand around the theatre to include everyone. "My brother and I would like to take this opportunity to thank both you, our audience, and our colleagues behind us for tonight's splendid and final performance of Maestro Giacomo Puccini's wonderful opera, *La Bohème*."

"Encore! Encore!" some wag called out in the gallery, causing the audience to burst into laughter, which then turned into loud applause.

Holding my hands up for calm once more, I continued, "Unfortunately, the hour is too late to encore the entire work. However, Theo and I have news! Backstage, while the scene change was taking place between Acts Three and Four, my brother and I shook hands with Mr. Arnold Willings, the manager of the Theatre Royal, and we are very pleased to announce that we will be remounting a further five performances of this theatrical masterpiece in August—"

"And there's more!" Theo shouted over the loud applause and cheers from the gallery. The clapping was definitely more energetic from those behind us. I could already feel letters arriving at our hotel over the coming days, announcing availability and desire to be involved in the return season. "Surely there's not one of you who has not heard the sad news of the death of our dear friend Howard Talbot. Tomorrow, at two in the afternoon, in this very theatre, a benefit performance will be held to raise money for our friend's widow and family. Not only will my brother and I perform, but every single one of the people you see on the stage behind us will donate their talents."

"But not only these generous colleagues," I added. "But variety performers from all over town. Every theatre will present something from one of their current productions. There'll be choruses, large dance numbers, and even perhaps a magician and his assistant on a flying horse!"

The crowd roared its approval. Theo bowed and then raised his hands until there was quiet once more.

"There's another incentive to attend, apart from supporting a grieving widow and her three children, ladies and gentlemen," he said, his voice ringing through the theatre. I could hear it rebounding from the back wall of the auditorium, behind the stalls. "Mr. Willings has announced that by presenting a ticket stub from tomorrow's benefit at the theatre box office next week, on Wednesday, Thursday, or Friday, there will be a discount of sixpence on any ticket, for any seat in the theatre, on the opening night of our new showing of *La Bohème*!"

The audience went wild, as we knew they would. I guarantee our proposed season would sell out within a week of tickets becoming available. I knew the first tickets sold would be those up there in the upper balcony, the part of the theatre known as "the Gods". For the same seat they'd sat in tonight, they'd pay one shilling, a saving of sixpence. Sixpence could mean a nice supper, and perhaps a carriage ride home if two of them took advantage of the discounted price and came as a couple. Perhaps one or two might still fork out one and sixpence and buy a ticket for what would normally be a two-bob velvet-plush seat with a back on it in the upper circle? When I was on my uppers, I would have jumped at the chance to leave a long performance without an ache in the small of my back.

Theo took one step backwards and left me alone at the front of the stage. I waited until the audience stood and then gestured into the pit. A spotlight at the back of the gallery swung onto me, bathing me in a gentle straw-coloured glow. I watched the orchestra leader stand, hold his violin to his chin and begin to play an introduction to the National Anthem. I cleared my throat as the rest of the orchestra joined in and then sang:

> *God save our gracious king,*
> *Long live our noble king,*
> *God save the king.*

And then the cast and the audience began to sing along with me. Thousands of voices rang out:

> *Send him victorious,*

Happy and glorious,
Long to reign over us.
God save the king!

It was one of those moments that I felt proud to be a member of the theatre and of the British Empire, and from the volume and enthusiasm in the voices that filled the auditorium, I suppose the rest of those around me felt somewhat the same.

★★★★★

"Gideon told me you were flirting with each other," Theo said as he slipped into bed.

"You took your time," I muttered, glancing at the clock on my nightstand. He'd been gone an hour.

"Ah!" he exclaimed, rolling onto his back and placing one forearm over his eyes. "At forty-two, I've not the stamina I had as a twenty-year-old."

"How did you smuggle … which one was it?"

"Ethan," he replied and then chuckled noiselessly.

"Why the laughter?"

"It's been a while, Eddie. He was reluctant to leave."

"So?"

"So what could I do but offer an encore?"

I tsk tsk'd and was then told I was jealous. He wasn't far off the truth. It had been such a very long time since I'd …

"I've a mind to offer him a position, if you'll agree?"

I sat up in bed. "Really?"

He nodded and then removed his forearm. There was enough ambient light from outside for me to see the sincerity and the shine in his eyes.

"I'm going to need someone when our house is done and we move in."

"Oh! You mean offer him a position as a manservant?"

"No, I mean something else altogether."

"Well, strike a light!" I said. "How long has this been gathering?"

"For a while. I've been thinking about my future. Either of us is yet to meet the right person, and I think if I don't make an effort, I'll end up like old Mr. Grouser. You remember him? Sitting alone in his cubby room in India, mending our shoes. No family, no friends, no one to kiss goodnight …"

"Do you love him?"

"Do you mean, am I in love with him? If that's what you're asking, then the answer is no. There's no throbbing behind my temples, desperation to hold him in my arms. Yet, when he kisses me and looks into my eyes … well, let's say it's a thing I could never tire of."

I said nothing. My brother paid both Ethan and Lucas.

"I know what you're thinking, brother mine," he said, poking my ribs playfully.

"And what do you believe I'm thinking?"

"Does it rhyme with Clive Willings?"

I laughed. "Five shillings? Well, isn't that how much you pay him?"

He shook his head and then drew me into his arms. "He hasn't taken money from me for over six months."

"Are you sure about this? He's been in your room so infrequently of late—"

"Ah, Eddie, this hotel is full of nooks and crannies. Butler's pantries, four on each floor, empty guest rooms aplenty."

"Why were you hiding him?"

"I wasn't hiding anything. Lots went on here while you were out in the theatre or rehearsing. Your practice hour in the reading room is often more than enough. But sometimes it's very arousing to be making love in a broom cupboard, or on a dining table in a suite, or—"

"Enough, for heaven's sake," I said, laughing softy. "Have pity on me, if you please. Think of my delicate condition …"

"He looks at you as if he's trying to discover your soul," my brother said, his voice suddenly calm, sober.

"Who? Ethan?"

"Come now. You know I understand you better than that. Andrew is who I mean."

I didn't know how to reply. I hated the way that something inside me was driving my attraction to a relative stranger. We lived in a strange age; one in which men shared deep, bonded friendships and spoke of loving each other in quiet, private moments. However, those friendships were generally accepted if only couched in fraternal demonstrations of affection.

Confirmed bachelors and their male companions made up sets of gentlemen in both the middle and upper classes. Those sorts of attachments were rare among the working classes, where expectations were different. True, I'd seen many close friendships and even committed connections among labourers, dockers, and navvies, but there was greater social pressure for poorer working men to conform and to get married, whether they wanted to or not. When the need came upon them, those men made excuses and left their wives at home for the evening, and went out into the night to do what they had to, away from prying eyes.

When I did not reply, Theo continued. "Gideon told me you were in each other's arms."

"I was showing him how chests can vibrate in sympathy with another person's voice, if their physiques are similar enough."

"He also told me that instead of his arms being around your ribcage, as one would have expected, his fingers were interlaced and his hands were resting in the small of your back …"

I had noticed. I'd lived through that moment while he'd sung, as if time had suddenly come to a halt. His arms around me, the feeling of his chest pressed against me, and with one of his feet between both of mine, our shoes touching, I'd felt the contents of my posing pouch nestled gently against his private parts. At the time I'd not thought it sexual in the least, but intensely sensual—two quite different things. I'd almost jumped out of my skin when Gideon had spoken up.

"*Ami balalama 'yathesta na'*, Theo," I said, the words falling quietly in the room.

"You told him our word?"

He was so surprised, he almost spoke on the intake of breath.

Translated, what I'd said to my brother, in Bengali, was that I'd told Andrew I found him moresome.

Theo got out of bed and walked to the window, standing with his hands on his hips and looking down over Philip Street. "My advice is to go no further until you understand the man, Eddie." He turned to look at me, leaning against the windowsill. "He's charming, handsome, and probably one of the best catches either of us has had the luck to run across. But, just be careful it's not you who is caught. For all his charm and friendliness, he's a policeman. In the theatre what men do behind closed doors is no one's business. However, out in the 'real' world—"

"Yes, yes, I know!" I said, turning onto my stomach to hide my face in the pillow. "There's no need to remind me. Why do you think I'm not next door sitting on the edge of his bed and throwing out a line to see what I can reel in?"

"Well, for one, that would be so unlike you it would be impossible, I couldn't believe you'd ever be so forward. If you were that sort of person, you'd not have had an empty bed for such a long time."

My brother was right. I'd no real talent for approaching men. Unless, of course, they were working-class men who called a spade a spade and were happy for half a crown and a bit of no nonsense. Besides, I hadn't been "slumming" for years. I had no wooing skills. I'd been a virgin until the age of eighteen, and my first time would not have happened had it not been for the other man being both older and understanding of my shyness.

"He is truly moresome, Theo," I mumbled.

"Perhaps he is, my fair-haired boy, and perhaps he's lying in bed next door thinking that you are somewhat moresome too. However, as your older brother and caretaker in life, I'd suggest that any attempts at further intimacy than your current level of friendship be delayed, at least until after they find out who this maniac is who is out to kill you."

"Come back to bed," I said.

He did so, and as he wrapped his arms around me, I curled up into a tight ball.

"Is everything all right, Eddie?" he whispered into my ear while stroking my arm.

"I worry he's attracted more to Edward Murray than to Édouard Marais."

We'd all had them, backstage Johnnies. Men and women who were smitten by the stage persona, with no real knowledge of who we were underneath the greasepaint.

"From what I've seen, he's a man of discernment. He can tell the difference between a set of fine cufflinks and the case they come in."

I didn't reply for a moment, and then said, "I like Ethan. He'll be very good for you."

My brother kissed the back of my neck. He understood that I'd run out of words and wanted to change the subject. I needed time to think and not to speak.

"Thank you," he replied and then snuggled into my back.

I lay quietly, my eyes open in the darkened room, inspecting the patterns of the Wunderlich pressed metal ceiling as I matched my breathing to that of my brother. Finally, my eyes began to close.

CHAPTER 6

The sun was streaming through the window. I looked at the clock. Nine o'clock. Had I been so exhausted I'd slept for almost twelve hours straight?

We'd spent a few hours in the theatre after the benefit yesterday, supervising the packing up of the sets and costumes, ready to be delivered to a warehouse we'd rented in nearby Darlington, where everything would remain under sheets until it came time for the revival of *La Bohème* in August.

After that, we'd had an early supper in the hotel dining room. Thoughtfully, Monsieur Hilaire had recognised my need not to be bothered, and had placed us in a corner far from other guests. Constant solicitations were appreciated, but in small doses and not while dining.

As they'd attended the benefit concert, we'd invited Andrew's family to sup with us, and I'd felt very comfortable in their presence. It had been charming how Andrew's mother, Wilma, had noticed Cooper seated by himself on the other side of the room and had asked the maître d'hôtel to ask him to join us. Perhaps it was only me who'd noticed the excitement hidden behind his feigned reticence. I'd stood when he'd arrived and offered him my chair next to Andrew's sister, Louise. The soft colouring that had spread across her bosom led me to believe that she was not indifferent to his company, despite her shy glances at him from under her eyelashes.

When I'd moved, it had disturbed the symmetry of our positions around the table, and I was "obliged" to sit between Andrew and my brother. I rather hoped the man on my right had not heard my brother's inappropriate snicker from my left-hand side, or had noticed his less than subtle poke in my ribs with his elbow. I'd not planned it, but was content it had turned out so.

After calling for a carriage to take the Bolton family home, it had been all I could do to get undressed and throw myself into bed, telling Theo I'd prefer to sleep alone. It was our understanding that at times it would be so—usually when either of us was really drained. I'd bade Andrew goodnight and left him and Theo in our living room, playing cards. I'd heard neither of them go to bed.

However, the following morning, I found Russell Ward sitting in an armchair, its back up against the door to our apartment.

"Good morning, Russell," I said. "No, don't stand, go on reading your paper. Do you know where everyone is?"

"Chief Constable Bolton has gone for a swim, Mr. Murray—I think I heard him return a few minutes ago—and your brother has gone to a studio in the Paling's building in George Street to rehearse for his benefit concert on Wednesday night. He said to say I was to wake you at half past nine, but if you rose earlier to tell you he's ordered you a cold collation to be sent up. He'll be back in time for lunch at half past one. Coffee's already here; it's on the spirit burner on the sideboard, turned down low so it doesn't spoil."

I felt I needed something that stuck to my ribs, so rang the concierge to ask for a cooked breakfast to be sent up instead of the plate of cold meats and cheeses. I asked for it to be delivered in half an hour, which would give me time to shower and shave, after which I could eat, and then set about writing a few letters. I'd start my vocalising by eleven thirty, which would make me ready for Miss Fischer, who I'd arranged to arrive at midday. I needed to go through my music for tonight's

Fledermaus. I knew it, but hadn't sung the role in some time and wanted to refresh myself on the ensemble after my character, Falke's, big "*Dui Du*" solo in Act Two.

After my shower, I was busy fussing over my hair when Andrew knocked at the bathroom door.

"Good morning," I said.

"You slept soundly," he replied, poking his head around the door.

"How was your swim?"

"Wonderful. I really needed it. You should come with me sometime."

"How about Thursday morning?"

"That sounds splendid."

"After Wednesday evening's *Faust* and my brother's benefit concert, I've no more performing for over a week until the opening of *Don Giovanni*. There'll be rehearsals, but I'm looking forward to having a few days to myself."

"I have to admit I'd no idea the life of a singer would be quite so busy," he said. And then, after asking permission to enter, came into the bathroom and took my scissors from my grooming set and the comb from my hand, ordering me to turn around to face him.

"It's not usually quite so busy," I said as he started to work with no small amount of deftness and expertise at the hair above my ears, where it never sat smoothly, no matter what I did. "It's the tail end of the summer season, and everything simply happened to pile up. I will have had three closing nights within the space of five days. *Bohème* last night, *Fledermaus* tonight, and *Faust* on Wednesday."

"You have very good hair that's been cut badly. Who does it for you?"

"The barber downstairs, as a rule."

"I'll get Father to come over one morning to do you and your brother."

"That's a terrible imposition. We couldn't possibly—"

"If he happened to arrive for the appointment early and was able to hear you practise, it would make his day."

His smile convinced me. In fact, at that moment, he could nearly have convinced me to do anything. Clad with only a towel around my waist, still warm and glowing from my shower, him standing close to me, his face not twelve inches away, he combed my eyebrows and tidied them.

"Why are you smiling?" he asked.

"Did you know one of your canines is longer than the other?"

He snorted and rolled his eyes. "Trust you to notice. Mother has been on at me to get my tooth filed, or whatever they do."

I grabbed his wrist. "Don't," I said. "Whatever you do, resist the temptation. It sets off the perfection of the rest of your features."

I suppose he was now a little used to my unconventional protestations, as he merely laughed and then put down the scissors and comb and ran his fingers through the hair on either side of my head before massaging the scalp above my ears vigorously. It felt wonderful.

"All better?" he asked, turning me around so I could inspect myself in the mirror.

"My scalp feels wonderful," I replied. "My hair's a bit of a mess, though."

He winked and then picked up my comb and my brush. In less than a minute, I whistled quietly. I'd never seen my hair so neat and orderly.

"You're what they're calling a strawberry blonde these days," he said in response to my broad grin as I inspected my new trim in the mirror.

"Howard used to say I had hair the colour of a five-rupee spittoon."

Andrew laughed. "No, it's a much more attractive colour than brass. There's no red in it."

"And yours?" I asked.

"Oh, I'm very modern," he said with a small laugh, smoothing his hair back as he spoke. "I'm popularly known as an ash blonde."

I was aware that his physical proximity had begun to stir things I'd rather not let show through my towel. So I excused myself and went to my bedroom to get dressed.

It didn't take me long, and when I returned to our living area,

Andrew was in his suite, and Ethan had appeared with breakfast for two and was laying it out on our dining table.

"Theo's practising," I said, noticing the two settings.

"Yes, I saw him earlier, before he left for town," he replied. "The other breakfast is for Mr. Bolton."

"Ah, thank you, Ethan," I said. "I'd like to find a quiet moment with you to speak about my brother."

"Of course, sir."

"It's nothing serious. I just want to make sure ..."

"As I did, Mr. Murray," he replied. "My intentions are as honourable as those behind your question." The light in his eyes as he spoke told me all I needed to know. I was now fairly sure I'd have no objections to his future relationship with my brother.

"Then we've no need for this conversation, Ethan. I have nothing but respect for you and look forward to getting to know you away from the Metropole."

I held out my hand and he removed his white cotton glove before shaking it. "I look forward to that too, Mr. Murray. Thank you."

*****

I sat at the writing desk in the reading room while Cooper practised his scales.

I was used to being surrounded by music and people practising. It didn't bother me at all. It was one of those things musicians could do: to listen selectively, to filter out music we didn't need to pay attention to. His repetitive arpeggios, preceded by major, minor, and then both melodic and harmonic minor scales, faded into the background.

I'd decided I could write my letters anywhere, and as Cooper was to play at his mother's concert on the coming weekend, I'd suggested that while Andrew went to Phillip Street, the young constable could practise and keep an eye on me at the same time.

Most of my correspondence had to do with Howard's funeral service, which was to be held next Monday, one week from today. I'd cabled his brother, Lincoln, who'd also been one of the "Mullins Boys" with us in India, but who'd worked after leaving the troupe as a steward on one of the P&O Orient steamers before settling in Auckland, where, for the past ten years, he'd been the senior hotel valet for gentlemen of influence who stayed at the Grand Hotel, in Princes Street.

Howard's body lay in the refrigerated storage compartment at Hudson's funeral parlour, awaiting Lincoln's arrival by steamer next Sunday. It would be an enormous funeral; it always was when one of us theatre people passed on. Most of my correspondence this morning was addressed to the Mullins Boys I knew of who'd come back to settle in Sydney, to ask them to stay after the services at St. James's church and the burial at Rookwood Cemetery. A special train would be put on from the mortuary station at Central, and then, after the interment, Theo and I wanted to have a quiet, special celebration of Howard's life with those we'd suffered with in India. We'd hold it quietly in the private lounge in the Lord Wolseley pub in Ultimo, in the area a lot of us grew up in before we were "adopted".

One special letter was destined for Lester Palmer, at the *Freeman's Journal*. I hoped he could get the notice of the church service and burial in this Wednesday's edition, so men I did not know how to contact, and who lived close enough to travel, could see it, and perhaps make their way to Sydney to attend. After Mullins had died, we'd learned that some seventy boys had survived from the period of twenty years he'd been back and forth to Calcutta where his company had been situated, and half as many girls—many, many more had died of typhus, cholera, and dysentery. We'd lost contact with dozens of the girls, who'd either changed their names or had married and wanted no part of what had happened during their time in the sub-continent.

I sealed the last letter and then reached for a telegram, which had been delivered this morning while I was still asleep. It was a return cable to one I'd sent on Saturday morning, cancelling my overnight stay at the Australia Hotel later in the week.

SEVERELY DISAPPOINTED BUT UNDERSTAND STOP WILL ARRIVE ON THE MORNING OF MAY SECOND STOP ADVISE AS TO YOUR SITUATION CLOSER TO THE TIME STOP LOOKING FORWARD TO YOUR LETTER STOP SANDFORD.

Garrick Jones

There was no way I would have been able to meet up with Sandford this Thursday evening, even though he'd planned a special trip down from the country. Not only would we have no privacy, but he was an extremely jealous man. Were he to catch one glimpse of my constant protector, Chief Constable Andrew Bolton, there'd be no end of disagreeable and unreasonable behaviour to cope with. It was one of the two associated character traits that had prevented me from making some kind of permanent commitment to him. The first was jealousy, the second, his sense of entitlement and ownership.

*****

I'd met Sandford Clarkson in 1881. I was eighteen at the time, and he thirty-one.

It was during the country tour that Elias Solomon had sent me on, not long after we'd auditioned for him. I'd gone off around New South Wales for six weeks with my newly met accompanist, Hilda Fischer, and her chaperone, while Theo had been cast as Jimmy Quick in the vaudeville review at the Lyceum.

Sandford had approached me after the concert we'd given in the Victoria Theatre in Newcastle. We'd been surprised at the turnout, as the Montague–Turner Opera Company had not long finished a season of *Faust*, *Lucia di Lammermoor*, and *Il Trovatore*. However, the theatre had been full. A great surprise for an eighteen-year-old with no reputation. Miss Fischer had suggested my programme itself had been the reason the concert had been sold out. I'd decided to sing six songs from *Die schöne Müllerin* by Schubert, some lieder by Mendelssohn and Brahms, and a selection of popular ballads by Balfe, Bishop, Sullivan, and Wallace.

There had been twenty songs in the programme. However, with a young, flexible voice, I'd found it not the least bit tiring vocally, but emotionally demanding, mainly due to the constant changes of sentiment needed for each of the songs. We'd split the evening into two halves, the "serious" music by the German composers in the first half, and the ballads in the second.

I'd thought half the audience may have fled after the interval, but when I'd walked back out onto the stage after the very long intermission, the theatre had been packed to the rafters—news had spread of "the young man with the golden voice", as I was described in the *Newcastle Morning Herald* on the following morning. I'd later learned that servants had been despatched by some of those in the audience to fetch others who'd not bought tickets for an unknown eighteen-year-old tackling *"one of the most refined and exquisite vocal collections of the Romantic period, followed up by songs dear to the hearts of nearly every man and woman in the land."*

The reviewer had been overflowing in the generosity of his praise.

Sandford Clarkson and his mother had made themselves known after the performance and then had delivered a calling card on the following morning with a note inviting us to their city house for lunch, before our train journey on to Maitland at six in the evening. A coachman had been waiting downstairs for our reply. Miss Fischer and her chaperone had demurred, but I had been interested enough to want to see some of the town, so the coachman had told me he'd return at a quarter to twelve to collect me.

The city house was a grand building of some elegance, not more than fifteen minutes from the theatre, set in huge grounds and overlooking a park. Curiously, Mr. Clarkson's mother had greeted me when I'd arrived, but had then excused herself, leaving her son and me alone. He was delightful company, charming, educated, and extremely well dressed. There had been something about him that fascinated me: his self-assured manner, engaging conversation, and very striking looks.

He'd asked about my career, and I'd managed to frame it in such a way it did not betray my background, twisting the facts slightly and reporting that I'd been a touring performer for the British Raj in India—which I had been, in a manner of speaking, for we had entertained them quite often. He'd asked how I came to be singing in Newcastle, so I'd told him about Mr. Solomon, and how the impresario had taken both me and my brother into his stable of performers.

It had been a very pleasant lunch and he didn't cross my mind much thereafter, until the very last week of our tour, when we'd arrived in Scone and I'd found a letter waiting from Elias, informing me that Mr. Clarkson had contacted him, offering to engage both Miss Fischer and I for another performance at the Victoria in Newcastle, followed a few nights later by one or two songs at a ball he and his mother were to be hosting at their property, Cliften Grange. The fee had been truly astonishing, so we'd agreed readily.

As the concert would be "own choice", she and I had put together a programme consisting of songs, arias suitable for my voice, some piano solos for her, and one or two "descriptive pieces" that were all the rage. I enjoyed the declamatory style and the challenge of acting, trying to match Miss Fischer's nimble fingers and oft-times thundering piano interludes with my own theatrical delivery of the story that accompanied them. As for the one or two songs to be performed at the ball, I'd left that choice up to Mr. Clarkson, and we'd decided we'd discuss it with him when we arrived.

We'd sent a cable the following morning accepting the offer of the engagement. For one thing, the idea of an own-choice concert and a few songs at a gathering, separated by a few days of leisure, sounded excellent to me. Besides, I'd not long ago signed a contract with Mr. Solomon and hadn't wanted to appear churlish by refusing the offer of a very well-paid engagement, no matter how arduous the travelling of the past six weeks had been.

Cliften Grange was a sprawling property, situated on the Hunter River, and consisting of fifteen thousand acres of mixed grain farming, sheep, and cattle grazing. The main house was a glorious two-story affair, surrounded on both levels by wide, spreading verandas. Miss Fischer had been lodged at the rear of the house, and I in a large bedroom at the front, with French doors that opened out onto the veranda. The view, down over the grounds to the river, had quite taken my breath away, as had Sandford Clarkson's quiet arrival through those doors into my bedroom, late on the first night of our arrival.

I'd been standing outside leaning on the balcony rail, smoking a cigarette, wearing nothing but my long johns, and rubbing my hand over my stomach and chest, idly pulling the hair above my navel between my fingers. The moon had been new and cast a faint pale silver gleam over the river. It had been very beautiful.

"Need a hand with that?" he'd asked, coming up silently along the veranda, wearing only his shirt, which had been unbuttoned halfway down his chest.

"What, my cigarette?" I'd asked.

He'd smirked. I'd known what he meant. Although I'd never previously done anything more than handholding, one didn't stay ignorant when one had a brother who slept with men, and who liked to share tales of his experiences. I'd also shared accommodation for eight years with dozens of other boys, adolescents, and young men in barracks in India and had seen and heard everything under the sun.

I'd not been saving myself up on purpose. To be honest, it had been because of Theo. He used to tell me I was different and that my attraction to other men was merely a phase, unlike his own confirmed Uranism. However, the phase had never passed, and at the age of eighteen I'd already confirmed to myself that I would most likely never marry. For about a year I'd thought that I'd like my first time to be with someone older; someone experienced, well mannered, and gentle. Such a person had sidled up to me and had been standing, barelegged, dressed only in his shirtsleeves—fate had made the decision for me.

So, I'd offered him a cigarette from my case, and we'd stood side-by-side, smoking in silence, until I'd said goodnight and then turned and gone into my room. I could have said I'd forgotten to close the door, but I hadn't. I'd leaned against the end of my bed, my heart pounding in my chest, and watched him unbutton the rest of his shirt. He'd stood in the doorway and asked if he could come into my room. I'd nodded but didn't speak. He'd smiled and then moved silently across the room to stand in front of me, our toes almost touching. His shirt had fallen open. He'd been naked underneath it.

It had been me who'd reached across and pulled him into my arms and then opened my lips to his kiss.

*****

I folded the letter and then wrote the address on the envelope.

Sandford Clarkson, Esq.
"Cliften Grange"
Via Woodbury,
Newcastle.
New South Wales.

If I posted it later this morning at the desk of the Metropole, he would receive it on Wednesday. In the letter I'd explained briefly what had happened since leaving the theatre last Thursday evening, and thanked him for understanding my reluctance to meet later this week. I felt a momentary pang of guilt when I thought of how much I was looking forward to swimming with Andrew on Thursday morning, intending to ask him to accompany me to Birchgrove by tram afterwards so I could inspect what progress had been made on our house, and so I could talk to the builders.

If only I'd felt for one moment, in the twenty years I'd known Sandford Clarkson, what I felt when Andrew Bolton looked into my eyes ...

"There! That's done, Mr. Murray," Cooper announced.

I was vaguely aware that he'd been practising one of Chopin's pieces. "Was that the A flat Polonaise?"

"No, sir. You have the key right, it's the third Ballade, opus 25 ..."

"I'm sorry. I was concentrating on my correspondence."

"Let me play you the last section again. You can hear Chopin's voice so clearly in the writing." He sat back down at the piano and replayed the last few pages of the work, occasionally glancing over and smiling at me, despite the dazzling display of effortlessly sounding and beautifully phrased playing. "See! It's so cleverly crafted, and truly delightful under the fingers."

"I'm rather puzzled, Cooper."

"I think I know what you're going to say. It's about my seeming lack of interest in the classics, isn't it?"

"Well, I am rather perplexed you play with greater élan than most I've heard, other than professional concert performers, and yet you understand the genius of the composers ..."

"Perhaps I can use an example, Mr. Murray," he said. "Your Miss Blanchard, with whom you'll be performing tonight? There are postcards of her everywhere. She's elegant, has beautiful, small white teeth, lustrous golden hair, possesses a magnificent, statuesque figure— the perfect woman. I can see and appreciate her as an item of beauty, but she does not stir anything within me."

"Like Miss Bolton?"

"At least there's a chance with a woman like her—"

"It's your mother, isn't it?"

"Mother?"

"Cooper, you may tell me to mind my business. I won't be the least offended. However, I distinctly remember you saying, after your dazzling rendition of the Gottschalk, '*there were a few imperfections. Mother would have been furious*'."

"Mother is a hard taskmaster, or rather, mistress."

"And of course that's the reason you play so brilliantly. But, if I were to suggest that now you're a grown man, you should play to either please yourself or someone other than the person who is your harshest critic. No doubt, if I were to hazard a guess, when you play your ragtime and cakewalks, and the classical repertoire at the ballet school, everyone is enthusiastic about your playing?"

He nodded. "But—"

"But can't you see? You're a grown man, Cooper—a man of no small ability on the pianoforte. When you play serious music, you must let go of that hard taskmaster who seems to be criticising every tiny moment of your playing. For, as long as she is breathing over your shoulder, you will never attain satisfaction from what you do."

"But isn't that what you strive for, Mr. Murray? Perfection?"

"Yes, it is, Cooper. But unlike you, I know it's not attainable, and I content myself with the knowledge I've done my utmost, and I congratulate myself on small victories. I sing and perform for those my voice speaks to; to the audiences everywhere who admire me for my ability to touch their hearts while I sing. If I can do that by singing a street song, or a country ballad, or one of Signor Verdi's arias, surely you could do that as easily with Chopin as you do with your popular scores."

"You have a greater deal of confidence in my ability to do that than I seem to have myself."

"You may believe me or not, as you wish, Cooper. But both Miss Fischer and I have performed together for over twenty years and we know and recognise true talent. We have both seen that you possess it in bucketfuls. No one is suggesting you should turn your life upside down and embark upon the life of a concert pianist. I'm merely telling you, as someone who has a certain reputation in the music world, that you can learn to love performing anything, as long as you don't self-criticise over every note while you are performing. Criticism is best kept to quiet moments, by yourself and to yourself, and with great care, sympathy, and kindness."

He sat quietly for a moment, twisting his fingers, and then looked at me. "How should I start?"

"Perhaps there is someone you might hold a picture of in your mind while you are playing and imagine them smiling at you as your hands go about their work? Think of them clapping with delight at your performance, of reaching out to give you their hand after you've played, of perhaps brushing your cheek with their lips. The reward for letting go and allowing the muse, and not the mother, to be your guide."

It was the most simple of things: to learn from a teacher who taught with strictness, but not severity. Instruction combined with care and not a small amount of encouragement and affection. I supposed he'd had plenty of the tough and not enough of the love.

"Now tell me about the Chopin you were playing. It's not a work I know."

"I thought Miss Bolton might like to hear it, so I'm refreshing my memory, in case I'm asked for a second encore on Saturday."

"Oh, what's your first?"

"Well, as you're attending, I thought I'd brush off the Liszt 'Faust Waltz', in your honour … it's like anything, Mr. Murray," he explained in reaction to my raised eyebrows and soft exclamation of surprise. "It's just a matter of practice. Surely you understand that?"

"Of course, yes. You're perfectly right, Cooper, and I shall be delighted if you think of me while you play it, knowing that any minor imperfection will merely enhance my appreciation of you as a performer. All of us make mistakes, even the greatest of musicians."

His look was initially one of puzzlement, which gradually turned to a small smile, as if he'd processed what I'd said and had accepted it. "I promise you I'll try, Mr. Murray," he said, standing from the piano stool and then crossing to where I sat at the writing desk. He held out his hand and I shook it. "I appreciate that you have given me good advice from the heart, sir. I mean it. And now, I've taken up some of your own practice time, so I'll pick up my book and find a corner in the room to read and relinquish the piano to you."

To his complete surprise, I smiled and then pulled him into a quick embrace, patting his back. "Any time you need advice, I'm here, Cooper. I must warn you, however, that in matters of the heart I am a very good listener and have broad shoulders upon which to weep, but as for advice in those areas, I'm afraid I'm a complete novice myself."

I tidied up my letters and then walked to the piano, gave myself a note, and then began my own vocal practice.

*****

Miss Fischer and I ploughed through the *Fledermaus* ensembles. It was as easy for me to sing as always. We'd not had to fix one thing and I was pleased at how fluid it felt.

"You've a new sound in your voice in the '*Dui Du*'," she said.

"I have?"

"There's something very tender there I've never heard before."

"Maybe it's because I'm feeling vulnerable? Having a madman trying to take your life would do it to anyone."

"I think not, Mr. Murray." She peered at me over the top of her spectacles for a moment and then turned back to the keyboard abruptly. "Let me hear the Schumann '*Widmung*'."

"Why?" I was painfully aware that my new sound had been due to the man who'd returned from police headquarters, and who had been sitting quietly, listening to me practise. I caught his eye and felt the colour rising in my cheeks. He smiled.

I stood transfixed for a moment, at once aware of why she'd suggested Schumann's song of love, composed for his wife, Clara Wieck. Like all of his songs devoted to her, "*Widmung*", or "Dedication" in English, was about commitment, frustration at their separation at the time, hopes, aching passion, his dreams of their eternal love, and a lifetime together as man and wife.

I couldn't help it. I sang with feelings from within I did not know I possessed. Not grand, sweeping, passionate, theatrical announcements of love and longing, but gentle, aching, tender feelings that came unbidden from somewhere deep within me. As the last chords sounded from the pianoforte, I realised my eyes were wet and dared not allow my gaze to wander to the man who sat silently near the doorway to the reading room.

It was only when Miss Fischer stood and excused herself, saying she needed a moment of air, and then pushed past me drying her eyes, that I glanced at Andrew, who was dabbing at his own with his handkerchief.

"Thank you, Mr. Bolton," Miss Fischer said to him as she left the room. "I've been waiting for that moment for over twenty years."

I'm sure he did not understand her, but I did. My God, why him? Why me? And why now?

*****

I almost ran from the practice room, such was my embarrassment.

Theo was just leaving our apartment and I grabbed him, asking for a cigarette, which he lit for me. I scurried to the end of the hotel corridor and pushed open the glass-paned door that opened onto a small stone balcony, overlooking Bent Street.

"Eddie?" My brother closed the balcony door behind him and then put one arm around my shoulders. "What's wrong?"

"Nothing."

"With you, 'nothing' usually means 'everything'. Come on, tell me—"

"I think I may have inadvertently played my hand." Even I could hear the misery in my voice.

"What have you done?"

"I sang to him."

"As you said 'to him', I suppose it is Chief Constable Bolton you're referring to, and it was a little more than mere practice."

"Damned Hilda! It's all her fault."

"You'd better explain."

"She said there was a new sound in my voice and then asked me to sing ' *Widmung*'."

"The Schumann?"

I nodded.

"I didn't look at Andrew while I was singing, but she thanked him when she left the room, saying she'd been waiting for me to sing it like that for twenty years."

My brother pulled me into his arms and hugged me hard. "I'm glad you did, Eddie," he said against my ear. "It's been a long time coming."

"But I've made a fool of myself. What will he think?"

"Ultimately, if he's not interested in you in the way you'd like him to be, then it's of no consequence what he thinks. But, hold onto whatever it was that caused Hilda to make that remark. Just think, you now have a new something inside you; something you can feed into your other performances when it's called for. We're artists. We need new vocabulary all the time. Feelings are our words, without new ones, we'd be writing the same prose for the rest of our careers. How lucky you are to feel something new like that ... was it what I think it might be?"

I nodded and then sighed. My brother began to rock me in his arms and kissed the side of my head.

"I'm thirty-nine, Theo. Surely at this age I'd know better than to throw my heart after someone for the first time who's not of the same persuasion."

"You've known him barely a few days. Perhaps it's a case of delayed puppy love? And, surely it's better late than never."

"I feel so embarrassed. How will I ever face him?"

"How do you know he even realised what was behind what you were singing?"

"He was wiping his eyes when I left."

"Everyone is moved by your voice, Eddie. I even cry when you sing 'Mandy Lee'."

I laughed loudly, and then he sang a few lines out over the street, using his growly negro minstrel voice:

> *Mandy Lee, I love you, 'deed I do, my Mandy Lee,*
> *Your eyes shine like diamonds, love, to me.*
> *Seems as though my heart might break without you,*
> *Mandy Lee,*
> *Cause I love you, 'deed I do, my Mandy Lee.*

I joined in on the last two lines. It was normally a favourite barbershop quartet, but he and I had sung it together at the pub as a lark, more than once, when we'd had a pint or two. It broke my mood, and we ended up laughing, both leaning on the stone balustrade of our balcony and looking down over the people walking along the street below us.

"He doesn't know what he's missing," Theo murmured.

"Who?" asked a voice from behind us. It was Andrew, who we hadn't heard open the door behind us, and who had also obviously come outside for a smoke. There was an unlit cigarillo hanging from the corner of his mouth.

"Hello," I said, braving the moment.

"Room for one more?"

Theo ushered him in between us and put an arm around his shoulder. I felt Andrew's arm go around my waist. I don't suppose he would have done that had I offended him in some way, so I pushed my anguish deep down inside and took another of my brother's cigarettes.

"Have you organised something for lunch, Theo?" I asked.

"I've sorted something to be sent up," Andrew said, answering instead of my brother. "I've had news from headquarters, and I'd like we three, with Braxton Miller and Cooper, to sit down together. Your impresario, Mr. Solomon, will be here too," he added, looking at his watch. "He'll be here right on half past one, which gives us fifteen minutes to have our cigarette and before our food is delivered and your manager arrives."

He smiled in turn at both of us, and Theo and I exchanged quick glances. My brother tilted his head minutely. He didn't need to tap the side of his nose with his fingertip, telling me to keep my emotions under control, the look in his eyes was enough.

*****

Elias arrived right on the dot of half past one, accompanied by Braxton. They'd run into each other in the hallway outside the elevator.

The dining table had been laid out for six. George waited beside his chafing trolley, white-gloved and ready to provide silver service for our lunch.

"Superintendent Morris has provided me with an expense account while I'm staying here, gentlemen," Andrew said as he waited for us to take our seats. "Lunch is courtesy of the police department."

When I asked why we'd been assembled and whether there'd been any developments, he said we should enjoy our meal first and discuss his reasons for bringing us together after. His glance at George, from the corner of his eye, indicated what he had to say would be best left until after the pantry butler had finished serving our food and had left us alone.

It was a perfect meal for a performing day. I tended to eat lightly on days I had to sing and then have something either when I got home from the theatre or tuck into a big breakfast the following morning. The four courses were simple but appealing: *vol au vents à la financière*; steamed asparagus with hollandaise, which George prepared *à la minute* on the spirit burner of his trolley; and then finely sliced rare roast beef with tiny potatoes, rolled in butter and sprinkled with parsley, accompanied by greenhouse French beans. Finally, Lucas arrived with the dessert trolley. On it a large frosted silver tub of vanilla ice cream and choice of a delicious-looking lemon tart or a fresh fig and strawberry compote.

I'd found dessert in any situation never to be a leisurely affair, especially when it came to frozen ices. Within the space of five minutes our plates were cleaned, only a few remaining traces of pink from the compote and a few crumbs from the delicious shortcrust tart remained on our plates as evidence that anything had been served at all.

"Another slice of *tarte au citron*?" George asked Cooper, who, during the course of the meal, had stared in astonishment as each dish was presented.

"Go on, Cooper," I said with a wink, after Braxton had also demurred. "There's but one portion left."

"Very well, Mr. Murray, if you insist. My mother always says we should not leave food uneaten. Her favourite admonition is to 'think of the starving children in India',," he said and then reddened as my face fell. "I'm sorry ... have I said something amiss?"

"Not at all, young man. I only wish I could do as much justice to the food on the plate before me as you do. We more mature gentlemen have to watch our waistlines."

"Mature, Edward?" Andrew said with a small chuckle. "You and I are much of an age, and I'd be happy for a physique such as yours. What waistline?"

Everyone smiled. It had been the perfect thing to say. He'd noticed my reaction, as had Theo. My brother and I had known hunger as children, more than most, both on the streets of Sydney as bantlings, and then thereafter in India when times were tough and the Mullinses had been skint.

"I shall look forward to comparing waistlines on Thursday morning at the baths. Rowers are renowned for their slender midriffs."

He patted his tummy, refusing the last ladle of fruit, which George had offered from the near empty *compotier.*

"I've never eaten such a delicious lunch," Cooper said. "It's steak and kidney suet pudding and treacle tart in the police kitchen most days."

Coffee was served by Lucas, who, although thoroughly professional and as friendly as usual, refused to meet my brother's eye. I guessed he'd heard the news about Theo and Ethan.

"Now, I suppose you're all wondering why I've asked you here?" Andrew said after the table had been cleared and both George and Lucas had left us. "Fetch Constable Whitley please, Cooper."

The young constable opened the door to our apartment and poked his head out into the corridor, talking to someone who was standing outside. He returned to the table, followed by a uniformed police officer who sported the most splendid bushy mutton-chops and a sweeping moustache. He was introduced merely with his surname, Whitley, and took a seat slightly behind Andrew, resting a satchel on his knee.

"I was called into Phillip Street this morning for a meeting with our new dactylographist, Constable Whitley, who will explain his findings."

"Thank you, sir, gentlemen," the man responded, nodding to each of us as he opened his satchel. He withdrew two sheets of paper and held them up. On each was drawn an enlarged fingerprint. "I used a magnifying glass and a pantograph to draw these two illustrations. They come from two fingerprint impressions. The first is from the top of the blade found in Mr. Talbot's back; the second is taken from the inside flap of the envelope that was left at the hotel desk for Mr. Murray on Saturday last. The person who stabbed Howard Talbot was indeed the same person who sent the letter."

"Explain why this is important, Whitley," Andrew said. It was very impressive to see him at work in his role as a detective. There was an authority and kindness in his voice that was notable. Other policemen I'd met over the years tended to be matter-of-fact, oft times gruff.

"Well, now that we know it was the killer who wrote the letter, we have a sample of his handwriting. It also means we can prove his identity to a judge and jury if the case comes to court. Dactylography is rather new, but handwriting comparisons are no longer scoffed at when produced in court. There are barristers who will argue it as nonsense, but most reasonable jurors will agree they can identify the handwriting of differing members of their own families as belonging to the person who's laid pen to paper."

"But how does that help us if we have no one to compare the handwriting to?" Theo asked.

"That's why I've asked you all here this afternoon." Andrew thanked Whitely, who returned to the hallway outside. "One of my men spent a lot of time on Sunday morning, and in the evening after the benefit performance, with Mr. Willings, the manager of the Theatre Royal, and Braxton here, going through the rosters, contracts, and engagement chits for the season of *La Bohème*."

"Are you still thinking it might have been someone in the theatre?" I asked. It was hard to understand anyone who'd been involved in the production could do such a thing.

"We need to start with the most obvious, Edward. When there's a murder, we usually start with the nearest and dearest to the victim. The husband, the wife, the lover … in nine times out of ten, the perpetrator is known to the deceased."

"There is no one in my life like that," I said. Sandford was the only person I had an ongoing liaison with, and although he was jealous, he would never resort to violence.

"No jealous lovers, rebuffed suitors? Over-zealous admirers?"

"There are always plenty of admirers for someone of Edward's standing," Elias Solomon said. "I receive all of the correspondence that's sent by devotees and theatregoers. There are always one or two who are tiresome, but on the whole the letters are usually requests for signed photographs, or merely expressions of appreciation."

"I see," Andrew said. "Are any of them from an admirer named James Kane?"

All eyes turned to our agent, who looked as if someone had slapped his face.

"Mr. Solomon?" As my agent seemed to have lost the ability to speak, Andrew prompted him to answer.

"He's one of the more ardent correspondents, yes."

"And …?"

"And he's a young singer with no great talent who's persistent in applying for auditions when he's been told over and over again that he is not someone my agency could possibly represent."

"Has he ever been angry when you've told him so?"

"The last time he turned up for open auditions, I wouldn't even hear him. He slammed the door as he left. That's hardly violent."

"But he writes to Mr. Murray?"

"He writes to a lot of my artists. He's obsessed with the theatre. But, his letters to Edward can be … difficult. I suppose that's the best word."

"Difficult in what sense?"

"He often asks for personal articles for his memorabilia. Handkerchiefs are the most frequent requests."

"Have you ever sent any?"

Elias Solomon spluttered his answer. "No! Of course not! That would be a betrayal of the most heinous magnitude. Those sorts of letters go into a box with others of the same ilk, in case Mr. Murray ever wants to peruse all the communications from his admirers, including the less salubrious ones. They are his property after all. I forward on all the rest."

I was astounded. I left that sort of thing up to Elias. When I had time, I replied to everything I received from admirers, usually enclosing a small, signed photographic portrait. Elias and his secretary had become adept at shielding me from those missives that were either from people asking for money or letters from religious fanatics who railed against both my Catholicism and my unmarried state. Bachelors past the age of twenty-five were considered blasphemous, merely for their existence, in the eyes of some.

"This James Kane, why do you mention his name, Andrew?"

"Well, Edward, as I told you, my team spent a long time with Mr. Willings and Braxton, and the only member of the entire production who did not return for the final performance was Mr. Kane."

"I've never heard of him," I said.

"Yes, you have, Eddie," Theo said and then went to his room. He returned a few moments later with a small, cardboard-framed photograph of a young, fair-haired man, wearing only a posing pouch, standing in an attitude that showed a very finely chiselled musculature. It was obviously taken to entice or to titillate. "Athletic studio posing photographs", they were euphemistically known as. In some of the more expensive versions, the fig leaf, or the posing pouch, covering the model's private parts, could be removed with a sponge and water. It was done to circumvent the law, and the "wet and reveal" photographs of handsome young men sold for guineas, not for shillings.

I recognised the face immediately.

"Edward?" Andrew asked.

"He also goes by the name of Bruno Little in the theatre. That's how I know him. It's not unknown for performers to take on a stage name. He is, as Elias said, an aspiring young singer with absolutely no talent whatsoever."

"It's me who knows him," Theo said. "Not Edward."

"May I ask the nature of your acquaintance with this Kane fellow?" Andrew asked, turning the photograph in his fingers.

"I can tell you where he lives," my brother said. I knew from the look in his eyes that James Kane, or Bruno Little, or whoever he liked to call himself, had shared my brother's bed; most probably on more than one occasion. The man in the photograph was exactly Theo's type. "He has lodgings at Milton House on the Broadway, on the left-hand side of the street, on the corner of Abercrombie."

Andrew tapped the photograph against the back of his hand, staring at my brother. "We'll talk of your acquaintance privately, Theo, if it suits you," he said and then turned to Cooper. "Get some men over there now. I'd like to have a talk with this Mr. Kane."

I swallowed. If it was as I suspected, Theo would most likely either lie or twist the facts in a way that would not incriminate him in any activity that could be considered illegal.

"He's been reprimanded twice that I can remember for being in parts of the theatre where he did not belong," Braxton said.

I'd been wondering why he'd been invited to be part of the group.

"Perhaps you'd like to elaborate, Mr. Miller?" Andrew asked.

Braxton was less used to discussing personal matters than any of us, so it was with some effort that he eventually spoke. "I suppose Mr. Willings told you I knew things."

"He did, but did not reveal what you knew. I have a feeling that you're uncomfortable about whatever it is. Please, you may tell us in your own time," Andrew said.

"He's taken to offering services to chorus men, stage hands, and mechanics in the men's dressing room on the top floor of the theatre. There's a small storeroom off the main area that's out of the way, behind the fly tower. The gentlemen's chorus dressing room is at the top of several flights of stairs. Management rarely goes up there. Someone left a note on my desk informing me that inappropriate shenanigans were taking place after performances of *The Barber of Seville* last month, and more recently after *La Bohème*, when most of the male chorus members had left to go home."

"Services?" I asked.

"Services, Edward. Do I have to spell it out?"

"Surely not," I said.

"He's a supernumerary with a very good physique, a handsome face, and no sense of decency."

"One could say that about any number of both chorus men and women ... and many of the carpet layers."

"Yes, but it's the first time I've heard of any of them taking on all comers for sixpence a shot. Most keep their business away from the theatre."

I laughed. It was terribly inappropriate. But, a man of his looks, and his age, distributing his largesse for half a shilling? I couldn't believe what I'd heard. "Are you sure this isn't theatre gossip?"

Braxton shook his head. "Since we started rehearsals a few weeks ago, I've discovered him at the receiving end of a small queue more than once," he said, looking acutely embarrassed. "On the second performance, I found him in the trapdoor space, underneath the stage during the intermission, with three men at the same time—two stagehands and the second bassoonist!"

"I'm sorry, I don't quite understand. At the same time?"

"I'm not sure I'm up to descriptive euphemisms."

"Then be blunt," Andrew said. "Cooper, you may leave the room if you wish."

"No, Mr. Bolton. I've seen and heard everything there is. Nothing offends me."

"Well, this might," Braxton said and then, after clearing his throat and adjusting the knot on his tie, spoke. "He was bent over, being sodomised by one stagehand, while performing fellatio on the other, with the bassoonist on his knees doing the same to Mr. Kane."

There was a moment of silence while each of us exchanged glances, until finally, it was Cooper who, after sipping at his wine glass, wiped his lips with his napkin, and then muttered under his breath, "Popular lad."

We all began to laugh, one after the other. Elias Solomon was the only one around the table who did not join in. He sat, his eyebrows raised, eyes wide, shaking his head slowly in disbelief.

"Well then, Constable Haddley," Andrew said to Cooper, "you'd best go find this prodigious sybarite and bring him in for questioning. Make sure you search his room after he's been taken away. I want anything you can find with his handwriting on it. If it matches the note sent to Edward, we have our man."

"I have several bundles of his correspondence in my office, too," Elias said. "Would you like me to fetch it?"

"I'd be extremely grateful, if it's no trouble, Mr. Solomon."

"Very well, then I'll be on my way. Allow me to offer you a seat in my carriage, Constable," our impresario said to Cooper. "I can drop you off outside Phillip Street on the way to my office. I'll send a boy with the letters to the police station, to be delivered to you, shall I, Constable Bolton?"

"That would be excellent. Thank you very much." Andrew rose from his chair. "I'll meet you back at the station in perhaps an hour or so, Cooper."

"Very well, Mr. Bolton. I'll see you then."

After Cooper and Elias had left the apartment, Braxton also made his excuses, saying he'd be at the Prince of Wales tonight for the last *Die Fledermaus*, as the guest of Sir Horace and Lady Blake. Andrew escorted him to the door and thanked him for coming, and apologised for putting him in an uncomfortable situation. He returned to his chair and offered us both a cigarette before speaking.

"Perhaps it is time for me to speak plainly, my friends. Although I'd sworn to uphold the law, I consider myself a man of the world. Although an innocent myself, I am not unaware of what gentlemen get up to in private. I've seen enough things, both in the army and as an officer in the morals enforcement branch of the police, and then as a student at the University of Sydney, not to make judgements. In the time I've known you, you've shown me nothing but respect and kindness. I don't care what you get up to behind closed doors. Full stop! So, Theo, when you and I go outside for a stroll down to Circular Quay while Edward is having his afternoon rest, I'd like you to be as open and honest as you can be, with the knowledge that the information will stay with me, and only with me. Do we understand each other?"

Theo smiled—a bare smile, but it was one of relief. I knew he hated lying. My brother wasn't one bit embarrassed about what he did with other men. He'd always protested that if both parties were willing, then it offended no one, nor was it anyone else's business. I also knew that he was probably more worried about upsetting Andrew than about lying or twisting the facts.

"Understood," my brother said and then returned Andrew's proffered handshake.

"That goes for you too, Edward."

"I'll shake your hand if you offer it, Andrew, but I've little to hide."

"That's hard to believe, if I may be so bold. A man of your consequence?"

"Circumspection is the result of consequence, Andrew. My private life is not what most might imagine, I'm afraid."

He laughed. "If that's truly the case, you are most certainly wasted, Mr. Murray."

"Sometimes the most ebullient of men are timid when it comes to such things, Constable Bolton." The use of our surnames loaned lightness to an otherwise awkward conversation.

"You, sir, are a man after my own heart. Shall we shake hands in any case?"

I may have imagined it, but the strength of his handshake and the look in his eyes was one of something akin to relief and vulnerability. It was all I could do to release his hand from my own.

CHAPTER 7

"Is there any of that roast beef cold in the larder?" I asked the concierge. We'd only this minute returned from the theatre, and I was tired and hungry. "If there is, I'd like a few sandwiches with some horseradish and a small salad. Andrew, will you have something to eat?"

"I dined before the performance, Edward," he replied, "but I'll keep you company."

"How about some pommes frites with mayonnaise? Surely you could handle a few of those?"

"Well …"

"Very good," I said to the concierge. "I'll have two small bottles of stout to go with the sandwiches, and a newly charged gazogene with some lemon syrup and a bowl of ice for Chief Constable Bolton. If you can send it up in half an hour, I'd be more than grateful."

"Of course, Mr. Murray. If there's no roast beef, will you be happy with our smoked ham in your sandwiches?"

"As long as there's Keen's on the side."

"You take your life in your hands," Andrew said to me in the elevator. "I can't cope with that really hot mustard. I like it French."

"As do I, but not only when I'm talking of food," I said with rather more lewdness than I'd intended.

He laughed. "I'm sure I have no idea what you could possibly mean."

"Oh, I'm fairly sure you know exactly what I meant."

"Theoretically, yes."

Even the elevator attendant smiled at our banter as he opened the grille of the lift compartment. He wished us a good evening and then, as we walked along the corridor, I heard the lift's motor fade as it returned to the ground floor.

"All's well, Russell?" Andrew asked of the young policeman, who'd been sitting outside the apartment door when we approached it. Despite my eyeroll when it had been suggested, it had been decided that even though the suite was locked when neither my brother nor I were there, a policeman should stand guard, in case an attempt to enter was made while we were off about our business.

"Yes, sir. It's been nothing but quiet," the man said and then tipped his hat to me. "Thank you for your kindness, Mr. Murray. The supper you ordered for me was delicious."

"It was nothing, Constable Ward," I replied.

"You had something sent up for him?" Andrew asked once we were inside the apartment.

"Of course. He's been sitting outside since half past five when we left for the theatre and it's nigh on midnight. You can't have the man fainting with hunger."

Andrew chuckled. "We get used to it. It's part of our job."

"Well, it's not part of my job—not being considerate. Now, shower before we eat?"

"Yes, I'm desperate to have a quick rinse. I've no idea how you bear the heat in the dressing room at the Prince of Wales."

"You get used to it. Until a few years ago, every dressing room was gas lit. It's a luxury to have electricity in those that have already converted. And, of course, four of us in that small space too."

"Your Mr. Darencourt is a great deal of fun. I so enjoyed his Eistenstein."

"It suits him well. He has a great ability at comedy, and *Die Fledermaus* is a wonderful vehicle for him to show off his talents. You'll see him in *Don Giovanni* too. He's sharing the role with Mr. Greco, who's to be the principal Don Ottavio."

"His voice is a little lighter than Mr. Greco's."

"He's a lot more comely," I replied with a small chuckle, "and younger. It's easier not to suspend belief Donna Anna could be so enamoured of him."

"Do you mind if I don't dress again after my shower?" Andrew asked. "I won't be long out of bed after we've eaten. I've a bathrobe, if you don't think that's too *déclassé*. After all, there's only the two of us."

"Mr. Bolton," I said, grinning broadly. "If it wasn't for decorum, after the food has been delivered, I would normally be having my dinner with nothing but a linen serviette across my lap."

"Very well, bathrobes in fifteen minutes is it, then?"

"If I must," I said with an exaggerated, theatrical sigh.

He smiled and then went into his apartment while I made my way into my bedroom and got undressed. My gloves and topper went into the appropriate drawer and tall hatbox, as did my cufflinks and studs into my jewellery case. I put my shirt, socks, and underwear into the laundry basket, which the maid would collect when she came to do the apartment, and then took my tails from where I'd strewn them across the bed and arranged them on the valet stand. My evening wear could go into the wardrobe in the morning after it had been aired overnight. I put the shoe trees into my pumps and then placed them on the internal window ledge. They'd also be put away in the morning.

As I stood under the shower, I allowed myself to ponder about the revelation that James Kane had not been at his lodgings when the police had arrived. All Andrew had told me was that he appeared to have done a runner. He was sparing with any more information, telling me he'd let me know more after my performance, and that I needed to concentrate on *Die Fledermaus*. I'd been on the point of telling him I could sing Dr.

Falke in my sleep, but he'd been trying to be considerate, and if he had anything of urgency or danger to impart, he would have told me.

"*Although an innocent myself, I am not unaware of what gentlemen get up to in private*," he'd said earlier that afternoon after lunch, when he'd spoken privately with Theo and me.

I hadn't been able to get that phrase out of my head. He was a mystery to me. There were moments when I thought I saw something in his eyes, and yet I was confused. Perhaps I'd fabricated those moments to suit my own yearnings? Tonight, in the dressing room, Gideon had been busy, looking after both Mr. Darencourt and myself, and Andrew had helped me change during the interval after Act One. I'd shivered involuntarily as he'd helped me on with my trousers while I was busy putting the studs into my dress shirt. The knuckles of his thumbs, on the inside of the waistband as he'd drawn up my trousers, had grazed along the length of my thighs. I'd abandoned my cufflinks and speedily buttoned up the waistband and flies myself. I hadn't been sure that my body would not betray itself, had he started to fiddle with the buttons on those areas of my strides.

"You fool!" I said to myself, bending my head underneath the stream of water from the showerhead. I stood for what seemed an age, my chin on my chest, one hand on the flat of my belly and one leg barely bent, the other raised on the ball and toes of its foot. It was one of the reflective poses of Hindu yoga, a practice of meditation and self-examination that no one seemed to have ever heard of away from India. It had been hard to be an inquisitive child in Bengal without finding the culture fascinating as well. The stance often helped me deal with anxiety and other unbidden, strong emotional forces.

I'd dreamed of him last night. It wasn't an erotic dream, and that's what had bothered me. Men I'd found attractive in the past had stirred something below my waistline. Andrew Bolton seemed to have ignited a passion of a different type; one with which I was entirely unfamiliar. It was not unlike the type of closeness I had with my brother—an affinity of the soul, to use a rather hackneyed phrase. I wanted to share his life in some manner, to find out who the man was, rather than share our bodies. Although …

"Food's here," he called out, after knocking at the bathroom door and then poking his head around it.

"You were quick," I said, snapping out of my reverie.

"You've been in there for twenty minutes," he said with a broad grin. "Don't be long, the frites will get cold."

I must have been daydreaming for longer than I'd thought. I dried my hair hurriedly and then ruffled it into place with my fingers, before running the towel over my body. I wrapped it around my waist, and then, before I left the bathroom, glanced at myself in the mirror and gently slapped my face twice.

"You fool!" I said again to my reflection.

*****

"There are a few things that have been puzzling me, Edward," Andrew said.

We'd finished our late-night snack, and despite his assurance that he'd eaten and wasn't hungry, before I knew it, he'd polished off most of the pommes frites and one of my sandwiches. I didn't mind, we'd had a great chinwag while eating, and he'd sat most of the time on the sofa, his long, shapely legs and strongly developed calves stretched out into the space between the edge of the sofa and the low occasional table on which George had served our food.

"Aren't you going to tell me about James Kane?" I asked. He'd been avoiding any mention of what had been found at the man's boarding house. All I knew was what he'd told me—that Kane seemed to have scarpered.

"I will, I merely wanted to check one or two things that don't make sense first, if that's all right with you?"

"Of course," I replied, opening my second bottle of stout and then filling my glass.

"What I don't understand is how Kane could have surprised Howard. Surely your friend would have at least heard the door open?"

"That stupid door in the Theatre Royal has complained for years. It was like a cranky cow that wouldn't budge, stuck in the middle of the road."

"What do you mean?"

"The hinges were stiff, so one had to push hard, or pull with all one's might, and it creaked like Grandma's joints as it opened."

He smiled. "So many similes."

"I was so sick of it never being attended to, I asked Howard to fix it at the start of the *La Bohème* run. After he'd rehung it, people were so unused to it being properly balanced and oiled, they'd often either throw themselves from outside in the corridor into the dressing room with the momentum, having prepared to put their shoulders to it, or slam their hands against the dressing room wall when it opened effortlessly, after they'd gathered their strength to pull it open. Besides, the way the dressing room is arranged makes it hard to see if anyone is standing more than a few paces to the right when you're sitting in front of the makeup mirror. There's a clothes rack built so it blocks the immediate view of anyone entering the room. It was put in for modesty's sake."

"I thought you said theatre people were used to being in a state of undress?"

"They are, on the whole. However, there are some famous, voluptuous ladies of the stage who would never like to be discovered in their undergarments. Too much of their shapely figures is due to stuffing and corsetry, rather than gifts nature has bestowed."

"The other thing that puzzled me for quite a while is why, all of a sudden, did a bothersome admirer suddenly turn to murder? And why the heart around the hilt of the dagger, and your birth name written on Mr. Talbot's corpse, rather than your stage name?"

"My birth name? You didn't mention that before?"

"I thought you knew? I'm dreadfully sorry. I'd forgotten you declined to look at the photographs of Howard's body. *Édouard Marais* even has the *aigu* accent over the initial letter of your Christian name. Does that make a difference?"

I shook my head. "I suppose not, Andrew. My birth name isn't hard to discover. It's on any legal document and on the census of March last year. We were already living in Hunters Hill in our rented accommodation. We moved there in January of 1901, and the census was in March. As for the heart and the sudden attempt at my life, I've no idea."

He scratched at the top of his thigh, a few inches above his knee. I was transfixed by the golden hairs that covered his legs so thickly. They shone in the electric light. I couldn't wait to get a proper look in the daylight when we went swimming on Thursday morning. It was one of my fixations, and one of the things I admired so much about Sandford—his hairiness. Not dense, but befurred in a defined pattern over the grazier's chest, stomach, and legs.

"There's something you're leading up to, Andrew," I said. "I've been aware of it all evening. I respond best to plain speech."

"Your brother told me of Kane's few visits here while you were away in Brisbane last year. It's most likely that while your brother slept, he took the opportunity of obtaining a few 'souvenirs' from your bedroom."

"Souvenirs?"

"He's been a bowerbird when it comes to you. Objects that have been probably taken from various dressing rooms, as well as your underwear drawer here."

"Underwear … I'm not sure I like the sound of this."

"Most men keep a hand towel close to the bed."

"For emissions?"

He reddened. "I was thinking of a more roundabout way of saying it. But, yes, emissions."

I chuckled. "I told you to speak plainly. We call those 'exchequers' in the theatre."

"Exchequers?"

"Somewhere someone makes a deposit."

He laughed loudly. "That's a new one to me. However, Kane had an impressive collection of men's handkerchiefs, underwear, and other personal items, wadded up in a drawer of a small nightstand beside his bed."

"Oh …"

"One of the articles was a dance belt. I wouldn't have known what it was, before I saw you put one on. It had *EM* embroidered into the waistband."

I began to get a sinking feeling. To be honest, I felt no sense of personal danger. I was more than able to take care of myself, and with Andrew at my side, or Cooper, or Russell Ward, or any of the other ever-vigilant policemen, it was doubtful that Kane could get anywhere near me. But, these new sexual overtones to his admiration made me feel quite uneasy.

"And?" I asked.

He cleared his throat before continuing. "Edward, I'm sorry to tell you this, but some of the soiled undergarments and handkerchiefs were also embroidered with your initials."

"Until this moment, I was feeling rather blasé about him. But now, I feel rather grubby. You said he'd scarpered?"

"His clothes were gone, and his landlady said he'd paid three months in advance, saying he was going to visit his aunt in Adelaide."

"Surely that's good news? If he's out of the way in South Australia, he can do me no harm. If you check which steamers are headed to Adelaide, you could alert the police there?"

"We could do that, but because it's a different State, legally we are required to have one of our own men on the ground to arrest him. I've assigned one of my colleagues with the task of checking sailing lists in the newspapers and then double-checking passenger lists. The problem is he could travel with any name he wanted to. We could be looking for Bruno Little—his stage name—or James Kane, while he's booked passage with a different name altogether."

"Was there anything else?"

"At his lodgings?"

"Yes. I can see you're holding something back. What could be worse than discovering someone who has tried to murder you has been fetching off into your pilfered underwear?"

He stared at his hands for a moment before answering. "There are some things I'd rather you not know, but—"

"Andrew, this is unfair! You must not protect me in this manner. I'm not a child."

"No, you're not. I beg your pardon, Edward. Very well, I have an idea why his fascination may have turned to hate. Pinned to the inside of his wardrobe door were two pieces of correspondence, both received in the days immediately previous to Mr. Talbot's death. The first is a letter thanking him for his query, but stating you are not accepting private students."

"All of those letters are sent directly by Elias. I get so many requests, and to be perfectly honest, I don't have time to teach—not with any regularity, that is. His secretary sends out a letter to every query, every one of them the same. It's a standard reply. Everyone gets the same wording."

"Next to it was pinned your adjudication for the recent *Daily Tribune* singing competition two weeks ago, in which he competed. The letter was dated three days before the rejection letter for singing lessons."

"Those adjudications are only sent upon application. They are not normally given to entrants as a matter of course, mainly because there are just too many of them. He must have written and asked for it, and then the newspaper has sent a copy of what I wrote for my own notes."

"I see ... he did not like what you'd written about him."

"I can't remember what I wrote. I remember his singing, which was poor, but I have no recollection of the exact words."

"I have it in my room."

"The copy of my report?"

He nodded.

"I'd like to see it please."

"Are you perfectly sure?"

"Of course," I said and then started to wonder why he would be so reticent to show me something as innocuous as a singing competition report.

When he handed it to me, I could not help but notice that half of the bottom of the page had been torn off. I looked at him with a raised eyebrow, but when he did not react, I read the copy of what I'd written:

> *Mr. Kane's time would be better-spent undertaking tuition*
> *with a serious teacher. He lacks the basics of rudimentary*

technique. The voice is unfocused, gripped in the upper register, and has no support. His choice of aria and his song repertoire were demonstrated to be beyond his current ability.

"So he got your adjudication and, as you can see, underlined the first sentence in red. He wrote to Mr. Solomon on the same day and received this the day before he killed your friend." He handed me the letter that had come from my agent.

Thank you for your letter enquiring about private singing tuition with Mr. Edward Murray. Unfortunately, <u>Mr. Murray only accepts singers of the very highest level of ability</u> and is, at this time, not taking any new students.

He'd also underlined the beginning of the second sentence in red, and in the margin had written a particularly vulgar four-letter word.

"What was on the section that was cut? I presume it was intact when you found it, otherwise you wouldn't have been so reluctant to show it to me."

"Dried human faeces," he replied.

His blunt statement had the effect he intended. It shocked me.

"That's not all, Edward."

I stared at him blankly. I was still processing my despoiled underclothing and handkerchiefs, the letters, and the filthy curse word.

"We found a small suitcase in the bottom of a refuse pit behind the boarding house. His landlady told Cooper she'd seen him through her kitchen window throwing items into it on the day he'd told her he was going to Adelaide. In the case was a large collection of bits and pieces of greasepaint and other makeup items; dozens of programmes of your performances with intimate dedications to him written on the cover—"

"No!" I interjected. "I never sign across the cover—"

"It's his own handwriting. The graphologist assures it and will confirm in a day or two. And then, finally, a score of pornographic drawings of men engaged in intimate acts, labelled with your initials and his."

"Good God!"

"He'd defecated on the contents of the suitcase before closing it and throwing it away."

I sat in silence. For the first time since stepping foot on the steamer that had taken Theo, Madeleine, and me to India, I felt disoriented and vulnerable.

"Are you all right, Edward?"

"I will be, thank you," I said, my voice sounding weak, even to myself.

He put one arm around my shoulders and drew me close. I hesitated for perhaps a second or two before resting my head on his shoulder. We seemed to sit like that for an hour, only moving apart when the door to the apartment sprung open and Theo and Cooper burst in laughing.

"Eddie?" Theo asked, his face falling as he looked at me. "What's wrong?"

I stood silently and walked into my bedroom, closing the door behind me.

"Eddie?" he said, knocking lightly at the door.

It was the first time in my life I ever remembered shutting a door in my brother's face. I needed to be alone.

*****

I awoke in the dark.

I'd been dreaming of something, but it was one of those dreams I couldn't remember, even though I'd woken with a jolt right out of the dream. I sighed, turned onto my back, and ran my fingers through my hair. I plumped up the pillow behind my head and reached for my fob watch, which always sat on the bedside table next to a glass of water.

Three o'clock. My door was still closed. I began to remember what had happened last night. The dreadful, demeaning insanity of Kane, defiling my personal belongings—the man was deranged; there was no other explanation for it.

I sat up in bed and switched on the lamp on the other bedside table, and then wondered where my cigarettes were. Then I realised I didn't have any. I usually smoked Theo's … curious how my mind had leaped back five years, when I'd decided that I wouldn't buy them anymore and only smoke when offered cigarettes from someone else and on a social occasion.

I threw back the covers and tiptoed out into the living area. Cooper's head snapped up. He'd been lying on his side on the sofa in its place up against the doors of the apartment.

"You sleep gingerly," I whispered to him.

"The light from your room when you opened the door woke me up."

"Sorry, Cooper. I couldn't sleep. I was looking for a cigarette."

"Don't smoke, Mr. Murray. There's probably a package in Mr. Bolton's room."

"It's all right," I said all of a sudden aware that once more I'd appeared naked. "I'll grab one from Theo—"

"Mr. Bolton's will probably be handier, sir. Your brother has company."

"Oh …" I didn't know what to say.

"It's none of my business, Mr. Murray. My next brother in age has similar interests. It would be churlish of me to make judgements when I accept and love my brother for everything that he is."

"That's very understanding of you, Cooper."

"Not really, sir. When you're brought up in a poor house in a rough area, you learn not to assume what people do is any indication of who they are inside."

I smiled. There was probably enough light spilling through my partially opened door for him to see it. "Thank you, Cooper. You're a true gentleman."

"I hope to be so one day."

"If you'd like my opinion, I think you've made a very fine start. Now, I'll let you close your eyes again and I'll look for a cigarette in Mr. Bolton's living room. Please excuse my lack of clothing … again."

"As I've told you already, Mr. Murray, one of six boys."

"Goodnight, Cooper."

"Goodnight, sir."

The door to Andrew's apartment was ajar. I slipped inside and looked around, and found his cigarettes and matches on the sideboard. I hoped he wouldn't mind, so I took one and then cupped my hands around the match as I lit the cigarette.

I sprawled in the armchair that he'd placed against the door to his apartment, the back of it under the doorknob. I drew in a long, slow lungful of smoke and then leaned my head against the door behind me, closed my eyes, and tried to remember if I'd ever done anything to encourage Kane.

I barely knew the man. In fact, I was really unaware of him. Had the competition not been so recent, I think I might have strained to even imagine I'd ever met him. There'd been a madman in India. Jalai was his name. Jalai meant someone who'd been born in water. Ganga was his last name, the name of the sacred river that ran through Calcutta. For that reason, Jalai Ganga had been left alone. He was treated almost like a sacred cow. People would touch him for good luck. He wasn't a holy man, but there was a certain respect paid to him because of his name, despite his sudden outbursts of anger, screaming at the sky, rubbing dung into his hair, and drinking his own urine, which he did in the middle of the street, bending his head down to micturate into his own mouth.

That sort of madness I understood, for it seemed rational in its simplicity. He was mad—all of the time. Staring into the clouds, rolling in mud, yelling nonsense in his own incomprehensible, made-up language ... one didn't expect moments of sanity.

That's what worried me the most. Someone who could fester within over an invented relationship, while seemingly going about a relatively normal day-to-day existence in the theatre. Word would have spread like wildfire about any instability. Theatre people didn't mind promiscuity, or inappropriate jokes, or coarse language. But anything that might jeopardise a performance, like erratic behaviour, would have been seized upon and rooted out post haste.

It was one thing to have a stranger give you an unsolicited pat on the arse, or a furtive grope in a crowded pub—mostly done in good humour and with a smile—but Kane's behaviour was a completely different thing: unwanted attention, with no encouragement, redolent of threatened violence and degradation. I still felt sickened by it.

"Can't sleep?"

Andrew's voice frightened me. I sat up with a jolt. He was standing in the doorway of his bedroom, his dressing gown hanging loosely around his shoulders, revealing his bare chest down to the navel. My voice stuck in my throat. The high-backed settee was positioned between us.

"Is that one of my cigarettes I can smell?"

"I'm sorry," I stammered, trying to keep my gaze fixed on his face. "I didn't have any and Theo was—"

"With Ethan. Yes, I know. Are you all right, Edward?"

"Yes, thank you. I can't stop thinking about … James Kane." I could barely bring myself to say his name.

"Have no fear, my friend. We'll make sure he's tracked down. No one will do you any harm."

"Go back to bed," I said. "I'm sorry to take up your space. I didn't want to disturb Cooper."

"You can stay here if you like. It won't bother me. I can sit with you if you need the company?" He ran one hand through a lock of his hair that had fallen over one eye. I hadn't realised that ungroomed it was so long. Rather like my own before I brilliantined it into place.

I shook my head, almost violently. "No, the cigarette has calmed me down."

"Goodnight, then," he said with a gentle smile and then went back into his room. He didn't close the door after him.

I sat for what seemed like an age, wondering whether the open door was an invitation. It was a foolish thought. He'd told me twice he was inexperienced. No one with that level of innocence would be quite so forward. Once more, I was sure I'd invented something that wasn't there. So, I lit another cigarette and went back into my own bedroom. I stood at the window and stared down into the empty street below. There were still gaslights in this part of the city, glowing greenish-gold.

The wicks needed trimming, I thought, trying to distract my mind from the image I'd been trying to forget—Andrew standing, the greater part of his chest bared, some ten paces away from me, only separated by a piece of furniture.

His upper body was well defined, as I knew a rower's would be. That was not what had taken my eye. As I stubbed out my cigarette and got back into bed, pulling the covers over me, I swallowed deeply. I wasn't really salivating, it was that I'd been so transfixed in my thoughts that I'd allowed my spit to collect in the back of my mouth.

"Édouard Marais ..." I scolded myself, closing my eyes against the memory of the thick mass of blond curls across Andrew's chest and down over his stomach to as far as I had been able to see, at the point a little below his navel, where his dressing gown had been loosely gathered, closed by its cord around his waist.

I wasn't sure why I hadn't stood before he'd gone. Perhaps things left unseen were best left to the imagination, but I sorely wanted to see more of pale blond thicket below his navel and over the tops of his thighs. As for the rest? Well, I supposed when we went swimming on Thursday morning I'd allow myself the briefest of glimpses of his hairy backside.

And perhaps, if my hand brushed against his arm while we were swimming, my morning would be complete, although when I began to drift off to sleep my mind was full of images of running my fingers through the golden threads of his hair.

CHAPTER 8

The auditions on Tuesday morning for Howard's replacement had been dismal.

It was as if most of the applicants hadn't bothered to read the basic requirements in the newspaper advertisement. We had men turn up who were twelve inches shorter than I, twenty pounds heavier, some who even had no idea what a dresser was. At the end of the morning, after the last man had left, Elias had suggested that he pay Tanning's for a replacement costume maker for Gideon, who, although he could never stand in as my double, at least knew the theatre back to front. And, as he'd constructed most of my costumes, knew better than anyone how to help me get in and out of them speedily.

I suggested a short-term solution might be to hire someone who was skilled at fencing and could take notes of my placements on the stage if I was unable to attend rehearsals. There were plenty of older thespians who had the skills. In the long run, payment by the hour would account for shillings, not pounds. I'd simply have to forego trying to palm off a double in front of an audience during bows on the odd occasion when I needed to leave the theatre early. In any case, I reminded Elias, we'd be off to New Zealand in a few months from now, and I couldn't think of an occasion when I'd need a body double. If such an offer was made before we sailed, I gave him instructions to refuse it, if it meant passing someone else off as me.

"But—" he'd said.

"No more double bookings. Please, Elias!"

"It would be ever so convenient to have someone on hand though, Edward—"

"No!" I'd said as he'd thrown a wistful glance in Andrew's direction. "He's a policeman, for heaven's sake."

"But, he could pass for you with makeup and at a distance."

"At a distance and in low lighting. We look nothing alike. He's far more fetching than I am."

My impresario had given me a double take and shaken his head slowly while tut-tutting. "You'd think that after all these years, you'd have realised you're much more attractive than—"

"Well I haven't!" I'd hissed, under my breath, and stomped out of the room.

★★★★★

Faust went splendidly. Elias Solomon had solved the problem of appearing in two theatres on the same evening, and to his own ultimate advantage.

I didn't know what he'd had to promise Mr. Willings at the Theatre Royal to allow me to leave after Act Four, but Braxton had made an announcement before the curtain had risen at the start of the performance, stating that due to the sudden unavailability of one of the feature acts at my brother's benefit for the boys' home at Petersham, Mr. Willings had released me, so I could "hurtle across the city to save the day".

Even I'd been impressed by the spiel.

So, after the curtain fell on Act Four, I was paged between the front tabs, where I took my bows.

"Encore! Again! Again!" the audience yelled. I looked down to the conductor, who made a great play of pretending to want to get on with the opera, but encouraged by the public to accede to their requests, raised his baton.

I sang Valentin's aria, *"Avant de quitter ces lieux"* for a second time. This time the lights in the auditorium were raised slightly, my new burnished gold costume gleaming in the light. I was renowned for my cadenza at the end of the aria. Miss Fischer had devised it for me, based on the notes of the dominant seventh of the tonic key. It culminated with a sustained top A flat—one of those "money notes", as Elias was fond of calling them. When I was in fine voice, they were effortless, and I loved the moment when I felt them fly from my throat and ring around the auditorium.

Tonight's second A flat was even more heroic and resonant than when I'd sung the aria in Act Two. The audience went wild with applause. When I bowed, I saw that not a few of the ladies had handkerchiefs to their eyes, and the shouts and applause from the gallery, accompanied by the stamping of their feet on the bare boards under their benches, caused me to grin and to blow kisses to those up in the sixpenny seats in the Gods. As I rose from another bow, and over the din, I heard a soft bravo from my left-hand side and glanced in that direction. Andrew had been observing me through the space between the back of the proscenium arch and the carpenter's scene.

He opened his arms to me when I came off stage. "Bravo! Bravo!" he whispered into my ear, after wiping his eyes with the back of his hand. "How do you do it, Edward? I thought my heart would burst with the love in your voice. It stirred something deep within me I didn't know was hidden there. Thank you."

His cheek was pressed against mine, and it was all I could do to control myself and not turn my head to kiss him. "You have makeup and rouge all over your face," I said, grinning at him, and then, after being prised from his arms by the stage manager, was pushed back out onto the stage to take a few more bows.

Cooper and Gideon were waiting outside the stage door in a cab. We had five minutes to get to the Adelphi Theatre for my appearance at Theo's concert. The driver snapped his reins and the horse took off like a rocket. We hurtled through the streets, me laughing, and Cooper, Gideon, and Andrew holding onto their hats for grim death with forced smiles plastered across their faces.

"Did you hear any of that, Cooper?" Andrew asked.

"Too right, Mr. Bolton, and it was smashing, if I may say so, Mr. Murray."

"High praise indeed, young man. I might convince you yet that high-class music is something you can learn to appreciate."

He smiled, but before he could reply, the cab drew to a halt outside the stage door of the Adelphi. One of the assistant stage managers had been waiting outside for us and ushered us swiftly through the backstage and into the wings. I stood near the prompt corner to get my breath, glancing to the other side of the stage where my brother was standing in the opposite prompt corner behind the first tormentor leg. He gave me a thumbs up and pretended to wipe his brow in relief, with an unvoiced "phew!"

The Adelphi had a large revolve, and the act just finishing was an equestrian performance. I caught a glimpse of four horses, hitched in pairs, pulling a chariot. On their backs the whole Frangore Family was stacked on each other's shoulders in a tower. It was a true feat of athleticism and balance. They were one of the best vaudeville acts in the country. Theo must have moved hell and high water to get them to perform this evening.

As a painted backdrop was flown in over the applause for the Frangores, Theo strode onto the stage and then peered theatrically in my direction, raising his hand to his brow, as if he was a shepherd peering for his lost sheep. It made me smile.

"The scene should be Germany in the reign of Charlemagne; but, as you can see, due to budget restraints, the scene behind me displays the Bay of Naples with Vesuvius in full eruption," he said, standing to one side, and with a grand gesture, indicated the backdrop. The orchestra played a loud "Ta da!" The audience laughed and then applauded. "However, the backdrop serves for nothing other than to complement the costume and the voice of my beloved brother, one of our country's finest treasures, the man with the golden voice. Please welcome, straight from the stage of the Theatre Royal, Australia's Son, Edward Murray!"

Garrick Jones

I bounded onto stage from the wings in my beautiful burnished gold tunic and yellow ochre tights, my sword in my hand, and then, at centre stage, turned to face the audience, and assumed an en garde! position with the my épée thrust forward over the orchestra pit.

Vaudeville and variety audiences were unlike opera audiences. Unlike the earlier ovation during *Faust* at the Theatre Royal, the crowd at the Adelphi roared and cheered and whistled their applause. Their acclamation was more riotous than refined. The orchestra struck up the famous march from the same Gounod opera in which I had just performed, while I bowed and blew kisses to the stalls, the balconies, and then finally, the Gods.

I loved the opera, but the rawness of this type of audience spoke to my heart in a different way. It was from this society of people that my brother and I had sprung. Maybe they were better dressed and not as poor as our family and neighbours had been, but they lived and worked in the less affluent areas of this great city, and when they loved someone or something they didn't sit on their hands when it came time to show it.

When eventually they'd calmed, I held up my hands for quiet. "A few minutes ago, I walked from the stage at the Theatre Royal after the curtain at the end of Act Four of Gounod's *Faust*—in case you were wondering whether I normally went about the town in tights and a tunic." Some wag in the Gods wolf-whistled.

"For the third time tonight, and as my first song for you, I'd like to sing Valentin's aria, '*Avant de quitter ces lieux*', which many of you will know better by the title in English, 'Even bravest heart may swell'. It's the song that the character I perform sings in Act Two, when he goes off to war, leaving his sister in the care of Siebel, one of his friends. In 1872, my brother Theo and I bade farewell to our sister, Madeleine, not leaving her in the care of a dear friend, but in the arms of the Lord above. It will be thirty years in two days from now since that dreadful day. And so, tonight, I'd like to dedicate this rendition of Valentin's song to the memory of our dear, sweet, and still beloved sister. To Maddie," I added, with a gesture to the conductor, indicating I was ready to perform. The lights on the stage dimmed, and a bright, rose-gold spotlight appeared at my feet. I stepped forward into the light and began to sing.

After I'd finished, there hadn't been a dry eye in the house. I'd taken more bows after it than at any time during my entire career. I fought back the urge to cry myself. Real tears hampered the ability to sing. Choked throats, runny noses, and tears do not a happy vocalist make.

I stood in the spotlight, my jaw clenched, and my fists gently trembling, trying to pull myself out of the world into which performers could so easily be transported when practising their art. Singers, instrumentalists, actors—we were all the same. I was aware of the cheers and the uproar from out front, the clapping and bravos from the conductor, and the stomping and applause from the orchestra, who'd risen to their feet.

Slowly I bowed, and then, when I straightened up, found myself in the arms of my brother, who'd made no attempt to hold back his tears. I waved once or twice to the audience and then exited into the wings. It was some time before the audience had quietened enough for my brother to speak.

"Can you see why I love him so much?"

The same wag who'd whistled earlier, called out, "Me too!"

Everyone laughed. It was a plant, of course, someone pretending to be a regular theatre attendee, but skilled in encouraging applause when needed, or catcalling, or cheering. They'd existed in variety theatre for years.

Theo performed one of his comedy routines, a complex and deft collection of snippets of popular ballads and joke telling. He was famed for his ability to move seamlessly between prose and melody.

I tried to watch as much as I could, but the head male dresser of the Adelphi had arrived, followed by Gideon, who'd draped my tails over his shoulders in a way that made it easy for me to take the trousers and then the jacket and slip into them. I had no more than four minutes to get completely changed into evening wear.

"Excuse me, Andrew," I said as Gideon swiftly undid the laces at the back of my tunic, which Mr. Bailey lifted over my head while Gideon fell to his knees and pulled off my tights. It was done in a trice. There was a set routine for quick changes among experienced dressers, and these two men were as swift as any I'd ever met. In one moment, I'd been in full *Faust* costume, twenty seconds later, totally naked except for my ball bag, and then, almost in a trice, wearing my best set of performing tails.

I was ready in time to hear the final playout of Theo's routine. I cleared my throat and bent forward while Gideon took off my wig and the stocking cap and then brushed my own hair into place. "Turn around," he whispered to me and then dabbed at my makeup with a sponge to hide the pale strip that had been underneath the front lace of the wig. As I stood, waiting to move onto the stage, fiddling with my white waistcoat and adjusting the button on my gloves, Andrew turned me towards him.

"Here," he said, taking the white rose boutonnière from his lapel and threading it into mine. But, before I could thank him, I felt the stage manager's firm hand in the middle of my back, directing me to stride out onto the stage once more, for a bracket of duets that Theo and I often trotted out as part of our regular repertoire. Audiences who knew them loved the three duos: the duet for the two gendarmes from *Geneviève de Brabant*, by Offenbach, followed by an arrangement of "Yes, Let Me Like a Soldier Fall" from *Maritana*, by Wallace, and finally "Excelsior!"—the song by which Theo and I had entered the professional world as performers.

All three duets had been wonderfully arranged and skilfully segued by our Miss Fischer, who was more than just an extraordinary accompanist. She'd scored the music for orchestra and had written out the parts in her own neat hand. Few could believe it when they learned. I could never believe their prejudice—why shouldn't a woman be as accomplished as a man when it came to arrangement and composition?

At the end of our bracket of songs, and after the applause had faded, I gave a short speech, exhorting the audience to be generous, reminding them every penny donated to the Petersham boys' home was a penny that might help a young man into a trade, and to steer him away from a life of crime.

I nodded to the leader of the orchestra, who gave me a G. Unaccompanied, I began to sing:

> *Australia's Sons are now united, as a nation they will*
> *stand,*
> *Side by side in peace or war with the motherland.*
> *For freedom's flag floats proudly o'er our race by land or*
> *sea,*
> *And to all nations of the world mean liberty*

And then, there was a whoosh of air behind me. It told me the backdrop had been swiftly flown up into the fly tower. At the end of the verse, the orchestra began to play, and Theo took my hand. We sang the first chorus together:

> *Australia's Sons are ready any time when e'er the need*
> *may be,*
> *To fight for fair Australia's land, the land of liberty*
> *And side by side with England we will stand to help in*
> *peace or war.*
> *Our nations' cry will always be the same, Australia!*

Behind us, the entirety of the performers who had given their services at the benefit joined in on the second verse; and, as they did so, to my surprise, the audience also rose to their feet, almost as a man, and began to sing along at the tops of their voices.

> *Our sons have proved by deeds abroad they can uphold*
> *our name.*
> *Beside the good old Union Jack, have brought our*
> *country fame.*
> *Long may those colours famous be for liberty they fly.*
> *Our Empire echoes all around one battle cry!*

And then, as the final repeat of the chorus rang through the auditorium, streamers, confetti, and favours fell from the flies above us.

I glanced behind me. Enormous versions of the Union Jack and the newly approved Australian flag were strung across the back of the stage, filling it from side to side and from top to bottom.

> *Australia's Sons are ready any time when e'er the need*
> *may be,*
> *To fight for fair Australia's land, the land of liberty.*
> *And side by side with England we will stand to help in*
> *peace or war.*
> *Our nations' cry will always be the same, Australia!*

It took twenty minutes before we were able to move five paces backwards, upstage behind the curtain line, to take our final bows.

*****

The following morning, as we made our way through the Botanical Gardens on route to the Corporation Baths, I was aware that something had changed.

I'd asked Theo and Cooper to join us for a swim, and the four of us were chatting, laughing, and telling jokes. It was a twenty-minute walk from the Metropole to the baths in Woolloomooloo Bay.

Casually, Andrew had threaded his arm through mine as we walked. It was done with such nonchalance it had taken a few minutes for his action to register with me. At first, I'd wondered if it had been the result of the accumulated time we'd spent together and his gradual acceptance of my proffered friendship. But then, I realised it was probably due to something that had happened last night.

We'd arrived home late, and Theo had gone straight to bed. It had been Cooper's night off, so he'd headed home immediately after the performance. Russell Ward had been on duty guarding our door, and he never came inside the apartment, preferring to stay outside. Andrew and I had chatted for a while, and then he too bade me goodnight and had gone to his rooms, telling me he'd leave his cigarettes on the aspidistra stand, outside his bedroom door.

I had been too excited to go to sleep right away, so had had a shower, and had then wandered around the apartment while I'd dried my hair. The lights had been off, so when the flicker of a flame from Andrew's apartment had briefly flashed, I'd known he was still awake too.

"Smoking?" I'd called out.

"Want one?" he'd asked.

The door between our living spaces had been half-closed, so I'd pushed it open and walked into his room. He'd been leaning casually against the doorjamb of his bedroom, holding the packet out to me.

"You're shaking," he'd said as I'd taken a cigarette from the pack.

He'd been completely naked, only a towel around his waist. Now that his entire torso had been laid bare to my eyes, it had been everything I could do not to reach over and trace my finger over his shoulders.

"I'm just coming down after the exhilaration of the performances tonight," I'd lied.

"You were wonderful."

"Thank you for your compliments, Andrew. What you said to me last night, standing in the wings at the Adelphi—"

"I meant every word of it," he'd said and had then reached over and run his fingers around the back of my neck. I'd felt his thumb resting against my jaw. He'd withdrawn it promptly, but I'd grabbed his wrist and then held out my other hand.

"I'd like us to be friends," I'd said. "When this is all over, I mean."

"I already think of you as a friend," he'd said, taking my hand and shaking it. "Is this some secret theatre ritual? Or perhaps it's an American Indian ritual, or one from the Bengal—smoking peace pipes, almost naked, exchanging secret handshakes."

I'd laughed. "It's whatever you wish it to be. And, if we're to be friends, then when we're alone you must call me Eddie."

"Very well … Eddie. I have no shortened version of my name. I'm not sure what you should call me."

I'd had a few ideas of what I'd like to call him, but I'd smiled and then shaken his hand again. "Friends?" I'd asked.

"Friends!" he'd replied.

Then there had been one of those moments when things could have progressed, questions answered, longings realised …

But I'd been too doubtful of myself. I'd released his hand and rested my head against the wall, smiling into his eyes. I don't know what he was thinking, but he'd too leaned back against the inside of his bedroom doorjamb, returning my smile. Neither of us had spoken. We'd smoked our cigarettes, and then, when they'd been all but spent, I'd taken the ashtray from him and stubbed mine into it. The moment had been broken.

"Goodnight, Andrew," I'd whispered.

"Goodnight, Eddie," he'd said, and then as I'd walked away, he'd turned and gone into his bedroom.

I think it was that moment, in the doorway, when we'd been smiling at each other without speaking that had precipitated the change I felt this morning. There was something about him that seemed more "open" to me. It was the only word I could think of to describe the slight lowering of his polite, professional, yet affable behaviour. There was an almost intimacy. It showed in the way his arm was through mine and the way he looked at me when I spoke, and laughed when I laughed.

Perhaps that's what modern pals did. I had no point of reference. But I did like it—I liked it very much.

There was no one at the baths when we arrived. Mr. Elder, the attendant of the men's changing room, who Theo and I only knew in a passing manner, appeared to be good friends with both Andrew and Cooper. Andrew, I understood, as he'd already told me he swam there a few times a week. But it didn't take me long to realise that Cooper haunted the place. He was an otter; there was no other word for it.

Although compact in size, and seemingly quiet and serious, another creature stepped into his shoes when it came to swimming. He came alive in the water, like a six-year-old with an over-abundance of energy after eating too many sugary treats. He'd been the first of us to throw off his clothes and run outside onto the boardwalk, whooping at the top of his voice. He dove into the water and sliced through the grey-green of the harbour like a porpoise, rising into view, his face shining with laughter and sheer joy. "Come in! Come in!" he called to us, diving under again and then resurfacing with a loud "Huzzah!"

While Andrew did steady, paced lengths of the pool using the crawl stroke—arm over into the water in front, pulling his body forward, turning his head to one side to breathe—Cooper plummeted to the depths like a merman, shooting up out of the water with hoots of laugher, spurting jets of brine from his pursed lips high into the air, and then laughing as he rolled onto his back and tried to catch the last drops into his open mouth as they fell. His energy seemed boundless, climbing the rope net over and over again, and then throwing himself into the pool in a series of graceful dives, alternated by mid-air tumbles, and not a few on-purpose back-thwacks to elicit groans of sympathy.

"He's very beautiful," Theo said.

"They both are in their way," I replied.

"You know who I'm talking about." He nudged my foot with his own.

We'd been lying in a sunny patch on the raised boardwalk that surrounded the inside of the men's enclosure, watching Cooper, who'd been driving poor Andrew spare, pleading time and time again to put his foot into Andrew's cupped hands, begging to be launched backwards into the pool, which, from where they were standing, was some two feet behind and four below them. "Come on, Mr. Bolton, please won't you? Just once more!" he cried, and then faked misery when his return was greeted with an unconvincing protestation of, "Enough!" Andrew invariably gave in.

Although Andrew's skin was pale, it wasn't white. Rowing had tanned his forearms, neck, and legs below mid-thigh, and his regular visits to the baths, swimming in the early morning sun, had faintly bronzed the rest of his body. I was transfixed by the tendons at the backs of his knees as he strained to launch Cooper into the air.

"You looking at his bum?"

"No, Theo. I'm looking at his legs, and those few pale moles under his right shoulder blade."

"And …?"

"The other side is very fine too," I said.

"Hm," was my brother's response.

I'd read a page or two of the *Kama Sutra*, the Indian book of pleasures of the flesh, in the tone of that soft hum.

"Shut up," I said and then we both burst into laughter.

Andrew looked over his shoulder at us. "What are you two laughing at?"

"Brother talk," Theo said and then patted the wooden deck beside him.

Andrew came over, declining Cooper's request for one more throw, and sat down beside me, not next to Theo. "This is enormous fun," he said. "Normally, I swim lengths of the pool and then go on my way. I've never sported in the water before like this."

"Never?"

He shook his head, flicking his hair out of his eyes, and then began to rub the tops of his thighs, staring off into the distance. "I wish I wasn't so hairy," he said idly.

Theo and I protested at the same time. "You look like a golden god when the sunlight hits you," my brother remonstrated. "You aren't a gorilla by any means, Andrew. What would bring you to make such a remark?"

"Well, look at you two, and Cooper," he replied and then began to run the fingers of one hand absentmindedly through his chest hair. I'm sure my eyes were on stalks. "None of the three of you is hairless, but your covering is more modest."

"Modest?" I asked, almost spluttering my amazement.

"Well, perhaps that's not the word that describes what I want to say. But look at my shoulders … you could almost plait it."

I laughed. "Hardly. But it makes you who you are. Wanting to be otherwise is like wishing for different colour eyes, or bigger feet."

"Mother makes me clean out the sink hole cover after I've had a bath …"

"Is that what worries you?"

"No, of course not. I merely think perhaps it's de trop."

"Unwelcome? Unattractive?" Theo laughed. "You two are a pair, you and my brother. He thinks he's plainer than bread flour too."

"Surely not, Mr. Murray." Cooper had just arrived, and protested, seemingly outraged at such a suggestion. "Why all three of you are so well put together … just look at me!"

Our banter soon turned into laughter as we assured each other that none of us was homely, pointing out each other's best features. It was very affable, and it wasn't too long before I realised I'd draped my arm around Andrew's shoulder. I made to move it, but he stopped me. "No, leave it be. It's perfectly happy where it is," he murmured.

"For my tuppence worth, I think you are perfectly right, exactly the way you are, hairy tummy and all."

"Stop it," he said, "or I'll start to believe you."

I shook his shoulder with my hand and then squeezed it. He returned the favour to my knee. Although he had more hair than either Theo or I, it was hardly a thicket. Not dense and bushy, except across his chest, but fine, golden, soft-looking hair. Even down below, where mine was brown, his patch was fair, like burnished bronze.

Theo's quick glance was not annoyed, but I read the warning in his eyes. *My advice is to go no further until you understand the man, Eddie*", is what he'd said to me a few nights before. He was afraid I might get hurt. It was in his nature, and I loved him for his caution, so I merely smirked and returned his look with raised eyebrows.

"If we're to have breakfast, and then get to Birchgrove before eleven, I think we should get moving, don't you?" I said as I got to my feet. I reached out and Andrew took my hand. I pulled him to his feet rather too powerfully and he overbalanced. I caught him in my arms and then quickly moved away. Our bodies had been pressed together, chest to chest, and I'd felt the soft warmth of his groin against mine.

I turned away to hide the redness that I knew had flooded up over my neck and face, and dogtrotted off towards the dressing room, calling out over my shoulder for the others to follow.

I'd barely reached the doorway into the men's changing rooms when I heard yells and shouts of laughter from the pool. Cooper had pushed and pulled both Andrew and my brother back into the water and they were busily thrashing around, splashing water at each other. I shook my head and then rang the bell on Mr. Elder's cage, in order to retrieve my cubicle key from him. After a minute or two he hadn't appeared, so I rang it again, and then called out through the grill on his hatch. Leaning forward, I noticed a key sitting on the desk. It was tagged with my cubicle number, so I took it.

Three paces from the door I stopped. It was ajar. I walked briskly back to the entrance to the changing shed. "Theo, Andrew!" I called out.

Andrew was clambering out of the pool when he heard me call. He quickly dried his feet and then ran to me. It was all too easy to slip on wooden decking when dripping wet. "What's wrong, Eddie?" he asked.

"I'm not sure, but Mr. Elder wasn't in his cubby-hole, and now I find my cubicle door's unlocked and open."

"Wait here," he said, "I'll have a look." He went into the change shed warily, and then, a few paces from my cubicle door, pushed it wide open with his foot. It was empty. My clothes were gone.

"Mr. Elder didn't come when I rang the bell and called out to him," I explained. "My key was on the countertop and I merely took it."

"I'll go see if I can find him," Cooper said. He and Theo had arrived just in time to see Andrew kick the cubicle door open.

"Very well, but be careful," Andrew replied and then turned to me. "You'd better wait outside, Edward, and you too, Theo."

"Not likely," my brother said. "Both Eddie and I are trained with our fists. It's best we all stay together—"

His voice was cut short by Cooper's loud yell. "Mr. Bolton, come quick!"

We ran towards his voice, which issued from the far end of the corridor on the other side of the attendant's hutch. Cooper stood, his hand to his mouth, staring into the last cubicle at the end.

On the floor, a man's feet protruded into the passageway that ran between the rows of facing cubicles. "Just stay here for a moment, please," Andrew said. "Let me see what the problem is first."

I was about to ignore him, when Theo grabbed my arm and shook his head. "Wait, Eddie," he murmured, craning his head to see what was going on.

"Gah!" Andrew said under his breath, a few moments later. "What a mess."

He was standing with his feet spread wide, his hands braced against the uprights of the doorframe, leaning into the cubicle to get a better look at whatever was inside. For a moment, I thought his stance odd, until I noticed a dark pool on the floor. It was fairly clear he was trying to avoid standing in what appeared to be blood issuing from beneath what I assumed was the body of the men's change room attendant.

I'd put two and two together almost instantly. Kane had followed us and had attacked Mr. Elder. It could be nothing else. Another death, another warning, and for what? I brushed past Cooper and Theo, but wasn't prepared for what I saw on the cubicle floor. "Dear God!" I muttered, and then crossed myself in haste, with a final kiss to the knuckle of my curled index finger—it was a reflex action. I didn't think I'd made an involuntary *signum crucis* for more than twenty years.

Mr. Elder lay on the floor of the cubicle. His eyes were wide open, fixed sightlessly at some spot on the ceiling. His throat had been cut.

My vision blurred briefly, and at the same time, I felt my stomach spasm, as if someone had punched me in the solar plexus. It wasn't a reaction to the sight of a dead man, or even to the amount of blood— I'd seen plenty of violence in India, and much worse than a cut throat.

It was that an awkward attempt had been made to dress Mr. Elder's body in my clothing.

"On the wall, above his head ... the knife," Theo murmured. I hadn't heard or felt him come up behind me.

Embedded in the wall, at head height, was a distinctive, bloodied dagger. A trail of red trickled down the panelling of the cubicle, as if the knife itself was bleeding from its tip, an inch below the surface of the wood.

"It's one of Naddo's," I heard myself saying. I recognised it from the red and black striped leather narrow strips wound around the handle, and by the polished bronze of the quillon and the cap covering the pommel.

As Andrew and Cooper turned to look at me, astonished, Theo grabbed my arm, and whispered hoarsely, "I think you're right, Eddie … Holy Mother of God!" I grabbed his arm as he fell to his knees.

"Who's Naddo?"

"A man who died six years ago, Andrew," I said quietly, kneeling at my brother's side and pulling him into my arms. "Theo killed him."

*****

Neil Adam Doland, known in the theatre as "Naddo", a contraction of the first syllables of his full name, was a variety artist who specialised in juggling, sword swallowing, and knife throwing.

When Theo had first started off in *Jimmy Steals the Show*, Naddo had been one of the feature artists. Twenty years ago, it was not uncommon to insert variety acts in the middle of longer works, either during the performance or as intermezzi, in front of the curtain while a scene change was taking place.

Although married, he'd a reputation for being a ladies' man, and at the time when we'd first met him was tall, athletic, and a superb performer. That had changed very quickly after his wife Nancy's premature death, when he'd taken to the bottle. He'd made a few unfortunate mistakes while performing under the influence, and in no time at all, his engagements had begun to fall off.

We'd only heard of him again in 1896, when my friend Sandford had asked me if I knew of a knife artist called Naddo. I'd told him that I thought he'd given up. It had been years since I'd heard the name. Sandford had recounted an appalling tale of a private "gentleman's showing" he'd been invited to at the disreputable Knighthawks Club, in Chinatown. I'd heard rumour of this type of act for years, but had believed it was merely a fabrication, a legend, something to titillate, not something that had ever been done.

It was called Death's Kiss, for the very real reason that it was incredibly dangerous. Supposedly invented by the great eighteenth century Italian *Il Muletto*, the act revolved around the cutting of garment strings on a pair of young lovers who stood facing the audience with a backing board behind them. Gradually, the four ribboned attachments that held the garments together on each of the young people were severed by a thrown knife, leaving them completely naked.

Sandford had witnessed an incident during the performance he'd attended, and had come to me to ask for advice. I had been not only astounded to hear the act had in fact been performed, but that he'd been there to see it. He'd looked mortified, so I hadn't pressed the point. I knew gentlemen of the upper classes tried to outdo each other in daring exhibitions, or challenged their peers to stay calm under duress. It was considered a test of their so-called "breeding", and often included debasement of those in social levels below them.

My friend had recounted how he'd held his breath while each of the thrown daggers had severed the ribboned knots, held by the young couple in turn, mere inches away from their bodies.

"Left shoulder!" Naddo had announced. The blade had thudded into the backing board, leaving no more than an inch of clear space between shoulder and fingertip, cutting the tie neatly. "Right shoulder!" The ritual had been repeated until eight knives had been thrown and the young man and woman had been left standing exposed, their garments a soft pile of white cotton around their feet.

But that hadn't been the end of it. "Open!" Naddo had called out, and then both the man and the woman had moved their feet apart. The two remaining daggers on his table had been rapidly picked up, one after the other, and thrown without pause. Sandford had gasped. Each of the last two daggers had hit, fractions of an inch below the private parts of the two assistants. The fear in the young man's eyes had told my friend that it had been too close for comfort. He'd watched as the man had surreptitiously run his hand over his testicles as he'd moved forward to bow, and had inspected his fingertips. There'd been no blood, but the ferocious glare at the knife artist had not gone unnoticed by Sandford.

My friend had recounted that he had been sickened by it. But, at the end of the performance, he'd followed the couple into their changing room while Naddo had been swaggering about with the host, waiting for his payment for the night, and organising gentlemen for five minutes alone with either, or both, of his assistants, at a guinea each.

"They told me he was their father," Sandford had said to me at the time. "I'm not sure if that was true, or if, like yours and Theo's situation in India, they were owned by the wretch—it was obviously part of the act to make the situation more scandalous and therefore more titillating." The girl had showed him a bad scar on her shoulder and another across her calf from near misses when Naddo had been drunk. The boy had parted his hair above his ear to reveal another long white mark in the flesh. The lad had been furious, saying that despite his promise never to drink when they were to do the Death Kiss, his "father" had been drunk again. When Sandford had heard Naddo call them back into the main room, he'd given them a guinea each and had told them to keep their mouths shut, and that he hadn't been here. The young man had introduced himself to Sandford as Mason. "He looked into my eyes, Edward, as if he knew what my private tastes were. It shook me to my soul," my friend had told me. "And, as I left, he told me he could be found most nights late, at the Sailor's Bristle, down near Fort Macquarie."

I'd been so appalled by the story of Death's Kiss, and the prostitution of the two assistants, I'd shared it with Theo. My brother had been furious and had gone to the management of the Queen's Theatre, where Naddo had been booked to make a return appearance, in the form of a three-minute intermezzo between the first two acts of the play that had been running at the time. They'd not only cancelled the act, but had not been discreet, and had revealed that it had been Theo who'd told them about Naddo's illegal and immoral sideline. If it had got out that he was performing for private parties, passing off his assistants as his own children, and then pimping them out to punters, it would rebound on any theatre that had engaged him. No management would want to get their fingers burned by association.

Four days later, after leaving a performance at the Criterion, Naddo had set upon Theo, coming at him out of the dark, and in his cups. There had been a struggle and Doland had died as a result of his own knife being turned against him. My brother was strong, agile, and trained to defend himself. Fortunately for Theo, there'd been a few chorus members, stragglers, leaving late from the theatre, who'd seen what had happened. Theo hadn't been charged, and Naddo's "children" had never been traced.

His set of knives had been legendary at the height of his fame. Reputedly forged from a meteorite and tempered in the great eruption of Vesuvius in 1861, their handles were said to be bound with dyed strips of skin from the sacred goats on the slopes of Athens, and the bronze accoutrements beaten from the bronze of Achilles' shield.

His daggers had been more famous than he was, and one of them had just been used to kill an innocent man, who'd been draped in my clothing, and displayed as some sort of stratagem to make me afraid.

It had not worked. I'd felt initially sickened, but now I felt a growing rage within me. Kane had crossed a final line. I no longer felt like a victim, I could sense the growing awareness of the hunter within me burning in my veins. For the time being, it would remain my secret. I'd tell no one; not even Theo.

*****

"It was exactly the same as the dagger used to kill Howard. One of a matched pair," Andrew explained to me twenty minutes later.

We were sitting outside, waiting for more policemen to arrive. Cooper had run to the ladies' changing area and had raised the alarm with the attendant there, who'd told him where the groundsman could be found. Cooper had despatched the man with a shilling in his hand to run to Phillip Street police station.

I was dressed in ill-fitting clothing, borrowed from the storeroom of garments left behind by bathers.

"Who leaves their trousers behind?" I'd asked in amazement, and then was told that people left all sorts, even artificial limbs.

I told Andrew about Doland and his famous knives.

"Had I been brave enough to see the photograph of Howard's corpse, I surely would have recognised the dagger," I said. "Theo and I may have been able to make connections, find out who bought his daggers after his death, and perhaps you might have snatched James Kane before he did a runner."

"There are so many instances in murder investigations of 'if only' and 'perhaps'. You mustn't blame yourself. Had I not been acutely aware of how distressed you were to learn of Howard's death, I might have insisted you look at the photograph to see if there was anything you noticed. It's my fault as much as anyone's. I was trying to be sensitive to your pain at the time. Perhaps, too much so ..."

I patted his knee affectionately. "You protect me too well. I could get quite used to it."

He laughed, despite the serious nature of our situation—a body sitting inside the changing shed, not twenty feet behind us, with its throat cut.

"Why do I get the feeling that you think it's you who is protecting me?" He placed his hand on top of mine.

"Perhaps I'm protecting you from myself."

"Perhaps I'm not as fragile as you think I am, Eddie. I'm a big, strong lad."

Maybe I'd revealed more than I'd really wanted to. But I was feeling, at the same time, both vulnerable and angry. I smiled at his response. He regarded me with kindness and openness. I would not interpret his words. I took them for what they seemed to be. I was past agonising over possibilities. It was time for reality.

"We can still be there by midday," I said. "The builder will have brought his lunch. He won't mind if we disturb him."

"You can't possibly think of still going to Birchgrove? It's madness! James Kane is obviously insane. He must have followed us on our way here—"

"Do you think I'm going to let him intimidate me?" I pounded my fist on the decking of the boardwalk. He looked startled at the vehemence in my voice. "No, Andrew. I'm no coward. If he wants me then he should blasted well make his move in a way I can confront him. I won't hide myself away with the curtains drawn. I shall go about my business as if nothing has happened. I don't care if my apparent indifference infuriates him. Perhaps it will lure him out of his fantasies and challenge me with whatever it is he thinks I've done. The angrier he becomes at my feigned nonchalance, the more likely he is to make a mistake. Let him try! My dander is up now. Fuck him, I say!"

Andrew stared at me in amazement, and then slowly a grin spread across his face. "I think it's he who wants to fuck you, Edward," he said.

I could not help myself, gradually dissolving into laughter, which he joined. It was one of those slap-your-knees moments, of incipient hysteria. He ran his hand around the back of my neck and laughed into my eyes.

I leaned forward and took his head with both hands and then gently kissed him.

It was a beautiful, soft, yielding kiss, and my heart was pounding in my chest. It lasted for what felt like an age and was only broken when he gently ran his fingers around my wrist and drew my hand down onto his chest.

"I can't ..." he said, his voice a mere thread.

"I'm sorry," I whispered.

He said nothing, but lowered his head, shaking it softly.

"I'm sorry, Andrew. Really, I shouldn't have—"

He raised his head abruptly and returned my kiss, his mouth lingering against mine.

"We'll speak of this later," he said and then rose to his feet and half-ran back into the changing sheds.

*****

At half past eleven we'd reached Rowntree Street, and Andrew made a move to stand.

We were sitting at the front of the tram on one of the two forward-facing benches, the driver standing in front of us. I loved this view from the tram as we rattled down the centre of the street: horse riders, carriages, hawkers, bicyclists, and pedestrians parting swiftly to either side of the road as the driver sounded his bell.

Ding, ding! Chugga-chugga. I also loved the sound of the tram bell, and the noise the compressor made when it was replenishing the air reservoir for the brakes.

"I thought we were getting off here?" he said to me, after the tram began to move, the hum of its electric motors rising in pitch as it gathered momentum, and its wheels protesting with a squeal against the steel of the tramway tracks.

"No, we're getting off at the next stop. Eaton Street, right next to the park. There's someone I think you should meet. It's nigh on midday, and I always know where to find him at this time of day."

We'd originally planned to travel to Birchgrove by ferry, but I'd changed my mind after seeing Naddo's daggers. Tram from the city to Balmain, a meeting in the pub, and then a twelve- to fifteen-minute stroll to our building site. We'd be there at half past twelve.

"I've never been to this part of the city," he said. "There are some very fine buildings. Which park is this we're passing right now?"

"Gladstone Park, it's where we'll alight. On the opposite side of the road is St. Andrew's Church. It's another beautiful structure."

"Thank you, Mr. Murray," the conductor said as we stood on the footpath and tipped our hats to both him and to the driver, who'd recognised me the moment we'd boarded the tram in the city.

We watched it whizz off down the slope to the east, in the direction of the wharf, a cloud of sand from the traction box whirling in its wake and bright blue sparks falling from the overhead wires onto the roof of the tramcar. The conductor leaned out the back of the vehicle and waggled the connecting rope to reset the tension of the pole, so the groove of the conductive wheel sat where it should. The sparking stopped.

"Brave, aren't they," he said. "Even in the pouring rain, they still have to manage those sorts of problems while on the move."

"Shall we?"

"Before we proceed, is everything all right, Edward?"

I squeezed his elbow. "Yes, everything is as it should be. I've been quiet for no reason other than I sang a complete opera last night, followed by a benefit concert. Three renditions alone of the aria from

Faust in one evening is enough to do anyone in. I'm trying to rest my voice a little. I promise you that's all."

"Are you sure?"

"You said we'd talk later. I know you to be a man of your word, and so I'll wait until the time is right. I regret nothing, and I have no expectations, Andrew. I seized a moment, and if I'm to suffer for it, then at least I will have a memory of something extremely pleasant. I'm feeling quite mellow; thank you."

"I—" He started to say something more, but I was not ready to hear anything in the middle of Darling Street, Balmain, and a dray was bearing down on us. We'd stopped to have this conversation in the middle of the roadway.

"Next on the right is Jane Street," I said. "The building on the far corner is where he'll be."

"It looks like a pub."

I smiled. His voice held a hint of discomfort. I'd no idea what was going through his mind. All I knew was that he'd returned my kiss, and his lips had not been tight, nor had it been an apologetic peck. Neither was it a token kiss from someone who had found the task unpleasant, yet felt it his duty to return one. His mouth had been yielding against mine and his lips slightly parted, soft, and pliant. It had been beautiful. I knew a meaningless kiss when I felt one, but his kiss had held nothing but promise.

"The public house, The London, where we are to meet with an old theatrical friend of Theo's and mine."

"And may I ask why?"

"For fifty years, he was the most famous impalement artist in the country."

Fabrice Evans was leaning against the bar in the far corner of the pub, a pewter stein in front of him. He was peering at the newspaper through the same gold-rimmed glasses I'd remembered him wearing when I'd first met him, twenty years ago.

"Another of the same, Fabrice?" I asked, coming up behind him and putting my arm around his shoulders.

"Good Lord, it's you!" He grasped the handle of his walking stick.

"No, don't get up. Stay where you are, old friend."

"My, my, my. Édouard Marais, what a sight you are for feeble old eyes."

I glanced at the dartboard on the wall behind where he was sitting. It was a rosette of bullseyes: six darts smack on the red centre spot, fanning out like some vicious flower, whose petals were feathers, and with stamens of bronze.

"Is that what you tell those you batty-fang?"

"Batty-fang?" Andrew asked from over my shoulder.

"It means to take advantage of gullible punters."

"Good day to you, sir," Andrew said, holding out his hand.

"This is Andrew Bolton, a friend of mine," I said hastily. I knew Fabrice would never open up to a copper, although I suspected it wouldn't take him long to work out Andrew was a member of the constabulary. Men like Fabrice, who weren't totally above board in their daily dealings, seemed to have the knack of spotting the law.

They shook hands and Andrew ordered from the barman.

"What's that you're drinking," Fabrice asked, suspiciously, smiling at the long glass of pale brown liquid.

"Sarsaparilla," Andrew replied and then patted his tummy. "Liver problems." He said it so easily, I guessed it was his regular excuse when he felt abstinence would be an inappropriate explanation.

"Ah! You're not very yellow, but biliousness is a dreadful thing. Does it keep you up at night? My old Maisie, the sister what—"

"Two of Naddo's daggers have turned up." My interruption was on purpose. Fabrice, once he got started, tended to go on and on.

"Where?"

"One in Howard Talbot's back, the other in a wall in a changing room at the swimming baths, covered in the blood of the man whose throat it had been used to cut."

Fabrice turned to his tankard and took a deep swallow. He removed his glasses and took out his handkerchief and cleaned them, nodding his head slowly.

"They was sold, so I heard."

"No, you heard no such thing, Fabrice. Remember who looks after you."

"And who said I'm not grateful for what you and your brother send me—"

"It could stop in a moment …"

He glared at me, and then his features softened and we both burst into laughter. Andrew shook his head and rolled his eyes.

"You old arse-fart," I said.

"You fell for it," he replied, giggling into his Guinness.

"Oh, spare me! I may have fallen for it when I was eighteen, but no longer."

He smiled over the rim of his tankard, staring at Andrew and waggling his eyebrows.

"No," I said. I knew his gesture was one asking about whether my companion was more than a mere friend.

"But you'd like to?"

"Naddo's daggers?" I changed the subject. Fabrice knew all about Theo and me. He'd taken us both under his wing after sharing a dressing room with us during a variety show, a month or so after I'd returned from the concert tour during which I'd met Sandford. Oddly enough, Fabrice was related to our grandmother on our father's side, but would not talk of our father, promising one day, if he got really drunk, he'd loosen his belt and tell us some home truths we'd probably not be happy to hear.

"Second house from the corner of Collins Street and Trafalgar in Annandale," he said. "Out the back, there's a factory. He's got a room upstairs."

"Who?"

"Neil's brother, Paul."

"Paul Doland is still alive?"

"He was four weeks ago. But he's got a dowager's hump these days. Stooped over and in pain. Hands all bumps and knobbles with that painful joint fever some of them get. I don't remember what the doctors call it? Only in his sixties too … no way he could even hold a knife."

"Rheumatism," I explained. "Tell me something, Fabrice. Did Naddo and Nancy have children?"

"A boy. Only one. She died in when was it?"

"1882," I said. "The year after *Jimmy Steals the Show*. It was about six months after we first met you. I don't remember any children at the funeral?"

"They only had the one child; born six years before she died. He was put in a home while they toured. Poor mite was never around. Passed from one to another, so's I heard it. As for poor Nancy, they put it about she'd died of consumption, but the truth was she got blood fever off one of those 'Missus Whatsis' up behind Kings Cross. Got the heat in her body and the purple bruises all over and was dead in four days."

"They got rid of a child? An abortion?"

"Abortion is a fancy word for what they called 'ripping' in those days," Fabrice said, wiping his mouth on the back of his sleeve. "Rumour goes it wasn't his, and he wasn't having none of it."

I could feel Andrew fuming at my side.

"Do you remember the boy's name?"

"He was christened just across the road there at St. Andrew's. It'll be on the register. Nasty piece of work."

"What? The foeticide or her death from infection?"

"No, they was bad enough, I meant the kid."

"You knew him?"

"Saw him with his uncle a few weeks back. Paul had him with him, running a 'deceit' at the Carpenter and Pistol. I do the rounds of the pubs, where I keep my head down, and where no one really knows me, and put a bet up on a quick round of darts on the chalkboard. Always walk away with some silver in my pocket. I don't bet big. Small change usually, it doesn't draw any attention to me. I miss a few throws on purpose. Too easy to end up with a black eye rather than five or six bob."

"What was the deceit?" Andrew asked.

"The knife game. They was raking it in until the publican threw them out."

"What's the knife game?" Andrew asked.

"Here, spread your hand out on the bar, fingers apart," Fabrice said to Andrew. "Borrow your pickle fork, Arnold?" he called out to the barman, who sighed and then retrieved it from the tall jar on the counter, wiped it on his apron, and then handed it to Fabrice.

"Hold perfectly still," I said with a grin, holding Andrew's wrist tight against the countertop of the bar.

"Ready?" Fabrice asked.

Andrew nodded.

And then, despite his eighty years, the retired vaudeville artist stabbed the counter between Andrew's fingers with the fork, moving between each of them so rapidly his hand was a blur.

"That's the knife game, Mr. Bolton, and for a copper you hide it pretty well," Fabrice said with a chuckle.

"Don't you laugh!" Andrew said, as rebuke to my chuckle. "That was extraordinary. I'm astounded, Mr. Evans. You have a true talent."

Fabrice gave me a cheeky look. He didn't need to say anything. He approved of Andrew.

"You said nasty piece of work? About the boy? Neil's son?" I couldn't let something like that go unexplored.

"Word has it Naddo was planning a comeback years back, way before he died. Circuses, a few guest spots at cheap fleapits, that sort of thing. His son was going to be the assistant. They found some girl off the street—sweet little thing with no morals. But then she disappeared, the son went off to do something else. Neil hit the bottle bad again, and then your brother killed him. Could have knocked me over with a feather when I saw Paul Doland with Neil's son at the pub."

"And you say the boy is living with him in Trafalgar Street?" Andrew asked.

"No, sir. I said no such thing. Paul Doland is living there. His nephew is working for one of the circuses or the carnivals, don't remember which he said. He and his uncle don't get along. I don't know where he's got lodgings—if anyone will have him, that is. Probably got a bed with the circuses he's working for—they run doss houses for those what's not working, or in between tours."

"Which circus, do you know?" I asked. "Wirth's, Ashton's, St. Leon's?"

"None of the big ones, Eddie. Most likely one of them touring tent shows. You know, boxing kangaroos, freaks, sideshow nonsense, not like a proper business."

"What did he do, do you know?"

"Inside the tent? He did physique shows. General roustabout when it was a church town."

"What's a physique show?" Andrew asked.

Fabrice smirked and then coughed into his hand. "Posing, copying ancient Greek and Roman statues, wearing a pouch for the main showing, and then after the tuppeny tickets file out, the pouch disappears for those who'd forked out a zac. They're allowed to touch from the navel up, and the knees down."

"Does such a thing go on? I've never heard of it."

"It's all under the guise of physical development. They hand out a cheap flyer to the punters with a few exercises printed on it. Keeps it legal."

"And that's all there is to it?"

"Well, as you're a man of the law, I don't think I can rightly say what goes on after hours."

"At the end of the night, those who've made a special arrangement with the sideshow owner can return and have a private exhibition in the man's tent," I explained. "Both ladies *and* gents."

"Oh!" Andrew said, looking mildly shocked.

"Good with words your copper mate, isn't he?" Fabrice said. "Young man with a big cock, lots of muscles, and no inhibitions ... I'd take ten percent of what he earns after hours and still be happy."

"Good grief!" Andrew said.

"Good money, Mr. Bolton. Grief has nothing to do with it!"

We chatted about other things for a short while, until I became mindful of the time, so we bade Fabrice Evans adieu, with the promise of calling in to see him again. I said I'd make sure Theo came next time. Fabrice threw me a sour look and rolled his eyes. We lifted our hats to him and made our goodbyes.

We were almost at the door of the pub when he called me back. "Did you remember something?" I asked him.

"No, it was something I had in my mind to tell you but then we got shunted onto other topics. About them daggers. I can put word around and find out who Paul sold them to, if you like."

"Sold?"

"Well they was Naddo's trademark, Eddie. Without them, his brother Paul is nothing. He's not even a good impalement artist. He must be hard up to want to sell them. I've heard nothing, but knives as famous as those, even if they went to a private collector ... well, let's say word would get around."

Andrew opened his *porte-feuille* and gave Fabrice a pound note, and his calling card. "Here, take this," he said. "Telegrams are sixpence each. You hear anything, and you send a telegram to me." He scribbled the address of the Phillip Street police station on the back of his card with a propelling pencil.

"No need to write down the address of the city clink," Fabrice said. "I know where it is."

"I bet you do," I replied.

"What do I do with the change from your twenty-bob note, Mr. Bolton? I think one telegram will most likely suffice. That is, unless you want one word of my long explanation on each cable?"

Andrew laughed and then nodded at the pint of Guinness on the bar. "Use the rest for your lunchtime tipple, Mr. Evans. One a day should see you through the rest of that quid until the end of next month."

"If I was wearing a hat, I'd tip it to you. Thank you, Mr. Bolton."

"Good day to you, sir," Andrew replied, touching the brim of his boater.

"Far too good for you, Eddie," Fabrice whispered to me as I turned to follow Andrew.

"I fear you may be right," I said.

"Get on with you!" he said and then poked me in the backside with his walking stick as I walked away.

★★★★★

The church was packed and in the middle of a wedding—the couple were exchanging vows when we arrived. There was no way we could interrupt the vicar to ask whether we could see the register of births.

Andrew read the list on the porch door and saw that the last ceremony was scheduled for five o'clock.

"I'll send one of the boys around when we get back to the hotel. Now, is there anywhere we can eat, or do you want to go straight to your house?"

"There's a workman's tea place, right next to Mort Bay Park. You can usually get something handmade there; a sandwich or a pasty, perhaps even a steak pie. We could sit in the park to eat it, and then it's five minutes to the house. What do you think of that?"

"Sounds bonzer to me, Eddie. Lead on!"

As we turned into the street named after it, he launched into an explanation of the etymology of the name of the river that ran through the centre of London.

"It was originally called the Tems, and then Romans renamed it the Tamesis …"

He could have talked about the price of eggs for all I cared. I was happy simply walking in the sun by his side. I could get very used to it.

CHAPTER 9

"This whole frontage is yours?" Andrew asked, standing on the other side of the road with his hands on his hips.

"Yes, it's a wide block, but only one hundred and fifty feet deep."

"That's enormous!"

"That's the size it came in," I said. "All the lots along this side of the street were the same. We bought this one mainly because of its ocean pool."

"There's a pool?"

"Stop sounding so astounded. You're making me feel more entitled than I am. Theo and I have put the greater part of our life savings into this house—the earnings of twenty years in the theatre. It will have to last us the rest of our days. The property even has a jetty with a small boathouse at the end."

"Fish for dinner!"

"Neither of us are fishermen."

"I am!"

"Are you moving in already?"

He didn't answer, but turned to look at me, smiling with his eyes. I nudged his elbow with my own, which caused him to change the subject.

"The fence is splendid," he said. "Such beautiful brickwork. I've not seen an inverse arch set with wooden palings. I would have expected wrought-iron upright rails, like those in the square-built brick fences one sees everywhere these days. You know the type I mean? Each rod topped by a spike, or an ornate fleur-de-lis? One could curl up in the curve of these arches, or lie flat on one of the stretchers across the top of the uprights. It's lovely."

"It was Theo's idea. He has a very keen idea for what suits what."

"It's a shame you can't see the house from the street though, Eddie. Those trees are enormous."

"They're for our privacy. You'd be surprised how many gawkers pass by houses of theatre people, on the off-chance they might get an autograph or a glimpse of us when we're not on show."

"You were lucky they were right where they are in that case."

"No, it's not as you think, Andrew. We planted those two bull magnolias here fifteen years ago, not long after we bought the land, and they've rocketed up since then. We found them by mere chance. They were building an extension to the asylum at Callan Park Hospital, and the trees were right where the new annexe was to go. The hospital advertised them for sale. It was Theo who saw the advertisement, so he dragged me down there to have a look. Of course, they were perfect, so we bought them. We couldn't get a permit to bring them here by road, so we hired a barge. It was such a sight watching them sail down the harbour, and then be winched onto a dray, one at a time, and hauled up the site into holes we'd already had prepared. The one on the left is called Théodore and the one on the right is called Édouard."

He laughed. "Perfect! They must be how tall now? Forty, fifty feet?"

"The telegraph poles are forty, so you're about right. I love the fact they give us privacy, and the bonus of the large round leaves and enormous cream flowers. They were half that size when they were planted. I so love them."

"Mother likes lawn."

"Neither of us likes to mow."

"Why is the gate to the driveway so wide? Are you going to invest in a pair of carriages? Drive them through the gate side by side?"

"No," I replied, smiling at his joke. "Although if Theo has his way, we'll have one of those new steam or electric-powered motor cars. The carriage house not only has room for a motor vehicle or a coach but there's also a storeroom on the side for our costumes and other theatre bits and pieces. The gates are as wide as they are to allow something the size of a bullock wagon to deliver set pieces, if we ever need to store large pieces of scenery we own."

"I thought your costumes and sets were owned by the theatres?"

"Sometimes they are; but most principal artists own a collection of their own costumes. We have hundreds between us, if you count the number of productions we've mounted as impresarios, not to mention pieces of stage furniture, and properties for Theo's vaudeville acts."

"Wait," he said. "I'm not quite sure I perfectly understand. You said you bought the land fifteen years ago, and yet the house is still not finished?"

"It's a matter of finances, Andrew. We were lucky enough to find a builder who would work in stages, and as we could afford it. The house has been a long time coming, and it's finally almost ready for us to move into."

"Come, then," he said. "I can't wait to see what's behind those magnificent trees."

We crossed the street and I opened the front gate to him. The first thing I noticed was the bricklayers had finished the front path up to the house: a herringbone pattern with very nice rounded-topped terracotta edging bricks at the sides, which framed off the garden beds, already lush with rosemary and lavender, interspersed by native laurel. It was small shrub, rather like English box, with small pink and white flowers and dark green glossy leaves. Its botanical name was *Anopteris* something or other. I couldn't remember all of the Latin name, but it set off the soft greys and lavenders of the other planting to their advantage.

I turned to speak to Andrew, but he was staring at the house with his mouth open.

"It's ... magnificent, Eddie. There's no other word for it. I'd expected a sprawling bungalow, or a cottage, not a two-storied Queen Anne style modern house. What a joy it is. Who designed it?"

"That would be me, sir," a voice said from behind us. It was Geraint, our builder. I'd heard the pony trap arrive, but although Andrew had looked over his shoulder, I hadn't turned to see who it could be.

"Andrew Bolton," my friend said, introducing himself.

"Geraint Blethyn." The stocky Welshman wiped his hands on his apron before shaking Andrew's.

"Well, Geraint Blethyn, you've an eye for perfection."

"Thank you, sir. Have you an eye for architecture?"

"I've an eye for good bricks and mortar, Mr. Blethyn," Andrew replied. "But alas not the pocket for it."

"That makes two of us, sir. Would you like me to show you around?"

"I'd really like that very much. Edward?"

"You go ahead. I want to wander around a bit. I'll join you upstairs in a few minutes."

"I'm supposed to be looking after you ..."

"Geraint's son is over there, just near the back stairs. He's the same age as you, and he's as nimble as a hare and as strong as an ox. He can keep an eye out if you're worried. However, I'll remind you—"

"That you're perfectly capable of looking after yourself."

I smiled at him, but even so, I saw him having a word with the man before he went into the house. Geraint's son touched the tip of his cap when I caught his eye. I returned his gesture with a wink. I wasn't going far, or out of sight. I just wanted a few minutes alone in the garden to take in its beauty—it gave me such enormous inner peace, something that in recent days I'd been finding elusive.

We'd planted most of the garden at least ten years before we were able to afford to start on the house itself. Poor Geraint's heart had sunk when we'd showed him the site and when I'd told him the garden must stay intact while he was doing the building. He'd insisted it was the wrong way around, but I'd told him that gardens take longer to grow than houses to construct. So, he'd sighed and then worked out how the building materials could be delivered, and how most of the construction could be made from the driveway at the side of the house, where there were no plantings and where the garage now stood.

The walls, roof, and major internal structures had been finished two years ago, and since that time, the garden beds below the front verandas had been planted, and were now bursting with pale, creamy white hydrangeas. "Lace caps" they'd called them at Lady Fielder's villa in Darjeeling, where we'd performed for a week and where we'd first seen them, massed under huge weeping figs.

At the western edge of the garden, in full sun, were our Indian plants. Gingers and herbs from the subcontinent—those that could survive in Sydney's cool winters. Much of the lowlands, from where our plants had come, had a similar climate. I longed for a mango, or a clump of papayas, but until someone could breed a cold-tolerant variety, they'd remain on my wish list and in my dreams. We'd planted leafy trees eight feet apart for hammocks to be slung in their shade on hot summer days, and a large terrace of lawn ran right across the back of the house for parties or badminton games. On the other side of the garden, on the eastern side, behind the garage, was a tennis court. It had been one of the first areas we'd levelled out. There'd been a "Theatre Monday" on which we'd invited dozens of fellow performers, offering them lunch in return for a spadeful or two of shifted earth. For years, apart from the garden, the tennis court, with its lonely-looking storage hut for the net and push mower, had been the only construction on the site.

Despite his quick word with Geraint's son, I wasn't surprised when I glanced up at the veranda surrounding the first floor. Andrew was standing with Geraint in the doorway of one of the bedrooms, obviously keeping an eye on me. I shook my head and rolled my eyes, and then pointed at the builder's son, who was not far away, out of line of sight for Andrew, and waved that all was well. He smiled at me and then disappeared back into the house.

I was surprised when I entered the house from the back veranda.

So much had been done since my last visit, two weeks ago. The workmen stopped what they were doing and shook my hand, removing their caps. I removed my own. I came from a poorer background than any of them and felt it was ridiculous to be shown respect for no other reason than being their employer. I'd rather them slap me on the back and call me Eddie. However, manners were everything to most people, so I was as affable as I could possibly be, enquiring after their wives and children, passing them chits they could redeem for a pair of balcony seats for Theo's next show at the Tivoli in Castlereagh Street. I'd given up offering tickets to my concerts or opera performances. They found the whole idea too daunting.

These little things cost Theo and me very little in terms for what we got back in return. Our genuine interest in them as men and in their crafts, together with the odd theatre ticket, was repaid with building schedules finished either on time or early, meticulous attention to detail, and great care not to damage my garden.

I called it my garden, because although Theo loved it, it was me who was passionate about plants. I put it down to an early childhood in the slums, not a stick or a bit of green to be seen, and then, in India, my first gift from Mrs. Mullins on my premiere performance in *Martha* by Flotow. She'd given me a rectangular, terracotta pot, the size of two fists, in which sprouted a tiny bush of fragrant Indian jasmine. I never knew the real name for it, but it had had the same sweet smell as the climbing jessamine, and grew along the marshy banks of the Ganga. In my darkest and most unhappy times, I could sit on the corner window ledge in our barracks room and rub its leaves between my fingers and sniff its perfumed white star-shaped flowers, telling it that one day I would put it outside into a huge garden where it could put its roots down to spread and flourish, just like I wanted to do.

Of course, Mr. Mullins had taken it away from me in a fit of anger one day, when he'd found me with one of its tiny flowers through my buttonhole; but from that small plant, a love for flowers, herbs, and trees had grown in me.

"And what will this room be?" I heard Andrew ask Mr. Blethyn as

I reached the top of the stairs. The bannister rails hadn't been sealed yet, but I'd rubbed my hand over them as I'd mounted the stairs, feeling the smooth surface of the Tasmanian oak slide underneath the soft kid of my gloves.

"That's my study," I said. "Theo has one of his own on the other side of the staircase."

"Geraint told me you were going to occupy the rear bedroom on the eastern side of the house?"

"Yes, it has splendid views down over the harbour."

"I love the idea of the French doors that open onto the veranda."

"Mr. Murray sent me up to the Hunter Valley to see the house of a friend of his up there. Most of my design was built around the plan of that house, although on a smaller scale," the builder said.

I handed him an envelope from my inner pocket.

"What's this, Mr. Murray?"

"You'll find this is the final payment for what we owe you, Geraint."

"But, sir. This is not normal. Usually the client pays after the building work has been done to his satisfaction."

"Off and on, for the best part of five years now, you've been about building this house for Theo and me, Geraint. You've never once complained when we've run short and you've had to put your men off. On that cheque you'll find there's an extra hundred pounds as a bonus. I'll leave it up to you as to how you use it."

"Why, Mr. Murray, please let me shake your hand. That's exceedingly generous of you if I may say so, and unnecessary. I think I can split the bonus up between us all as an early Christmas present."

"I certainly hope you'll be done before Christmas."

"The plasterwork cornices and ceiling roses in the music room, the main sitting room, and the breakfast room downstairs are still to be done. Up here everything is almost finished. Only the surrounds of the marble fireplaces need to be polished, and the door furniture attached throughout the whole of the top floor. It will take half a day with three of us at it. The stained-glass panels for the main door and the transoms will be fitted on Tuesday next. And then there's the sinks and tubs in the laundry—the cooker arrives from England in ten days, and then the kitchen will be finished. I reckon we'll be done and dusted in here in five weeks from now. Give the oil on the woodwork a week to dry and cure, and you can move in in six weeks. How does that suit you?"

"Mr. Blethyn, you are a miracle!"

"Far from it, Mr. Murray; but I've enjoyed this build. It's a house I can only ever dream of for my own, and I will be proud of every nail and inch of timber that went into her."

"What shall you call the house?" Andrew asked. "It must have a name."

"There can only be one choice," I replied. "Theo and I decided long ago. It will be called *Madeleine.*"

*****

We spent another half an hour walking around the house and grounds. Andrew was entranced and didn't want to leave. I promised him we'd make regular visits and next time we came I'd bring towels so we could play tennis and swim. He asked if he could bring his father, who loved to fish, and would be happy sitting on a portable canvas stool on the end of the pier.

I suggested we'd make a picnic of it and invite everyone we'd come to know. His parents and sister, Cooper, and Russell Ward. "Not Russell, please," Andrew begged. "He's as dry as a loaf of last week's stale bread."

"Very well," I replied. No Constable Ward, but I'll ask Ethan if he's free if you don't object. After all, he's going to be living with us here.

"Why should I mind? I know about Theo's private life and I've already told you I don't judge. Besides …"

His voice trailed off and he reddened slightly.

"I'd like you to get to know the house well, too, Andrew," I said. "You must know that."

He didn't answer, but continued to walk at my side, twirling his cane and occasionally stopping to ask me the name of plants, or pointing out a new vista across the harbour that he happened to glimpse.

All too soon it seemed, he glanced at his pocket watch and suggested we should get moving. It was at that point, when he moved his hand to retrieve the timepiece, I became aware we'd been walking arm in arm—it had felt so natural I hadn't noticed it.

*****

The ferry master's hut had a telephone, so, after we'd bought our tickets, Andrew showed his badge and asked to place a call. He spoke with Cooper, who was at the Metropole, and told him to meet us at the Quay, giving him the arrival time of the ferry. He also told him to phone Phillip Street and ask for two junior detectives to accompany him. He wanted Cooper to stay with me while he and the two other policemen went to find exactly where Paul Doland lived and to talk to him about his nephew.

We sat outside on the ferry when it arrived. The sun was on the water and there was a slight breeze. I really enjoyed a bit of salty mist on my face, so we found seats near the bow. The trip was over far too soon. How I longed to be in our own house, twenty minutes from the ferry terminals at Circular Quay and then a short tram ride to whichever theatre I would happen to be working in. There were plans for a tram service, which would terminate almost opposite our house, on the other side of the park at Birchgrove, but I'd heard it might be years off yet.

I decided, on the spur of the moment, that I'd take Andrew and Cooper out to dinner that evening. Despite this morning's terrible turn of events, I was determined to go about my life unhindered. A public appearance at Chiffonier's would bound to have a mention in the society page on the following day, or on Saturday, and perhaps it would infuriate James Kane enough to make an unfortunate, ill-timed move. I had no doubt Andrew and I could overcome him. I'd been rattled by Mr. Elder's death, of course—who wouldn't be? But it was the theatricality of dressing him in my clothes that made me wonder. If he wanted to kill me, why hadn't he made an attempt? I was starting to speculate if perhaps there was some method in his madness.

Cooper's face fell when I told him about dinner. He had no evening wear, and refused, despite my offer to pay, to pick up a hired set at the tailor Theo and I used.

"You planned this, didn't you?" Andrew said to me, under his breath, as we moved away from the others to have a cigarette.

"What? Planned what?"

"You and I dining alone together."

"I'm happy for you to invite your sister, or your parents, if you feel uncomfortable."

"No. I was teasing you, Edward. It will be very pleasant to have dinner somewhere nice and to chat about everything other than James Kane. There's lots about you I don't know."

"As there is about you, my friend. Take care of yourself. I'll be interested to know what Naddo's brother has to say."

"I'll send one of the men to the church after we've spoken with Paul Doland. He can have a look through the register. I should be back at the hotel, all things going to plan, around five, and my man should telephone to let us know what he's found close to six, assuming the wedding is running on time."

"Righto! I'll book for eight, if that suits you."

He tipped his hat and then went to collect his two colleagues.

"Practice, Cooper?" I said. "I've a good book to read and I'm happy to sit while you do your scales."

"That would be excellent. Thank you, Mr. Murray."

"Let's go, then."

We headed up Loftus Street. Five minutes later, we were walking through the front doors of the Hôtel Metropole.

*****

I'd put my book down twenty minutes beforehand and was replying to a few letters when Andrew returned. George followed him through the door with a tea trolley, on which a coffee service was laid out, and with it a tall, tiered, silver cake stand laden with sandwiches and jam tarts.

"I didn't know if you preferred lemon or raspberry, so I've ordered both," Andrew announced.

"I'm happy for both, Mr. Bolton. Thank you, sir!" Cooper said, bounding up, mid-phrase from a Bach prelude he'd been playing.

"I was talking to Mr. Murray, Cooper. But you're welcome."

"You look annoyed," I said.

"He refused to speak with anyone but you and Theo ... together."

"About what, and who are you referring to?" Theo announced, having walked into the room. He picked up a lemon tart from the cake stand and popped it whole into his mouth. I threw him my napkin. He invariably ended up with cake crumbs everywhere.

"Paul Doland," I said.

Theo swallowed abruptly. I hadn't seen him since Andrew and I left that morning, and I hadn't told him about my intended visit to Fabrice Evans either.

"Neil's brother is still alive? I thought he'd dropped off the perch years ago."

"Alive is a comparative term, Theo," Andrew said, pouring coffee for us all. "He's bent almost double and can barely feed himself. His hands look like a pair of gloves full of marbles. He's crippled with arthritis. The wife of the owner of the factory looks after him, cooks his meals, and cleans a bit. I don't know how he affords it."

"The knife game scam he runs with his nephew, most likely. Most punters will throw in a threepenny bit; especially if his hands are as knotted as you say they are."

"Nephew?"

"Stop gaping, Theo," I said. "It seems Neil and Nancy had two children. One a son, born six years before she died, and then another which Naddo made her have aborted. That's what killed her. She got an infection after the procedure."

"Dear God!" my brother said, sinking onto a chair next to the tea trolley. "I heard it was tuberculosis. How did you find this out? I distinctly heard Andrew say Paul would only speak to you and me together."

"Fabrice Evans told me."

"Fabrice? You went to visit Fabrice?"

"He said to say hello."

"I doubt that. He doesn't like me."

I smiled. "I was being polite. No, he didn't ask after you. But he did take a shine to Andrew. Do you remember, six years ago, that story Sandford told me? The Death's Kiss at the Knighthawks Club. The thing that sparked off his attack on you outside the Criterion?"

"Oh wait, yes, I remember ... do you think that it was really his son? That boy in his act ... you think he was really pimping out his own flesh and blood? I'd always thought the word 'son' was a figure of speech, just like Mullins, who used to call us his children. But, I do remember it made me see red when you first told me about it."

"I'm not surprised," Andrew said. "It made my flesh creep too when Edward told me."

"I've got a terrible feeling about this, Eddie," my brother said.

"How terrible?"

He reached into his pocket and withdrew a small brown paper package, tied with bright yellow string. "Here! Show one of these to Sandford and ask if it's the same boy he saw in the Death's Kiss and spoke to after the performance."

I unwrapped the package. In it were six photographs of James Kane—expensive photos—those in which he was totally nude.

"Where did you get these?"

"The name of the studio and its address is stamped on the cardboard frames of the photographs. The photographer has premises a block away from where I was rehearsing. They cost me an arm and a leg ... and a bit of blackmail."

"Oh dear," I said, passing the last two to Andrew.

"These are obscene," he said.

"It's only an erection," I replied.

"It's more than 'only'."

"He was rather blessed," Theo said. "But ..."

"But what?"

"I think I know what's going through my brother's mind, Andrew," I said. "I've been wondering the same. Could it be that James Kane or Bruno Little, whatever he wants to call himself, is actually Neil Doland's son?"

Andrew stared at me for a moment. "But it was Theo who killed his father, not you. Why does he want revenge on you and not on your brother? It doesn't make sense."

"He relieved his bowels all over my photographs, programmes, and memorabilia," I replied. "I don't think sense comes into it at all. It's more likely his mind is deranged and he resents the fact that I didn't praise his singing in the competition. Either that or the letter Elias sent, which, although generic, could read as if I didn't want to teach *him* in particular. Perhaps both were enough to tip him over the edge. If he's unstable, that's more likely the cause of his violence, rather than some incomprehensible revenge for his father's death, six years ago."

"Perhaps you're right? Anyway, there's no way of finding out. Neil Doland's son could be anyone. It's a fancy, a mere suggestion, that Kane is the same person. At the moment we've no idea of who he actually is. Still, I think it's a good idea if one of my men was to show your friend, Mr.—"

"Clarkson. Sandford Clarkson."

"Mr. Clarkson, and ask him if they're the same person."

"He'll never do that, Andrew," I said. "Speak to someone he doesn't know about such a delicate matter. He's extremely private. If I went, he would, but I think the best course of action is for me to post one of the photographs this evening and then call him on the telephone on Saturday."

"Where does he live? Is it local?"

"He's the gentleman Geraint told you about. The man with the large house in the Hunter Valley, after which Theo's and my house was modelled."

"Wouldn't it be quicker to phone him tonight, and then both of us catch the train up there tomorrow morning? He could meet us at Newcastle station, and we could take the same train back to Sydney. We'd be there and back the same day."

I shook my head. Sandford would never understand a trip up and back without spending a few hours with him, and if Andrew were to accompany me ... well, that would be a dreadful mistake. "My plan is a better one," I said. "I know him well. Trust me on this matter. I'll put one of these photographs in the mail this evening. With luck he'll get it on Saturday morning. I'll call him tonight before we go out to dinner and let him know it's arriving."

"Very well—"

The telephone rang in the corner of the reading room. Cooper went to answer it, and then spoke for a few minutes, drawing out his notepad from the pocket of his waistcoat and scribbling in it.

"That was interesting," he said after he'd hung up. "It was Billy, calling from Balmain nick. The bride was late, so he was able to talk with the vicar before she arrived. He was shown into the vestry and given the parish registry to go through."

"And?" Andrew asked.

"Father: Neil Adam Doland. Mother: Nancy Kayne Doland, née, Nancy Kayne Little. Son: baptised, fourth of March, 1876."

"And the name, Cooper?"

"Oh yes, sorry. Adam James Bruno Doland."

I reacted, even though I wasn't totally unprepared for what I heard. I held out my coffee cup to Andrew and asked for a refill.

"Are you all right, Edward?"

"Yes, thank you, Andrew. At least we know who we're dealing with now."

It all made sense, the two aliases. He'd devised his false names from a combination of his own middle names, his father's middle name, and his mother's maiden name.

James Kane, or Bruno Little, however he wanted to call himself, was Naddo's son, and he was out to kill me.

*****

"I can't believe we're dining in Chiffonier's again. It's not quite a week since we had dinner here with Sir Horace Blake," Andrew said when we finally sat down.

It had taken an age to get to our table. News had hit the afternoon papers about a second attempt on my life at the baths that morning. There was no stopping some of the gutter press from publishing sensationalised inaccuracies. Only Mr. Palmer, from the *Freeman's*

Journal, had bothered to contact me before writing his article. When I'd disillusioned him of any direct harm to me, he'd written a well-structured report, in which he'd noted I'd not been intimidated by such cowardice, and I believed the perpetrator to be the lowest scum of the earth for attacking innocents in an attempt to frighten me. Andrew had not been well pleased, saying he thought my attempts to publicly goad Kane in such a manner unwise.

Gentlemen had risen from their seats as the maître d'hôtel had shown us to our table. I'd been obliged to stop to shake hands, to accept wishes of safety, to kiss ladies' hands, and to introduce my companion. There'd even been a smattering of applause, and a soft bravo from the Lady Mayoress, who'd clutched her hands to her bosom and expressed admiration at my bravery. The Lord Mayor had pumped my hand so ferociously, I'd thought my fingers might break.

"This is such a treat, Edward," Andrew said. "But I simply can't accept your generosity. You must allow me to contribute something towards the meal."

"I appreciate your offer, my friend, but I don't pay for it. I never have to pay here, no matter how many guests I entertain."

"Please don't tell me you're going to have to stand up and sing for our supper?"

"Not this evening, no. But once a month Miss Fischer and I perform a salon concert here. The tables are all stowed away, and there's perhaps sixty guests who listen to an hour of our music. It's quite delightful, really. We both really love it, as we get to perform music that's not part of our regular concert repertoire."

"So, in return for an hour a month, you—"

"Both Miss Fischer and I are able to dine here whenever we wish, and with whomever we invite. She often comes with her beau, but I don't take advantage. In fact I sup here rarely. I'm usually too exhausted during the theatre season, except for when I need to impress someone."

"Miss Fischer has a beau? I've met her several times and she's always unaccompanied. Surely her gentleman—"

"Did I say it was a gentleman?"

"Ah!" he said, showing no surprise, merely raising an eyebrow. "She's a very beautiful and talented woman. Her companion is indeed lucky."

"Indeed she is," I said, smiling at his tacit understanding of my accompanist's "situation".

"Edward, I'm puzzled. Not over Miss Fischer, but over something else you said a minute ago. Why would you need to impress someone? I don't understand."

"Remember what I told you about being an entertainer and moving in the circles both Theo and I do? Well, we've lived in rented accommodation for the past twenty years, so we can't reciprocate our dinner invitations in the same style as the rich and famous. We're often invited to their homes and we're expected to return the favour, even though we're nearly always encouraged to 'sing for our supper', as you put it. So, dinner at Chiffonier's is our home away from home when it comes to entertaining."

I was about to explain more, but the maître d'hôtel arrived with menus. The sommelier hovered at his elbow.

"I think the plat du jour menu might suit me, Edward," Andrew said. "It sounds delicious."

"Indeed it does, but I've a hankering for oysters," I said.

"There are excellent oysters from the Georges River, Mr. Murray. Freshly arrived by cart and packed in ice, not more than two hours ago," the maître d'hôtel explained.

"Very well, then. Unless you've changed the menu since last week, I'll have a dozen *huitres au naturel*, on the shell, followed by the *bouillon gras de lapin*. For the entrée, *poulet à l'estragon*, with the same seasonal vegetables as Chief Constable Bolton, and then I'll see if I can manage some dessert after that."

"Very good, Mr. Murray. There are fresh strawberries with *petites meringues* and vanilla ice this evening, if you'd like me to put a punnet or two aside for you and your guest."

"Strawberries? At this time of the year?"

"The *Celeste* docked this morning from Brisbane, Mr. Murray. Greenhouse, but large, sweet, and delicious."

"Then I'll say yes now. How about you, Andrew?"

"I think I've changed my mind," he said to the waiter. "I'll forego the special menu and I'll have exactly what Mr. Murray has ordered."

"Very good, sir."

He left and the sommelier took his place.

"I remember you from last Friday, Mr. Bolton," he said to Andrew. "I remember that you don't partake. But we do have a splendid sparkling gooseberry and elderflower flavoured concoction, which looks exactly like champagne, but which has no alcohol."

I found it hard to look at him during the first course. It was the way he tipped back his head and slid the oysters into his mouth from the shell. It was all too sensual. I, too, ignored the tiny seafood fork and followed his example. They were precisely how I'd imagined them when thinking about what to order. They tasted of iodine and the sea, sharpened by the merest hint of the lemon half I'd squeezed over the entire dozen. I could have easily eaten another twelve.

"I've been meaning to explain something," I said to him, as our waiter removed the huge linen serviettes he'd tied around our collars, to protect our dickies.

"I hope it's to explain whether napkin or serviette is the correct term," he said with a twinkle in his eye, as he raised his glass to me.

"Nothing quite so vexatious and confounding as that," I replied with a chuckle. "Now may I continue?"

"Explain away."

"Ever since I met you, I've been feeling uncomfortable about our apparent lifestyle."

"I've absolutely no idea why you think I should make any judgement, but please, go on, if you feel you must."

"Well, most of it is for show. My brother and I are obliged to appear to lead an existence that would be far beyond our means, were it not for engagements that come as a result of attendance at society functions. Theatre performers, even those as well-known as Theo and I, don't earn the fabulous sums that most believe us to receive. Unless we mount our own productions, which are very risky, we're lucky to each make five or six hundred a year from performances in the major theatres, and our costs are enormous."

"I don't need to know about your finances," he said.

"I'm only telling you as I want you to know something about who Theo and I are, Andrew. You did say there was a lot about me you didn't know. I know it's still considered vulgar to talk of money, but please hear me out."

"I'm sorry; please continue."

"Despite appearances, we'd both be quite happy living in a humpy somewhere near the sea, wearing hand-me-downs, and eating simply. We were brought up with nothing, we moved to India, where we had next-to-nothing, and then returned to Australia, and for two years went back to a life of bare survival. Once we started to earn decent money, we've been very careful in the management of our finances. The land at Birchgrove was bought for a pittance. It was in the middle of an economic downturn and they couldn't give land away. We were merely very fortunate with the timing. However, the house has cost us a fortune. It's our insurance against anything that might go wrong. At least we'll have a roof over our heads, which we can sell for a decent sum if we face some tragedy in the future. All the evening suits, the beautiful clothes, and the expensive jewellery is for show. It's lovely, but if, like I told you when we had lunch at Central Railway last Friday, I'm to be engaged to sing at Government House at ten guineas a throw, and then at society weddings for the same sum, I need to look and behave like those people."

"Ten guineas to sing at a wedding?" he sounded astounded.

"At a New Year's Eve party, I'm paid twenty for six songs from operetta with the orchestra, over the course of three hours. The prices paid bear no comparison to each other, Andrew. It's the prestige value. If Lady X is able to boast to her friends she paid Edward Murray the sum of ten guineas to sing at her daughter's wedding, it's less about the sum and more about her self importance ... and of course the value of using my name ostentatiously."

"Good heavens, I'd no idea."

"It's like good costuming and wonderful, world-class singers at the opera," I explained. "The higher the quality, the more you can charge for the stalls and the boxes."

"And that's why you do two engagements in one evening, and perform at the variety theatres and make guest appearances at the vaudeville."

"Correct, Andrew. It's not greed, it's for our future, for when we are too old to continue performing. We must earn enough while we can, and invest in a way that allows us never to become so poor again that we might be forced to boil our shoes and eat them."

He chuckled. "Your metaphors," he said.

"That example is not strictly a metaphor, my friend. We've been very close, once or twice, and that's no joke."

Our broth arrived, straw yellow and fragrant, dotted with tiny dumplings.

"What's in the floaties?" he whispered across the table to me.

"Rabbit. Didn't you know what you were getting when you ordered?"

He shook his head. "You ordered yours with such aplomb, I thought it must be good."

I chuckled, and once again, he smiled into my eyes.

*****

I couldn't stop smiling when I got into bed.

It had been the most wonderful evening I could remember. I lay on my back, the covers up to my waist, with my hands behind the back of my neck, thinking of the light in his eyes and the way my gaze had darted to his uneven smile. Had that canine been a little shorter, I doubt he would have been quite so handsome to my mind. I'd juggled a triangle of glances all evening, from eyes, to teeth, to lips, where my gaze had lingered perhaps a little longer than necessary. The memory of his returned kiss early this morning burned in my mind.

I was starting to drift off when I saw a glimpse of light. Someone had opened my bedroom door. As I presumed it was Theo, late home from the theatre, I pulled back the covers and patted the sheets next to me.

"Hop in," I said and then nearly jumped out of my skin when Andrew's voice replied.

"I'd rather stay on top of the sheets right now, if you don't mind," he said, pulling the covers back up over me.

He slid down onto the bed and stretched out on his side.

"Hello," I said after what felt like an interminably long silence.

"Hello, Eddie," he replied.

"Is this a social visit, or ...?" He laughed, so I rolled onto my side to face him. "What are you doing here?" It was an enormous effort not to reach out and stroke his lower lip with my thumb.

"I need to tell you a few things, Edward. I don't think I've ever had such an agreeable evening in my entire life. In fact, this past week has been unparalleled. The theatre, the music, Chiffonier's, Theo, and ..."

"And?"

"You know what, Édouard Marais."

"Say it again."

"What, your name?"

I nodded. "But wait, I want to open the curtains first." The room was very dark.

"Why?" he asked, as I leaped out of bed.

"So I can watch you while you speak it. Only Theo calls me Édouard," I said while drawing back the curtains. When I turned around, my heart caught in my throat. "You're naked," I said.

"I think you should go to detective school," he said with a laugh. "My dressing gown's on the hook on the back of your door."

He rolled onto his stomach and waited until I got back into bed.

"Pull the covers back up over your waist," he whispered.

"Why?"

"If you want me to say your name in French, then you'll do as I ask, and then I'll tell you why."

I leaned on my elbow, watching his face, as he carefully smoothed down the counterpane over my waistline. "Édouard Marais," he said, running his hand over my ribcage.

"Look at me and say it again, please, Andrew," I whispered.

He leaned forward and kissed me, as he had done this morning. It was such a hesitant kiss, yet soft and yielding, his fingers trembling as they brushed against the side of my neck, underneath my ear.

"I'm sorry," he whispered, "I'm not very good at this."

There are times in every man's life when he knows when not to speak. This was one of them.

"I said I'd talk to you, and I meant it. I've been avoiding this moment most of my life, Eddie. I'll be thirty-six years old in a few weeks from now, and meeting you has stirred something within me that I've been trying to control for twenty years."

"What?" I was puzzled, not amazed.

"In fact, these three kisses we've exchanged today have been the first since I was sixteen, and the most intimate I've ever been with anyone in my entire life. I know you well enough to believe you will make no judgement when I tell you the reason for my self-imposed celibacy, avoidance of any intimate friendships, and taking the pledge. I promised myself I would avoid all three as penance for something truly terrible that happened back then."

I could see the pain in his eyes and longed to reach across the eighteen inches that separated us to run my hand over his back, to offer him some encouragement to proceed and some comfort while he explained.

"I had a brother," he said. "Harris was his name. My little Harry. He was kidnapped and then found dead three days later."

"Oh my God!" I said. "But surely it wasn't your fault?"

"That's where you're wrong, Eddie. I've never told anyone, not even my parents, but it was my fault that he was taken."

"You don't have to—"

"No, I do! Don't you see! Talking with you and seeing how unashamed you are of where you came from, the circumstance of what your mother was forced to do to feed you, and how you and Theo have risen above all that. You've owned your past. I've tried to bury mine."

"Come here," I said and opened my arms.

"Let me speak first. I've thought of nothing else but holding you in my arms, or feeling myself enfolded in yours. There, I've said it plainly now. I've owned up to my most hidden secret. I suppose there's no turning back. I've barely dared admit it to myself, if truth be told."

"You've said nothing more than one intimate friend would say to another, Andrew. The door's over there. Now's your chance."

"I was supposed to be looking after him." He rolled onto his back.

"Harris?"

"Yes, my little mate, Harry. He was at the front gate playing with his hoop and his top when he was taken. One moment he was there, laughing, calling out to me. I can still hear his little voice 'Andy, Andy, come play with me'. 'In a moment,' I called back, and then the next minute I heard him screaming. A man on a black horse had him by one arm, trying to pull him up into the saddle. I ran down and grabbed the man's leg, but he kicked me. I held on for dear life, with every fibre in my body, but the man put his heels in and dragged me after them as he galloped off on his horse. Eventually, he kicked me free and they disappeared. I lay on the road sobbing, calling out for Harry, whose screams became fainter and fainter."

"It was a dreadful thing, Andrew. But why do you blame yourself? I don't understand."

"I wasn't doing what I should have been doing, Eddie. Instead of watching after Harry and playing with him, I was sitting twenty feet away, on our local doctor's front porch, holding hands and exchanging pecks on the cheek with his son, Stephen. I was sixteen and smitten. On the second kiss of my life, my brother was snatched away, and because of my handholding, a stranger took him from our lives and murdered him."

I was stunned.

In music, the silences between notes are often more important than the notes themselves. Rests, pauses, rallentandi … these are devices to allow the music to breath, to give light and air and time to appreciate what has come before and what is yet to come.

This was one of those moments. I reached over and pulled him into my arms and held him as he wept softly.

"I'm so dreadfully sorry," he said minutes later.

"Sorry for what? Sorry for being human?"

"It's the reason I made the pledge, and why I joined the army, and then why I became a policeman."

"And why you deprived yourself of the balm of affection?"

"Balm of affection? That's something my grandfather would have said, but coming from you, the phrase sounds so poetic, and beautiful somehow." He chuckled and then sniffed. "Do you have a handkerchief handy?"

"No," I said. "I've an exchequer under the pillow though."

He laughed. "I'd like to blow my nose, not excoriate it, thank you very much."

"Use the corner of the sheet," I said. "They're due to be changed tomorrow. Housemaids see far worse on bed linen, I promise you."

My silliness caused him to laugh and turn in my arms so we were face to face.

"Do you really—?"

"No, I was making light of things. There's nothing under my pillows but loneliness, Andrew."

He nodded, as if processing that we were not unalike in that. Single men, lonely beds, unfilled hearts. "I've a confession to make, Eddie. I've never ..."

"I know," I replied. "And it's not expected of you either, Mr. Bolton. If it's to happen, it's you who'll come to me when and if you decide that's what you want."

"I know you don't give lessons in singing, but ..."

I couldn't help but smile. There were some things that were more difficult to discuss than others. It was our age, the time in which we lived and how we'd been brought up to behave. We tended to interrupt streams of conversation with diversions, to allow ourselves time to regain composure. It was quite ridiculous, but I respected him for his awkwardness. I'd not been able to speak of bedtime subjects with Sandford either; not for quite a long time. But, in that last utterance he'd told me he wanted me, even though he hadn't said the words, and that he was apprehensive about his lack of experience.

"I suppose joining the army was somehow learning to take care of yourself—had you been stronger, you may have been able to save your brother? Is that why you wrestle and row? To become stronger? And then becoming a detective because you'd lacked the skills to trace who'd taken him—"

"And a lawyer to know the intricacies of the law so that offenders might face true justice. Am I that transparent?"

I kissed his nose. "No. In fact, it's exactly what Theo and I have done. Two gutter children who've made it out of the slums and risen out of poverty and deprivation. It's precisely what you've done. Except that in the doing of it, you've blamed yourself for your circumstance, and then deprived yourself of nature's greatest healer."

"Is it really so, Edward? Tell me the truth. Surely man must fight his own demons, find succour within his own breast?"

"Of course he must, but it's easier with someone at your side."

"Have you ever had one?"

"I've had opportunities, but met no one I've ever wanted to be part of my soul."

"At least you have Theo."

"That's true. I do love my brother, Andrew. I love him with every fibre of my body. It's what kept me alive in the darkest days—my love for Theo. When he was ill in India, I gave him my own food when there wasn't enough for both of us. I begged in the streets; tough competition when there are so many young native boys doing the same. I allowed old white men of the Raj to touch me wherever they liked for money to buy medicine for Theo. I never let them do anything but touch, I swear on my honour that's the truth. I stole, I lied, I did everything humanly possible because I loved him, and he repaid me not with admonition for my wrong-doings, but with love. I would do anything for Theo. Yes, even kill someone if it meant saving his life. But, there's another sort of love too, you know. Love between two people that's a melding of the spirits. Romantic love. I might be being selfish, but I'm not alone in the world of wanting that for myself too."

"May I kiss you again?" he asked, after the briefest of pauses.

"There's a coverlet between us."

"For a very good reason," he said. "Edward, there's another struggle going on inside me, that has to do with you."

"You policeman, me the person you're supposed to be protecting?"

"Yes. I'm happy for us to have what they call a platonic friendship, but I'm afraid that I can't cross any lines while in the performance of my duty. Until Kane is caught, I must be beyond reproach. If I was to repeat the same mistake that happened twenty years ago …"

"There's plenty of young men out there in the world who, like 'passing women', have acknowledged 'romantic friendships'. I'm happy for that if it's what you want. As for later on, who knows?"

"I suppose so."

"You must try to realise that giving up alcohol might be a beneficial thing for your health, but giving up the chance of a life of happiness … Tell me, Andrew, just one thing, please answer me this honestly."

"I promise."

"The fact you gave up so much for your brother means you loved Harry. You cared for him. Am I correct?"

"Of course," he mumbled. At that moment I was fairly sure he knew what I was going to say.

"Do you really think Harry would not have wanted you to be happy, to be fulfilled in your life? To what end, had he lived, would he have rejoiced in your loneliness, in your—"

He seized the back of my neck with one hand and gently pulled my mouth to his. After a few seconds, he drew back, resting his forehead against mine, and panting slightly.

"Was that what they call a French kiss?" he asked.

"It was more like a Belgian kiss," I replied. "Borderline."

He laughed. "Show me, please, Eddie."

"Are you sure?"

"I shall lay asleep wondering why you refused."

"I'm sure this goes against my better judgement," I said. He understood I was teasing him and searched my eyes as I ran my hands up over his jawline and cradled his face.

At the touch of his lips, I opened mine barely, and then slid my tongue into his mouth. He moaned against me, wrapping his arms around me and pulling me closer as he reciprocated the kiss.

It was far too much. I could feel my pulse racing and a familiar ache down below. I pulled away.

"Why did you stop? Did I do something wrong?"

"No, no, you sweet man. You did nothing wrong. Quite the opposite, in fact. But the heat was growing in my ears. Had we continued, I may have found it hard to respect your boundaries."

He sat up against the headboard of the bed, and then glanced down. "Oh God!" he murmured, raising one knee to hide his tumescence.

"Don't be ashamed," I said. "I've been the same for the past half hour, ever since I first drew the curtains. It's another demonstration you're simply another human being—a very beautiful one, if I may say, Andrew. Your body's merely giving you the same sort of message that it gives every man in a situation like this."

"And what sort of situation is that?"

"You're a big boy, as you're so fond of telling me, Chief Constable Bolton. I'm sure you can work that one out for yourself."

*****

When I woke in the morning it was still dark, and Andrew was snoring gently in my arms, under the coverlets. It was the smell of his moustache wax that had woken me, that soft, beautiful combination of honey and tar.

I didn't remember him actually lifting the sheets and getting into bed with me. I must have been sound asleep. Perhaps it was merely he felt cool during the night, lying on top of the covers. I didn't mind. My nose was pressed to the back of his neck and my arms wound tightly around his chest, the fingers of one of his hands laced through those of one of mine.

I dared not breathe in case I broke the spell, nervously and carefully moving my arse back in the bed, away from him. My erection was painfully hard and had been pressing against his buttocks. For some reason it felt too soon and I felt awkward, until he snuffled in his sleep and nestled back against me.

It wasn't a sexual thing. I recognised it for what it was. That luxurious, wonderful feeling of complete body contact and the comfort cuddling gives. Tummy against back, knees spooned up behind each other, breathing in a regulated synchronous rhythm. I kissed the back of his neck, careful not to wake him, and then allowed myself to relax against his back, no longer fearful that my arousal was anything more than a natural reflex.

He was the one. I knew it already. It was too soon, far too soon, but I could hear Howard's voice in my mind. Every morning, while we were in India, he'd say hello when he woke up, look around at our miserable living conditions, and then smile at me. "Don't worry, Eddie. One day we'll all be happy. Truly happy," he'd say. "You and me, we'll both find the thing that makes us as happy as Larry."

I'd wanted it to be true so much it hurt back then.

And I still wanted it to be so, but in the present, and with Andrew Bolton.

CHAPTER 10

I woke to the sheets being violently ripped off me.

I knew it could be only one person. "Theo ..." I grumbled, pulling the pillow over my head. He pushed me onto the floor and I landed with a thud, but laughing.

"What are you doing up there?" I asked.

"Checking to see whether the sheets are soiled."

"Good Lord—"

"Fee, fie, fo, fum," he chanted, "I smell the scent of a copper's bum."

I roared with laughter and then rolled onto my back on the carpet, my fingers intertwined, resting on my belly.

"So ...?" he asked, hanging his head over the edge of the bed and waggling his eyebrows. I said nothing. "Any exchange of bodily fluids?"

"Theo Murray, you are not fit for polite company." I could barely control my laughter.

He passed a theatrical glance around the room. "I see no polite company, only my wanton brother, who, when I arrived home, was lying asleep with his head upon a policeman's shoulder, and he with his arms around you."

"Crickey, it wasn't half lovely either."

"Uh huh?"

"We kissed."

"And?"

"Proper kisses."

"Oo!" His voice ranged up and down through two octaves.

"I don't know what I'm going to tell Sandford," I said suddenly serious.

He leaped off the bed and sat at my side. "Really? Are you quite sure?"

"You know me, Theo, I'm not given to histrionics, unless I'm paid for them. Yes, I'm sure. He's the one."

"But are you the one for him?" He lay down beside me, resting his head on my chest.

I shrugged. "Only time will tell, I suppose. But—"

"Shall I book the church?"

"Daft bugger! No! It will take time, but I'm prepared to wait."

"And if nothing ever comes of it?"

"Then at least I'll have known what it is to feel like this."

Theo said nothing, but kissed the side of my face. I knew he was both happy for me and anxious at the same time. I'd never felt quite as protective of him as he was of me—possessive perhaps, but he'd never suffered for me to look after him, unless he was sick, of course. Knowledge of the bumps and scrapes in Theo's life had come to me after the fact, while he had gone out of his way to prevent any such disasters in mine—not always successfully either.

"I think it's quite fortunate we put in four bedrooms in *Madeleine*," he said.

"I can't see it ever coming to that. We don't live in those sorts of times yet. People will understand with you and Ethan. He's ostensibly our gentlemen's gentleman if anyone comes calling. But Andrew? With his parents living so close by? If it ever came to be a relationship of an intimate nature, I think it might be 'too late to get home' excuses, and perhaps weekend parties and sleepovers. Of course, there's always the

visits to our pool to swim, or to play tennis … what are you thinking?"
I could see his eyes glaze. A sure signal his mind was wandering.

"Wouldn't it be nice if one day two men could live together
openly."

"We both know plenty of confirmed bachelors who share
lodgings, Theo. How they manage their passion for each other in public
is beyond me. I suppose it's something I'm going to have to discover for
myself, if he finds it in his heart to return my feelings."

"Why is it that you are starting to sound like me all of a sudden?
Those words could easily have issued from my own mouth."

"I don't know," I said. "Perhaps I'm finally starting to grow up?"

"Heaven forbid," he said, grabbing the pillow that had followed
after me onto the floor. He hit me with it. "Now, the object of your
affections is pretending to read the newspaper and waiting to have
breakfast with you. He keeps glancing at the clock and at your bedroom
door."

"You should have let him wake me, Theo. Such meanness."

"It will do him a world of good to wait. Go have your shower and
get dressed. Perhaps I'll send him in with a bar of soap and a brush to
scrub your back?"

I pulled my brother to me and hugged him hard.

"No, you're right," I whispered against his ear. "Too much of a
good thing. I'm all for old-fashioned courting."

"Old-fashioned courting with tongue kisses by the sound of it."

"Well, progress is progress. We no longer live in the nineteenth
century, in case you hadn't noticed."

"If you really believe in progress, why don't you bounce out there
stark-naked and stir his coffee with your prick?"

*****

I couldn't believe the shambles Paul Doland lived in.

I'd done my vocalises after breakfast and then had sat at the piano,
learning notes for a concert performance of a relatively new work in
operatic terms. One I was familiar with, but which I hadn't performed—
other than the baritone aria, "*Si Può*". Ruggiero Leoncavallo's opera, *I*

Pagliacci, although first performed in Italy some twelve years ago, hadn't seen the light of day in Sydney. In 1893, thirteen performances had been shown at the Princess's Theatre in Melbourne, but no impresario in Sydney had felt confident enough to mount a production; perhaps because it was a short work and needed another piece to balance the second half of an evening at the theatre. Nonetheless, I'd always had a very positive reception when I'd sung the aria at symphony concerts. With its high tessitura and sustained top notes, it suited me to a T.

We'd all four of us taken the tram, alighting at the corner of Booth Street. Naddo's brother lived above a factory, as Fabrice had told us; but what he hadn't told us, and what Andrew had also neglected to say, was one half of the factory was a tannery, and the other a wrought iron manufactory—they made gates and cooking trivets, at least that's what the sign said over the door to their half of the building. The stench from one and the noise from the other were quite awful.

"Hello, boys!" he said, struggling to rise from his armchair, which, like him, had seen better days.

"Stay where you are, Paul," Theo said, stripping off his gloves. He pulled up a fiddle-back chair and sat at Paul's side. He'd always been very fond of Paul, despite being the author of his brother's death.

"Oh, my dear boy, look how you've grown," Paul Doland said.

In his attempt to smile, I noticed he'd lost all his teeth. He had that sunken cheek, gummy mouth look that so many had who couldn't afford dentures.

"Only sideways, Paul." Theo took his hands and rubbed them between his own.

"Hello, Eddie," he said. "Still as handsome as ever."

"Thank you, Mr. Doland," I replied. "Shall I put the kettle on?"

"You'll have to go down the iron stairs at the back to get some wood for the stove. I know it's a bother, but I find it hard going, and I'd love *a dish of tea*."

Theo and I both laughed. "*Mistress Angoul and the Raven of Doom*," Theo explained to Andrew and Cooper, who'd both looked dreadfully confused at our outburst of laughter. "It was a melodrama I featured in. Dreadful piece really, but Paul made a guest appearance, dressed as the vicar, having to throw cutlery at a stuffed raven, which was flown above our heads on wires. He was supposed to hit it at expressly the correct moment, so that it plummeted into Miss Angoul's cup of tea."

"Instead it landed on her hat, which was so securely attached to her wig she couldn't remove it," I said, "and in an effort to continue with the story, she tried to stab it with her cake fork, while saying, 'Oh dear! I'd only wanted *a dish of tea …'.*"

"It was the one time I was incapable of delivering my next line," Theo said. "None of us have ever forgotten that evening. I laughed so much I had to hold onto my sides—"

"And the audience was howling with laughter—"

"He knocked me down and stole everything," Paul said, suddenly solemn, interrupting our laughter.

"Who did?"

"Adam. Isn't that why you're here? I haven't seen either of you for years and then you turn up after policemen came here, rattling my bones and asking about my nephew?"

"I'll get the wood and light the stove," Cooper said. I smiled at him. The more I got to know him, the more I realised how kind and considerate he was. I thought him a perfect prospective match for Louise Bolton.

"To be honest, we heard you'd passed away," Theo said gently. "Maisie Wilson at the Adelphi told me she'd gone to visit you at that actor's boarding house you used to have a room in, what was it called again?"

"Akhust's," he said.

"Yes, that's it. Well, Maisie told us all you'd disappeared. She returned, telling everyone at the theatre you'd said to the landlady you were going to do a bit of fishing ten days beforehand, and you never came back. Maisie checked your room and all your belongings were there. The police said you'd probably fallen into the harbour."

"I went up the coast for a bit, and then when I came back, Akhust's had let my room to some blackguard, who'd thrown my things out in the street," he explained. "There was a new landlady, who knew nothing of me, and said she'd call the cops on me if I didn't clear out."

"Why didn't you come to us? You know we'd have helped you out."

"I felt like no one wanted any part of me; that's why. People saw me coming and turned their backs."

"That's not fair, Paul," Theo said. "You took yourself off away from everyone, refused any offers of help, after ..."

"After you killed my brother."

"It was he who attacked me, Paul! What's got into you? I can't believe that after all these years you've suddenly decided I'm the villain. It was Eddie and I who took you into our house, remember? We looked after you until you got back on your feet. We paid for both Nancy's and Neil's burials. We set up a trust for your welfare—"

"I'm sorry," he said, and then put his head in his hands and began to weep.

I recognised it for what it was. Loneliness. I looked around the flat. It was merely one large room with a cooking range at one end, a small curtained-off area, in which I could see a dirty tin hip-bath, and a door beside it, which I took to be a lavatory. Around the walls were faded posters of him and of his brother in their heydays. Coloured engravings, popular at the time, had been pasted up over walls and sidings all over the city. It was very sad to see how low he'd sunk.

I walked around the room, taking it all in while Theo chatted with him, and then when Cooper returned with a large basket of wood, I helped him lay the fire in the grate. I picked up the enamel ewer from beside his tin bath and smelled the water inside it. It was fresh enough, so went about looking for the tea makings. Every so often, I glanced over my shoulder at Theo, who'd curled up next to Paul with his arm around his shoulder, chatting quietly to him.

"Andrew?" I called out, aware I hadn't seen him for a while.

"I'm here!" He was standing outside, on the landing at the top of the stairs that led up to Paul's flat, leaning over the railing, and seemed to be conversing with someone below in the factory forecourt.

"I've sent a boy to the corner grocer with the wheelbarrow from the tannery and a crown in his pocket. I told him to tell the grocer to fill it up with what was on the list I threw down wrapped around the coin," he explained when I'd joined him.

"Let me—"

"I can afford five shillings, Edward. Keep your silver in your pocket. Perhaps you can take me on another ferry ride with it, and use the change for our supper."

"Now there's an offer I can't refuse." I turned, leaning on the railing to look inside, but at the same time moving closer to him, so the backs of our hands were touching.

"How did you sleep last night?" he whispered.

"I'm not quite sure, Chief Constable Bolton. I think I might need another such visit to judge the level of my slumber."

"Well, I've never experienced anything like it," he said under his breath, facing out over the courtyard below so his voice could not be heard inside. "It was the first time I've ever shared a bed with anyone, and I'm still trying to evaluate the effect it's had on me. Your tender embrace, the feel of your chest rising and falling in rhythm with my own … I can't help thinking it's the way people were meant to sleep— all safe and warm."

"Perhaps I can offer more of the same on a regular basis," I said and was about to continue when Cooper appeared in the doorway asking for help. The flue damper was stuck closed and the range was smoking like billy-oh.

Tea finally made, we pulled up chairs around Paul and sipped from our tin mugs quietly.

"As I said, Adam knocked me down and stole everything. He was unbalanced, you see … and violent with it."

"Did you know he killed Howard Talbot?" I asked.

Paul Doland nearly dropped his mug, such was his shock. "I'd no idea—"

"And the attendant at the Corporation Baths," Andrew added.

"Using Neil's daggers, too," Theo said and then took the mug from Paul's hands. He'd begun to tremble so violently, the tea had started to splash all over his shirt. It was obvious Paul had no idea of his nephew's doings.

"He's after me, Paul," I said, when I saw tears begin to gather at the corner of his eyes. "It's me he wants to kill."

"But why, Eddie? He idolised you. I simply don't understand. Why on earth would he want to kill you?"

"We've simply no idea, Mr. Doland," Andrew said. "And that's why we're here."

We chatted for perhaps an hour, only interrupted by the return of the lad with his barrow full of dry goods, soaps, candles, and other household items Andrew had put on his list.

Paul was as reluctant as we were to share much information. It seemed common decency to keep the details of his nephew's sexual adventures from him, and the news that Neil had recruited his own son for the performance of Death's Kiss, which Sandford had attended.

We left with promises of rallying his old theatre friends to visit him, and a postal note for two shillings and six pence, which we would post to the corner grocer every week to be redeemed for goods only from the shop. There was a fund actors put threepence a week into to help out their fallen comrades in times of trouble. My brother managed it. Neither Theo nor I needed to say it, but we didn't want Paul to end up on the bottle like his brother had.

"So where do we go from here?" Andrew asked. I knew it was a rhetorical question. He was merely speaking to himself aloud. We were standing at the tram stop, waiting to return to the city.

"What do you mean?"

"How on earth do I use what he told us in order to proceed with our investigation?"

We'd learned that James Kane had confronted his uncle a month ago, wild, desperate, and angry, shouting obscenities at him. He'd come back again two weeks later, his face black with rage, and had assaulted

Paul, stolen everything of value, including the set of his father's knives, which had been locked in a strongbox, hidden under his uncle's cot.

That was the last Paul had seen of him, presuming him to still be in his lodgings in Broadway.

There was some connection with the timing of all of these events, but it escaped me. Perhaps, like most puzzles, it would mull around in the back of my mind and slowly crystallise. However, in the meantime, Theo and I needed to call in to see our manager.

Mr. Solomon had sent around a letter earlier that morning asking us to pay him a visit. In it, he'd said he needed to discuss bookings for a country tour, which he proposed might take place after we'd returned from New Zealand. Theo and I both had a month free from engagements after the proposed dates for the remounting of *La Bohème*, and Elias wanted to send us, with Miss Fischer, on a state-wide tour.

It would be fun reviving our act, *A Little of What You Fancy*. We'd toured for years all over the country and in New Zealand in the early nineties. It had been five, if not six, years since our trio had last seen the light of day.

I'd never admit it to anyone, but I secretly hoped I'd still be alive when it came time to travel. Paul's revelation that his nephew's violent behaviour seemed to be fuelled by anger, rather than lunacy, had really disturbed me. It seemed to have purpose rather than random madness.

"I'll see you later," Andrew said, lifting his hat to us as he stood ready to alight from the tram on the corner of King Street. He intended to spend the afternoon at police headquarters with a few of the old-time members of the force, trying to work out where James Kane may have been and what it was he had discovered that had caused him to become so aggressive with his uncle. That violence and the two ensuing murders had to be connected. It was a needle in a haystack, but when I'd suggested he start at the Sailor's Bristle, the pub Kane had told Sandford he'd frequented, Andrew suggested he might go there straight after calling in at Phillip Street to see if anything new had come to light.

"I hope you're going to find something to change into," I said. "You can't go down to a rough-house pub looking like that, all spic and span, and shiny clean. No one would ever talk to you."

Theo stood. "I'll go with him, Eddie. You sort out the business with Elias. It'd be you doing most of the negotiating anyway. I'll rustle up some clobber for this galoot and we'll go in our crusties."

"Where will you find clothes to fit him?"

"His name's Billy Carter. Remember him? The man who works in the basement of the Metropole, who's the possessor of the biggest—"

"Coal shovel anyone can lift," I said, interrupting him, and blushing along with it.

The tram rattled to a halt and the conductor rang its bell. "Be careful," I said to Andrew, who was standing in the middle of George Street, next to Theo, waiting for the tram to move onwards.

"Sounds like this Mr. Carter, with the impressive shovel, is probably more dangerous than James Kane," he said, with a slight hesitation on the word "shovel".

"Anything's a weapon in the wrong hands," Theo quipped as our tram set into motion. I almost laughed, but controlled the urge, waving to them as they crossed the street in its wake.

"Crusties?" Cooper asked.

"Old clothes. Working men's trousers and jackets."

"Why do they call them crusties, Mr. Murray? I'm confused."

Ours was the next stop, so I stood and smiled at the conductor, indicating we wanted to alight.

"Because the blokes who wear them seldom wash," I said to the young policemen, over my shoulder.

*****

Later that night, we ate in the Metropole dining room.

Theo and Andrew had reported their visit to the Sailor's Bristle had not yielded much—Kane hadn't been seen there for well over a year. There'd been a bit of tattle, which had abruptly come to a halt when Andrew had taken offence at a tradesman's inelegant, and unsolicited, grope of his privates.

"Lucky stiff," I'd whispered into his ear so that none of the other diners could hear.

"Wrong on both counts, Eddie," he'd replied, surreptitiously squeezing my knee under the tablecloth.

The only information Theo had been able to find out before the pushing and shoving had started was Kane was still occasionally seen hanging around the wool clipper docks at Woolloomooloo at night. It was a well-known place to procure male prostitutes, or for lonely men to meet others of the same ilk. There were plenty of dark corners and empty warehouses in which no one was likely to be disturbed. It was a rough area and even the police didn't like to go there after dark.

"Why would he do such a thing?" Cooper had asked. "I've seen his picture. It's not as if he's not young and athletic?"

"Perhaps he simply likes it?" Theo had replied. "The physical act, I mean. There's plenty who do, Cooper."

"It can't be that good, to let your scruples fall so low."

Theo winked at me. One day Cooper would find out for himself. However, we'd known so many, many men and women who'd fallen under the spell of the pleasures of the flesh. It was like anything addictive that gave physical satisfaction. Some people saw it merely as an activity that felt good, rather like eating an excellent meal, being in the winning team at sport, or even spending a night in the theatre. But, all the moralising in the world would do nothing to change those who were obsessed with erotic indulgences.

Cooper was on duty, sleeping on the sofa, which we'd pushed up against the inside door, as we always did when he stayed on guard, so Andrew came to my room after everyone was sound asleep. He tiptoed into my room, saying he couldn't spend the night with me with Cooper outside. I told him I understood and he lay down next to me for a few minutes, pulling away breathlessly and vowing he had to go after a long, very passionate kiss.

I jumped out of bed as he went to leave, and stopped him before he got to my bedroom door.

"What?" he asked.

I lifted his nightgown over his head and threw it on the floor, and then drew him into my arms. He moaned against my mouth, one hand clasping my buttock, the other threaded through the hair at the back of my head, devouring my mouth with the passion of his kisses.

"Eddie … that's not fair," he said after we'd pulled apart.

"I know," I replied and then helped him back into his nightshirt. "But sometimes being fair is not what life's about, Andrew Bolton."

"I could get very used to that, you know."

"What? Me helping you in and out of your clothes?"

"Well, that too; but what I really meant was the feel of your naked body pressed up against mine. I promise you, Eddie, on my brother's grave, I will come to you when this is over and I'll not hold back. I need to know what it is to make love, and there's no one in the world I'd rather have teach me than you."

He kissed me on the cheek and then left my room before I could answer.

*****

The six Haddley boys sat in the front row of the Academy of Music.

They looked like a row of Russian dolls. Those carved wooden babushkas one opens to find another slightly smaller version of the same inside, and then another one inside that, and so on. All identically dressed in the same dark coloured smart suits, with pale blue spotted brown bow ties. I idly wondered whether their parents had gradually run short of "child stuff" when they were producing their boys, for even though they were grown men, they ranged in height from Francis, the eldest and tallest, to Cooper, the youngest and shortest.

Our party had been delighted at the end of the first half. The concert producing one excellent player after the other over the course of an hour. The four eldest boys finished it off with an eight-handed, two-piano version of the overture from *William Tell*, by Rossini. It was truly very skilfully delivered, lacking neither in dynamics nor in shading or nuance. The Bolton family, Theo, and I were all entranced.

"If only they would relax a little," Theo had whispered to me during the short interval, while we were having a cup of tea. After having been introduced to Cooper's mother, Adelia, we chatted with her for a short while. She'd looked embarrassed that we'd been there, immediately apologising for the capability of her students, and then wincing with disbelief when we'd both assured her that not one of them we'd heard so far was in the least way lacking.

It took me less than a minute to realise why Cooper was so judgemental about his own playing. She appeared to be a termagant. My heart bled for him as she launched into a criticism of all of her students, her face wreathed in frowns. Poor Cooper, I thought. No wonder he thought so little of his ability, with a mother so forceful in her denunciations of him and of his siblings.

While Adelia Haddley was held forth, I caught a glimpse of Cooper standing shyly in the corner of the hall, glancing nervously across the room at Andrew's sister, Louise, who'd been returning his shy smiles. I pardoned myself and then made a beeline for him, taking his cup from his hand and threatening to march him over to her if he didn't take the initiative, something that I knew would embarrass him beyond belief. So, he swallowed, adjusted his shirt cuffs, and sallied forth. A few minutes later, they stood, a few feet from her parents, talking to each other. My heart did a little flip of happiness when I noticed they both were blushing.

The second half of the concert consisted of piano duos and duets, one of the most impressive, although it irked me to admit it, was Mrs. Haddley herself, who played the first movement of Beethoven's fifth piano concerto, with her eldest son, Francis, playing a piano reduction of the orchestral score on the second piano. She indeed did possess a very finely honed ability, although not nearly on the same level of technical finesse as her son. Perhaps it was jealously that Cooper far outshone her own prowess that made her so critical of him? The thought was beneath me, but I accepted it as a strong possibility.

The last student of the concert, immediately preceding Cooper's appearance as guest artist, was his next older brother, Hillary. He was the boy who Cooper had described as having "similar interests" as Theo—and presumably me as well. I hadn't enquired whether anyone

had told him, or if he had twigged that both my brother and I were
Uranists. Pale, and nervous, but with beautiful hands and a lovely smile,
Hillary announced he would play the Valse Romantique by Debussy. It
was exquisite. He poured so much feeling into the phrasing, and his
hesitations immediately leading into the natural cadences in the work
were achingly beautiful. I was entranced. He didn't have Cooper's
virtuosity, but by jingo, that boy could touch one's heart with the
loveliness of his performance. The lightness of his touch alone was
something to marvel at. Miss Fischer almost leaped in her seat with
approval when he stood to bow.

At the other end of our row, another young man, his face streaked
with tears, clapped loudly. I turned to look at him and he caught my eye
and smiled. It was obvious he was Hillary's beau.

So, when it came time for Cooper to play, he announced that as
he'd been in my constant company for over a week, and had attended
my performance of *Faust* last Wednesday, he wanted to dedicate his first
work to me. I'd been extremely embarrassed, not wishing to draw
attention away from him. It was his moment to shine, not mine. But I
stood and nodded to the audience members as they applauded.

"He's playing Liszt's Faust Waltz Paraphrase?" Jacob Bolton
whispered to me when I sat. "That young policeman we met at the
theatre last week? Can it be true?"

"Just wait until you hear it, Mr. Bolton, and then make your
judgements."

Halfway through the performance, I noticed a movement from the
corner of my eye. It was Louise, fanning herself vigorously, her eyes
shining brightly and her face flushed with excitement. I could not have
been happier for Cooper at that moment had I tried.

"Was that truly him?" Jacob asked Andrew, leaning across me,
almost shouting over the tumultuous applause.

Cooper had performed faultlessly and with great passion in his
hands. I'm sure his mother was not used to such rowdy folk as my
brother, Andrew and his family, and me, as we called out our loud
bravos. His brothers were all on their feet too. It was very moving.

She looked as if she was about to move onto the platform and say something, but when he announced he would play the Gottschalk as his encore piece, Andrew's father applauded louder than the rest of us.

"The boy's a miracle," he said.

*****

"Father was very taken by him, as we all were," Andrew said.

We'd put his family on a tram home, and he and I had decided to call in at the Strand Arcade on our way back to the hotel to see if the tea shop was still open. Even though it was a Saturday afternoon and all the shops were closed, there was usually a brisk trade at this time of day, as the matinees of all of the surrounding theatres finished about now.

"I hope you'll put in a good word for him," I said as we turned into the arcade.

"Who, Cooper?"

I nodded.

"But a good word to whom? I don't understand you, Edward."

"To your father, Andrew. He'd like to step out with Louise, or at least have permission to call upon her."

"Really?"

"You object?"

"No! No, it's merely that I never thought of it ... oh, wait a moment. How do you know of this? Have you been the architect of some plot I'm unaware of?"

He was smiling, so I knew he didn't object to the idea. "No, I was merely the older man who offered advice to a younger man who solicited it. He's a wonderful young fellow, Andy, and although right now he's at the bottom of the ladder in the police force—"

"You called me Andy," he said suddenly.

"Oh, I'm sorry, I—"

"No, don't," he said, pulling me into the recessed entrance of one of the closed shops. "Say it again, but I want to look at you when you say it, like you did when you asked me to say your name."

I gently stroked his chin with my thumb. Right where I'd banged it with my forehead on the night we'd first met. "Andy," I murmured.

He stared into my eyes. It was all I could do to stop myself leaning forward and taking him in my arms. I was about to run my hand around the small of his back when, from the corner of my eye, I caught a glimpse of a man dressed in black, his arm raised on high, and then before I could react, there was an almighty bang. Clouds of smoke filled my eyes. Women screamed and men shouted in alarm. The man grabbed Andrew and pulled him out of our alcove, throwing him onto the floor. I tried to restrain him, but he landed a punch right on my jaw, knocking me backwards. I could see Andrew's form spread out across the tiles of the arcade floor, and then I jumped in fright when I saw who it was who'd hit me.

Although he was wearing a black wig and a false moustache and beard, I recognised Kane instantly.

"James! Stop!" I yelled, grabbing his raised arm. He fought with me for control of his dagger, our arms trembling with the effort and our bodies hard up against each other, our feet struggling for purchase on the tiled floor as we wrestled to gain advantage one over the other. He kept throwing quick glances at Andrew's prone figure, struggling to release himself from my grip. All at once, I understood it was my companion he'd intended to hurt, not me. He saw the fright in my eyes as I realised his purpose, and grinned. With one enormous effort, he hurled me backwards.

"No!" I shrieked as he threw himself onto his knees, raising his arm to strike, just as Andrew moaned and rolled over, holding his hands up to protect himself. My voice roared around the enclosed space, and as it did so I heard a policeman's whistle.

Kane glared at me, cursing loudly, and then took off like a rabbit. Instinctively, I took chase after him out of the arcade and across George Street. He ran between carts and horses, flying through the masses of people who'd been walking down the street out of the theatres in Pitt and George Streets, heading down to Circular Quay to catch ferries home.

"Stop that man," I screamed as I hurtled after Kane, his tailcoats flying behind him as he dashed down King Street, knocking pedestrians aside in his haste to get away. At the corner of York Street, he collided with a woman and her daughter who were waiting to cross the road. It gave me just enough time to reach him. I grabbed the back of his collar, but he continued to run, shrugging his arms free of his overcoat, leaving me holding it, and then yelled as he dived between the wheels of a beer wagon, which had been trundling across the intersection. I cursed and ran around it, calling out his name.

"James!" I yelled, almost breathless, my ribs aching. I could go no farther and leaned against the sandstone façade of the post office on the corner of Sussex Street. "Stop! *Adam*, please, stop!"

It looked as if he'd been punched in the middle of the back, so violent was his reaction at hearing his name. He braced himself against a lamppost, breathing hard, and then turned slowly, one of his father's daggers in his hand, watching me warily as I moved cautiously towards him with my hands up, showing I was not armed.

"Adam," I said. "I meant you no harm. The letter came from my agent, not from me. Adam, please—"

He lunged forward, swiping at me with the dagger. I pulled backwards. Its tip passed a few inches in front of my chest.

"It's not about the fucking singing!" he screamed and then threw his knife at me.

I'd seen the gathering momentum of his arm and threw myself sideways into the gutter. The dagger passed inches above my shoulder and clattered on the footpath behind me. Sprawled out on my face on the ground, I watched as he tore off, jumping through the open carriage of the toast-rack tram that was crawling up the incline from the wharf in Darling Harbour.

I'd been spread out in the gutter for no more than a few seconds when I heard the slap of feet pounding down the footpath towards me, and Andrew's voice calling out my name. I sat up as he reached me and fell to my side, pulling me into his arms. "Did he hurt you?" he asked, his cheek against mine. I could feel him trembling.

"No," I replied. "He's gone now. Jumped onto one side of a tram, ran through and out the other."

"Everything all right, sir?" a voice said, startling me. Andrew pulled away quickly.

"Yes, he went that way, down towards Darling Harbour," I said to the policeman, who'd obviously been chasing after Andrew down the hill. Hot on his heels were a few chaps who'd seen him run after me and were also giving chase. One, who must have run all the way from my arcade after him was bent double, red in the face, and puffing heavily.

"Go into the post office and bang on the door," Andrew said to the policeman. "It's Saturday afternoon, but the postmaster probably lives above. If he's there, ask him to use his telephone. Connect to Hyde Park 102. Can you remember that number? It's the private home of Chief Superintendent Morris. Tell him what's happened and where we are. He'll organise to send men."

*****

The detectives' room at Phillip Street police station was pandemonium, packed with policemen both in uniform and in informal clothing.

"Now the man's made a public nuisance of himself, we must take firmer action," Chief Superintendent Abel Morris said to the twenty or so men assembled in the room. "It's unthinkable what might have happened had his bomb detonated in a main street. Just think of the chaos! One only has to cast one's mind back to the day Harry Wilson shot his mistress in Pitt Street in the middle of the day. There were dozens injured by stampeding horses and runaway carriages. The collision of the omnibus and the tramcar, with its subsequent derailment, caused two deaths. But an explosion of a magnitude far greater than a pistol shot—"

"It was a flash pot, sir," Andrew said. He and I had been perched side by side on the edge of one of the large desks in the office. I couldn't stop glancing at his cheek. He'd grazed it when he fell and it wouldn't stop bleeding. He caught my eye and smiled, still embarrassed he'd hit his head and had lost consciousness for a few minutes when he'd been pushed onto the floor of the Strand Arcade."

"It wasn't a bomb, then?" the superintendent asked.

"No, sir," Andrew replied, getting to his feet and accepting my offer of a handkerchief. His was quite bloodied. "Mr. Murray assured me it was a device used in the theatre. It would explain how the explosion was set so rapidly."

"Perhaps you'd like to explain to us, Mr. Murray?"

"Of course, Superintendent. Flash pots are used to create those flashes of light and clouds of smoke that magicians are so fond of using, usually to mask a disappearance. Normally, in the theatre these days, the powder is ignited by an electrical charge, which is initiated from the wings. However, in the old days, they were set off either by a fuse or by a contraption that tipped a lighted candle or lamp into the powder. Small enough, and easily hidden by something twelve inches high."

"So you think James Kane knew where you'd be and arranged to place this device in advance?"

"No that's impossible," I replied. "We'd decided at the last minute to go to the Strand Arcade to have a cup of tea. He must have been following us. That tin, the one used to contain the explosive powder, it's a coffee can. The lid was in his coat pocket."

One of the constables held it up and showed it around the room, like a magician's assistant might have done.

"I think it was opportunistic. He'd probably been following me all day on Saturday. Mr. Palmer's article in the newspaper on Thursday afternoon may perhaps have riled him up. That's my guess. The pockets of his overcoat are voluminous! He must have been carrying the tin around, waiting for an opportunity, and when we stopped to light a cigarette in the recess of the shop in the arcade, he removed the lid from the container, placed it on the floor out of our line of sight, and then probably ignited it by throwing his lit cigarette into it. It's an old stage trick."

"But where would he get the powder?" Andrew asked.

"Any of those oriental shops in Dixon Street," I said and then explained further when I saw puzzled looks from some of the policemen. "Chinatown. Fireworks. Those large 'letterbox bomb' firecrackers you all hate. Each one of those contains about four ounces of black powder. A skyrocket holds four or five, depending on the size.

Two of each is over a pound of gunpowder. Loose, in a tin, and uncontained, an ignition would produce a loud report, masses of smoke and a flash of light, but no shrapnel. It was opportunistic, not planned."

"Why did you move into the recess to light a cigarette, that's what I don't understand," one of the men asked.

I wasn't going to give the real reason, that we wanted to speak intimately, so fabricated my reply. Another benefit of being an actor: the ability to ad-lib. "The wind," I said. "The wind howls down the Strand Arcade sometimes. We had to take shelter as my matches kept blowing out."

"Are you all right, Mr. Bolton?" I heard Cooper whisper to Andrew. He'd arrived while I was talking and was hastily pulling on his jacket. "I'm sorry I'm late. I had to get changed out of my concert clothes."

Andrew shushed him quietly, patting his forearm, while Superintendent Morris spoke.

"I believe we need to take an aggressive stand," he said. "I'd like Mr. Murray to sit down with an engraver to create a portrait of Little, or Kane, or however he calls himself. I want it on every front page of every newspaper. The public must be made aware of the danger."

"We do have a photographic portrait of him, sir," Andrew volunteered.

"I'd still like Mr. Murray to sit with the engraver. Photographic reproductions in newspapers are still costly. The press would prefer an engraving. Are you happy to help, sir?" he asked of me.

"May I be so bold as to propose an alternative course of action?"

"Please, Mr. Murray, let's hear what you have to say."

"I think such a public exposure will make him go to ground. He might even flee elsewhere. It will not solve the problem if he's still at large, as he will merely return later on when he thinks the coast is clear. It's my belief he somehow wants to goad me into a private meeting. I've no idea why yet. But, he needs to be captured before anyone else gets hurt."

"A private meeting, you say? But surely he had the opportunity when you waylaid him at the bottom of King Street?"

"There's no way he could not have seen Chief Constable Bolton and the other officer running down the hill, they could only have been twenty or thirty paces away. He feigned a knife throw at me to allow himself time to get away."

"So, what is your suggestion?"

"I'll not allow another innocent soul die because of me. Had I not shouted my head off, and had not the beat policeman sounded his whistle at the same moment, Chief Constable Bolton might well be laid out in your morgue downstairs right now. I'm sure you won't agree to me wandering around by myself to draw him out; however, I propose that we continue as before, with either Mr. Bolton, Mr. Haddley, or Mr. Ward at my side while I go about my normal routine. In pantomime, if you can remember back that far into your childhoods, gentlemen, the audience is often asked to keep an eye out for the villain, and to shout out when he appears. My suggestion is, Superintendent, you assign some members of your collection of brave men to follow discreetly at a distance, to intervene if Doland makes another move, which I'm sure he will do."

"I understand. But if the distance is too great, he might do his mischief before anyone is able to reach you. No, I can't risk your safety, or any of my men," the chief superintendent said.

"While I understand your concern for my safety, Abel," I replied, using his first name on purpose, "I cannot spend the rest of my life looking over my shoulder. I had not finished, if you will allow me to continue?"

Abel Morris smiled at me. We'd been friends for such a long time. He'd understood the use of his first name was to impress upon his men whatever operation was to take place, then it was of personal concern to him. Those who succeeded would do well in his eyes.

"Of course, Edward. Go on, I do beg your pardon."

"I'll draw up a plan of every day's activities in advance, which can be distributed among your men. There can be police officers following not only behind, but on the opposite side of the road, or walking discreetly a dozen or so paces ahead. This coming week, apart from

Howard's funeral, I'll be attending rehearsals every day in the hall behind the Theatre Royal for the season of *Don Giovanni*, which opens this coming Friday. Although it irks me beyond belief to carry on my life with such close surveillance, I do appreciate he must be caught. If I'm to be the bait, we should put a big worm on the hook."

"And your meaning?"

"I intend to go about my normal routine, as I have done this past week, but with a greater police presence hidden in plain sight, if you understand my meaning. The bait is this: someone surely can draw up a list of places that may seem like good opportunities for him to make a move, but which will also afford observation and quick access to me. I'd like to try to lure him into a trap."

"It makes good sense, Mr. Murray," Andrew said. It felt a little odd hearing him use my name formally again, but understood the reason. "But as he's only attacked people around you and not you yourself, then when I'm with you, I'm more likely to be the victim than you."

"You'll be safe, Mr. Bolton, I can look after you," I said.

The men in the room laughed loudly. Andrew gave them a mock bow, taking the jest in his stride.

"Well, I think we should discuss this further, and in private, but in principle I'm happy to go along with your plan, Edward," Chief Superintendent Morris said. "Now, if you, Chief Constable Bolton, and Constable Haddley would like to come to my office in fifteen minutes?"

*****

"He missed on purpose, Andrew," I said, dabbing at his face with Cooper's handkerchief, which I'd purloined for the purpose.

"Ouch," he said, "that stings."

I'd wet the corner of the handkerchief with some brandy. One of the men had a flask in his desk drawer. "I'd offer to …" I said, smiling, but Cooper was standing next to us, watching, with his hands in his pockets.

"Don't mind me," Cooper said. "My brother Hillary is always spitting on his handkerchief and wiping off scrapes and bumps. He always gives it a kiss better."

"That's your brother, Constable Haddley, not Mr. Murray," Andrew said, trying to sound gruff, but failing in the attempt. I winked at Cooper, who beamed his brightest smile at me.

We were standing in the washroom of the lavatory on the first floor of the police headquarters. It was a splendid affair, accessed by two sets of doors at either end of a long corridor, all cream and pale green tiles, with a long row of hand basins along one wall, twelve in all, above each a large bevelled-edged mirror. There were even soap dishes and rails upon which to hang hand towels. Andrew had told me many men performed their daily ablutions at work, especially those who lived in accommodation with shared bathrooms. There were shower compartments in another part of the building too. Police work was often a grubby business.

"Anyway, back to Adam Doland. There was no way he could have missed me, Andrew. We were but a yard apart. I wondered why his preparation to throw was so slow. He'd done it on purpose so I'd dive out of the way to give him time to get away. He'd only have needed to take one step forward and he could have stabbed me easily."

"But why didn't he?" Andrew asked.

"I have no idea, and that's God's truth. He looked as if I'd punched him in the gut when I called him by his name. He hadn't reacted at all when I'd called him James, but that mention of Adam stopped him in his tracks."

"And he said to you it wasn't about the singing?" Andrew asked.

I shook my head.

"But I'm sure that's not what you said, Mr. Murray," Cooper interjected.

"He said it wasn't about the *fucking* singing, Cooper," I said with a smile.

"Well, yes, Mr. Murray, but I couldn't use that word—"

"Will you stop calling me Mr. Murray when we're by ourselves!" I pretend-snapped with a wink. "Either call me Edward or 'you ugly bastard', or anything but Mr. Murray, Cooper. Surely we've passed that point in our friendship."

"Why thank you, Mr. ... I mean, you ugly bastard, sir. Truly, I'm very honoured."

I shook his hand and he wiped his eyes with the back of his after he'd returned the handshake. "I think I need to go ... um."

"Have a piss?" Andrew said, laughing.

"Right you are, Mr. Bolton."

"You may call me Andrew, Cooper. But only when we're alone. You and I have a work relationship and it would never do for us to sound too friendly while we're on the job, especially as I'm your senior officer."

"Good-oh," Cooper replied and then pushed open the door from the washroom into the lavatory area.

The moment the door closed, I took Andrew's face between my hands and kissed him. I meant it to be a quick peck and made a move to draw away, but he wouldn't let me go, opening his lips for a deep, luscious kiss. I laughed into his mouth, despite how lovely it was.

"Why are you laughing?"

"Because you're playing with fire, Chief Constable Bolton. I'm only flesh and blood."

He ran his hand over my shoulder down to my elbow, and held it, squeezing gently.

"I suppose I am being a bit mean," he said. "I made a vow. You didn't."

"I promised to respect your boundaries."

"Do you want me not to do that again?"

"Have you lost your mind? Of course I don't want you to stop! I'm just keeping you informed of my physical state."

"There was no need, I felt it prodding me while we were kissing."

I was on the point of saying something very flirtatious when Cooper returned and began to wash his hands.

"Shouldn't we get moving?" he said, drying his hands on one of the loops of towelling hung along the wall behind us. "The governor will be waiting."

"After you," I said.

Cooper left first, followed by Andrew, with me behind him, trying to arrange myself in my trousers so everything would be stowed away when we returned to the main office.

Nothing like a bit of almost being killed to rattle the stones, as Theo once had to say to me in a pantomime we'd performed in Nagpur over twenty years ago. We'd no idea what it meant at the time, but the gentlemen in the audience had howled with laughter.

Now that I was older, I realised that peril often stirs more than a sense of danger.

*****

Abel Morris had invited Andrew and me to sit. Cooper and two detectives I hadn't been introduced to were left standing near the door. The office was quite splendid, and the brown leather canapé settee on which we were seated was especially fine. Absentmindedly, I'd paid more attention to its beautiful craftsmanship when we'd entered than to what the chief superintendent had been saying to me.

"I'm sorry, gentlemen, we haven't been introduced," I said, rising from the sofa.

"I beg your pardon, Edward, remiss of me. I keep forgetting you're not one of our crowd. Our men normally introduce themselves in the course of their work."

The two men shook my hand in turn, introducing themselves with their surnames only.

"You are comfortable with your task?" I asked.

"Yes, sir," they both replied.

I'd suggested that a few young policemen, who came from working-class backgrounds, spend some evenings down at Woolloomooloo docks, wandering around and keeping their eye out, just in case Adam Doland was skint and needed to earn some change. Cooper had been sent out to choose them.

One of the men reminded me of Billy Carter. He'd refrained from meeting my eye when he'd shaken my hand. I knew the type and recognised that he was embarrassed to be chosen for the undercover job, perhaps because he was no stranger to the wool clipper docks after dark.

"You're not to get yourselves into trouble, mind you," I said. "If a gentleman makes a proposition, be polite, but make an excuse. Tell him, for example, you already have an appointment and are waiting for the person to arrive, or that you've recently been with someone else and are waiting to top up your reserves—you'll think of something. There's no point throwing your fists about, you'd only draw attention to yourselves. Understood?"

They both nodded and then left us after Abel told them to wait outside for further instruction.

"So, Edward," the superintendent said, gesturing for Cooper to take a seat. I patted the sofa and he sat between Andrew and me. "Have you any ideas why he killed Howard Talbot and then Mr. Elder at the baths, and yet left you unharmed?"

"At first, I thought Howard's death was a mistaken identity, as you yourselves did. Howard looking so like me in the darkness of the dressing room. But then, the heart drawn around the dagger puzzled me. What does 'you stabbed me in the heart' generally mean?"

"Some sort of romantic relationship come to grief?"

"But I barely know him. I may have spoken to him once, maybe twice, and that was to return his 'good morning', or 'good evening'."

"It could be something you've done has wounded him to the core?"

"Maybe so, but it would be entirely unwitting, I can assure you. I've no association with him. Why would he ejaculate on the dressing room mirror?" I said. "That bench is thirty-six inches deep. It's a prodigious feat at that distance for any man—"

"It was saliva," Cooper said. "I'm sorry, I thought you knew."

"The last I heard was when Abel and Andrew arrived at the hotel and informed me that you suspected it was semen?"

"We hadn't been to the scene when I told you that, Edward," Andrew explained. "It was merely the report handed to us downstairs in the foyer of the hotel by a policeman who'd come from the theatre with details of the initial inspection of the dressing room. What I said to you was we'd not yet scientifically determined exactly what it was. It seems I was in error, as the test is only available theoretically in textbooks, not in practice yet."

"So, he spat on the mirror?"

"Yes, the first police officer on the scene had a very active imagination. He saw Howard Talbot naked and assumed something untoward had happened during an intimate encounter, which had eventuated in murder."

"What is this policeman's name?" I muttered darkly. "He'd be useful writing scripts for threepenny melodramas."

Cooper was the only one who chuckled. "It was scraped off the mirror in the morning when dry," he explained. "A man's emissions produce either small flakes or a powdery residue. Saliva does not."

"Spitting is quite different than fetching off on something," I said. "To spit on something is to show your hate, defiling something, and defining it as beneath your contempt."

"It's not uncommon for murderers to ejaculate on their victims, Edward," Andrew said. "The world is a weird place. The act of killing another human being can be incredibly sexually arousing to some disturbed men. It's what we had originally supposed, before we established the defilement on the mirror was saliva, not semen."

"The daggers, Edward?" Chief Superintendent Morris asked me, he seemed to want the conversation to move on.

"Well, I did think about the daggers and their relevance, Abel. However, there's no way, unless someone told him, that Adam Doland could possibly have known we'd have recognised them."

"Why's that?"

"Well, Fabrice Evans told us Adam was born six years before his mother died, and before that, he'd been passed around from one to another. We'd never known they had a child until a few days ago. The boy wasn't at his mother's funeral. Theo and I paid for it, and Paul gave the eulogy. I'd remember if a child was mentioned. Neil stopped performing a year later. The boy would have been seven at the time I suppose. So he'd never have been aware that we'd been on the same stage as his father. Those daggers were only famous when Neil was performing. They disappeared when he stopped, and I never heard mention of them again until I saw one of them stuck in Neil Doland's corpse after he'd tried to kill Theo. The second was six years later, impaled in the wooden panelling of the dressing room cubicle, above Mr. Elder's body."

"So, you believe that Adam Doland had no idea you knew James Kane and he were the same person?"

"Not until a few hours ago," I said. "The anger in his eyes when he saw I'd recognised him under his black wig and false beard and moustaches was impossible to ignore. But, when I finally called him by his real name, Adam, it was as if I'd punched him in the gut. His reaction was physical. There was no mistaking his shock and surprise. I've not been taken aback often in my life, but when I tried to explain I had nothing to do with the letter from Elias, the hate in his voice made my blood run cold."

"If he hates you as much as you say, why didn't he kill you then? He had the opportunity?"

"Andrew and the other policemen were hard on my heels. There's no way he could have avoided seeing them tearing down King Street."

"Wait," Andrew said, "if that's the case, let's look at it logically. We've established he hates you for some unknown reason and he's killing people around you, most likely to heighten your sense of fear, and yet he doesn't take the opportunity to kill you? Even in the arcade when I was laid out, he made a move to stab me when he could have murdered you."

"He wants to tell you something before he kills you," Cooper said. "It's like a snake mesmerising its prey. He wants you by yourself, vulnerable, afraid, and caught off-guard, so you'll be too terrified to put up a struggle. It's then he'll tell you why it is he hates you, and then he'll kill you at his leisure."

"Why thank you, Cooper," I said with a slight chuckle to break the silence in the room. We'd all understood the truth of what he'd said.

"Oh! I'm terribly sorry, Ed … Mr. Murray, I didn't mean to sound so melodramatic."

I laughed. "You spoke the truth, Cooper, and you're a clever lad. I'm sure you've put your finger right on it. But, I can promise you one thing."

"What's that, sir?"

"Adam Doland has seriously underestimated me, Cooper. He doesn't know my background, my tenacity, my will to fight, or my training with fisticuffs and acrobatics. He's woken a sleeping giant. I'm not afraid of him. In fact, I now see him as the frightened rabbit, and me as the red-bellied black snake."

"Oh!" he said, his eyes wide.

"Yes, Cooper, it's Adam Doland who's now on my menu for dinner, not the other way around!"

*****

"What do you think his reaction will be?" Andrew said.

We'd been talking about my connection with Sandford Clarkson. The conversation had arisen because Sandford had telephoned to say he'd received the photograph in the mail and confirmed the young man he'd seen at the Knighthawks Club was indeed Adam Doland. He'd wanted to have a lengthy conversation, but as Andrew had been present, I'd felt awkward and had informed him I had company at the time and hadn't been free to speak.

"Oh, he'll be more than annoyed. Maybe a temper tantrum, perhaps not speak to me for a week? But we've been friends for over twenty years," I replied. "And, it's not as if he doesn't have fingers in many pies."

Andrew laughed. "I'm not sure that's an appropriate turn of phrase."

I smiled and kissed him behind the ear. We'd had a late dinner in the supper club of the Adelphi after deciding to go to see a performance. He'd chosen it: *The Night Before My Pants Caught Fire*. It was a trite work, but very funny. It had been the right medicine for the occasion, something light and frothy, to take our minds off the events of the day.

Andrew had gone into his apartment after we got home, and I'd chatted with Theo for a while before going to say goodnight to my policeman—for that's how I saw him in my mind now: *my policeman*. He'd been waiting for me, his jacket draped over the back of a chair, his shirt undone to the third button, and his shoes off, leaning into the angle of his sofa. He patted the space between his legs. I sat there and leaned into his arms, the back of my head on his shoulder. There was something about the way his hands wandered over my chest and forearms that made me aware he wanted more than kisses, despite his vow. I wasn't really sure he was aware he wanted it, but it was unmistakeable.

So, that's when I felt it my duty to tell him about Sandford, who was the only person with whom I'd been regularly intimate. Sandford and I had no commitment. It was a relationship of convenience. Convenient to both of us, with no promises on either side. However, he felt very proprietary of me when he was in town. It was something we'd argued over ever since I'd met him. He was due to arrive for the opening of *Don Giovanni* later in the week, but now, with my feelings for Andrew running so high, I knew I'd simply not be able to spend the night with him. I was not one of those sorts of men.

"I'll write to him in the morning, Andy," I said. "No doubt he'll still come down, but I want him to rage without me around and then have a few days to think through his reaction. He knows I never wanted a permanent relationship with him. We've argued about it forever. I think his fury will be disappointment, that he will believe himself lacking in some way, as if he was not good enough for me, and yet you are."

"I am?"

I turned my head and pulled his mouth down to mine. It was a gentle, exploratory kiss, but there was no mistaking on my part, anyway, that he was the man I wanted to make a commitment to, even though we were still basically at handholding stage.

"I'm not entirely sure what I feel, to be perfectly honest, Eddie," he whispered. "I've never allowed myself the dream of finding myself in this situation. I thought I'd go to my grave a lonely man. At the moment, everything feels overwhelming. My mind is telling me one thing and my body the other. It seems I'm constantly fighting myself ... but, you saved my life today."

"I did no such thing," I said, taking his hand in mine.

"Yes, you did. Had you not roared like an enraged bull, he might not have been so startled. His hesitation gave me just enough time to roll onto my side."

"I think he knows."

"About what."

"About what I feel for you," I said. "It was the way he smiled when he saw how panicked I was that he was about to strike you. You must be vigilant for your own safety now, not only mine."

"You know calling him by his real name will probably either infuriate him further or drive him into hiding?"

I nodded. "What about Theo? If he's really desperate to get at me, perhaps he'll try to hurt my brother?"

"We've already talked about that possibility at the station and it's been taken care of. Theo will be perfectly safe here, and next week two policemen have been assigned to accompany him wherever he goes."

"Well, he was going to spend the week starting to sort out the furniture and household goods in our rented house at Hunters Hill. We closed it up six weeks ago when we moved into the Metropole. Everything's packed into crates and the furniture's under sheets. He thought he'd make a start, ready for us to move into *Madeleine*. It's the first free period of seven straight days he's had in ages, until he starts rehearsing his new play on Monday week."

"I'll have a word with him. Under the circumstances, I don't think it's wise if, as you say, the house is isolated and there's no access except by carriage or ferry."

"We have a housekeeper ... well, she's not really that, but the wife of the assistant ferry master, who pops into the house at Hunters Hill once a week, to make sure everything's all right. She collects whatever mail is there and sends it on to us once a month. There's so little arrives, maybe one or two letters a month, that I've told her to hold onto it. We can keep Theo busy with other things if you'd prefer him to be close at hand in the city. Getting things ready for our move can wait until after the *Don Giovanni* season. I've a series of country concerts immediately after for two weeks, and then we're off to New Zealand."

"I shall miss you."

I rolled into his arms. "I haven't gone anywhere yet."

"Eddie, do you think it wise if I came to your bed tonight?"

I laughed. "No, it's not wise at all, but I should love you to."

"I'm simply afraid I might—"

"If you do, push me onto my back and climb on top of me," I said with a grin.

He laughed, covering his eyes with the back of his forearm.

"Well, that's not quite what I was thinking, but if I feel a spontaneous movement, then I'll take your advice, although I warn you, it might make a dreadful mess."

"I might really like that, Chief Constable Bolton," I said.

"Oh …"

His "oh" was one of surprise, but soft, as if I'd said something unexpected, but pleasant. I rolled over in his arms and then straddled his hips, running my arms up over the crisp, white linen of his shirtsleeves. I bent forward and nibbled his lower lip and then sighed.

"I almost feel like running down into the street waving my arms around and calling out, 'Here I am! Come get me!' just so we can get this business over and done with. I'm a strong man, Andrew Bolton, but sometimes, when I close my eyes, I see us in this precise position, but without our clothes on."

"Good heavens! Really?"

"Uh huh … and more."

He sat up and pulled me into his arms.

"Tell me," he whispered.

"No you don't, Mr. Bolton. The next time we have this sort of conversation, Adam Doland will be in prison, and you and I won't need words."

CHAPTER 11

But for his slightly protruding ears and lack of moustache, Lincoln Talbot could have been a twin for Howard, despite the twelve months difference in age between them.

Theo grabbed my arm when Lincoln appeared at the top of the gangplank, and I let out a muffled choking sound. The SS *Mahurangi* had docked exactly on time, blowing its horns as tugs nudged it alongside the wharf. The band played something bright and cheerful. It did nothing to lighten my mood, which was filled with sadness in anticipation of Lincoln's arrival.

Eileen smiled. I'd turned my head to see her reaction. She seemed stronger than either Theo or me, but she'd only met her brother-in-law Lincoln once, before the children were born, not long after she and Howard were married. We'd seen him three years ago in 1899, on our last visit to New Zealand, and of course we'd spent years with him as children in India and then back home here before he decided to move across the Tasman.

"He looks like Daddy," Gertrude said. Andrew was holding her up high, sitting on his waist, her arms around his neck. She'd taken to him when we'd visited on the day after Howard had been killed.

"That's your Uncle Lincoln," Eileen said. "Children, you must mind your manners. Shake his hand if he offers, but be polite. He's never met you before."

Her words were ignored as Lincoln pushed past the other passengers on the gangplank and ran to us, sweeping Eileen into his arms, and gathering the children to him. I ground my teeth in an effort not to break down while I watched the group of five huddled, all weeping at the same time.

Eventually, he pulled away, and then kneeled down, talking to each of the children in turn, kissing Gertrude and hugging each of the boys.

"Do I only get a handshake?" he said to me, his eyes full of tears.

I shook my head and then fell into his arms. He kissed the side of my neck, whispering, "Oh, God! How I've missed you both."

When it came time for Theo's embrace, he got a hand on each side of his face and a smack on the lips before the hug. They'd been closer when we were children. It was Howard who'd been my special mate.

"And I don't know who you are," he said to Andrew, after he'd released Theo. "Is it to be a hug or a shake?"

"Perhaps both, Mr. Talbot. I'm here professionally and as a friend of these two miscreants," he replied, smiling, indicating my brother and me.

*****

As Eileen and the children were still not ready to move back into their house, Theo and I had arranged for them to stay at the Metropole until after the funeral, when they'd travel back with her parents to their house in the country.

Fortunately, the Royal Suite was vacant, and although the management extended its friendship as far as Theo's and my accommodation, it was a different matter when it came to that particular set of rooms.

"Five pounds a night! Have you lost your senses?" Lincoln hissed at me when he learned how much we'd had to pay.

"It would have been twice that, and in guineas, had it been anyone else," I replied. "It's only for two nights. After that, you can go live in Howard and Eileen's house until she decides she's ready to come back, and then, depending on how long you intend to stay in Sydney, Theo and I will find somewhere for you."

Of course, the children loved the suite. Two enormous reception rooms and four bedrooms. It had a balcony that gave expansive views to the north over the few city blocks that separated the hotel from the harbour.

I walked out onto the balcony. My mind was still in turmoil. The events of yesterday, the explosion in the arcade and then the hate in Adam Doland's eyes had affected me more than I'd let on. It was only when Andrew had finally sneaked into my room an hour after we'd said goodnight to each other in his living room that I'd managed to fall asleep. He'd rolled me on my side and had snuggled up behind me. We'd chatted for a short while, but were both tired, and very soon after he'd arrived, we'd fallen asleep.

Behind me, I could hear the children laughing inside. It was a wonderful sound. I leaned on the balustrade, half-listening to their play while I watched a steam motorcar passing below in Phillip Street, almost out of view. As a craned my head forward for a better look, a pair of arms embraced me from behind. I knew who it was, even before he spoke.

"So, who's the looker then?"

"You know he's the policeman assigned to look after me, Lincoln," I said as he moved to stand beside me. I took his cigarette from his mouth and puffed on it a few times.

"Hm ... and?"

"Howard would have loved him."

"As you do?"

"I didn't say that."

"You didn't need to, Eddie. I saw something had changed the moment I got off the ship. And then, the intimacy between you both ... I could almost taste it. I'm happy for you."

"Ah, dammit, Lincoln! I can't help feeling it's not a silver lining, that we might have met otherwise had it not been for Howard, but—"

"Howard would be happy for you. As you would be for Theo if something happened to you and he found someone special because of it."

"What will you do the day after the funeral?" I changed the subject. I was still feeling too private about Andrew to discuss it, even with those very close to me.

"On Tuesday morning?"

"Yes. Will you go back with Eileen and the children or will you stay in town for a few days?"

"I rather hoped you'd invite me to the theatre to hear the sing-through of *Don Giovanni*. You know it's my favourite."

"It will only be with piano. No orchestra."

"I don't mind. You know how I miss the theatre, and your singing."

"Stop it," I said, laughing.

"No, really I do, Eddie. The job's good at the Royal Hotel, but I'd swap it for a position at the Theatre Royal … I should never have given up performing."

"Do you still fence? Dance classes?"

He nodded. "My old hips are stiff as anything, but I can still feint and parry, land a few once or twice in a bout with the youngsters."

"Youngsters? We're the same damned age." I poked his ribs and laughed.

"Of course I still fence, and dance, and keep my acrobatic skills up! It's in my blood, you cheeky bugger. How old were we both when we met on that blasted ship? Eight years old?"

"I'd offer you Howard's job in a flash you know, Lincoln. If you ever change your mind about where you want to live, let me know."

"I'll do that, Eddie, I promise you. Now, about the funeral service. If either you or Theo want to deliver the eulogy, I'll step aside."

"No, you must do it. We both still feel uncomfortable in Anglican churches. It feels like we're interlopers."

"But you don't mind singing?"

I shook my head. "It was Howard's wish. Whether he'd changed his mind or not, remember what he always said?"

"*When I die, I want to hover over the coffin for one last time to hear my friend, Edward Murray, sing 'The Lost Chord', by Arthur Sullivan.*" He said it with same intonation as his brother, his voice so similar to Howie's that I began to cry. It was all too much.

"Hey! No, Eddie, don't do that," he said, taking me into his arms. "He'll be there listening. You can't let him down."

I snuffled over his shoulder, and, my voice thick with tears, told him we'd arranged a small orchestra to accompany the hymns and my solo.

"Will you say something in Bengali before you sing?"

I nodded. It had been our secret language. The way we Mullins Boys talked about our secrets when we didn't want the grown-ups to know what we were talking about.

"Yes," I said. "*Prabhu'I amara mesapalakal amara ya kichu ca'I sabasamaya ami ta-neba …*"

"*The Lord is my shepherd, I shall not want?* The twenty-third psalm?"

"No doubt they'll sing it or say it in English, but it won't be the same now, will it?"

"No, Eddie, you're right. It won't be the same."

*****

The following evening, after the funeral, I fell into bed, exhausted.

Although I'd only had one or two beers at the pub after the interment with the rather large company of former Mullins boys who'd turned up, the reason for my fatigue was emotional. I remembered little of the ceremony itself, except for feeling so overcome when it came time for me to do my bit, that to steady myself I'd had to reach out to grasp the edge of the pulpit. I'd been told to stand there, above the heads of the congregation, to deliver my prayer in Bengali, and then to sing "The Lost Chord", which had been accompanied by the church organ and the orchestra from the Theatre Royal. Even a few of the ladies we'd known as girls in India had appeared at the funeral service and then had reluctantly joined us in the evening at the Lord Wolsey pub. The publican had been gracious enough to turn a blind eye to women drinking in public, even if we were in the private lounge.

The church had been packed for the service, many who'd attended unable to find a place inside and who'd spilled out into King Street. There'd been such a crowd of onlookers several policemen had been fetched to control road traffic and to keep order. The sight of the elite of the city's theatre performers had elicited soft applause as each of them had arrived at the church, and I'd been told the sound of so many trained voices singing the hymns had evoked much weeping from those on the street who were close enough outside to hear.

Just before he'd left the graveyard to return to the police station, Chief Superintendent Abel had reported to me that on top of the two thousand souls within St. James's church, another four hundred had gathered on the roadway and over Queen's Square. The theatre community had gathered en masse to honour one of its own, and as a result the public who supported them had come along to offer their own support to us. It was the way things happened.

The procession from the church to Central Station, in order to board the mortuary train, had been a terrible ordeal for me. Had I not been obliged to support Eileen on one side as we'd followed the hearse on foot, I think I might have fallen to my knees with grief more than once.

And then, at the cemetery, it had been all I could do to control myself as I'd thrown my handful of soil into the open grave and had said farewell to my dearest friend. Had I not glanced up right at that moment and seen my own pain reflected in Andrew's eyes, I may have sobbed out loud and howled my grief to the sky.

"*Bidāẏa āmāra priẏa bandhu,*" I'd said in Bengali. Goodbye, my dearest friend.

"*Ākāśa tōmāra prāṇa rakṣā karuka,*" fifty voices had answered, scattered among the crowd of mourners.

The soft response from all of those who'd been with us in Calcutta had been the final straw.

May heaven guard your soul, they'd replied. It had been more than I'd been able to bear, and I'd turned into Theo's arms and wept. I hadn't cared who'd seen me do it, or what they'd thought at my lack of decorum. My friend was dead, and the person who'd killed him had meant it to be me, lying at the bottom of a cold grave in a polished oak casket.

*****

On the following morning, I arrived at the hall in the laneway behind the Theatre Royal to see the director, Mr. McDaniel, waiting for me at the door. Despite the ordeal of the previous day, I'd decided that Howard would have expected life to continue as it would have done, had he still been alive. The first day of any rehearsal was an important day. I put on a brave face. Even though I felt sad, it helped to have Andrew at my side.

"Oh, Mr. Murray, there's been a dreadful accident," McDaniel said, rushing up to greet me as he saw us turn the corner from King Street.

My stomach went cold. I'd had news of too many accidents of late to hear any news without thinking of the worst. "What's happened?"

"It's Mr. O'Brien. He's broken his leg."

"That's a relief," Andrew said at my side. "Oh, I'm sorry, Mr. McDaniel, that must have sounded terrible."

"I quite understand, Chief Constable. It's a relief to us all not to hear news of another dreadful murder. But, what shall we do? We've no one to sing Masetto!"

"There's no telephone here is there?"

"No, Mr. Murray, the nearest is in Mr. Willings's office at the theatre."

"Leave it with me, Mr. McDaniel, I'll find us a replacement. I have someone in mind. Has Mr. Talbot, Howard's brother, arrived?"

"Yes, sir, he's inside chatting to the other cast members."

"Perhaps you could teach him the fencing moves for my fight with the Commendatore while I sort this out. I shan't be long. When we get to that section we can skip it, and I'll get Lincoln to teach it to me this evening."

"Very good, sir, and thank you, Mr. Murray."

"What will you do?" Andrew asked me, as we crossed the laneway to the stage door entrance of the Theatre Royal.

"The first thing I'll do when I get through the door is to drag you into my dressing room and have my way with you." He'd not come to my room last night, and I'd woken feeling quite abandoned.

"Ah, my kisses are a shilling a piece."

"I've a fiver in my *porte-feuille*; there's a hundred for a start," I said to him, and then, as we arrived at the rear entrance to the theatre, lifted my hat to Mr. Hobbson, the stage door manager. "Morning, Hobbson."

"Good morning, Mr. Murray, Detective Bolton. Is there anything I can help you with?"

"I'm going to pop into my dressing room for a moment. Is it clear?"

"Yes, sir, the ballet won't be in until after eleven this morning."

"Very good, and then I'm going upstairs to see Mr. Willings. I presume he's in?"

"Yes, sir. Shall I let him know you're coming?"

"Tell him I'll be there in ten minutes," I said over my shoulder as we walked down the corridor to the principal dressing room.

"Ten minutes?" Andrew whispered. "You piker!"

"Any longer than that, I'll have your strides off and then you won't know what's hit you."

He laughed, only stopping to push me against the back of the dressing room door and attack my mouth.

"For someone who, until a few days ago, had no knowledge of deep kissing, you've certainly taken to it like a duck to water," I mumbled, coming up for air.

"Shut up, Murray," he said with a smirk. "Maybe you've started something you'll live to regret."

"I certainly hope so—hmm."

*****

"He's not answering," I said, hanging up the connection.

"Who are you trying to reach?" Arnold Willings asked. I'd marched into his office, said a brisk, cordial hello, and then had requested the use of his telephone.

"Julius Harcourt," I said. "Robert O'Brien has broken his leg, and we need a Masetto."

"Julius is downstairs in the foyer. He came in early and asked if he might use the upright rehearsal piano to do some practice before the ballet arrives. Masetto? Are you sure, Edward?"

"He sang it for the touring performances in January. I heard it wasn't bad; apart from his attitude, and that's improved markedly after I had words with him and then gave him a solo in Howard's benefit concert. I'll make sure he understands it's another reward on sufferance of good behaviour, modesty, and hard work. It will do him good to sing with such a strong cast. Everyone is the best there is. Good enough for a *Les Huguenots*."

"What do you mean by that?" Andrew asked.

"Meyerbeer's opera is often described as 'The Night of the Seven Stars', and it's often touted as such, with the seven foremost singers management can find in the main roles."

"Ah, I thought it an overwrought work myself … and if I dare say so, overlong."

"You don't have to sing in it," I replied as we went downstairs to find Harcourt. "At least it's another one in which I get to die early and can go home to put my feet up before everyone else."

I could hear Julius Harcourt singing dominant seventh arpeggios as we came down the stairs towards the foyer. I hummed the foundation note of the exercise, and then smiled to myself. I was rarely wrong when identifying keys in my head.

"If you modify your 'ah' vowel on the third note of the arpeggio, you won't find the highest note quite so awkward," I said as I came up behind him. "Never change to the 'covered' note so blatantly when approaching it from below, Mr. Harcourt. The vowel modification should be subtle, not crash upon the ears like the grinding of tramcar wheels on a tight corner."

"Oh! Mr. Murray, you startled me!" He'd been standing with his back to us in his shirtsleeves. His jacket was draped over the bentwood chair accompanists used when playing the foyer upright piano.

"The highest note is a G? So, sing the first two notes of the four on an open 'ah' vowel. Tip the third note, the D, into an 'aw' sound while keeping the 'ah' space in your mouth, which will lower the larynx a little naturally, so that your high note will not stick out like dog's balls. Like this …"

I demonstrated.

"I shall never have such a ringing top as you, Mr. Murray," he said, his eyes alight.

"Just try what I told you to do." His resultant high note was very much improved. "You see? It would have been even better had you not arched your back. Posture is everything, Mr. Harcourt."

"Dog's balls?" Andrew asked with a grin.

"That's the technical word for it, Andrew."

He suppressed a chuckle at my dry retort.

"I should really like to press you once more for one or two lessons, Mr. Murray," Julius Harcourt asked, much pleased with his effortless top G. "I know you don't have time to teach, however—"

"However, nothing is impossible, Julius, and that's why I'm here. I won't beat about the bush, so I'll get straight to the point. At the beginning of the year you toured with Mr. Cantieri's production of *Don Giovanni*, which I believe was sung in Italian. Am I correct?"

"Yes, Mr. Murray, I sang the role of Masetto."

"I can hear the role sits a little low for you now. I noticed, when you sang at Howard's benefit concert, that your voice sits somewhat higher these days. However, I'm here to offer you an opportunity."

"An opportunity?"

"Yes, Julius. Mr. O'Brien has had an unfortunate accident, and we are now without a Masetto. I'm not the impresario for this production, but I have been asked to solve a problem. Therefore, I'm offering you the opportunity to perform the role, and to understudy me."

"You?" His voice came out almost as a squeak.

"Masetto does not appear until the third scene. I doubt if Mr. McDaniel will get that far with the plotting of the moves before eleven o'clock, so if you'd care to refresh your memory on the section with Zerlina preceding your first aria, we'll see you in the rehearsal hall in an hour."

"But, Mr. Murray … where shall I find a score? I never owned one of my own. It was loaned for the production."

I opened my music satchel and handed him mine. "It's signed by Joseph Beck, the famous Austrian baritone, and was originally his score. So I hope you'll take care of it, Julius … and by the way, when Mr. Solomon contacts you to arrange a contract, I wouldn't settle for less than four guineas a performance. I trust you remember our talk in your hotel room?"

He nodded, clutching the music score to his chest. "I'm very honoured, Mr. Murray—"

"You will find me a friend and a helpful colleague if you behave yourself during rehearsals, Julius. No grandstanding, do you hear me? Comport yourself with humility, take note and follow the professional behaviour of all of the other principal singers, and do not, under any circumstances, sing along with me as you did in *La Bohème*. Are we clear?"

He gulped and held out his hand. I shook it and then bid him good day.

"Plotting of the moves?" Andrew asked as we ascended the staircase.

"It means when the director positions the actors or singers where they're to be on the stage," I replied. "Moving the pieces around, like a game of chess."

"I do believe I may have just witnessed you do something of the sort with Mr. Harcourt, Eddie."

I smiled and squeezed his elbow.

★★★★★

"Is that him?" Sandford asked, nodding towards the corner table of the restaurant in the Australia Hotel.

"No, that's not him. What sort of a person do you think I am, Sandford? You've known me these twenty years. Have I ever been inconsiderate?"

He wiped his lips on his napkin and then snapped his fingers to a passing waiter for another. It was one of his more irritating habits, the public misuse of servants—that's how I saw it anyway.

"I suppose it's another of your conquests—"

I slammed my hand hard on the table. The cutlery rattled, and guests around us turned to stare. I pushed my chair back and stood, red-faced.

"I'm sorry, Edward, I'm sorry. Truly I am, please forgive me."

"I'm going outside for a cigarette and to calm down. I don't want you to come out after me if you don't want a punch on the nose." I beckoned Cooper to follow me onto the terrace, which ran along the building's façade, outside its first-floor dining room.

"I've never seen you with your dander up, Edward," Cooper said.

"It's not a pleasant sight, Cooper," I replied. "I'm sorry you have to witness it. But my nerves are frayed. It's been five days since the attack in the Strand Arcade and nothing. Not even the shadow of the man."

We'd done everything we could to draw him out. Solitary cigarettes outside the rehearsal room while standing in docking bays that were out of sight from the street; Andrew and I eating lunch at the single outside table of a Parisian café in Rowe Street; walking in the Botanical Gardens early in the morning, with not another soul to be seen. All around us, hidden from sight, policemen watching, waiting ... and yet he hadn't poked his nose above water. It worried me.

He patted my arm and smiled at me.

"Why are you smiling?" I asked.

"I'm no fool, Edward," Cooper said. "Chief Constable Bolton has come to life since we came to look out for you. He was an empty vessel before that; rather like those player pianos one sees in the shops these days—very capable but no soul."

I went to speak but he asked me to let him finish. "I know I'm the man who solicited advice from you, but although I'm inexperienced, I can read a man's worth by his ability to speak from inside, like music does to you and to me. Mr. Bolton is a different man in your company. Not only the one I've always admired and respected, but a man who smiles these days, and who is not afraid to let one see those tiny imperfections that make us more human for them."

"Why, Cooper, that's a beautiful observation—and astute," I said.

"I'm quiet because I observe, sir. It comes from being the youngest and being the most bossed about by everyone else. One learns to look for chips in people's armour, and then to judge whether they're weaknesses or strengths."

"Cannot some of them be a bit of both?"

"Like your love for your brother?"

"Come here and let me give you a hug, Cooper," I said. "It's one of affection, nothing more, and it's long overdue. No matter whatever comes of this dreadful situation, or whether your unspoken passion for Miss Bolton eventuates to an understanding or not, I'd like you to know that I now consider you part of our little family."

His embrace was initially stiff, but after a second or two, he relaxed and laughed.

"What's there to laugh about?" I asked.

"I almost fit under your arm, you tall, ugly bugger. Now, where's that smoke we were supposed to come out here for?"

When I returned to Sandford, I brought Cooper to our table with me. I could see the look in the grazier's eyes, and before he could say anything, I spoke. "I know a young man who once wore hired evening wear, Mr. Clarkson, and it didn't seem to bother you one whit in those days. My friend's suit is befitting a gentleman of his profession. Now, behave yourself. I'd like to present Constable Cooper Haddley, who is not only a fine young man, and now friend of Theo's and mine, but also a pianist of outstanding ability."

Cooper shook Sandford's hand, who had risen from his seat. I knew my mention of "outstanding ability" would pique his interest, as he knew me to be a musician who was known to be sparing with his praise unless it was well deserved. Sandford Clarkson was also an avid supporter of the arts, the chairman of the Hunter Valley Musical Appreciation Society, and the chairman of the governing board of the Newcastle Symphony Orchestra. He loved talent, and Cooper had it in abundance.

The main course polished off, and a cigar while thinking about dessert, I could see that Sandford's mind was working. He'd almost done a backflip when Cooper had casually mentioned his concert repertoire of last week, especially when I'd added that Miss Fischer had remarked she'd never heard either played better.

"Which brings me to ask a favour, Mr. Murray, if you don't think this is an inappropriate place to be talking of music," Cooper said.

Sandford chuckled. "There are few places I can think of where the talk of music is inappropriate."

"What's the favour?" I asked.

"Well, it's really in the form of advice."

"Please proceed. I'll do my best."

"Were you aware that your agent, Mr. Solomon, was sitting up the back at Mother's concert?"

"I may have had an inkling ..."

"Well, he's made Hillary and me an offer. Mother would hear nothing of it—"

"You leave your mother to me, Cooper. You're a grown man now. You must stand on your own two feet."

"She was fit to burst. I've never seen her so angry."

"Hell hath no fury than a jealous mother," I said, to Sandford, who'd raised his eyebrows in an "ah, one of those" gestures.

"What was Mr. Solomon's offer, Cooper? I'm interested."

"Well, he's asked Hillary if he'd like to play Debussy's *Suite bergamasque* in a concert at Marrickville Town Hall in August."

"And?"

"And what, Mr. Murray?"

"Oh, for heaven's sake, Cooper. What did he ask *you* to play?"

"It was all Hillary's fault."

"Do I have to put you over my knee and spank it out of you?"

He laughed and then turned the most profound shade of red. "The Mozart Piano Concerto, Number 23, in A major, with the Parramatta symphony orchestra."

Sandford nearly jumped out of his chair. "My boy, you must do it!"

"Well, Hillary volunteered me when Mr. Solomon spoke to us after the concert."

"When will it be, Cooper?" I asked.

"On the twentieth of July."

"Damnation! I will be in New Zealand by then. I would so have loved to hear it. I'm assuming you do know it?"

"Yes, that's why my brother opened his big mouth when Mr. Solomon asked me what I'd like to play."

"He asked *you* what *you'd* like to play?" my dinner host asked.

Sandford Clarkson was rarely lost for words. It was normal for the impresario to tell the soloist what they were to perform. I could see the wheels turning in his head, as I knew they would. The Newcastle Orchestra had a season still undecided in December. I knew, because he'd asked me to sing the *Lieder Eines Fahrenden Gesellen* by Mahler at the same concert, and he'd been worried what to choose for the first half to provide a good contrast and balance. I'd thought a Mozart piano concerto ideal, but I'd let him come to that conclusion by himself.

At the end of the meal, he accompanied us to the top of the staircase. I told Cooper to go ahead, I'd only be a minute.

"Shall we lunch tomorrow?" he asked me.

"I'm afraid I can't, Sandford. We have a flying rig rehearsal and we need to sort the trap out. I'll be in the theatre from twelve until two, and then I simply must get home to have a rest."

"I understand," he said. "I won't pretend I'm not disappointed about what you wrote in your letter, even if it is, as you said, my own habit to spread my largesse discreetly around the area, and it isn't as if there's been a commitment between you and me. I'm happy you've finally allowed yourself to feel for someone like you say you do. I'm only sad that person is not me."

"Were it to have happened, it would have been early on, twenty years ago, Sandford, you know that. I still care for you. It's simply that until I know whether this is really right for me or not, I can't extend any intimacy to you other than friendship."

He stared at me long and hard, holding my hand well after we'd stopped our handshake, and then sighed. "Goodnight, Eddie."

"Goodnight, Sandford," I replied, and then watched him walk to the elevator, whose operator was already standing with the cage door open, waiting for him.

At the bottom of the stairs, a tall handsome figure appeared from near the concierge's desk and joined us.

"Hello, Andrew," I said.

"How was dinner?"

I looked at Cooper. "It worked," I said.

Cooper's look of dawning realisation was a sight to behold. "You knew all along!" he said. "You planned for me to be here?"

"Well, I did arrange for Mr. Solomon to attend your concert, and he was genuinely enchanted. I had nothing to do with his offer, nor will I do when Mr. Clarkson writes to you to ask you to perform at the Newcastle Symphony Orchestra concert in December. But, I have to admit that I'd planned to introduce you to him at some stage during the evening, and had planned to casually mention your ability to play as well as you do. He's a powerful man in the north of the State when it comes to musical engagements, Cooper."

Cooper stopped in the middle of the street and stared at me.

"But, Mr. Murray, I'm a policeman, not a pianist."

"Perhaps you can do both, Cooper?" Andrew said. "Until one day, when you realise that the pianist has been there all along, merely passing time with a badge attached to his keychain."

"But Mother—"

"Mother will be no obstacle, Cooper," I interrupted. "She may be strong, and even angry, but she hasn't crossed swords with the Murray boys yet."

*****

"What's the problem with the trapdoor?" Andrew asked me.

We'd been waiting for half an hour on the stage while the mechanics fiddled around with the opening mechanism.

"It's not the trapdoor itself, but the elevator lift that's the problem. The restraining bar underneath the twin opening flaps has to be strong enough to hold my weight when I stand on them, but then be able to release suddenly, so that I plummet down into the stage void underneath. The audience will think I've disappeared. Closing the trapdoors is no problem either, but regulating their re-opening to coincide with the elevator lift as I rise back up into sight for my bows at the end of the performance seems to be the problem."

Braxton joined us. I couldn't help but smile, it was so rare I ever saw him in anything other than his fine tailored suits or evening wear. Today it was workmen's clothes, an open-necked shirt and flat cap, only the bracers to his trousers showing his expensive taste, they were hand embroidered with musical symbols and doves.

"We're ready for your test now, Edward," he said.

"Cooper is down below?" I asked.

"Yes, he wanted to see how the mechanism works."

The stage was painted in black and white squares, each thirty-six inches on a side. The two squares on which I would place one foot each were marked with red paint at the front edge, which could not be seen from the audience. They were also placed directly behind the centre stage marking on the old float panel, which was now rigged with electric footlights. There were many safeguards to make sure I was standing correctly, for, if I did not, it would be easy to either hit my chin or the back of my head with the sudden abrupt drop of eight feet into the under-stage void. Trapdoors were notoriously dangerous; there had been not one or two deaths across the world caused by malfunctions.

"Stand back, Edward," Braxton said and then gave a hand signal to two stagehands who loaded sandbags, corresponding to my weight, evenly distributed across the two panels. He stamped on the stage three times, and then the trapdoor opened, the sandbags plummeted below, and the trap closed over.

"There'll be a flash pot, right in front of the traps," I explained to Andrew. "By the time the audience's eyes have adjusted, it will appear to them that I've disappeared into thin air."

"May I go downstairs and look at what happens from underneath?" Andrew asked.

"Of course you may," Braxton said, and then called out for Simon, who'd been arguing with one of the flymen in the wings.

"Morning, Simon," I said. "How are you?"

"I'm very well, thank you, Mr. Murray. I have to say that I haven't stopped crying since your 'Lost Chord' at Mr. Talbot's funeral. I've never heard anything so beautiful in my life."

"Hear, hear!" Braxton said, accompanied by nods and agreement of the mechanicals who'd gathered around to help with setting the trapdoor.

"Why, thank you, gentlemen," I said. "I can't tell you how hard it was to get through to the end without my voice cracking."

"This way, Mr. Bolton, if you please," Simon said to Andrew, ushering him into the opposite prompt wings, to the door to the stairway that led to the under-stage area.

"Have you two ...?" Braxton whispered to me while we waited for Andrew to get into place.

"No," I whispered back. "But it was within a hair's breadth last night, I can tell you. I had to grab the base of my prick and squeeze my testicles to stop myself losing control."

"You should have asked him to do it for you," he said with a chuckle.

"He was sound asleep next to me. It was all I could do not to wake him."

"You sleep together?" I nodded. "My God, Eddie, how do you control yourself?"

"With extreme difficulty—"

"Ready!" Andrew's voice called out from under the stage.

I got into position, checked that each foot was dead centre in the middle of the two designated squares, and then signalled to the prompt corner that I was ready. *Kachunk!* I fell down onto a padded mattress. Terry Smith, the catcher, in place behind me to support me if I'd fallen backwards off the padded paillasses.

I helped him pull them out of the way and then stood on the riser platform. "Come," I said to Andrew, beckoning him to my side. I put my arm around him and told Terry we were ready. He pushed the lever at the side of the trap scaffolding, which activated the hydraulic system, and Andrew and I rose noiselessly into the light.

"And that's how it's done!" I said to my companion, whose face was bright with delight.

"You've six minutes down there while the final sextet is sung," Braxton said. "Have you decided whether you'll change into the first scene costume, or stay as you are?"

"As I'm nearly naked in both, I think I'll stay in the red tights and open doublet. I'll ask for a pitcher of water and mug, if you don't mind. There's a lot of running around in the last scene, and I'd like to whet my whistle before I reappear."

"Very good, I'll see to it," Braxton said. "Would you like to rehearse the balcony leap once more? It will only take five minutes to get the set into place."

I'd done it once or twice before, leaping from one balcony to the other, using the chandelier as a swing. It was a tried and true method for Don Giovanni to escape from the festivities at the end of the finale of Act One.

"Well, if it's no trouble, yes, that would be good. Perhaps someone can fetch Mr. Harcourt from the dressing room so he can try the trap before we do that? I'm not expecting anything to happen between now and tonight, but it would be terrifying for him if he hadn't done it at least once. After that, we can both take turns practising the balcony leap."

"Simon, fetch Julius please!" Braxton called out.

McDaniel's mise-en-scène was nothing out of the ordinary. I'd sung several productions of *Don Giovanni* that were as economical in their complexity of movement on the stage. This new mounting had splendid sets and sumptuous, eye-catching costumes. The singers were the best there were, so it would no doubt be a success.

There were far too many changes of clothing for my taste, but Andrew had assured me that the ladies would swoon in my first and last costumes, which had me bare chested, and there would no doubt be an ovation for the serenade at the beginning of Act Two. Upon entering the scene, I was costumed in a full-length dark blue velvet cape, wearing a "domino" carnival half-mask covering my eyes, and a large, beplumed tricorne. I always played my own mandolin when singing *"Deh vieni alla finestra*", and the cape was rigged so that it would fall from my shoulders during the introduction to the second verse, revealing me naked from the waist up and wearing only dark blue tights. It was still somewhat of a novelty in an era when ladies on the stage were covered from neck to knees in flesh-coloured, long-sleeved body stockings.

Mr. McDaniel certainly had an eye for the theatrical—and also for comely men wearing as few pieces of clothing as possible without the censor closing the performance.

I made the first few passes between the balconies easily. Unseen by the audience, a belt with two wires attached to the back prevented any serious accident. We were guided across the space by mechanicals in the wings who were trained in stage flying—the same tricks used by Theo on his flying horse in *The Arabian Nights*.

When it came to his turn, I could see Julius loved it. I remembered my first *Don Giovanni*, and how excited I'd been. Truth be told, Mozart's Count Almaviva in *Le Nozze di Figaro* was a finer role. There was so much more depth to the character, and the big aria was a wonderful showpiece. In the hands of an inexperienced performer, Don Giovanni himself could appear to be a secondary character in an opera that bore his name. One learned more about the inner workings of the man from those who sang about him than one did from the man himself. However, over the years, I'd learned much from working with and observing other men who'd sung the title role. The insinuations, shades of colour, and word use in the recitatives were the answer. The finesse of their delivery was what made a could-be pastiche melodrama villain into a believable man of substance and wicked purpose.

"Do you remember your first?" a voice said from my side.

"Oh, hello, Chase," I said, shaking hands with Julius Harcourt's romantic partner. "He's doing well, isn't he?"

"Who, Julius? Ever since your plain talk with him two weeks ago, he seems to have turned a corner. I think the opportunity you gave him to stand in for you at *Die Fledermaus*, and then his solo at Howard's benefit, and now this …"

"One forgets what it's like to be twenty-five," I said.

"That's how old you were when you sang your first Don Giovanni. I was there. Remember?"

"It was in the old Her Majesty's. How could I forget? You were so dashing back then, all the girls chasing you."

"You mean I'm not dashing anymore?"

I laughed. "You cut a very fine figure, Mr. Osborne. I'm sure Julius appreciates every inch of it."

He winked at me and chortled. Theatre talk.

"I've heard a rumour ..."

"Does anyone else know?"

"I haven't told him, if that's what you're asking."

"Well, I'd be grateful if you could keep it to yourself until it's certain. Theo and I are still negotiating to buy this production of *Don Giovanni* from Mr. McDaniel. He doesn't have the cash to travel it as we do. We wouldn't make a lot of money in Brisbane, but if we brought it back here afterwards, we'd cover costs for both cities and be able to put something aside for ourselves."

"When were you thinking of remounting it?"

"Well, if we can negotiate a suitable price for sets and costumes, perhaps next March, at the beginning of the season. *La Bohème* should be ready for a few more performances too, and then ..."

"And then?"

"Well, our idea is to mount our own four-week-long season of three operas. We've all but cleaned out the bank with the final payment on our house, and although there are plenty of bookings in our diaries, we'd really like to replenish our savings."

"The third opera?"

"Now, if I tell you, I might have to tie you up and punish you severely," I said with a chuckle.

"Now there's a threat I might quite enjoy."

We both laughed. There was nothing to it again. Merely theatre people exchanging unseemly banter between themselves.

"*Les Contes d'Hoffman*," I said in a whisper.

"It's no secret it's a work you've always wanted to do," he said.

"The aria you performed at the benefit is among my favourites that you sing, Mr. Murray."

"Well, if we do mount it, it will make taxing work for me. As they don't appear at the same time, I'll perform the three baritone roles in the opera. That means I might be prepared to hand over one or two matinee performances of *Don Giovanni* to a worthy understudy during the four-week run of all three operas."

"He'll be beside himself."

"Yes, perhaps. But not before it comes from the horse's mouth. Understood?"

"My lips are sealed. But, thank you, sir."

"It will depend on how well he sings his Masetto, of course."

"I promise I'll say nothing."

"Very good, Chase. I'll keep you to your word. And now, I'm being summoned to a late lunch and then a kip. I'll see you back here around six tonight."

"Good day to you, Mr. Murray … and thank you again. From us both. *Toi, toi, toi* for tonight!"

I patted his back and went to find Andrew and Cooper, who were chatting in the corner of the stage with Braxton.

CHAPTER 12

To non-performers, the concept of reciprocity between the artist and the audience sometimes leaves them bemused.

For example, a lacklustre audience can drag down the energy of the performers. Whether it's a matinee performance and the theatre is too hot, or famously, a Tuesday or Thursday night when audience members behave as if they'd rather be elsewhere, despite the cost of their tickets, an unresponsive audience can really sap the energy of we performers on the stage. Performances can feel either like pushing a laden cart up a steep hill, or be so exhilarating actors are unable to sleep with the rush of excitement they carry home from the theatre.

The very best presentations are those when the audience and the performers feed upon each other's enthusiasm and excitement.

So far, tonight's *Don Giovanni* had been one such occasion.

My fellow performers had been in splendid voice. The audience had gasped and applauded vigorously at the revelations of each new scene and after the appearance of each beautiful costume. They'd cheered and clapped in the stalls and the balconies, and stomped on the floor in the Gods while yelling for encores, but the conductor, Maestro Gagliani, and Mr. McDaniel, the impresario and stage director, had both decided that, apart from the traditional encore of *"Fin ch'han dal Vino"* or the "Champagne Aria", as it was commonly known, there would be no giving in to cries of encore!, no matter how long the applause held up the performance.

The second rendition of the aria, already very fast and full of words, was usually given at a brisker tempo, to showcase the performer's alacrity. I always had to have my wits about me when I sang it as an encore, one tiny slip of the tricky words, and bars would go past before I would be able to catch up again. I'd seen many performers stumble, and always cursed under my breath before I was to sing it— another example of theatre superstition, the use of foul language to ward off misfortune.

In our mounting, the opera was given in its entirety; something unusual of late, as most Mozart works were curtailed in some manner. It had been over a decade since I'd last performed in a complete version that included every note Mozart had written. I adored it, especially as our two leading ladies, the sisters Montessori, Olivia and Portia, were singing Donna Anna and Donna Elvira respectively. They were the stars of our times. Originally Sally and Dora Butterworth from Nyngan in outback New South Wales, a good teacher, a change of location, and exotic new names had propelled them into the public's eye as singers of exceeding reputation and ability.

Olivia Montessori's *"Or Sai Chi l'onore"* had stopped the opera for a good three or four minutes with applause, but her sister's wonderful *"Mi tradi"* in Act Two had left me breathless. I'd watched it from the wings. So rarely performed because of its impossibly long phrases, with seemingly nowhere to breathe, she'd thrown it off with aplomb, theatrical fury, and superb vocal colour and musicianship.

I was proud to be a member of an ensemble of superlative artists, not merely a group of very good singers thrown together, ad hoc, with no real sense of communication between each other, as was so often the case when performing with divas and divos.

I'd nearly laughed halfway through the serenade at the beginning of Act Two. As the cloak had fallen from my shoulders and I'd flung the tricorne from my head, a loud "oh!" had issued from the audience at the sight of my bare torso. My supressed laughter had not been because of the audience's "oh!" but because of Miss Portia Montessori, who had raised her fan to hide her face, and then had given me a saucy wink and a very lewd, open-mouthed passing of her tongue over her lips.

Without Howard to do his wonderful artistry on my chest, I'd called Theo backstage before the opera had started, and then during the interval to freshen it up. He didn't have Howard's hand, but he was very good, although a little heavy-handed. After his first attempt I looked rather less "athletic" in build and more like Eugen Sandow, the famous wrestler and strongman.

"Here, use your fingers and blend these shadows on his stomach while I outline his pectoral muscles," Theo had said to Andrew, with a sly wink aimed at me.

I'd caught his wrist after a few moments. "I don't need distractions of this sort, Andrew," I'd said and had then smiled at him.

My favourite part of the opera was the last scene, immediately before the concerted finale, the banquet at which Don Giovanni is consigned the eternal flames of hell. Most productions usually revolved around variations of the same action—Don Giovanni disappearing under the table in a clap of thunder and a flash of lightning. However, in this current mounting, Mr. McDaniel had produced a coup-de-théâtre.

The Commendatore's appearance at the banquet was an artful management of metamorphosis. Tables and chairs disappearing into the flies, or collapsing flat to the floor to give the illusion that they'd vanished. The players in Don Giovanni's onstage orchestra ripping hidden cords that turned their formal court musicians' costumes into those of demons, while others, suspended on wires, flew across the stage on high, trailing streamers of red, orange, and yellow, besparkled with sequins, which caught the light and gave the appearance of flames.

As these things took place, the large chair in which I'd been sitting at the head of the banquet table split open to reveal the Commendatore, clad in a costume that was the exact replica of his graveside statue. The audience gasped and cheered.

While the scene progressed, the demons swirled around me, plucking at my costume, and bursts of real flame shot up from hidden gas jets in the stage floor behind us. During all of this, there were three pounds, two shillings, and sixpence worth of fireworks being set off in contained areas upstage. I'd watched the technicians perform their rehearsal. It took my breath away—and I'd seen many such things during my days on the stage.

"*Pentiti!*" the Commendatore sang, urging me to repent.

"*No!*" I sang in reply.

This exchange was repeated several times, until I sang a final, declared, "*No!*", after which the Commendatore consigned me to oblivion, and I began to writhe, singing about the agonies of pain that already ran through my body in preparation for eternal torment.

It was at that point that placement became critical, and I began to move, surrounded by my tormenting demons, to get myself centre stage, so that I could make sure I was aligned correctly over the trapdoor openings.

"*Chi l'anima mi lascera?*" I sang, moving slowly downstage. Red and yellow lighting effects played over the scenery behind me—the flames of hell. I knew Catherine wheels had now been lit and were whirling, throwing out circles of sparks over strategically placed tin receptacles in the stage floor, as they rose up and down in the air on invisible wires.

"*Chi m'agita le viscere?*" I placed my feet securely in the centre of the squares that were the top of the trapdoor.

"*Che strazio, ohimè, che smania! Che inferno! Ah! Che orror!*" And then, on the final "*Ah!*", written on a D, the tonic note of the key, I instead sang my signature high note, one for which I was famous when performing this role: a long, sustained top A.

The audience roared its appreciation, the flash pot exploded, and I fell down into the subfloor area of the stage.

*****

For a moment I thought I'd hit my head, or something had fallen over my eyes. It was pitch black.

The thud from above made me aware the wooden carpenter's scene had been flown in and had bounced slightly on the stage floor. It was immediately followed by the soft whirr of electric motors as huge fans at very back of the theatre powered up, sucking the smoke from the stage behind the backdrop through large grilles placed high above the gridiron. I could hear the scrabble of technicians' feet as they rushed around, checking there were no sparks still glowing from the pyrotechnics.

"Terry?" I called out. During rehearsals, we'd arranged he would be standing next to the mattress at the bottom of the trapdoor scaffold, ready to catch me, in case I landed badly and rolled backwards. Every time we'd rehearsed the fall, he'd extended a hand to help me to my feet. However, there was no sign of him. I look around in the darkness, waiting for my eyes to adjust. There were normally two or three dim safety bulbs under the stage that lit up the space. Perhaps an electric fuse had blown? I got to my feet and reached out, fumbling for the wall opposite the trapdoor shaft, when something crunched under my feet. It was thin glass; it could only have been a broken light bulb.

My stomach went cold. "Terry?" I shouted, inching my way forward in the dark until I tripped over something, falling forward and landing on my knees. I felt about in the darkness and touched a man's leg. "Terry!" I yelled, running my hands up his body, thinking he'd had a heart attack … until my hands reached his shirtfront—it was wet and warm.

Above me, I could hear my colleagues singing loudly, demanding that Don Giovanni's servant, Leporello, tell them what had become of his master.

"Is anybody here?" I yelled. I could scarcely hear my own voice. It was drowned by the voices of my colleagues above me, and the sound of the orchestra through the back wall of the pit.

I scuttled backwards to brace myself against one of the uprights of the trapdoor scaffolding. I crouched on my toes, tensing my calf muscles, ready to spring away from any attack. Why was Adam Doland playing with me? It could only have been him. Surely he knew I was here?

"Adam?" I called out. There was no answer.

Gradually, as my eyes got used to the dark, I began to see a little. A small space around the former float well at the front of the stage area allowed a sliver of light to shine down into the gloom. Its illumination was barely enough to see anything, but better than the deep blackness I'd struggled with after falling down from above, out of the bright lights on the stage. I thought I heard a sound. For a moment I thought Terry Smith had regained consciousness and was not dead. I scuttled across to his body, still keeping low. "Terry?"

It was then, now I'd adjusted to the near darkness, I saw he would never respond. His throat had been cut.

I looked around me, trying to make out shapes in the darkness. Adam Doland must have been down here somewhere. I stood slowly, and then inched towards the entrance door to the under-stage space. I knew where it was, off to my left. If I could get there before he attacked me, I might have a chance to escape.

The singing above ceased and the orchestra fell silent. It was a natural cadence in the score, right before the point at which Don Ottavio sings his hauntingly beautiful, "*Or, che tutti, o mio tesoro.*" It was very lightly scored, and in the relative quiet, over Mr. Greco's floating tones, I heard a soft voice calling for help.

"Help me! Somebody help me."

"Cooper!" I screamed. What was he doing here? I ran towards the sound of his voice.

His legs appeared first in the gloom, and then, as I got even closer, I saw he was propped up against the door to the underfloor space, clutching his shoulder. A large, dark stain spread out over the floor next to him. This time, my voice was a shriek, "Cooper!"

"Oh, Mr. Murray, thank God you're here," he said as I crouched next to him. "He surprised me."

"Shh! Stay calm and try not to speak, Cooper. I'll get help!"

"Wait!" he said and then drew my head down close to his mouth. "I need to tell you what happened."

"Save your strength, it can wait."

"No, no. You don't understand, Mr. Murray. You need to know."

"Very well, but—"

He grabbed my bicep and groaned loudly, and then hissed between his clenched teeth. "Please, listen to what I have to tell you."

"Very well," I replied, "but make it brief, for heaven's sake."

"I came down here immediately after the start of the banquet scene to keep an eye out for you. It's where I was rostered to be this evening for this part of the opera. But when I got here, I found Mr. Smith's body. When I bent over to see if he was still breathing, someone jumped on me from behind."

The words came out in quick snatches, with pauses in the middle of his sentences. He was obviously not only in shock but also in a great deal of pain. The handle of one of Naddo's daggers protruded from between his fingers. He'd been stabbed in the upper chest, just below the collarbone.

"Was it Adam Doland?"

"I think it must have been. When I tried to grapple with him, he whacked me over the side of the head, knocking me to the ground. He kicked me and then said I should tell you that you're next."

"Did you see where he went?"

"Yes, upstairs. He locked the door behind him. I managed to get this far and tried to get out, but ..."

Even though it was still very dark, I could see much better now. A long streak of blood ran down the door from the handle and behind Cooper's wounded shoulder.

"I banged and yelled, but eventually my legs gave way, Mr. Murray. I'm so sorry ..." He began to cry. I knew it pained him to show such emotion as he kept shaking his head and saying he was sorry.

I shushed him and held his cheek against mine, careful not to jar the knife handle. "Save your strength, Cooper. I'll have a weep along with you once we get you out of here. Let me see how badly you're hurt."

I placed my hand on his jacket, directly underneath the dagger hilt. His coat was soaked in blood. I threw off my pump shoes and then ripped off my tights and pressed them against his chest, under the handle of the dagger, and told him to press them tightly against his chest. I got to my feet and began to bang with both fists as hard as I could against the door, calling out for help at the top of my voice over and over. I knew it was in vain, but I tried. There was simply too much noise from the combination of my colleagues singing above, and the sound of the orchestra.

"Mr. Murray, please help me, I'm afraid I'm going to—"

Up above us, Leporello had just finished his solo, telling the other five characters on the stage what he intended to do in the future—to find another master.

"Quickly, put your arm around my shoulder," I said, and then lifted Cooper into my arms. He screamed with pain, but I rushed to the lift platform and urged him to keep his legs and arms tight against my body. Bracing myself, I leaned over and threw the lever.

As my colleagues began to sing, "*Questo è il fin, di chi fa mal, di chi fa mal,*" I rose into view slowly from below, Cooper in my arms, his blood smeared over my body. Apart from my dance belt, I was naked and covered in gore.

It was Portia Montessori who alerted the audience that this was no theatrical effect. She stopped singing mid-phrase, screamed loudly, and then fainted, falling into the arms of Elio Greco. The orchestra stopped playing, and in the brief silence before the audience erupted with cries of horror and disbelief, I fell to my knees and screamed into the wings, "Andrew, for God's sake, get help! Doland's still in the theatre!"

Pandemonium broke out, both in the auditorium and in the wings. Andrew and Braxton almost collided, running in from opposite sides of the stage.

"Get a doctor!" I said urgently.

"Mr. Murray ..." Cooper said softly. "You're crying!"

"Hang tight, my friend," I whispered into his ear. I was crying with fright. He sounded so weak. "The most famous surgeons in the city are sitting out there in the audience. We'll take care of you, never fear."

Andrew caught my eye. I wondered if I looked as pale under my makeup as he did.

"Make way! Make way!" I heard and then looked up.

Maestro Gagliani was assisting Sir Terrence Molesworth, the Surgeon General, up over the apron of the stage from the pit. I guessed he was in his usual opening-night seats, centre front row of the stalls, and had climbed over the orchestra railing that separated the pit from the seats in the auditorium.

"Thank you!" I mouthed to the principal bassist, whose head was showing over the edge of the stage from the pit. Sir Terrence had climbed up on his shoulders, and was getting a hoist up onto the stage apron by several of the taller orchestra members.

*****

I was beside myself with anxiety, standing barefoot outside in the laneway, holding Cooper's hand as two assistants loaded him on a stretcher into the ambulance van.

"There are two horses, Cooper," I said fretfully, "you'll be at the hospital in no time."

"Thank you, Edward," he said, smiling at me wanly. "Look, I can wriggle my fingers."

It was the thing I'd been obsessing over—if he could move his fingers and his hands, no nerves had been severed. However, I did remember Sir Terrence whispering to me he wouldn't know the full extent of the damage until he removed the dagger.

It was raining lightly, and I became aware that I was still all but naked underneath one of the cloaks we used to protect our costumes when moving back and forth between the stage and our dressing rooms.

"Go back inside, Mr. Murray," the surgeon said to me. His carriage had arrived behind the hospital wagon. "If you come to the hospital in an hour, we'll have more news. However, I think it better that you return to your hotel and check with me in the morning. Try to get some rest. Have a strong cup of tea with plenty of sugar. You've had a very bad shock."

I felt Andrew's arm around my shoulder, and then Theo's voice begging me to get out of the rain.

"I'll see you shortly, Cooper, I promise."

"Please, Edward, send someone to tell Mother and Father, and apologise to Miss Bolton that I won't be able to call tomorrow afternoon."

"I'll look after that," Andrew said from my side. "Louise is very anxious for you."

"She is?"

"Of course, she is, Cooper," he said.

I leaned forward and kissed his cheek. "Be strong. I have to go. The ambulance is waiting."

I watched until they closed the twin rear doors of the vehicle, before turning to go back inside, accompanied by a round of applause from the members of the cast who'd braved the rain to see Cooper off. I'd done nothing, except think on my feet. I deserved no praise. It's what anyone would have done for a friend.

"Let's get you home to the hotel and into the shower," Andrew whispered.

I looked at him, desperate to kiss him, even though we were surrounded by people.

"What shall we do?" I asked.

"We can talk about that after I've scrubbed you clean."

"What did you just say?"

"You heard me, Eddie," he said, leaning close. "I'm not prepared to wait any longer ... had that madman—"

"I think I simply want to be held, Andy. I think I'd like that far more than anything tonight, if you don't mind."

"I'll see what I can do," he said as Theo reached us. "Although holding you is such a hardship." He squeezed my waist and winked.

"He got away," Theo said as he opened my dressing room door for us. "He ran up through the fly staircase into the loft, and then kicked open one of the old gas lighting ventilators. Three of the riggers ran after him, but he escaped across the roof."

"What?" Andrew said. "You mean he waited around?"

"It seems he was hiding backstage, waiting to witness the confusion he'd caused. One of the mechanicals noticed him take off like a rabbit when you appeared holding Cooper in your arms. The man who spotted him sounded the alarm and off they went after him."

"Where were you?" I asked.

"I'm sorry, Eddie. I know I should have come back to see if you were alright, but I know your body movements too well. I could see from where I was sitting in the front row of the circle with Andrew's parents you weren't injured. And then Louise fainted, so I carried her down to the foyer."

"Louise? Is she all right?" Andrew sounded alarmed.

"Yes, Andrew. There's nothing to worry about. Your mother brought her around in a trice with the vinaigrette from her reticule. No one but me had any idea which one of you was injured. But I knew immediately who'd done it. It could have been no one else but Doland. I left Louise with your parents on the chaise longue in the entrance hall and then ran through the theatre to the pass door. Men up in the gridiron were yelling he'd headed across the tops of the buildings down towards George Street. So, I tore out the stage door and ran down Rowe Street, looking up, trying to see where he might be heading. The three flymen were running over rooftops, calling out to one another, but there was no sign of him."

"Who made tea?" I saw the pot on my dressing room table.

"I did," Lincoln Talbot said, reaching out for my cloak.

I turned my back to him and allowed him to take it from my shoulders. He draped it over the chair in front of my makeup bench and then kneeled down to pull off my dance belt and ball bag.

"Where did you come from, Lincoln?" I asked. "I thought you were in the audience."

"I was, in the row behind Andrew's parents and Theo. Feels like old days, stripping you naked," he added with a grin.

"Really?" Andrew asked.

"Not like that, Constable. I've always been a petticoat man. But I did my fair share of work backstage, and more than once helping my brother in the dressing room. I'm a valet by trade these days. Seen more of these dangly bits than you've had breakfasts," he said, pinching my scrotum, and then ducking as I tried to slap him.

Lincoln and Howard both; no boundaries when it came to private areas of either Theo's or my bodies, but no interest in them either.

"Where's Gideon?" I asked. It should have been him helping me out of my clothes, not Lincoln.

"Here I am," the boy said, poking his head around the dressing room door. "Went to get this." He held up a bottle of very good brandy. "Mr. Willings will never know it's missing."

I lifted the lid of the teapot and poured the contents of my cup into it, and then held it out to Gideon. "Fill to the top, please," I said.

"I thought Sir Terrence said strong tea with sugar," Andrew said with a feigned frown.

"Two of these down the hatch, and then I'll be ready for tea," I said.

He shook his head and tsk tsk'd, but I pulled him into my arms and kissed him deeply in front of my brother and my friends. He barely resisted.

"That's my brother," Theo murmured. "Takes a murder to get him fired up."

"Oh, I've been fired up for quite a long time, Theo," I replied after I'd released Andrew's mouth from my own.

"It's been me that's been the problem," Andrew said over my shoulder to my brother.

"How pleased I am to hear you say those words using the past tense," Theo said. "I think I'd like to drink to that."

"That was a first for me, gentlemen," Andrew said, moving from my arms. "Embraced intimately by a naked man in front of three other fully clothed men. I think that's enough excitement for the moment. I need to see if my sister is all right. Would you show me the way, Theo?"

"Of course," my brother said and then threw down his full cup of brandy in three loud gulps.

"Don't go anywhere until I come back, you hear me," Andrew said to me.

"Yes, sir," I replied with a smile. He kissed my cheek and then made to leave with Theo, but stopped inside the dressing room door when someone knocked. Gideon opened it. I heard the man's voice and knew instantly who it was.

"Would you please tell Mr. Murray that Sandford Clarkson is here to see him?"

"Come in, please, Sandford," I called out.

It was the strangest of tableaux: Me, Theo, Lincoln—who'd known Sandford before he went to New Zealand—and Andrew, all caught frozen in mid-action as my old friend entered the room. Sandford made no move to embrace me, but his eyes flickered around the room to each of my companions, acknowledging Lincoln, smiling at Theo, his gaze lingering on Andrew.

"I've come to see how you are, Edward," he said, turning to me.

I moved to him and took him in my arms. I'd known him and shared his bed for twenty years. It was not that I did not care about him, and it was obvious he felt ill-at-ease and, at the same time, concerned for my welfare.

"Shall we leave, Eddie?" My brother was trying to be solicitous.

"Could you give us a moment please?"

Sandford smiled, shaking hands with Lincoln and Theo as they left the room. He asked Andrew to stay behind.

"Sandford, this is Chief Constable Andrew Bolton," I said, mindful they'd not been formally introduced. I'd known Sandford would feel uncomfortable until initial pleasantries had been taken care of.

"I was the first to jump to my feet when I saw you rise into view with Constable Haddley in your arms, Edward. I was about to leap onto the stage, until I realised the first person to arrive at your side was Mr. Bolton here …"

"Sandford—"

"No, no! I'm not here to make a scene, but I really wanted to thank you for the magnificence of your performance tonight, and to check you'd not been injured."

"No, thank you, I wasn't injured, merely scared for Constable Haddley's—"

"Please take care of him," Sandford said, suddenly, to Andrew, his eyes brimming with tears. "You are the luckiest man on God's earth—"

"Sandford, please," I said. "No one set out to hurt you."

"I think I should leave," Andrew said.

"Please, don't go, Constable Bolton. I wanted to meet you, for no other reason than to wish you both well while you were together at the same time and in the same place. I rather hope that when the dust settles, you both might visit Cliften Grange. Perhaps when Constable Haddley comes to play the Mozart concerto at the end of the year and when you're to sing the Mahler song cycle, Edward?"

"Then you've engaged Cooper?" I asked.

"I've sent the letter to Elias Solomon. Negotiations have begun. I'd rather like you to keep the news to yourself until the contract is issued?"

"Well, of course—"

A loud knock at my door and the announcement that his carriage had arrived caused Sandford to tell us he had to leave. He'd decided to return to Newcastle that evening, on the midnight train service.

"Please send me news of Constable Haddley? If there's anything he or his family needs, you know I'd be only too happy to help. Perhaps you could telephone me or send me a cable after you've been to see him to let me know how he's faring?"

"Of course I will, Sandford. He'll be touched at your concern."

"Goodbye, Constable Bolton. It's been a great pleasure," he said, extending his hand to Andrew, who took it and returned the same solicitation.

"Goodbye, Eddie," he said to me, standing back as I moved to embrace him again before he left, but holding out his hand to me instead.

"Travel safely, Sandford," I said.

He lifted his hat to both of us, and then left.

And then he was gone. Andrew folded me into his arms and swayed gently.

"Are you all right?" he said.

"Yes, Andrew, everything's as it should be, but I'm desperate to get home now."

"Shall I take you?"

I turned in his arms and kissed him. "Won't you be needed here?"

He sighed. "Most likely. I need to check on Louise before I do anything, but I'll be back at the hotel shortly. I'll get one of my men to stand outside your dressing room now and to escort you back to the Metropole. I'll be with you in half an hour; three quarters at the most."

"Ha! Unlikely, but please forgive me if I don't wait up?"

"Eddie …"

"Yes?"

"He's a real gentleman. I doubt if I'd have been so kind and solicitous had I been in his place."

"He knew it would happen one day. He's not the sort of person to make a scene, and from the way he looked at you I knew he was quite taken with you, Chief Constable Bolton."

"How could you tell that? He doesn't know who I am. He knows nothing about me."

"Taken, meaning he'd like to get his hands down your pants type of taken with you."

"Good heavens, Eddie. I think he was rather too upset to be thinking those thoughts."

I shook my head slowly. "Alas no, Andrew. And it's one of the reasons I was never able to fall in love with him. He desperately wanted me, but not just me alone, if you understand. Sandford is a man who thrives on adoration. He'd never have been happy with one beau. There'd still be a stable of others kept discreetly at a distance, and his eye was always roving, even when we were out together. It annoyed the tripe out of me."

"Even when you were out together, he was admiring others? I don't understand."

"There's no need, Andy. No need at all. Some men have straying eyes, and commitment is not for them, no matter how much they avow an eternal devotion."

"I couldn't live my life like that."

"Nor I, Mr. Bolton, and there's your answer."

"Answer? I wasn't aware I'd posed a question."

I laughed. "Very good. Just remember what I've said. It will save you asking me when it's time."

"I've no idea what you could possibly mean," he said, his eyes glowing, despite his disavowal. "Now, get some clothes on and go home. I'll be there in half an hour."

I raised my eyebrows. I knew he wouldn't be, but I smiled, nonetheless.

"You're shaking," he whispered into my ear, his arms still around me.

"It's starting to hit home. I think I need to sit down."

He strode to the door and pulled it open, speaking into the corridor. "Lincoln, can you see if there's a doctor around? Mr. Murray is not feeling well."

Lincoln burst into the room, but I laughed, waving my hand to signal I was all right. "I'm merely very, very tired, and I have had a bit of a fright. There's no need for a doctor."

"Are you sure, Eddie?" Lincoln tended to fuss, as his brother had. I appreciated the concern but asked him to help me get into my clothes.

"There's a crowd waiting outside the stage door," he said, as he helped me into my shirt. "A lot of those who've been cleared by the police have returned, anxious for your well-being."

I glanced at Andrew and sighed. "This is the life, my friend. I'll have to make an appearance at the stage door and wave to the crowd. One gets used to it."

"I'm looking forward to the opportunity," he replied.

Lincoln smiled as he inserted my shirt studs. "I'll add an amen to that," he whispered with a cheeky wink.

"Me too," I whispered back, but in Bengali.

CHAPTER 13

The sun woke me. I glanced at my bedside clock. It was nine already, and at my side the bed looked unslept in.

When I'd left the theatre last night, I suppose I should have realised Andrew wouldn't be coming home, as he'd said, within half an hour. There'd been police everywhere. The doors of the theatre and backstage had been locked and every single person in both the audience and backstage had been scrutinised by a member of the constabulary as they'd left, each one of whom had a small photograph of Adam Doland in his hand, checking faces.

Chief Superintendent Morris had insisted on it, even though Doland had been seen scampering across the rooftops away from the theatre. "He wouldn't be the first rascal to retrace his steps in the hope we'd look everywhere else than here," he'd said.

I pulled on my dressing gown and wandered out into the living area. I could smell coffee. The pot was on the spirit warmer and Constable Ward was sitting at the dining table, his legs crossed, reading the newspaper.

"You made quite a splash last night," he said, holding up the newssheet. On the front page was a melodramatic engraving of me standing in the middle of the stage, holding Cooper in my arms. I grimaced. I thought it looked like an advertising leaflet for a cheap act at the Tivoli. However, the article went as far as naming Adam Doland, with the superintendent's statement that he was believed to be linked to the other recent murders associated with my name.

I couldn't help think it was foolhardy; however, what was done, was done.

"Telegram for you, Mr. Murray," Ward said, sliding the envelope across the table.

"Chief Constable Bolton?" I asked.

"Got in half an hour ago," he replied. "Dead on his feet. Was at the hospital until six, after which he went to visit Constable Haddley's family."

I opened the telegram. It was from Andrew, written out by the telegraph officer in very bad handwriting. It crossed my mind that the early shift at the General Post Office must be staffed with exhausted clerks at the end of their twelve-hour rosters.

> *Cooper recovering well. Lost a lot of blood, but given time, he will regain full function of his arm. I thought you should know directly from me in case you woke early. I'm off to visit his mother and father to break the news of his successful operation. I'll go straight to bed when I get back to the hotel. Wake me when it's time for lunch. Andrew.*

No shorthand telegrams for him. It made me smile. I supposed the police department didn't have to pay by the word. I poured a cup of coffee and wandered into Andrew's apartment. He was stretched out, fully dressed apart from his jacket, face down on his bed, snoring quietly into the pillow.

I didn't know whether to wake him or leave him be, so merely took off his shoes and covered him with the counterpane, which had fallen onto the floor. I sat next to him on the bed for a moment, resting my hand in the small of his back, but as he didn't react, I assumed he was very deeply asleep.

I went to have a shower, shave, and get dressed. I planned my day:

after I'd had something to eat, I'd walk up to the hospital with Constable Ward to visit Cooper, and once Andrew was awake, when I got back, we'd talk about last night. I was feeling a little sad—in the nostalgic sense of the word. Sandford's farewell last night was heartfelt. His polite handshake instead of a hug signalled he'd accepted my situation. I couldn't help thinking of the old male of the herd finally relinquishing his place to the new, young blood bull. Sandford would survive. He had no end of willing stable hands and country boys at his beck and call. Wealth was an extraordinary enticement for those with limited means and from impoverished backgrounds.

After breakfast, I was checking my tie in my bedroom mirror, getting ready to leave for the hospital, when I heard the phone ring. Constable Ward answered it.

"It's for you, sir," he said, after knocking at my bedroom door. "A Mr. Julius Harcourt. I told him you were about to leave, but he was insistent, Mr. Murray. He said it's urgent."

"Very well," I said and then went to the telephone. "Good morning, Julius. How can I help you?"

"Good morning, Edward." My blood ran cold. "Now unless you'd like to hear me put an end to Mr. Harcourt while you're listening on the telephone, you'll do as I ask."

"Very well …" I said, unsure of what I should do.

"Is there anyone else there?"

"Yes," I said.

"Get rid of them."

I put my hand over the mouthpiece and told Constable Ward that my conversation was private and asked if he could give me a moment alone. He went into Andrew's apartment and closed the door.

"What do you want, Doland?" I spat into the receiver.

"You have twenty minutes to get here before I start throwing bodies out of the window," he said.

"Get where?"

"Julius Harcourt's room at the Gulgong Hotel. I'll be waiting downstairs for you to arrive. Come alone, Edward, and tell no one. I've been following you all week and I know the faces and the addresses of every one of your copper friends. If you're followed, I'll know. And then not only will it be Harcourt and his mate, Chase Osborne, but after them I might start with a blind man, his wife, and their daughter before I get to your fancy man. Do you understand?"

"Wait!" I said.

"Twenty minutes, and alone." He hung up the connection.

I didn't know what to do. My hand hesitated on the knob of Theo's door ... alone he'd said. I felt unable to think clearly. And then, ignoring what I knew was ill-advised, and the voice inside me that insisted I should not go, I grabbed my hat from the sofa where I'd left it, and let myself quietly out of the apartment door.

I couldn't risk another person's life for the sake of my own. He'd said he wanted to talk with me ... and yet, last night Cooper had told me he'd said I'd be next? Perhaps this *was* all about rejection: his singing competition report and Elias's letter stating I was not offering anyone private lessons. That was strictly not true, as I'd worked twice with Julius Harcourt during the rehearsal period of *Don Giovanni*. If Doland had been following me, perhaps his anger had been reignited when he'd realised that I'd been helping Julius. But ...

There were no more buts to be pondered at this very moment. Ignoring the elevator, I ran down the staircase and out onto the street, jumping into the first handsome cab in the rank outside the hotel.

"The Gulgong Private Hotel," I said to the cabbie, and then sat, concentrating on strategies to soothe whatever situation it was Doland imagined me creating.

The reception area was empty. He'd said he'd be waiting for me to arrive. I paced around the area, not knowing whether to ring the bell or not. The concierge had always been hovering behind her counter; it was odd she was not. I leaned over the reception desk, trying to see into her private room.

"She's a little tied up," Adam Doland said from behind me. I swung around, uncertain what to expect. "Upstairs," he added, gesturing towards the staircase with a flick of his head.

"Wait, before we do this, is Julius all right?"

He'd been standing with one hand inside his coat. He slowly removed it, producing a derringer pistol.

"Upstairs!"

He pushed open Julius's door with his foot, and then indicated I should enter the room first. I was more concerned for the young singer's safety than my own—my heart was in my throat as I walked through the doorway, but was relieved to see no one else was in the room. On the way up the stairs my mind had been working frantically, imagining Julius perhaps also dead at Doland's hand.

"Not there!" he snapped as I crossed the room to the window. "On this side of the bed where I can see you. Against the wall, between the door and the wardrobe."

"Adam, what's this all about—?"

"Shut up!" he snapped and then began to pace in front of the window. Through it, I could see Railway Square. Despite the precarious nature of my situation, it was odd my first thought was to think how noisy this room must be, with trams rattling past a few feet from the edge of the hotel's street awning, not six or seven yards from Julius's bedroom window.

"You know my name …"

"Yes, I looked it up in the church registry."

"Fabrice Evans didn't tell you?"

"No, he didn't! I swear it. How did you know I went to visit—?"

"Then why didn't you answer my letters?"

"My agent answers all my letters," I said. He was becoming agitated, rocking back and forth, muttering to himself, and running one hand through his hair as he continually raised and lowered the pistol in my direction. "It's a stock letter. He writes them to everyone who asks for lessons—"

"It's not *that* fucking letter!" he screamed.

I heard a soft whimper from beside me and glanced at the wardrobe.

"It'll take two bullets through the front of that piece of furniture and they'll both be dead, and it will be your fault!" He was beginning to sound incoherent, stumbling over words, red in the face, his eyes empty of anything but rage.

"And then you will shoot me with what?" I said. My fear was turning into anger. He'd most certainly tied up Julius and Chase and had gagged them and locked them in the wardrobe. The man was mad. There was no other word for it. He'd taken leave of his senses. I could see there was no reasoning with him.

Adam Doland had no reason to know of my background. I was a child of the streets, quick on my feet, violence still lurking just below the surface. I did not give in to threats, otherwise I'd never have survived the slums of Ultimo and then the life of a white child in India. I was not afraid; I was furious. I glanced around the room for something I might use as a weapon.

"There are only two bullets in a derringer!" I shouted at him. "Will you throw it at me after you've shot them both and then hope I'll not be able to duck in time? Is that what you want?"

"Shut your mouth!" he yelled. "Move back! Stand against the wardrobe."

As I did so, he pushed Julius's dressing table chair across the room, securing the back of it under the doorknob, to prevent anyone from coming into the room.

"No one's followed me. I did what you told me to. I've come alone." I tried to find the lock to the wardrobe behind my back, but it was too high, right in the middle of my back. I leaned against it. There was no key in the lock.

"But once I start shooting, they'll be all sorts banging on the door," he said and then smiled. He backed across the room to his place in front of the window. "But, when they do, it will be too late, Édouard Marais."

"Adam—" I took two steps towards him, my hands open in a gesture of appeasement.

"Stand back!" he said, his eyes blazing, prodding the derringer in the air in my direction. "Why didn't you answer my letters?"

"What letters, Adam? Speak sense or shoot me now."

"The letters I took to your home, blast you!"

I recoiled slightly. "My home?"

"Yes. Don't tell me you didn't get them, as I put both of them through the letter opening in the door. I knocked. I wanted to speak with you and hand the letters to you—to wait until you'd read them. There was no way they'd let me go up to your room at the hotel, or to visit your dressing room in the theatre—and they were personal, I didn't want them to be forwarded to your agent by either place. I wanted to give them to you and to see your face when you read them."

"Adam, you must believe me, there's no letter opening on our front door. The letterbox is at the front gate. I received no letters from you."

"Liar!" he shrieked, and then discharged the pistol into the wall, a foot from where I was standing. "On two occasions I caught the ferry to Hunters Hill and put the letters into your mail slot. Why didn't you answer me?"

I could hear noises in the hallway outside, and then a man's voice at the end of the corridor yelling out something I couldn't make out. His voice was muffled, but I could hear someone's feet pounding down the corridor as they ran towards Julius's door.

"Because our house is in Birchgrove, not in Hunters Hill, Adam," I said. "We haven't been to Hunters Hill in nearly two months."

He reacted as if I'd slapped him across the face.

"No … no! No! You read the letters. You simply didn't want to know about me. I fucking hate you, you stupid, stuck up, fucking bastard."

And then, someone began to bang on the door to the room, calling out my name. It was Lincoln; I recognised his voice.

"Get away from the door!" Adam Doland shrieked and then pointed the gun at me. "Tell him to stand away from the door."

"*Dure sara! Se ekati banduka ache!*" I yelled through the wall. Get away, he's got a gun, I'd said, in Bengali.

"What did you tell him, Edward? What was that?"

"I told him to move away from the door. Nothing more."

"What else?"

"Nothing," I lied. I didn't want Lincoln to be standing behind the door in case Adam Doland fired again and this time the bullet went through wood and not into plaster.

"I got no letters, Adam. On my mother's grave, I got no letters from you!"

He turned his back briefly, pounding on the wall with both fists. I was afraid the gun would go off. I thought for a moment I could leap over the bed and disarm him, but he swung around suddenly, and pointed his pistol at the wardrobe.

"I'll kill one of them unless you tell me the truth! One …two …"

"For Christ's sake, are you insane? I tell you I got no fucking letters, Adam. How many times do I have to tell you—?"

He shot a bullet into the top of the wardrobe. Muffled screams came from within.

"You have no more bullets in your derringer," I said and then started to make a move.

"Well, it's fortunate I have another gun," he said, reaching behind him and retrieving a long-barrelled pistol from the back of his waistband.

"You can shoot everyone, including me, if you want to, but it still won't make any difference," I said, and then shouted, as if yelling at a hard-of-hearing four-year-old, "I DIDN'T GET YOUR LETTERS!"

It was as if I'd pulled the plug in the sink of his hate. His eyes glazed and he began to keen softly. I suppose the vehemence of my rebuttal had finally sunk in.

"So, Adam, if you've killed all of those people because of me not replying to letters you sent to me, it's because I never got them in the first place—"

"No! No! It can't be," he said, starting to sob. "No—"

At that moment, I heard Andrew's voice out in the corridor and then loud kicking against the door. The chair gave way and went flying across the room, and as the door flew open Lincoln threw himself into the room, rolling into a ball as he hit the floor. Doland shrieked and discharged his gun through the open doorway.

"Andrew!" I screamed. My cry was almost instantly followed by the sound of smashing glass.

Adam Doland had leaped through the closed window, Lincoln jumping through after him. Andrew rushed into the room and grabbed my arm. Thank God he hadn't been in the line of fire. We ran to the window, just in time to see Adam Doland standing on the edge of the hotel awning, preparing to jump onto the roof of a passing tram. Lincoln reached him immediately he became airborne and managed to snatch hold of the hem of his trouser leg. Doland swung around, as if trying to kick Lincoln mid-air. The movement caused him to miss his leap. He fell sideways, clutching at the air, reaching for a pair of tramline rigging cables. A terrible flash of blue light erupted from his body, and then he fell, instantly followed by shrieks from passers-by in the street.

Adam Doland had grabbed hold of one of the rigging wires of the tramway. Unfortunately for him, it was the wire that supported the live power supply line. He'd died before his body had even hit the ground.

*****

Julius was hysterical when we'd untied him. I was as I'd thought—he and Chase had been bound and gagged, stuffed inside the large double-fronted wardrobe. Had they not been sitting on its floor, toe to toe, one of them might have taken a bullet to the head.

The mechanist was barely conscious. He'd lost a great deal of blood. One of Neil's daggers was underneath Chase's leg, lying in a pool of gore at the bottom of the wardrobe.

Doland had ordered Chase to tie Julius up first, and then, when he'd refused, had thrust his dagger through the back of Chase's thigh while holding his pistol to his head. I didn't know if I would have had the gumption to say no with a pistol pressed against my temple. Chase Osborne was a very brave man.

Mrs. Jamison, the concierge, had also needed to be taken off in a second ambulance. Doland had punched her in the face so hard she'd fallen backwards and hit the back of her head. He'd bound her with her electric fan cable, hence his not so witty rejoinder to me when I'd arrived, that she was "a little tied up".

"How did you get here?" I asked Andrew once we were alone in the room.

"Lincoln telephoned the hotel from Mrs. Jamison's office. He was arriving at the Metropole when he saw you jump into a cab by yourself. Thank heavens he had the wits to follow in another hansom. Of course, Russell Ward became suspicious when you seemed to be so long on the telephone and came to wake me up when he saw you'd gone. He told me Julius Harcourt had called. Theo came out, wondering what the ruckus was about, but I was on the telephone in my room trying to get the operator to find out from where the call had originated. We were about to leave when Lincoln's phone call came through in your apartment."

"You got here quickly," I said.

"You've no idea how fast a cabbie can go with five shillings in his hand."

"Those poor horses!" I said.

He nodded and then ran his hand over my thigh. "I came in a single carriage. It's lighter and faster. I was here in time to hear the first gunshot."

"That's the one he discharged into the wall."

"Oh, God! Edward," he said, breathing heavily. "If anything had happened to you ..."

"Well, it didn't, Andy. I—"

He pushed me back on the bed and rolled on top of me, kissing my forehead, my cheeks, my chin, and then finally, my lips. His kiss was desperate, as if he was trying to devour my mouth ... and then, I felt a tear fall onto my eyelid.

"Please, don't risk yourself like that again," he whispered, smoothing back my hair.

"I promise. On one condition."

"What's that?"

I thrust my hips against his and then wiggled them from side to side. He chuckled.

"I'm sick of waiting."

"Here?"

"No, you madman. But somewhere quiet, where we can be alone and make love to one another."

"I'm afraid," he whispered against my ear.

"I promise you there's nothing to be afraid of. I'll be gentle with you."

He chuckled. "Not afraid of that. Afraid that once we start, it won't be just our bodies we'll be sharing, but our hearts."

"But, Andy," I said, kissing his ear. "Didn't you hear me? I didn't say enjoying each other's bodies, I said something quite different."

"You said?"

"I said, 'making love'."

Had not Theo burst into the room, valiantly late, we may have consummated our connection right there on Julius's bed, surrounded by shattered plaster and shards of broken glass.

*****

By five o'clock Andrew hadn't returned and I was starting to get worried.

We'd come back to the Metropole together straight from the room in the Gulgong Hotel, and he'd telephoned Phillip Street police headquarters and had spoken to Superintendent Morris, saying he'd had no sleep and needed a few hours before he could even begin to think straight.

I'd undressed him and put him into bed, desperate to climb in with him, but only too aware he was exhausted. So, like he had done the first time he'd visited my bed, I lay down next to him, on top of the covers, holding him until he fell asleep.

Abel Morris had turned up at our hotel perhaps half an hour after I'd left Andrew's bedroom, and Theo, Lincoln, and I had given statements to him, which Russell Ward dutifully jotted down in his notebook. The superintendent had informed us that he'd already contacted the police station at Hunters Hill, and one of their officers had been despatched to collect our key from the ferry master's wife, and to gather whatever mail she'd been keeping for us, together with any that may have arrived since her last visit.

He'd asked my permission to read the letters from Doland before I did, in case there was anything in them that his men needed to follow up on. I'd told him to go ahead. I'd been in no mood to think about Doland just yet, and even though I was puzzled about what had driven him to murder, I'd simply wanted some time to clear my mind, and to try to come to terms with the events of last night in the theatre, and those in Julius's room this morning.

I'd woken Andrew at one; two hours of sleep had done nothing to relieve his fatigue, but he'd pulled me to him and had kissed me. "Was that French enough for you?" he'd asked with a smile as we'd drawn apart.

I'd taken his hand and placed it on my chest. "You feel that?" I'd said. "Well, it's not the only part of my body that's throbbing."

He'd laughed and pulled me against him. "Tonight, I promise," he'd whispered into my ear. "Now let me up, Eddie. The sooner I get into work the sooner I can be back here. We can lock the dividing door between our apartments and you and I can do whatever we wish, undisturbed."

He'd left at half past one after a sandwich and a glass of lemon barley water, saying he'd be back in an hour at most.

That's why I was concerned when the clock chimed five and I still hadn't heard from him. I'd been napping on the sofa in his room while Theo and Lincoln re-established their long-neglected friendship.

At half past five, the telephone rang. I heard it from the other room. Lincoln appeared in the doorway a few minutes later.

"That was Andrew," he said. "They'd like you and Theo to come up to Phillip Street at about seven."

"What for?"

"He didn't say, but he sounded very serious."

I sighed. "Very well, if we must, we must, I suppose. I think I'll call in at the hospital on the way. If I leave now, I'll have over an hour to spend with Cooper and to check on Chase to see whether he is all right too."

"What's up, brother mine?" Theo said, after tapping Lincoln on the shoulder and giving him the chin toss that said "hook it!" to any Australian. Lincoln left us alone.

"I feel so guilty, Theo."

He threw himself down on the sofa next to me and wrapped me in his arms. "You can't be guilty for the actions of a deranged mind, Eddie. There's nothing so bad you could possibly have done to cause a person to take the lives of innocent people. He was unbalanced. You told me so yourself. You must stop taking the weight of the world on your shoulders."

I kissed the crook of his elbow and then sighed once more. "Yes, but we all know feelings are irrational things. All I can content myself with is that I'm totally unaware of anything I may have done on purpose to upset him. I suppose we might never know?"

"I think we'll know not long after seven this evening, to be honest. Abel will have read the letters by then, and presumably there was something in them that caused him to ask us to go to the police station, rather than he come here."

"You're right," I said. "Will you come to the hospital with me?"

"Of course, I will. My guess is that we'll have to fight through a throng of Boltons to get to Cooper's bedside, but I'm game enough."

I laughed. "Me too," I said.

CHAPTER 14

Cooper was sitting up in bed when we arrived at the hospital, his mother seated in a chair against the wall of his hospital room, several feet away from her son, staring coldly at the Bolton family, who were gathered close around him. Oddly enough, I was not surprised to see Hilda in attendance as well. She was inordinately fond of Cooper, and had confessed she'd offered to be his mentor for both musical matters and for the advancement of his performing career.

Cooper's father, who was leaving to go to work, shook our hands enthusiastically in the corridor outside his son's room. He was a tall, thin, rather quiet man, who apologised in advance for his wife's extreme bad humour.

"I'm sure she's merely distressed about her son," I said, surprised to see the amount of care in the man's eyes as he talked about Cooper. I didn't know why, I'd assumed his father would have been an "absent" parent.

"My wife has always been gruff," he said. "We all try not to take it personally." By the tone of his voice, I assumed even he didn't believe what he'd said. We shook his hand and expressed our pleasure at meeting him.

Garrick Jones

The first thing I'd noticed upon entering the hospital room was Cooper's hand, lying on top of the sheets, Miss Bolton's index finger barely grazing the tip of his own. He was very, very pale, and his voice weak, but he asked me to embrace him. When I did so, his mother muttered something.

"Did I hear you say my brother's embrace was unseemly, Mrs. Haddley?" Theo asked sternly.

"It's not fitting, is what I said, Mr. Murray." She would not meet his eye.

"No doubt you'd be saying something else had you been required to arrive dressed in black," he snapped. "Had it not been for my brother, you'd be visiting the morgue, and not sitting at your son's bedside in hospital."

He turned on his heel and left the room. It was so unlike him, and so far beyond the tight rein he kept on his public behaviour and his meticulous manners, I couldn't believe it. No doubt he'd be outside, pacing and chewing his lip, disgusted at his loss of self-control.

"I should go to find him," I said, glaring at Cooper's mother, who sat, red-faced and fuming.

"No! I'll go," Jacob Bolton replied. "Guide me to the door, Louise."

"Let me take you, Jacob," his wife said.

When they'd gone, Hilda stood and asked Mrs. Haddley if she might speak with her outside in the corridor. No one was more surprised than I when Cooper's mother acquiesced. I sat quietly in the corner of the room and was about to speak when I noticed Cooper's quick nod and glance out into the corridor. When I turned to look, I saw nothing. But then, when he made the same movement immediately I turned back, I realised it was an invitation for me to leave him alone with Louise.

"Shan't be long," I muttered and then made myself scarce.

Outside, at the end of the corridor, I saw Hilda and Mrs. Haddley engaged in vigorous discourse. The sounds of their agitated and whispered conversation carried in my direction. However, Hilda seemed to be really fired up, shaking her finger at Cooper's mother, evidently giving her an earful about something or other.

I'd had a mother who'd given up Theo, Madeleine, and me for what she'd hoped would be a better life. I sincerely hoped my splendid and fearless accompanist was telling Cooper's mother she perhaps should let her son fly free, for if she did not, he might break from her chains and flee of his own accord, never to seek her out ever again. It was a subject about which my Miss Fischer was most passionate, for it had been her own experience. Her stepfather had been fanatical in his strict control over her life and had frequently forbidden her to play the piano in public. His rants and oft-times physical violence when she'd disobeyed had forced Hilda to leave home at the age of twenty-one, when she'd come of age and had inherited her father's money. She'd had no social intercourse with her stepfather ever since, and rarely saw her mother, who saw her as not only uncontrollable but living in an undesirable situation.

I watched as Hilda shook Mrs. Haddley's hand and then nodded in my direction. I touched the brim of my hat to the two ladies and waited. Shortly after, Hilda joined me.

"All in order, Miss Fischer?" I asked.

"Perhaps I've just made an enemy, but I needed to speak plainly. Although I may have overstepped the boundaries of propriety, I only have Cooper's best interests at heart. His prodigious talent is far too extraordinary to be crushed beneath his mother's disapproval and censure. It was my companion, Miss Frobisher, who saved me from my own parents' clutches, and it was when I was about the same age as Cooper. It was shortly after you and I returned from our first engagement together. Do you remember the concert and the ball at Sandford Clarkson's house?"

"Yes, I do. How could I forget it?"

"Miss Frobisher made a special trip to hear us perform, after which, outside in the garden, she told me plainly I needed my own life, and confessed she was prepared to be at my side if I wanted her as truest friend and confidante. I'm eternally grateful she did, for had she not, I would never have had the experience of her tender companionship, nor would I have formed the relationship I have had for twenty years with you, Mr. Murray, for my stepfather would have forbidden it. My connection with you and with Miss Frobisher has been all that any woman could possibly wish for. Both of you have made me who I am."

"You mustn't think I've not had the same thought myself, Miss Fischer. You are as part of my performing history and career as I am myself."

"Thank you, Mr. Murray. There's no need for you to pass such compliments, but I do know your feelings about our connection as artists ... and friends. How could I fail to? I've never uttered the words, but I've felt our performances together have communicated everything that's ever needed to be said."

"I couldn't agree more, Miss Fischer. But after what's happened to me this few weeks, I'm especially mindful of not taking any friendships for granted. I value yours as highly as is humanly possible, and I'm eternally grateful for not only your support as a pianist of extraordinary ability but for your constant and devoted friendship. I mean it."

"Thank you, Edward," she said.

"No; thank you, Hilda," I replied, and then we both smiled broadly, aware it was the first time we'd ever used each other's Christian names in direct conversation.

"Where's Mrs. Haddley?" I asked.

"I think she's gone to splash water on her face. I may have told her to regain her composure for the sake of her son ... or words similar."

"I suppose she didn't take kindly to your advice?"

"I think she believes her relationship with her children is no one's business but her own. I agreed, but warned her that ownership is something quite different than love, using the example my own estrangement from my family due to the circumstances similar to those of hers and her son's."

"Oh!"

"Yes, oh! To be honest, Mr. Murray, I'll make it my task to encourage Cooper to take the bit between his teeth and make his own life away from a desperately controlling mother. It will be harder for him, as he does not have his own Miss Frobisher, as I did."

"But he has me, Miss Fischer, and I'm more than ready to help you with your endeavour," I said. "I've been having thoughts of my own along those very same lines."

Our conversation was interrupted as Mrs. Haddley sailed towards us, having returned from a quick visit to the ladies' room.

I saw in her eyes the hurt the truth my friend, Miss Fischer, had shared. I'd seen it so often before in the theatre: parents who thought their child was their property, husbands who thought likewise of their wives. It never ended well. My career had been littered with the shipwrecks of glorious performers whose abilities had been crushed by possessive relationships.

"Shall we return to your son?" I asked, offering her my arm.

Hilda had left as Cooper's mother had arrived; no doubt to give warning to him and Louise they would shortly be interrupted.

Once everyone had eventually returned to Cooper's bedside, a cordial but cool atmosphere prevailed. I couldn't help but think he'd rather not have his mother there. She kept inspecting her small pocket watch, as if wondering when it would be seemly enough to leave, and throwing annoyed glances at Hilda. I'd rather hoped Miss Fischer's bluntness would have turned to some softening in her attitude towards her son. I could see she hated Louise already.

She eventually left, perhaps ten minutes before we did, and soon the room was filled with laughter and smiles, even a few from our "hero" Cooper.

Miss Bolton's fingertip touch had turned into a holding of his hand by the time we said our goodbyes. At least something nice had come to pass during these past horrendous weeks: Cooper and Louise. Had Andrew and his fellow officers not come into my life, the young couple may never have met. Perhaps my thinking was macabre, but after my life as a child, which seemed to be nothing but shades of grey, I couldn't help looking for the small flowering weed in the corner of the bare courtyard. There had to be something positive in every horrid situation—I'm not sure I could have continued to be the man I was without that thought.

*****

As Theo and I walked from Macquarie Street to Phillip Street, I was feeling very uneasy. I wasn't convinced I was ready to hear whatever it was the police had to tell us. We arrived at the police station a little after seven, just as it started to rain. Outside, there was the usual small gathering of newspaper reporters, eagerly juggling their notepads and umbrellas, to whom we were polite but firm. We knew nothing.

Inside, the desk sergeant showed us to a waiting room and told us he'd send word downstairs we'd arrived. A few moments later, Andrew came through the door in his shirtsleeves, his collar unbuttoned and tie hanging loose, his waistcoat flapping open. His hair was a mass of untidy strands and he looked exhausted—handsome and masculine, nonetheless. I couldn't help but think he looked as good when scruffy as he did when all neat and tidy.

"Hello," he said, closing the door behind him. He enfolded me in his arms. "Hello there, Theo," he said over my shoulder.

"What's wrong?" I asked after I moved from his embrace. There was the most awful sadness in his eyes.

"I hate to do this to you both, but I've no choice."

"Do what?" Theo asked.

"Downstairs. We have someone who has a confession to make."

He patted my shoulder and then opened the door to the waiting room. We followed him along the corridor and down a circular staircase at its end. A policeman stood guard outside a locked iron door, above which was written in copperplate on a varnished wooden plaque:

Detention Cells and Interrogation Rooms.

"Lincoln was supposed to join us here," I said.

"He's been here for an hour already. Patience. You won't like what you're going to hear, but all of the pieces of the puzzle have finally come together."

I couldn't imagine why Lincoln was here already, and had been for an hour? Theo raised an eyebrow at me and shrugged.

Andrew knocked at the door of one of the interrogation rooms and a policeman opened it from inside. Behind them I could only see half of the room. In the middle of it was a desk, positioned sideways to the doorway, seated at which was Abel Morris. He seemed to be talking to someone opposite him, but the person to whom he was speaking was hidden from my view.

As I came into the room, I saw Lincoln sitting inside the door at my right, hunched over, his head in his hands and long strands of his hair falling over and through his fingers.

"Hello, Lincoln," I said.

When he looked up, I saw his eyes were red, as were his knuckles. I was perplexed at why they should be so, until I caught sight of the other man in the room, sitting opposite Chief Superintendent Morris. I almost gasped with surprise. His hands manacled, and his face bloodied and bruised, sat Fabrice Evans.

"Fabrice?" Theo sounded stunned.

Evans looked up at us briefly and then turned his head to one side and began to sob.

"What the hell is going on here—?"

"Take a seat, Theo, Edward," Abel Morris said and then turned to Andrew. "Just make sure Mr. Talbot is comfortable, please, Chief Constable Bolton. There's no need for him to become so agitated again."

"I won't do anything. I won't lay another hand on him. I promise," Lincoln said, lowering his head and rubbing his knuckles. I could scarcely believe it. I'd never known him to be violent. Assertive, yes, but punches?

We sat and waited in silence until Fabrice's sobbing had stopped. "Edward—"

Abel Morris slammed his hand on the desk. "You'll have time to explain yourself when I allow you to, Evans! In the meantime, answer questions, otherwise keep your mouth shut. Understood?"

Fabrice nodded slowly, unable to look at either Theo or me.

"This is the first letter that Kane delivered to your house, Edward,"

Abel said, patting one of two letters on the desk. "Tell them why he went to Hunters Hill, Evans."

"Adam came looking for me. It was me who told him that's where you lived. I was drunk, you see, Edward … He got me drunk and I said things better left unsaid."

"What things, Fabrice?" I asked.

"I told him he had a sister, but Neil had made his mother get rid of her."

"Wait," Theo said. "You mean he didn't already know? Surely his uncle must have told him?"

"No, Paul would never speak of such things. He disapproved greatly, you know. It happened back in his real religious days. But me? I knew lots of other private family goings on that even Paul didn't know—or closed an eye to. Me and Neil were close, you know, like that." He crossed the index and middle finger of one hand and then winced as the manacle bit into his wrist.

"How did Adam even know you existed, Fabrice?" I asked. "What made him come to you in the first place?"

"I already told you and your friend here about the night I saw them at the Carpenter and Pistol doing their knife game swindle. I followed Paul and Adam outside after they'd got booted out, and Paul introduced the boy to me then. Told Adam that I was his Neil's best mate, and then said what I told you two at the pub—get me drunk and I'd tell secrets about his father that not even Paul knew hisself. He said it as a joke, but I felt the spite behind it. Anyway, I learned out later on the boy took it for the truth and pressured Paul to tell him where he could find me."

"And was it the truth?" Theo asked. "Did you know about things his uncle didn't?"

"Of course," Fabrice retorted. "Although the last thing I expected was to see the boy turn up at the pub with a pocket full of coins and offer to pay for me grog."

"Why didn't you tell me this on the day we visited you at the London?" I asked. "You seemed pretty happy to share other bits of information."

"Because I knew I'd made such an arse of things ... I was frightened, Eddie."

"Frightened of what? I don't see how telling Adam Doland where we lived—"

"I told him another secret. It came out before I could stop it. I was legless, you see. He'd been pouring neat scotches all the time I was on my Guinness. You know what it's like. A gulp of stout, a glass of whisky, and—"

"No, I don't know what it's like, Fabrice. I can hold my alcohol. Now, what was the other secret?"

"I told him who the father of the child was—the name of the man who got his sister on his ma."

"You told me it wasn't Neil already. Who was it then?"

"The man Nancy had been having an affair with for thirty years and more. She and him were sweet long before she even met Neil."

"Holy Mother of God!' I said. "Neil knew Nancy was having it off with some other bloke when they met, and yet he still married her?"

"Yes, Eddie. I know you'll find it hard to understand, but she was a real beauty back in those days. She met her gentleman friend in, let's see, when was it? Oh, yes, in 1851, and then Neil about ten years after that. She was only sixteen when she met the true love of her life. Neil was the second prize in the raffle. There was a famous stoush between them over her, backstage in the old Lyceum. I was a young man back then, probably twenty-four or twenty-five, but I remember the fight very well."

"What fight?"

"Neil Doland attacked her lover backstage during the interval of 'Little Nell'. He pulled a knife on him in the corridor. She stood between them and tried to hold them apart, but in the scuffle she got sliced across the breast—there was blood everywhere. The only reason the attack stopped was because she put her hands over her ears and screamed her head off at them both. I'd never heard such a ruckus. The corridor of the theatre was packed with people, probably expecting to see one of the men get killed ... pack of ghouls. Anyway, when they'd put their knives away, she said she'd marry Neil, but as long as she could go on seeing her fancy man."

"Really? It sounds like something from a penny dreadful."

"Well, the three of them moved in together for a few years, until it all came crashing down, as you'd expect. The boyfriend took off, but she still visited him, even after Adam was born, and …"

"And?"

He swallowed and then shook his head. "And then I told Adam Doland the last, great secret. One I could cut my tongue out for revealing."

"What was it?" I asked.

"That Neil Doland was not Adam's father either."

"What?" I wasn't expecting to hear that.

"Neil had girlfriends everywhere. Not one of them ever got knocked up. We all knew his seed was barren. Adam's father was the same man who got Nancy pregnant with the child Neil made her get rid of."

"You mean?"

"Yes, her boyfriend of all those years—"

It explained why Neil had sent the boy away to live with other people, and why we hadn't seen him at Nancy's funeral. He couldn't bear to bring up the child of another man.

"You keep saying 'her boyfriend', 'her lover', 'her fancy man', Fabrice," I said. "I'm not unaware you've been skirting around his real name. Who was it, then?"

"I can't say. I'm sorry. Please don't ask me, Eddie, I beg you …"

His look at me was so fearful, I started to feel sick. What was he hiding? It was obviously something he was very scared to tell me, but for the life of me I couldn't think what this unknown father of Adam Doland could conceivably have to do with me or my brother.

"This is ridiculous, Fabrice," I said. "What possible reason could you have of not telling me who it was?"

Lincoln jumped to his feet. "If you don't speak up, I'll knock it out of you again—"

"Please sit down, Mr. Talbot," the superintendent said, rising from his chair.

"I can't tell you, Eddie. I simply can't—" Fabrice started to say, and then his words disintegrated into a whimper. It was the sort of whine that children made when they didn't want to admit they'd done something wrong and they're afraid of some terrible punishment.

"Enough of this nonsense!" Andrew said. "Be a blasted man and tell Edward and Theo what you told us!" Fabrice Evans started to cry again, but Andrew leaned across the desk and grabbed him by the collar of his shirt.

"I was drunk. I promised never to tell!" Fabrice shouted, his spittle flying through the air. "Leave me alone … please!"

This stupidity was starting to make my blood boil. I got to my feet.

"Very well, Fabrice. I've had enough of you and your ridiculous carry on. You've obviously already told everyone else in the room apart from me and my brother. I've taken you for many things in my life: a friend, a colleague, and someone my brother and I have felt fit to support financially over the past ten years, but I'd never have taken you for a *coward*," I said, spitting the word out angrily. "I'm sick of this! Too many people have been killed, and I've been scared out of my wits for weeks. Stew in your own juices. I don't care what happens to you. You can go to buggery for all I care. Goodbye."

I'd just reached the door when he spoke.

"His father?" he said. "You want to know why I'm afraid to tell you who his father was?"

"Of course I damn-well do."

"Are you sure, Eddie … please, are you sure?"

I'd barely opened the door to leave the room when he spoke.

"It was Jacques Marais," he said. "I told Adam that Jacques Marais was his father."

I nearly fell over with the shock. Theo gasped loudly and jumped to his feet. Lincoln grabbed him, but my brother pulled away and threw himself against the wall, his head buried in his hands. I could hear him murmuring, "No, no … no."

I couldn't believe I'd heard correctly.

"Jacques Marais? The Jacques Marais who was our father? Are you telling me that Adam Doland was our half-brother?" I could barely get the words out.

Fabrice nodded.

My mind whirled, running dates through my mind. My father had been seeing a mistress all the time he'd been getting our mother pregnant, year after relentless year. He'd left her when I was three? That was 1866. Five years before that he'd been living with Neil and Nancy in an awkward ménage ... so, Theo, Madeleine, and I had all been conceived while he was passing back and forth between two households and the rest of my siblings while he'd been seeing Nancy Doland. The thought of it was repulsive. I was glad I'd never known the man.

At that moment, Abel Morris swivelled in his chair, his coat sleeve catching one of the letters and knocking it to the floor. As he picked it up, I began to think about the letters and their contents. It took me only a few moments to guess what was in Adam Doland's first letter. He'd written to me, probably with joy in his heart, telling me that he'd finally found a family.

"When did Adam deliver the second letter?" I asked Abel. It surprised me how contained my voice sounded. My hands were trembling slightly and my knees felt like jelly.

"Two days before he killed Howard Talbot. It was four days after he received the eisteddfod result, and the same day he got the letter from Elias Solomon telling him you wouldn't teach him."

The enormity of the situation hit me like an avalanche. It crashed into my brain, screaming at me, overwhelming my thoughts with its impact. I tried to get back to my chair, but my legs were like rubber.

"May I have some water, please?"

The policeman who'd been in attendance left the room, returning a few minutes later with a carafe and a few glasses on a tray. I slurped down two glassfuls and then offered one to Theo, who shook his head. I could see the horror in his eyes, and knew it for what it was. He'd realised he'd conducted a lengthy sexual relationship with our half-brother.

I wasn't feeling particularly calm when I eventually spoke, but breathed deeply to still my inner turmoil. "I still don't understand why you're here, Fabrice, and in handcuffs," I said.

"I turned myself in," he said, refusing to look at me.

"Turned yourself in for what? Police don't restrain people for betraying family secrets. Why are you manacled to the table?"

"Because I killed him," Fabrice said. "I killed your father."

"What! When?" I fell heavily back into my chair, such was my astonishment.

When he didn't answer, it was Andrew who explained. "The day after Adam murdered Howard, Edward. On the night we attended Theo's last performance of *The Arabian Nights* at the Royal Standard."

"You're telling me our father was still alive until two weeks ago?" Theo almost shouted his question. I stared at my brother. We'd merely assumed that he was already dead when we got back from India.

"Yes." Fabrice Evans' reply was no more than a whisper.

"And did he know that we were here, in Sydney, these past twenty years, and never once made move to contact us?"

Fabrice nodded.

I was astounded. What sort of man could abandon their children not once, but twice? I leaned forward in my chair and banged my forehead on my knees. I was too horrified to cry, but I felt the anger and tears gathering, held inside like some great plug in a volcano, waiting for the right moment to explode.

"Why did you kill him, Fabrice?" I asked. Although I wanted to scream it, I spoke quietly. I was determined to remain level-headed until I knew everything.

"Because once Adam had visited Jacques, your father would know it was me who'd blabbed. I was the only one who knew he was still alive, and the only person who knew Jacques Marais was Adam's real father. He once threatened to kill me if I ever told anyone—and that was no idle threat, either. Your father was an evil, nasty, violent piece of work,

Edward. You don't remember, you were too little, but all of you Marais kids were always covered in bruises. Just ask your brother … he remembers."

I looked at Theo, who shook his head slowly and shuddered. He didn't need to reply, I could see it in his eyes, and wondered why he'd never spoken to me of it.

"Go on, Fabrice," Theo said, breaking his eye contact with me. It said everything when my brother could not meet my gaze. His voice was thick with supressed rage. "My brother asked why you did it, not for a character assessment of our father."

"Well, Adam burst through my front door on the day before he killed Howard Talbot, demanding to know where Jacques was living. He knocked me to the floor and then pulled out one of Neil's daggers and held it to my throat. I had no choice. I told him where your father had lodgings. Adam went to find him, but they argued, and Jacques kicked him down the stairs and threw him out into the street. Adam came straight back to me and told me what had happened; gave me a few punches as good measure. I knew I was dead meat if I didn't get to Jacques first, before he came looking for me. So, I took the tram into the city that night and climbed up into the room he kept in Dawe's Point. I found him senseless, drunk in his cot, so I stabbed him in the throat and cut him from his balls to his chin, and then tipped his corpse out the window."

"We found the remains of your father's body under a pile of timber and corrugated iron a few hours ago," Superintendent Morris said with great sadness.

I felt vomit rising in my throat but pressed both hands over my mouth. Apart from Theo's muffled sobs, the room remained very quiet for a very long time. Eventually, I covered my eyes with my hands while I tried to process everything I'd just learned.

"There's only you and me now, Eddie," Theo said.

"That's all that's ever mattered since Maddie died," I whispered.

"What shall we do? About Father's body?" he asked, his voice nothing but gravel.

"We must bury them. Both he and Adam," I said quietly, a few minutes later.

Theo crossed the room and kneeled next to me, his arm around my shoulder. I kissed the side of his head and gave him a sad half-smile.

"What? After what they both did to you?" Chief Superintendent Morris could not have sounded more astounded had he tried.

"Yes," I replied. "They were still our flesh and blood, no matter what they did."

"I don't understand you," the superintendent said, shaking his head.

"Matthew, chapter five, verse forty-four," I said.

"I thought you two buggers didn't go to church?" Andrew asked. I could see the pain he felt for me in his eyes. His kind and gentle smile felt like a beam of light in the darkness.

"Not anymore, Andrew; but you never forget your scriptures when they're beaten into you as a child, even if you don't know what the words mean at the time. It's only when you get older, and get to see the wisdom hiding behind the dogma, that you really understand the message. There's a similar saying in Bengali. Christianity doesn't have a monopoly on forgiveness, you know."

"I'm not sure I ..." Chief Superintendent Abel Morris obviously didn't go to church either.

"*But I say unto you, love your enemies, bless them that curse you, do good to them that hate you, and pray for them which despitefully use you, and persecute you,*" Andrew explained.

"Is there anywhere I can have a cigarette?" I asked.

"You can smoke here, Edward," Superintendent Morris said.

"No. I need some fresh air too, if that's not too much of a conflict of ideas."

"I'll take you out into the exercise courtyard, Eddie," Andrew said.

"Thank you." I smiled at Theo's kiss against my neck. He'd heard the "Eddie" too. "That would be absolutely perfect."

*****

It had stopped raining.

The "exercise" courtyard was anything but. The only creature that might have gained any benefit from exercise in the space would have been a small rodent, or an anxious cat. It was merely a stone-paved rectangle, four yards to a side, in the middle of the police station complex, open to the air above. A door led into it, otherwise it was a box of four brick walls.

A police officer unlocked the door for us, and Andrew told him we'd bang on the door when we'd finished. The moment it closed, he took me in his arms and rocked me back and forth.

"What will happen to him?" I mumbled into his neck.

"Who? Fabrice?"

"Yes."

"He'll hang. He confessed to a murder and we found the body where he said it would be. Your father's body was cut open, exactly as he said it would be … I'm sorry, Eddie."

"Had he only told Adam where we really lived …" My voice caught in my throat.

"I know, I know. But he didn't. You can't blame yourself."

"I suppose the second letter is full of hate?"

"You can read them both later. But, yes, the second letter is quite vitriolic. It's almost incoherent to be honest. You didn't reply to his first letter, in which he revealed he was your lost half-brother, and then he received your blunt assessment of his performance in the eisteddfod. In it you said he needed lessons, so he wrote to your agent, and then … well, you know what happened after that. That second letter made very hard reading. He seemed to be incredibly overwrought when he wrote it. In it, he said if you didn't meet him at the Sailor's Bristle at seven in the evening of the sixteenth, the night before he killed Howard in your dressing room, he'd take it for granted you'd rejected him, and he'd punish you for it."

"Even if I'd only received that second letter and not the first, I would have gone to meet him to find out why he was so angry, and then Howard would still be alive, as would Mr. Elder at the baths, and Terry Smith at the Theatre Royal. I keep thinking how close we came to losing Cooper—"

I simply couldn't hold back anymore, I'd been holding too much inside, and it burst out in a sudden torrent of misery. I began to sob into his shoulder. He pulled me tight against him and kissed me over and over on the neck and behind my ear, whispering soft, soothing words.

"Six deaths, if we include his, my father's, and Fabrice's, Andy," I whispered. "All because of a simple, insignificant error of judgement—Fabrice Evans just gave the wrong address to a madman."

*****

That night, I told him I'd come to him.

I stood in his living area for a moment, trying to calm myself. I couldn't stop shaking. It was ludicrous, as it wasn't the first time we'd spent the night together. But now we were about to embark on a new adventure. Sail seas together, explore virgin lands, conquer the skies. Poetic thoughts perhaps, but for the first time since I was a child, I felt my life was about to radically change direction. I knew I'd go on as I had done before, but with a new reservoir of strength in my soul. One that was no longer fed by my brother, but by a man with a perfect blond moustache, who smelled of honey and tar, and whose perfection was only marred by one, slightly longer canine in the row of his otherwise perfect upper teeth.

He was waiting for me when I pushed his bedroom door open. Stretched out naked on his back, one hand behind his neck, the other resting on the knee of a bent leg spread out to the side. He glowed; the hair on his body a golden sheen, illuminated by the electric light on the bedside table.

"May I?" I asked softly, standing beside him as I ran my hand over his shin and up to the hand on his knee. He entwined his fingers through mine.

He nodded and drew me down on top of him, wrapping his heels around the backs of my calves as I kissed him.

"I want that to be the very last time you ask my permission," he said.

"Even if I do this?" I asked, and then kissed the base of his neck, in the notch between his collar bones.

He laughed.

"How about this?" I asked, as I placed my hand between our bodies, feeding the hair on his tummy between my fingers.

"No," he replied.

"How about—"

He threw me onto my back and ran his lips down over my body. I sighed with the pleasure of it.

"Stop!" I said.

He lifted his head. "Did I do something wrong?"

"Have you been taking lessons behind my back?"

"No, why?"

"How did you know how to do that?"

"Court reports, of course, silly."

"They write about those things during trials?"

"They surely do," he replied, and then ran his hand down between our bodies, as I had done, but lower.

"And those things too?"

"Oh, I've read about lots of things—I've simply been waiting for the right man with whom to try them."

"Have you found him yet?"

He lay very still in my arms for a moment and then kissed me very deeply. I fell into that kiss. I didn't need to hear his affirmation, for I felt it within my heart.

For the first time in my entire life, I didn't feel the tiniest little bit alone.

*****

The following morning, after breakfast, I could bear it no longer.

I went to my bedroom and retrieved the first of Adam's letters and went into the living room. I threw myself into the corner of the sofa, twirling the letter between my fingers, hesitant, not knowing whether I was ready to read it or not.

Eventually, sick of the whole business, I retrieved the four neatly written pages from the envelope and began to read:

Milton House,
Broadway.
Sydney.

Wednesday, 2nd April, 1902

Dear Mr. Edward Murray,

Perhaps you will not remember me; there is no reason you should. I've written to you countless times over the years, and your agent, Mr. Elias Solomon, has been kind enough to send me signed portrait photographs and newspaper cuttings of the reviews of your performances I have missed for my collection.

My name is James Kane, and I work at times in the theatre as a supernumerary, having appeared many times on the stage with you. I've always gone out of my way to remain quietly at a distance, greeting you when the occasion should happen that we pass in the greenroom, or at the stage door. You have always tipped your hat to me and returned my good mornings with polite and respectful wishes of your own. Your good manners and courteous demeanour are something I've tried hard to emulate in myself.

I am your greatest admirer. I don't think there's a performance you have given in the past six years I have missed. I go home and practise the imitation of your voice, as I too, one day, hope to be a performer. I know that I could never become one with such authority and beauty of voice as you. However, I will continue to try my hardest. You are "Australia's Son", the symbol of manhood that we others in our great country should strive to imitate.

Perhaps you get many such letters as these; this is why I decided to deliver it in person. I hope you will forgive the forward nature of my communication, but you see I bear important personal news of a hitherto unknown connection between you and me, and your brother, Theodore.

After visiting a mutual friend very recently, I have learned that our connection, formerly as performer and audience member is indeed of another nature ...

I could read no more when I reached this point in his letter. Although formal, there was a great deal of hope and happiness written between the lines. Besides, my eyes were so filled with unshed tears the words were simply too blurred to continue.

I handed it to Theo to read, who'd been watching me anxiously, tapping his foot while he waited for me to finish.

"Here," I said to him. "I can't read any more of it, Theo. You'll have to finish it for me."

Australia's Son, the symbol of manhood that we others in our great country should strive to imitate, he'd written. How ironic and bitter those words felt in my mouth right now as I listened to my brother's stifled choking while he read Adam's letter. Who knew what had tipped him into madness, for indeed that's how I perceived him to have been in that room at Railway Square.

It could not have come from that single incident of not receiving a reply to his letter. A sane person might have enquired further, especially if, as he'd said in his letter, he perceived me to be a man of good manners and courteous demeanour. What person such as that would ignore what he'd written to me?

Perhaps it was the result of a dissolute life, of having to prostitute himself to survive, or having an alcoholic "father" who'd pimped him out, or perhaps it was because he'd been shuttled from house to house as a child, while knowing his parents were still close by and didn't want him? Now he was dead, we'd never know. The only way we could find out would be to frequent the places he had, and seek out those who knew him, or knew of him.

In the time after we'd left Australia and before we'd returned, six of our siblings had died. The thought of the loss of another, even though I had not known of his existence, tore at my heart.

I'd known what it was to be lonely, to grieve, and to lose a father. Perhaps it was the loss of Neil Doland that had tipped him over the edge? He'd been twenty at the time, and had just been rediscovered by his father, only to find out that it was not paternal love that had driven Neil Doland to seek him out, but financial gain and a form of sexual exploitation. How Naddo must have rubbed his hands together to find a son who was happy enough to sleep with ladies and gentlemen for a price.

As for the news of the death of my father? Well, I'd had no truck with him I could remember. His presence wasn't even a vague shadow in my mind like my siblings were—pastel, blurry shapes against the background of our slum-dwelling home. What you didn't have, you couldn't miss. There was no way I could grieve for an abstract idea—I had no concept of "father". Theo had been everything to me a father could possibly have been. Protector, carer, and sharer of my joys and my miseries—companion in my life both off and on the stage. Jacques Marais' only contribution to me had been his ejaculate, which had brought about my conception.

I would not grieve for him, as I would for Adam, for whom I felt some pity. We'd bury them both, and then visit their graves dutifully, as we would have had we known where our mother and our other brothers and sisters were laid to rest. I'd discussed it with Theo over breakfast. We'd have a small mausoleum erected for all of the family, even those whose bodies we'd never found. One day in the future, there'd be eleven names on it, starting with my mother, and father, and our five siblings who'd died here, Adam's, and eventually Theo's and mine. Even though she was buried in India, Maddie's name would come immediately next to my brother's and my own.

I went to put my arms around my brother, who was bent double, sobbing his heart out, having finished the letter, when I could not. I'd already formulated the reason Adam had written to me and not to Theo; not only because he idolised me but also because he was most likely ashamed once he'd discovered our family connection, that he'd conducted a sexual liaison with his own half-brother. Perhaps there was some contrition in the unread pages I'd been unable to face—excuses and mortifications … even pleas for forgiveness? Perhaps that was what had left my brother so desperately heartbroken.

Right now, I had no interest in finding out. I'd read the rest of Adam's words when I had the strength.

I pulled Theo close to my chest, as we had done with each other so many times during our lives since we were children, and let him bury his head under my chin. I felt too numb within myself to do anything but rock him gently in my arms and murmur soft, soothing sounds of comfort.

The letter slipped from his hands and I watched the pages flutter to the floor. They were spread out over the carpet, one page resting on the toe of my shoe. As I stared at it, I had only one thought:

"Poor Adam. There but for the grace of God go I."

CHAPTER 15

EPILOGUE

The passenger terminal was thronged with people. Hundreds had turned up to greet the Melbourne Williamson Company, who'd sailed up the coast on the SS *Rangitoto*, and to farewell us Sydney performers who were to accompany them on the voyage across the Tasman Sea to New Zealand.

Some of Australia's most famous theatre performers from down south hung over the ship's railings, waving and blowing kisses to the crowd on the dockside.

"Take care of Cooper, won't you, Louise," I said to her with a wink.

His arm was still in a sling, which he was allowed to remove for a few hours a day. He'd begun to practise again, with no ill-effect other than the ache of holding his arm up unsupported at the keyboard for any length of time.

"Cooper," I said, chucking his chin, "I'd like to make sure that you listen to Louise. Eventually, through her, I'm sure you will gain your love of 'high-class' music. It's not enough to be able to perform it, and to pour your soul into it when you play, you have to learn to adore it. Will you keep trying?"

"Of course, I will, Edward. It's not that I don't like it, but I've realised it was Mother, with her constant criticism, that made me shut my heart to it. Perhaps I voiced my preference for cakewalks to thwart and aggravate her. She's not an easy person to stand up to, except passively."

"So, things are improving since you moved in with Hillary and … what's his name again?"

"Avenal," he replied.

"I should have remembered that. The bachelor's life suits you then. All three young men sharing digs …"

"If it hadn't been for your generous gift of a pianoforte, I don't know what Hillary and I would have done. As it is, we split shifts, and there's a silent damper pedal for late at night."

"The benefits of a detached cottage in Hunters Hill, Cooper. We've paid the rent to the end of the year, so you're welcome to stay there as long as you like. The rent is cheap. I'm sure you'll come to love living there—it's only a ferry ride to the city."

"Edward, how can I ever—"

"By learning to love your art, Cooper. Let it be as dear to you as any person you care about." I smiled at Louise, who beamed at me, blushing heavily. "And remember, although I won't be at your concerto performance in person, it doesn't mean that your 'guardian angel' won't be hovering over the audience and beating his wings with excitement while you play."

Ignoring all dictates of correct behaviour between gentlemen acquaintances in public, he threw his arm around my chest and began to cry. I held him until he'd quietened and then handed him my handkerchief. "Keep it," I whispered. " Put it in your pocket while you're performing, then I'll be happy to know that at least part of me will be up there on the stage with you."

"Thank you, Eddie," he said, his eyes still liquid. I kissed the top of his head, as an older man might do to a favourite nephew, and was about to say something else when the ship sounded her horn. It meant I had twenty minutes before she cast off.

"And now, I must bid you adieu, Jacob, Mrs. Bolton, Louise, Cooper. Lincoln, Ethan and Andrew took our cabin baggage aboard, and I must get them off the ship, otherwise they'll end up halfway across the Pacific with no ticket!"

"Goodbye, Edward," Jacob Bolton said to me. "May I accompany you to the foot of the gangplank?"

"Of course, sir."

"I'm not sure what you had to do with it, but Andrew's promotion is surely your doing, Edward; as is his three-week placement in Auckland, training detectives in the latest forensic skills. Odd that it coincides with your last three weeks over there."

I heard no accusation in his voice, merely the hint of a smile. "Indeed a great coincidence, Jacob. Nothing to do with me I'm afraid. Chief Superintendent Abel Morris was very taken with your son's knowledge of criminal investigation and the new sciences that go with it."

It helped that not only was Abel Morris my good friend but Lieutenant Colonel Arthur Hume, the New Zealand Commissioner of Police, was one of Theo's greatest fans. It had taken some delicate negotiations, but in the end we'd got the result we wanted.

"And you'll travel home together?"

"Yes, sir, we will. He'll be in Auckland to see me in the last of our performances with the orchestra and choral society, and in both *Don Carlos* and *La Traviata* in the Williamson's season at the new His Majesty's Theatre."

"For a long time, I thought he would lead a lonely life, you know. The loss of our other son, Harris, and Andrew's belief that he was somehow responsible, made him very isolated in his connections with other young people of his own age. However, since he's been looking out for you, Mr. Murray, he seems a different man, one we haven't seen since he was in his early teen years. It's as if some quiet piece of furniture in our house has suddenly sprouted leaves, burst into flower, and bedazzled us all with its beauty. Yours is an acquaintance that Mrs. Bolton and I both approve of. Your kindness is exemplary and your friendship to our boy inestimable. I am truly in your debt."

"Why thank you, sir," I said.

"Take care, Edward, and bon voyage."

Andrew was stretched out on my bed in my cabin when I got there.

"Ah, on your back waiting for me, again, Andy? I could get quite used to that, you know."

"Shall I take my trousers off?"

I laughed and sat astride his hips on the bed.

"You'll have to get going, I'm afraid. We've about ten minutes before they hoist the gangplank."

He pulled me down to him and kissed me.

A knock on the door and "All passengers ashore, thank you!" announced that what I'd thought was correct.

"Walk me out to the gangplank, Eddie," he said after I'd pulled him to his feet.

"That's what your father said to me not more than ten minutes ago."

"When Father asks for those sorts of things, I usually get an uneasy feeling …"

"No need this time. It was more of an affirmation he thinks I'm good for you."

"And me for you?"

"He didn't need to say that, for you and I both know it's true."

"See you in three weeks," he said with one hand on the cabin doorknob.

I kissed him again, and then pushed him out into the corridor, where Theo, Ethan, and Lincoln were waiting for us.

"All set, Edward?" Lincoln asked me.

"All set, Lincoln," I replied, patting the breast pocket of my jacket. "I'll hand in your letter of resignation to the manager of the Grand Hotel the moment we register. Are you quite sure you don't want to go back?"

"I've spent too long away from my sister-in-law and the children, who I'm just getting to know. And, now that you've offered me a theatre position as your permanent factotum, how could I refuse an opportunity to get back into yours and Theo's lives as well?"

"Make sure you follow our plan for the placement of the furniture, Ethan," Theo said to him.

"Lincoln, Andrew, and I will sort it all out, don't worry," the young man replied shyly. "It's going to be odd for you both to return to your new house with it already occupied for six weeks."

"Odd?" I said. "Not at all! We'll be coming home to our family."

Theo and I stood at the top of the gangplank, where the purser was checking off the names on the list of visitors. "Last three, gentlemen," he said, saluting Andrew, Ethan, and Lincoln. "As soon as you're ashore, we'll cast off."

We watched as the gangplank was retracted and the railing gateway secured.

"They're waiting for you on the first-class promenade deck," the purser said. "As soon as you both arrive up there to join the other guests, we'll sound the horn again and then set sail."

I smiled at the set sail. There hadn't been a rigged passenger liner out of Sydney since I was a lad.

When we arrived on the deck, we were greeted by fifteen or twenty other performers who we knew well, and who'd embarked on the *Rangitoto* in Melbourne. Theo and I moved to the rail, our pockets full of brightly coloured rolls of paper streamers. The band was playing selections from the new musical *The Messenger Boy*.

"Look, down there," Theo said. "Eileen and the children are pushing their way through the crowd. Their train must have been late arriving from the country."

I watched as Andrew picked up Gertrude and hoisted her up onto his shoulders. We waved and blew kisses, and as we did so, the ship sounded its great foghorn three times. The band stopped playing their selection and launched into a fanfare. There was no need for anyone to guess what was about to come, for, as the tugs took the strain on the ropes to pull the ship away from the quayside, we threw the last of our streamers and emptied our boxes of confetti out over the growing rift between the vessel and the wharf. All of us on the promenade deck, joined by the hundreds on the dockside, began to sing:

> Australia's Sons are now united, as a nation they will stand,
> Side by side in peace or war with the motherland.
> For freedom's flag floats proudly o'er our race by land or sea,
> And to all nations of the world mean liberty.

I waved at Andrew. I had eyes for no one else. He blew me a kiss, which could have been seen as being sent to any number of beautiful young women in our group, but as our eyes were locked, I knew it was for me. I threw one back at him and we both laughed, in time for the rousing rendition of the chorus:

> Australia's Sons are ready any time when e'er the need may be,
> To fight for fair Australia's land, the land of liberty.
> And side by side with England we will stand to help in peace or war.
> Our nations' cry will always be the same, Australia!

The great ship was towed out into the bay by the tugs, who let her go at Dawes Point, where it was hoped that one day the largest bridge in the Empire would stand. Her bow now pointing towards the heads of Sydney Harbour and the ocean beyond them, she gave another long toot of her horn and we gathered speed, away from the wharves at Darling Harbour.

Even though I could barely see anything but indistinct figures on the quayside, I kept waving. My heart was tied to one of those tiny dots on the wharf, and I knew he would still be waving back at me.

AUTHOR BIO

From the outback to the opera.

After a thirty year career as a professional opera singer, performing as a soloist in opera houses and in concert halls all over the world, I took up a position as lecturer in music in Australia in 1999, at the Central Queensland Conservatorium of Music, which is now part of CQUniversity.

Brought up in Australia, between the bush and the beaches of the Eastern suburbs, I retired in 2015 and now live in the tropics, writing, gardening, and finally finding time to enjoy life and to re–establish a connection with who I am after a very busy career on the stage and as an academic.

I write mostly historical gay fiction in two distinct styles; books that are erotic and those that leave things up to the reader's imagination. The stories are always about relationships and the inner workings of men; sometimes my fellas get down to the nitty–gritty, sometimes it's up to you, the reader, to fill in the blanks.

Every book is story driven; spies, detectives, murders, epic dramas, there's something for everyone. I also love to write about my country and the things that make us Aussies and our history different from the rest of the world.

I'm research driven. I always try to do my best to give the reader a sense of what life was like for my main characters in the world they live in.

Website – https://garrickjones.com.au

Facebook – https://www.facebook.com/GarrickJonesAuthor

ALSO BY GARRICK JONES

The Boys of Bullaroo: Tales of War, Aussie Mateship and More (Nov.2018), MoshPit Publishing, Australia
Six tales of men and war, spanning sixty years, and linked by a fictional outback town called Bullaroo. From the deserts of Egypt in 1919 to the American R&R in 1966, the stories follow the loves, losses and sexual awakenings of Australians both on the battlefield and in the bush.

The Seventh of December (Jan. 2019), Manifold Press, UK
As bombs rain down over London during the Blitz, Major Tommy Haupner negotiates the rubble-filled streets of Bloomsbury on his way to perform at a socialite party. The explosive event of the evening is not his virtuosic violin playing, but the 'almost-blond' American who not only insults him, but then steals his heart.

The Seventh of December follows a few months in the lives of two Intelligence agents in the early part of World War Two. Set against the backdrop of war-torn occupied Europe, Tommy and his American lover, Henry Reiter, forge a committed relationship that is intertwined with intrigues that threaten the integrity of the British Royal Family and the stability of a Nation at war.

Neither bombs nor bullets manage to break the bond that these men form in their struggle against Nazism and the powers of evil.

Rainbow Bouquet: an anthology from Manifold Press, (Feb 2019),UK
Authors featured are Harry Robertson, Edward Ahern, Victoria Zammit, Erin Horáková, Cheryl Morgan, Sarah Ash, Kathleen Jowitt, Sean Robinson, Garrick Jones and MJ Logue, and the settings vary from a mediaeval monastery to the 'final frontier', give or take the odd supernatural realm along the way. Stories of love in the past, present and future – all as fascinating in their variety as love itself.

The Cricketer's Arms (July 2019) MoshPit Publishing, Australia

Clyde Smith is brought into the investigation of the ritualised death of pin-up boy cricketer, Daley Morrison, by his former colleague, Sam Telford, after a note is found in the evidence bags with Clyde's initials on it. Someone wants ex-Detective Sergeant Smith to investigate the crime from outside the police force. It can only mean one thing—corruption at the highest levels.

The Cricketer's Arms is an old-fashioned, pulp fiction detective novel, set in beachside Sydney in 1956. It follows the intricacies of a complex murder case, involving a tight-knit group of queer men, sports match-fixing, and a criminal drug cartel.

Was Daley Morrison killed because of his sexual proclivities, or was his death a signal to others to tread carefully? Has Clyde Smith been fingered as the man for the case, or will the case be the end of the road for the war veteran detective?

All available from your favourite on-line retailer